I0688351

Douglas William Jerrold

Fireside Saints, Mr. Caudle's Breakfast Talk, and Other Papers

Douglas William Jerrold

Fireside Saints, Mr. Caudle's Breakfast Talk, and Other Papers

ISBN/EAN: 9783337254520

Printed in Europe, USA, Canada, Australia, Japan

Cover: Foto ©Andreas Hilbeck / pixelio.de

More available books at **www.hansebooks.com**

FIRESIDE SAINTS,

MR. CAUDLE'S BREAKFAST TALK,

AND

OTHER PAPERS.

In all thy humors, whether grave or mellow,
Thou'rt such a touchy, testy, pleasant fellow;
Hast so much wit, and mirth, and spleen about thee,
There is no living with thee, nor without thee.

MARTIAL, *as translated by* ADDISON.

FIRESIDE SAINTS,

MR. CAUDLE'S BREAKFAST TALK,

AND OTHER PAPERS.

BY

DOUGLAS JERROLD.

A fellow of infinite jest, of most excellent fancy.

SHAKESPEARE.

NOW FIRST COLLECTED.

BOSTON:
LEE AND SHEPARD, PUBLISHERS.
NEW YORK:
LEE, SHEPARD AND DILLINGHAM.
1873.

Entered, according to Act of Congress, in the year 1873,

By **LEE AND** SHEPARD,

In the Office of the Librarian of Congress, at Washington.

Stereotyped at the Boston Stereotype Foundry,

No. 19 Spring Lane.

NOTE.

LEIGH HUNT, in a little speech at the Museum Club, said that if Jerrold had the "sting of the bee, he had also his honey." In this volume there is, undoubtedly, more honey than sting; though, it must be confessed, there is also plenty of the latter, particularly in "Mr. Caudle's Breakfast Talk," "Silas Fleshpots," "Michael Lynx," and "The Tutor-Fiend and his Three Pupils"— a story or allegory almost as grim and ghastly as anything in Spenser. But if these papers, and perhaps one or two others, are full of caustic humor and biting wit, keenly and unsparingly exposing "the hypocrisy of life," many of the essays, sketches, and stories in the collection are remarkable for their pleasant satire, and easy, good-natured Rabelaisian philosophy. Even the "Hedgehog Letters," which are nothing if not satirical, are not very bitter or ill-

6 NOTE.

natured in their assaults upon cant and humbug in
church and state in England. "The Recollections of
Guy Fawkes" is a paper nearly as genial and pleasant as an essay by Leigh Hunt or Charles Lamb.
And the "Fireside Saints" are, I think, the sweetest
and sunniest of Jerrold's writings. The fancy, grace,
and humor of these little thumb-nail sketches will
be appreciated by the reader, who, after perusing
them, and others of kindred excellence in the volume, will, I hope, say, with Hawthorne,* "I like
Douglas Jerrold very much."

None of the papers in this volume are included
in the collected works of Douglas Jerrold.

J. E. B.

MELROSE, July 24, 1873.

---

* English Note Books, vol. ii. p. 11.

CONTENTS.

———◆◇◆———

7

FIRESIDE SAINTS.

SAINT DOLLY.

AT an early age, St. Dolly showed the sweetness of her nature by her tender love of her widowed father, a baker, dwelling at Pie Corner, with a large family of little children. It chanced that, with bad harvests, bread became so dear that, of course, bakers were ruined by high prices. The miller fell upon Dolly's father, and swept the shop with his golden thumb. Not a bed was left for the baker or his little ones. St. Dolly slept upon a flour-sack, having prayed that good angels would help her to help her father. Now, sleeping, she dreamed that the oven was lighted, and she felt, falling in a shower about her, raisins, currants, almonds, lemon-peal, flour, with heavy drops of brandy. Then, in her dream, she saw the fairies gather up the things that fell, and knead them into a cake. They put the cake into the oven, and dancing round and round, the fairies vanished, crying, " *Draw the cake*, Dolly ; Dolly, *draw the cake*." And Dolly awoke and drew the cake ; and, behold, it was the first Twelfth Cake,

9

sugared at the top, and bearing three images of Faith, Hope, and Charity. Now, this cake, shown in the window, came to the King's ear ; and the King bought the cake, knighted the baker, and married Dolly to his grand falconer, to whom she proved a faithful and loving wife, bearing him a baker's dozen of lovely children.

SAINT PATTY.

St. Patty was an orphan, and dwelt in a cot with a sour old aunt. It chanced, it being bitter cold, that three hunters came and craved for meat and drink. " Pack," said the sour aunt ; " neither meat nor drink have ye here." " Neither meat nor drink," said Patty, " but something better." And she ran and brought some milk, some eggs, and some flour, and beating them up, poured the batter in the pan. Then she took the pan, and tossed the cake once ; and then a robin alighted at the window, and kept singing these words: " *One good turn deserves another.*" And Patty tossed and tossed the cakes, and the hunters ate their full and departed. And next day the hunter baron came in state to the cot, and trumpets were blown, and the heralds cried, " *One good turn deserves another.*" And in token whereof Patty became the baron's wife, and pancakes were eaten on Shrove Tuesday ever after.

SAINT NORAH.

St. Norah was a poor girl, and came to England to service. Sweet-tempered and gentle, she seemed to love everything she spoke to. And she prayed to St. Patrick that he would give her a good gift, that would make her not proud, but useful; and St. Patrick, out of his own head, taught St. Norah *how to boil a potato*. A sad thing, and to be lamented, that the secret has come down to so few.

SAINT BETSY.

St. Betsy was wedded to a knight who sailed with Raleigh, and brought home tobacco; and the knight smoked. But he thought that St. Betsy, like other fine ladies of the court, would fain that he should smoke out of doors, nor taint with 'bacco-smoke the tapestry. Whereupon the knight would seek his garden, his orchard, and in any weather smoke *sub Jove*. Now it chanced, as the knight smoked, St. Betsy came to him and said, " My lord, pray ye, come into the house." And the knight went with St. Betsy, who took him into a newly-cedared room, and said, " I pray, my lord, henceforth smoke here : for is it not a shame that you, who are the foundation and the prop of your house, should have no place to put your head into and smoke?" And St. Betsy led him to a chair, and with her own fingers filled him a pipe ; and from that time the knight sat in the cedar chamber and smoked his weed.

SAINT PHILLIS.

St. Phillis was a virgin of noble parentage, but withal as simple as any shepherdess of curds-and-cream. She married a wealthy lord, and had much pin-money. But when other ladies wore diamonds and pearls, St. Phillis only wore a red and white rose in her hair. Yet her pin-money bought the best of jewelry in the happy eyes of the poor about her. St. Phillis was rewarded. She lived until fourscore, and still carried the red and the white rose in her face, and left their fragrance in her memory.

SAINT PHŒBE.

St. Phœbe was married early to a wilful, but, with-al, a good-hearted husband. He was a merchant, and would come home sour and sullen from 'Change. Whereupon, after much pondering, St. Phœbe, in her patience, set to work, and praying the while, made of dyed lamb's-wool, a door-mat. And it chanced from that time, that never did the husband touch that mat that it didn't clean his temper with his shoes; and he sat down by his Phœbe as mild as the lamb whose wool he had trod upon. Thus gentleness may make miraculous door-mats!

SAINT SALLY.

St. Sally, from her childhood, was known for her innermost love of truth. It was said of her that her heart was in a crystal shrine, and all the world might see it. Now, once, when other women denied, or strove to hide, their age, St. Sally said, "*I am five-and-thirty!*" Whereupon, next birthday, St. Sally's husband, at a feast of all their friends, gave her a necklace of six and thirty opal beads ; and on every birthday added a bead, until the beads amounted to fourscore and one. And the beads seemed to act as a charm ; for St. Sally, wearing the sum of her age about her neck, age never appeared in her face. Such, in the olden time, was the reward of simplicity and truth.

SAINT BECKY.

A very good man was St. Becky's husband, but with his heart a little too much in his bottle. Port wine — red port wine — was his delight, and his constant cry was a bee's-wing. Now, as he sat tipsy in his arbor, a wasp dropped into his glass ; and the wasp was swallowed, stinging the man inwardly. Doctors crowded, and with much ado the man was saved. Now, St. Becky nursed her husband tenderly to health, and upbraided him not. But she said these words, and they reformed him : " *My dear, take wine, and bless your heart with it; but wine in moderation. Else never forget that the bee's-wing of to-day becomes the wasp's sting of to-morrow.*"

SAINT LILY.

St. Lily was the wife of a poor man, who tried to support his family, — and the children were many, — by writing books. But in those days it was not as easy for a man to find a publisher as to say his Paternoster. Many were the books that were written by the husband of St. Lily ; but to every book St. Lily gave at least two babies. However, blithe as the cricket was the spirit that ruled about the hearth of St. Lily. And how she helped her helpmate! She smiled sunbeams into his ink-bottle, and turned his goose-pen to the quill of a dove! She made the paper he wrote on as white as her name, and as fragrant as her soul. And when folks wondered how St. Lily managed so lightly with fortune's troubles, she always answered, that she never heeded them, for, "*That troubles were like babies, and only grew the bigger by nursing.*"

Saint Fanny.

St. Fanny was a notable housewife. Her house was a temple of neatness. Kings might have dined upon her staircase! Now, her great delight was to provide all things comfortable for her husband, a hard-working merchant, much abroad, but loving his home. Now, one night he returned tired and hungry, and by some mischance there was nothing for supper. Shops were shut, and great was the grief of St. Fanny. Taking off a bracelet of seed pearl, she said, "*I'd give this ten times over for a supper for my husband.*" And every pearl straightway became an oyster; and St. Fanny opened, and the husband ate, and lo! in every oyster was a pearl as large as a hazelnut; and so was St. Fanny made rich for life.

Saint Jenny.

St. Jenny was wedded to a very poor man; they had scarcely bread to keep them; but Jenny was of so sweet a temper that even want bore a bright face,

and **Jenny** always smiled. In the worst seasons Jenny
would spare crumbs for the birds, and sugar for the
bees. Now, it so happened that an autumn storm
rent their cot in twenty places apart; when, behold,
between the joists, from the basement to the roof, there
was nothing but honey-comb and honey. A little
fortune for St. Jenny and her husband in honey.
Now, some said it was the bees, but more declared it
was the sweet temper of St. Jenny that had filled the
poor man's house with honey.

Saint Florence, or Saint Nightingale.

St. Florence, by her works, had her lips blessed
with comforting, and her hands touched with healing.
And she crossed the sea, and built hospitals, and
solaced, and restored. And so long as English mistle-
toe gathers beneath it truthful hearts, and English
holly brightens happy eyes, so long will Englishmen,
at home or abroad, on land or on the wave, so long —
in memory of that Eastern Christmas — will they cry,
"*God bless St. Florence! Bless St. Nightingale!*"

NOTE. — These little sketches, so graceful, genial, and fanciful, appeared in
Punch's Almanac for 1857. "They are holy little presences these," says Mr.
Blanchard Jerrold, "with each her special shining virtue to be imitated. Any
home shall be the better for looking at — for studying them. They were the
author's last marked success in *Punch* — that is, the last thing of his which the
public seized upon and welcomed, acknowledging their author." — ED.

MR. CAUDLE'S BREAKFAST TALK.*

CHAPTER I.

*How Mr. Caudle married Miss Prettyman, and
how he " nagged" her to Death.*

WHEN Harry Prettyman saw the very superb
funeral of Mrs. Caudle, — Prettyman attended
as mourner, and was particularly jolly in the coach, —
he observed that the disconsolate widower showed
that, above all men, he knew how to make the best of
a bad bargain.   The remark, as the dear deceased
would have said, was unmanly, brutal, but quite like
that Prettyman.   The same scoffer, when Caudle
declared " he should never cease to weep," replied,
" he was very sorry to hear it ; for it *must* raise the
price of onions."   It was not enough to help to break
the heart of a wife ; no, the savage must joke over its
precious pieces.

The funeral, we repeat, was remarkably handsome :
in Prettyman's words, nothing could be more satisfac-
tory.   Caudle spoke of a monument.   Whereupon
Prettyman suggested " Death gathering a nettle."
Caudle — the act did equal honor to his brain and
his bosom — rejected it.

Mr. Caudle, attended by many of his friends, returned to his widowed home in tolerable spirits.

* This " Breakfast Talk," which is a fit and characteristic sequel to "Mrs.
Caudle's Curtain Lectures," will please the women, who have always looked
upon Mrs. Caudle as a witty libel upon the sex.   "Mr. Caudle's Breakfast
Talk " was originally published in " Punch's Almanac " for 1846. — ED.

Prettyman said, jocosely poking his two fingers in Caudle's ribs, that in a week he'd look " quite a tulip." Caudle merely replied — he could hardly hope it.

Prettyman's mirth, however, communicated itself to the company ; and in a very little time the meeting took the air of a very pleasant party. Somehow, Miss Prettyman presided at the tea-table. There was in her manner a charming mixture of grace, dignity, and confidence — a beautiful black swan. Prettyman, by the way, whispered to a friend, that there was just this difference between Mrs. Caudle and his sister — " Mrs. Caudle was a great goose, whereas Sarah was a little duck." We will not swear that Caudle did not overhear the words ; for, as he resignedly stirred his tea, he looked at the lady at the head of the table, smiled, and sighed.

It was odd ; but women are so apt ! Miss Prettyman seemed as familiar with Caudle's silver tea-pot as with her own silver thimble. With a smile upon her face — like the butter on the muffins — she handed Caudle his tea-cup. Caudle would, now and then, abstractedly cast his eyes above the mantel-piece. There was Mrs. Caudle's portrait. Whereupon Miss Prettyman would say, " You must take comfort, Mr. Caudle, indeed you must." At length Mr. Caudle replied, " I will, Miss Prettyman."

What then passed through Caudle's brain we know not ; but this we know : in a twelvemonth and a week from that day, Sarah Prettyman was Caudle's second wife. Mrs. Caudle, number two. Poor thing !

CHAPTER II.

How Mr. Caudle begins to show "off the Fiend that's in him."

"IT is rather extraordinary, Mrs. Caudle, that we have now been married four weeks, — I don't exactly see what you have to sigh about, — and yet you can't make me a proper cup of tea. However, I don't know how I should expect it. There never was but one woman who could make tea to my taste, and she is now in Heaven. Now, Mrs. Caudle, let me hear no crying. I'm not one of the people to be melted by the tears of a woman; for you can all cry — all of you — at a minute's notice. The water's always laid on, and down it comes if a man only holds up his finger.

" *You didn't think I could be so brutal?* That's it. Let a man only speak, and he's brutal. It's a woman's first duty to make a decent cup of tea. What do you think I married you for? It's all very well with your tambour-work and such trumpery. You can make butterflies on kettle-holders; but can you make a pudding, ma'am? I'll be bound not.

" Of course, as usual; you've given me the corner-roll, because you know I hate a corner-roll. I did think you must have seen that. I *did* hope I should not be obliged to speak on so paltry a subject — but it's no use to hope to be mild with you. I see that's hopeless.

" And what a herring! And you call it a bloater, I suppose? Ha! there *was* a woman who had an

eye for a bloater, but — sainted creature ! — she's here
no longer. You *wish she was?* O, I understand
that. I'm sure, if anybody should wish her back, it's
— but she was too good for me. 'When I'm gone,
Caudle,' she used to say, 'then you'll know the
wife I was to you.'   And now I do know it.

   " Here's the eggs boiled to a stone again !   Do you
think, Mrs. Caudle, I'm a canary-bird, to be fed upon
hard eggs? Don't tell me about the servant. A wife
is answerable to her husband for her servants.   It's
her business to hire proper people : if she doesn't, she's
not fit to be a wife.   I find the money, Mrs. Caudle,
and I expect you to find the cookery.

   " There you are with your pocket-handkerchief
again ; the old flag of truce ; but it doesn't trick me.
A *pretty honeymoon?* Honeymoon? nonsense ! People can't have two honeymoons in their lives. There
are feelings — I find it now — that we can't have
twice in our existence.   There's no making honey a
second time.

   " No ; I think I've put up with your neglect long
enough : and there's nothing like beginning as we
intend to go on.   Therefore, Mrs. Caudle, if my tea
isn't made a little more to my liking to-morrow — and
if you insult me with a herring like that — and boil
my eggs that you might fire 'em out of guns — why,
perhaps, Mrs. Caudle, you may see a man in a
passion. It takes a good deal to rouse me, but when
I am up — I say, when I am up — that's all.

   " Where did I put my gloves? You *don't know?*
Of course not: you know nothing."

CHAPTER III.

Showing how Mr. Caudle could go out and enjoy himself.

" By the by, Sarah, just put half a dozen shirts, and all that sort of thing, in my portmanteau. I'm going — There you are with your black looks again! I can never go anywhere, just a little to enjoy myself, but you look like thunder. What! *I might sometimes take you out?* Nonsense! women — that is, women when they're married — are best at home. What can they want to go out for? It's quite enough for them to go out to hunt for husbands; when they've caught 'em, let 'em sit at home, and sing with the kettle and the cat; their best place is their fireside.

" Half a dozen shirts, I say, and my shaving tackle. Do you hear me, Mrs. Caudle? Perhaps when you've done counting the legs of that fly on the ceiling, you'll attend to me. Eh? *I think you never want to go out?* Quite the contrary; it's my belief you'd always be out. If you wanted to go about like a June fly, why did you marry?

" I should have told you where I was going; but as you've shown your temper, I won't tell you a syllable. No; nor I shan't tell you whom I am going with, or when I shall be back. When you see me, then you may expect me; and not before. And mind all the buttons are on my shirts — that's all.

" *It's miserable always being left by yourself!* Yourself, indeed! Arn't there books in the house?

There's capital company on the shelves if you'd only get acquainted with them. I'm sure you'd be none the worse for 'em. Besides, there's the cookery book: read that. A wife can't study anything better.

"The fact is, Mrs. Caudle, I've indulged you too much. I've made a fool of you. *No, I haven't?* Well, then, who has? If I haven't, somebody has, it's plain. Going out, indeed! I've no opinion of any woman who wants to go out at all. Women were never intended to go out; only the fact is, we've let you have your own way. Ha! they manage these matters much better in the East.

"I'm generally a pretty quiet man, Mrs. Caudle, and you know it. Nevertheless, I have a little of the lion in me; just a little. Don't rouse it, that's all.

"There you are, with the pocket-handkerchief again. Always hoisting that signal of distress. No, no; I'm not made of sugar, like a twelfth-cake image; I'm not to be melted with tears: let them be as many and as hot as they will. Besides, as I say, you can all do it when you like — every mother's soul of you. But I'm not to be washed off my legs by any river of the sort.

"All I say to you is, stay at home. You've a needle and thread, haven't you? and I'll be sworn for it, plenty of things to make or to mend. And if you haven't, cut holes, and sew 'em up again.

"Now, see when I come home that my portmanteau's ready. What's o'clock? You *want five minutes to* —— *?* No doubt: the old story; you're always wanting something."

CHAPTER IV.

Showing how Caudle, having lost Money at Cards, determines to abridge the House Expenses.

" I DON'T know how it is, my dear; but when I remember there's only you and myself — just two of us, and I eat and drink next to nothing — and when I see what other people do with half our money, I do think you might be a little more careful. I'm sure I spend no money on myself — none. Nobody can be more watchful of every sixpence; but, of course, a man can save but little when he knows, or, that is, when he fears he knows, that everything's going to waste at home. Besides, it's a woman's place — particularly a woman's place — to save. Women were designed for it. Economy is one of the noblest virtues bound up with matrimony. There can be very little real love, Mrs. Caudle, where economy's neglected. A woman can't truly care for a man's heart, unless she has an equal regard for his pocket: the things go together, and always did from the first.

" No, Mrs. Caudle, I did not lose at my whist club last night, that is, only next to nothing; in other words, nothing to speak of. Now, that's like your sex. You always set about hunting for some foolish, shabby motive for whatever your husbands complain about. Because I lose at cards, I *don't* want to get the money back out of your cupboard. No: I want to save money, that, should I be taken from you — and life at all times is uncertain, Mrs.

Caudle — you might be left snug and comfortable —
that's my object.   But I never knew any woman yet
— except one, rest her sainted soul ! — who had the
mind or the generosity to allow a truly noble motive
to what her husband should do, that is, if it went
against herself.   You can't help it, poor things ! —
nevertheless, when a man is depriving himself of
every little enjoyment that he may lay by something
for a rainy day, it *is* hard — a little hard, I think — to
have a woman spend what you do in housekeeping.

" Now, Mrs. Caudle, be rational ; and, for the thousandth time, let me beg of you not to cry.   You only
waste your trouble and your tears.   Both are thrown
away upon me.   I'm not one of the people, I tell you
again, to be melted with a little soft water.   My expenses, that is, *your* expenses, are dreadful.   Your
grocer's bill — and when I never taste sugar in my
tea — is preposterous ; enough to ruin a man of ten
thousand a year.   What?   *I take sugar in my grog,
and so do my friends.*   Scarcely any — nothing to
speak of ; not worth naming.

" And then look at your butcher for the last fortnight.   Well?   I know I won't eat cold joints.   I
had enough of them with my first — that is, I can't
bear 'em.   Besides, with half the money you have, a
cold joint is an insult to any man.

" And finally, Mrs. Caudle, — for you know I hate
this talk at breakfast ; it's a meal of all others I like to
enjoy when I can, — finally, I have made a calculation,
and in the next month, come what will, your cupboard must do with ten pounds less.   It's for your
good, I tell you, when I'm gone, and ten pounds I
must have of you."

CHAPTER V.

Showing how Caudle came Home very late, and very vinous: he complains of Want of Sympathy.

"THE old story, Mrs. Caudle! Sulky again! But so it is with women of no intellect; they can never properly sympathize with a man. You make the tea as if you were making poison, and all because I kept you up just a little last night. Ha! I only wish you had half what I have upon my mind. What! *You wouldn't have half what I had in my head?* Indeed I know what you mean; but I only wish you had. You'd have a little more sympathy for what I have to go through; as I say, you don't know what's in my mind. Women, who have to sit quietly basking before the fire all day, doing nothing whatever, except, perhaps, a little sewing — women, in their snug homes, know nothing of what their husbands have to go through in the world; slaving and wearing, as I may say, their very souls out. Ha! I only wish I'd been a woman. O, you needn't sigh, Mrs. Caudle; you've all the best of it from the beginning.

"For how can you tell, when your husband is doing all he can to seem happy and delighted at home. What! *You never saw him in such a state!* You might, if you'd eyes like any other woman. I say, how can you tell at the very time he's full — running over, I may say, with smiles, and affability, and good temper — how can you tell that his brain isn't being torn into bits, and all to make his wife happy and comfortable at her own fireside? I must say it; I only wish you'd my anxieties, sometimes; just for half a day, that's all; you'd have more sympathy, Mrs. Caudle; a little more sympathy. There you go on again, — with your woman's argument. *If I have so much on my mind, I needn't stay out so late!* How can you possibly tell what it is that detains me? If I chose, like some men, to tell my wife everything, and so worry you and make you unhappy with all sorts of anxieties, — then, indeed, I dare say I might have a little more tenderness from you. *But*, precisely because I wish to keep you in clover — precisely because I won't let you be worried by worldly matters — you think I've nothing to contend with. Ha! Mrs. Caudle — I can't help saying it — if you only knew what was on my mind!

" What do you know what wine *will* do, or won't do? Besides, I'd taken but a poor half pint of the very weakest sherry last night! Only half a pint. But when I'm harassed you ought to know how a little tells upon me. I was not intoxicated, Mrs. Caudle; I was merely intensely anxious. And if you'd any sympathy you'd known it. Yes, a woman with sympathy would have felt for me; would have turned a face upon me beaming with love and comfort — and not have been all night making up looks of thunder to come to breakfast with.

" I'm going out, now, and I shall take the key; so don't sit up again. I promised to sup at Doubleday's to-night; and you don't know what's on my mind."

CHAPTER VI.

Showing how Caudle brought home some "Good Fellows" to spend the Evening, and found Mrs. Caudle with some Female Friends at Tea.

" I DIDN'T choose to say anything to you last night, Mrs. Caudle — no : you needn't tell me that ; I know I didn't open my lips ; don't I say so, woman ? — I didn't speak, because, indeed, I was too tired.   But I *do* think it hard that I can't leave the house for a few days but I must find it swarming with petticoats when I come back.   Your friends, as you call 'em ! as if women could ever be friends !   It's rather hard, with what I'm charged for housekeeping, that I must find the place like a fair.   *You didn't expect me home till to-morrow?*   O, no !   Else I should have found you alone, and as mute as a mouse ; and not a word would you have said to me about the pack of gossips you'd had about you !

" Now, Mrs. Caudle, for the future just remember one thing.   Never think to expect me ; for you shall never know the exact time when I shall come home. No : I shall always take you by surprise ; as every man who'd know what his wife's about should do.

" Well, I think I may guess now where the housekeeping money goes to !   Now I can account for the grocer's bills — and I can't tell what other bills besides — when I see the people you have to eat me up. And then when I bring home a few friends that I find aboard the steamboat — good fellows, I know, every

one of 'em; though I never saw them before — when
I come home, I find my house full of silks and satins
— a mountain of bonnets on my bed — and nothing
fit for Christians to sit down to. And after such conduct you'll expect me to keep my temper! Yes:
you'll open your eyes and affect to stare at me, if I
only swear the smallest in the world — when if you'd
married some men, Mrs. Caudle, the house wouldn't
have held you! Now, I should like to know what
my friends thought of me last night — what they
thought of you? Why, of course they looked upon
me as a fool for putting up with your conduct as
quietly as I did; whilst for you, but — I'll respect
your feelings — I won't say what they must have
thought of you.

" For an hour and a half, at least, did we wait for
supper — if supper, indeed, you could call it; for I
blushed at everything upon the table. An hour and
a half. *There was nothing in the house; everything was to be got?* Why, that's what I complain of,
woman. That's the very fault. I bring home a few
friends to supper, and there's nothing in the house.
But I come home, and I find you with I don't know
what cotton-box acquaintances, and the house smell-
ing of toast and tea-cake enough to ruin one.

" Now, Mrs. Caudle, if we wish to continue happy
together, understand that I won't have it. If I can't
give a little supper to friends at my own home, I'd
better give up housekeeping altogether.

" Where's my hat and gloves? I dine out to-day."

CHAPTER VII.

Showing how Caudle brought home a Newfoundland Dog, insisting that " The poor Animal can't add to the Expense."

" O, NO ! I know what the objection is, Mrs. Caudle. It isn't that the poor faithful animal will add to the butcher's bill — not a bit of it. No : it is only because the creature is fond of me, that you object to it. 'Tis only because of its love for its master — and it's well I can get somebody about the house that does love me — that you make an excuse of the expense. You can keep your canary-bird — that's rattling away all day like a whistle in hysterics — and I never complain of the expense of that. You can keep your half a dozen gold-fish too, and do I ever murmur at what they cost? I think not. And yet when I bring home a dog — a fine fellow as high as the table — instead of admiring the noble animal as any other wife would do, you begin to talk about what it will eat ! But that's like you, Mrs. Caudle ; that's the rock we've always split upon. You never had any sympathy — not an atom. True marriage ought to melt two hearts into one piece. Ours — I am sorry to say it — have only been tacked together. There *was*, indeed, a woman — but, sainted darling ! — why should I name her?

" I repeat it ; if you thought of me as you ought, you'd be delighted with the animal. A true wife would love even a crocodile or a boa-constrictor, if her husband brought it home.   But my wife's like no other woman — never was.   *You don't object to the dog if I chain it up?*   I think, Mrs. Caudle, you ought to know my principles a little better by this time.   No, madam ; liberty — though it's quite above the female intellect to understand its beautiful essence — but liberty I wouldn't deny even to a dog.   The poor beast shall have the run of the house all day, and — noble fellow — sleep at my bed-room door all night.   I'll have somebody near me that loves me — I'm determined !

"What are you whimpering about?   *The beast will kill your cat?*   Perhaps he may ; and what if he does?   Cats are plenty enough, I suppose.   I'm sure there's more in my house than catch mice ; I know that.   Not that I see the noble fellow need kill her unless you choose.   *What do I mean?*   Mean !   Why, lock her up in the cellar, or cupboard, or coal-hole.   He won't kill her, if he can't get at her.   I'll answer for him.   Eh?   *And yet I talk of liberty?*   To be sure I do.   But there's your great defect again, Mrs. Caudle ; you've no sympathy — none, or you'd know what I mean directly.   Liberty for dogs is one thing ; liberty for cats is another.   There's what I call a moral distinction entirely."

· CHAPTER VIII.

Showing how Caudle thought " that Bill" settled
a long Time ago.

" IF, now, I were to leave you, Mrs. Caudle, — if I
were to do what I really ought to do as a husband, —
break up the establishment and go myself into chambers, just giving you enough to live upon — of course
the world — the world that never can judge between
man and wife, but always will poke its nose in between 'em whenever they separate — the world, I've
no doubt, would begin to abuse me. *What's the
matter?* Matter enough, I think ! I'm called out,
from my breakfast too, and this, Mrs. Caudle, this
little bit of paper, put into my hand. What, have
you the face to ask, Mrs. Caudle? *What of it? Don't
I know I owe it?* Why, of course not ! I could have
laid my life that *that* bill was paid long ago ! I could
have sworn it ! *How was it to be paid?* You ask
that ! Why, with money, of course. *But I never
gave you the money?* Nonsense ! You're enough to
drive a man mad, Mrs. Caudle. I must have given
you the money ; of course I must. Else where can
all the money go to? *When did I give it?* Well,
if you are not the most outrageous, perplexing woman !
When did I give it, indeed ! As if, with what I have
on my mind, I can exactly recollect the day, and the
hour, and the place when I gave you the money for
that bill ! I, who am always giving you money for
bills. Do you think I'm a calculating machine, Mrs.

Caudle, — to remember everything, and with what I have in my head? All I know is — and that's enough for any reasonable man — all I know is, I must have given you the money. The bill's been delivered a month ago, the man told me; and you're not the woman, I know, to let me remain quiet for a bill so long. No, indeed; for if there's anything in the world gives you pleasure, it is continually coming to my pocket. And you must think I've a gold mine there; to dip as you do into it.

"There you are! crying again! That's the mean advantage you women always try to take of your husbands. What! *You wish I'd common feelings, and you wish you were in your grave?* Of course. A man can't open his mouth, can't make the slightest remonstrance, when a woman lets money matters go all wrong, but he wants feelings. Ha! He'd better want a few feelings than want money. And I'm sure, Mrs. Caudle, that's your opinion, if you spoke the truth. And then again, you must always be scratching your grave up before me! And only because I just spoke about a bill. Of course, you've paid away the money for something else — some new gowns, perhaps — and forgot it.

"However, Mrs. Caudle, it is not worth quarrelling about — certainly not. Besides, I hate quarrelling. However, this I have to say: as I'm convinced that I've given you the money for the bill, I'm not going to pay it a second time. You must save it out of something else. *What are you to save it out of?* Anything: cat's-meat and canary-seed! — but I don't pay twice."

CHAPTER IX.

Showing how Mr. Caudle objected to Mrs. **Caudle's** *Female Friend, a Visitor for a Month.*

"When a husband comes home to what he ex-
pects to find a comfortable house, it is a little — I say
a *little* annoying for him — to break his shins over a
heap of portmanteaus in the hall, and find, too, he's
saddled with a visitor, — some stupid Miss or the
other, with all her boarding-school starch about her.
Eh — what? *You told me you'd invited dear Miss
Loveday?* You took an advantage of me, then,
and told me when I was asleep. I don't recollect it.
And now I shall be stunned to death by her for three
months — for of course she plays the piano; and I
shouldn't wonder if she's brought a guitar besides
with her. For three precious months! What! *She's
only invited for one month?* Humph! Then she'll
stay three, of course: they always do.

"Nice breakfasts I shall have now — for she'll not
always stay in her own room; she won't always be
tired travelling. Nice breakfasts I'm doomed to!
What! *How will the dear soul hurt me?* O, in the
gentlest way possible — I know. She'll always be
reading the play-house advertisements in the paper,
and always be wanting to go to the opera, or concert,
or fireworks, or some show of that sort. I know the
sideway talk of such girls very well. But understand,
Mrs. Caudle, I'm not hampered with her. As you
say she was your school-fellow once — I suppose I

shall have all Minerva House here in their turn —
you alone must be troubled with her. I shall behave
as civil as I can — but don't expect that I'll take her
out, or spend money upon her; that's your affair,
not mine.

" No, I *don't* forget when I'd my three friends here
all together : not at all ; I was too happy ever to forget it. Jack Stokes — noble fellow ! What a song
he sang, and what punch he made : Tom Ryder — the
best fellow he at whist and a chorus : and Sam Slab,
who gave such a licking to the coal-heaver. Ha !
they were something like people to have in one's
house. What ! *You never complained of them, and
why can't you have a friend?* That's quite a different thing. Besides, as I say, women never have
friendship one among another — they don't know
what it means. No, indeed ; I *don't* think friendship's
a thing of cigars and brandy and water — not but
what all these are a very pretty mixture. They were
something like nights we had. *You never got to sleep
till four while my friends were here?* What's that
to do with it? Is that any reason you should bring a
lot of visitors to my house who can't say " bo " to a
goose? And when you know, too, how I like to
enjoy the comfort of my friends alone ! How I hate
that we should have anybody to disturb us ! And if
you loved me really, you'd hate it too — but it's a
bad business to have all the love on one side : I feel
that."

3

CHAPTER X.

Showing Mr. Caudle again perplexed with Domestic Finance.

" Is it not a most extraordinary thing, that I can't sit down to enjoy a bit of breakfast, but under my nose there's a paper for taxes? *It's just been left, and it's Sarah's fault?* No! — it's your fault, Mrs. Caudle: you know that such things at such a time always affect my appetite, and it's my belief that you have 'em put there to save your cupboard. Taxes — taxes! What! *You don't pay 'em?* No: but what's quite as bad, you are always plaguing me about them. I can't help saying it, Mrs. Caudle, but what a much nicer wife you'd be, if there was no money!

" But I know it: when a woman likes to be extravagant, let a man do what he will, he's no match for her. I see that every day. Only yesterday I saw an old coat of mine — a very good coat too — on old Digges. Ha! my dear first wife used to turn my left-off clothes into beautiful mugs. But then, to be sure, she had some respect for my exertions. She used to calculate how and where the money came from. But — I must say it — I've no confidence in what's spent here.

" No, indeed, Mrs. Caudle. I'm not a cruel, unjust man — nor have I anything of the tyrant about me, — not a bit. But when women happen to be a little younger than their husbands — and that — I knew it,

to be sure — was your fault when I married you —
they are apt to indulge in expenses; and — I must
say it — that last hosier's bill that came in I don't at
all understand. I'm sure by the socks that's down for
me, anybody would think I was a centipede. Well,
I can't help sometimes suspecting — I should be glad
if I could be disabused — but I can't help thinking,
now and then, that what I've paid for hosiery you've
worn in velvet and silk.

" If I could only be sure of this, I should know very
well how to act. *Then* my course would be plain
enough. What? *If I'm not sure, why do I accuse
you?* O, there can be nothing lost by that. For if
a woman is blamed when she doesn't deserve it, she's
sure some time or other to escape when she does;
so there's nothing thrown away, blame her when
you will."

With this liberal axiom Caudle took his hat, observing to his weeping wife that he " might be home
to dinner, and he might not."

CHAPTER XI.

*Showing how Mr. Caudle thought something,
" very odd."*

" ANYTHING particular, my dear, in the paper —
I mean anything in the military way? *What do I
mean?* O, nothing. Ha, ha! A little joke of
mine — just a little joke. What do you think of the
cavalry regiment? *What am I driving at?* Noth-

ing at all. I thought you might have seen 'em.
They go by the window, you know, twice a day.
What of it? Nothing, to be sure. Only it is odd —
I must say it is odd, that one of 'em — a young fel-
low with sandy mustachios — always turns his head
towards this house. I say it's odd — slightly odd.
Now, you can't say he's looking for Miss Loveday.
She's gone — thank Heaven! at last. I waited till
she went before I spoke ; because I know how women
will stand by one another.

"Well, Miss Loveday is gone — do you hear me,
Mrs. Caudle? — and still that fellow with the sandy
mustachios looks towards this house. Now, I think
that's something very odd. And I should like to
know what he's looking for? What! *I'd better
ask him?* I shall take my own opinion as to that,
Mrs. Caudle ; but allow me to say this much — that
— ha! there *was* a woman — who never, never
caused me the finger ache. That I had never lost
that woman! Eh? *You wish I never had?* Ha!
She never gave herself airs about her beauty. What!
She couldn't? Mrs. Caudle, I don't wish to say a
harsh thing of you — far from it. But permit me, in
all good temper, to say, that you are not fit to stir the
tea of that blessed woman. She never looked about
her — never stared at anybody but her own husband
when she went out. She never thought there was
another such in the world. But I deserved to lose
her — I didn't think enough of her then.

"If any soldier had dared to look twice at any
house she was in, she'd have shown what she felt as
a wife, and closed every shutter. But she *did* know
her duty — I wish other people did."

Upon this, the second Mrs. Caudle — poor ill-used soul! — simply remarked that " she knew he was a brute," and left him with his own bad thoughts, and his own bohea.

CHAPTER XII.

Mr. Caudle's Defence of his Tyranny.

MR. CAUDLE, ere he left this world, had much more " Breakfast Talk " with his unfortunate wife ; but it is believed that we have given the principal heads of his discourses ; for his topics were like the church bells — they " nearly always rang the same morning peal." To the reader who believed in the declaration of the first Mrs. Caudle that her husband " was really an aggravating man," with her prophecy that " the world would at last know him as well as she did," the conduct of this individual towards the insnared and unfortunate Miss Prettyman, may not afford surprise. Caudle himself, however, set up an ingenious if not a credible defence. Prettyman, his brother-in-law, had now and then remonstrated with him. " I don't mean it, — upon my life, I mean nothing. I'm very fond of your sister — extremely fond ; it's only a habit, my ill-treatment — nothing but a habit."

" A habit ! " cried Prettyman ; " why, that's what we complain of ! That's what we want you to get rid of."

" Impossible, my dear boy — quite impossible. Having lived twenty years with the late Mrs. Caudle, though I believed her to be a sainted woman notwith-

standing — how was it to be expected that I shouldn't
make a natural use of my liberty?   You don't suppose
I was going to suffer Mrs. Caudle the second to be
only another Mrs. Caudle the first — so, you see, I
bent the bar the other way."

" And this is your defence," cried Prettyman.

" My excellent friend," said Caudle, " bad temper's
catching.   Therefore, let folks beware how they
come together.   If I've been a little bit of a tyrant in
my second marriage, 'tis only because I was a slave
in the first; and all tyrants, my dear boy, are only
slaves turned inside out."

" I can make nothing of that figure," said Prettyman, " but this: that in most marriages there are
faults on both sides."

" Exactly so," answered Caudle, " and both I've
known."

AN OLD HOUSE IN THE CITY.

ANTIQUITY hath abundance of charity — she
pleadeth for the mighty and the mean, the
magnanimous and the contemptible.   Touched by
her influence, we gaze with reverence at the great
pyramid, and can look with interest at a gibbet — we
venerate the dust of a sage, and linger even by the
mummy of a lawyer.   Placed in her circle, her host
of shadows passing before us, we not only bow to
poets and philosophers, but can nod and give a " good

den " to usurers and pickpockets. The veriest rascal, seen through the haze of centuries, becomes picturesque. Who, for example, can see Guido Fawkes as he really moved and lived? Who can place before himself the veritable Claude du Val? The vulgar, cold-blooded conspirator is a. fearful conjuration of romance, the highwayman a sprightly ill-used gentleman — the dark lantern of the fanatic is lighted with a fiery star, the fiddle of the cutpurse sounds in truth a most taking instrument. And why this delusion — why this charity towards the long departed? Is it not that we feel they are no longer partakers of our state of existence, but that they form a portion of that mystery, to the attainment of which life is but the preface? Is our homage that of ignorance towards intelligence? Is it, that, feeling a tree of knowledge springs alike through every coffin, our prejudices as to the peculiar earth are lost in speculation on the fruit? It may, we feel, be apples of Paradise — it may be apples of the Dead Sea; but whatever the produce, it can only grow from a dead man, and thus the corpse of the poorest slave has higher wisdom than a breathing Solomon. This, however, is more serious — if you will, more dull — than we intended. Only desirous of proving how time can plead for even antiquity, how evil may be hallowed by the consecrated garments of years, we break off our sermon. This we will say: such lovers are we of the real antique, that we would not destroy a single twig from a upas-tree, if the said tree had flourished for centuries — no, let pestilence drop from the branches, if the branches were really and truly old.

With such benevolent feelings have we many a
time gazed at the mansion of Messieurs Cat and
Condor — yes, with no less amiable emotion have we
beheld their "Old House in the City." We never
asked our friends, but have little doubt that the walls
were built of the first bricks imported by the Earl of
Arundel — to our eyes more valuable than the bricks
of Babylon — writ with far deeper, far more recondite
mysteries. Many a time, our back supported by an
opposite door, with upturned looks and folded arms,
have we contemplated the external features of that
"Old House." Yet ere we narrate our wayward
musings, it is right we give precedence to the opinions of "sage, grave men," of "great ones of the
city." We will inflict on the reader but two or three
examples.

"Pray, Sir (I am strange to business), what may
be the character of the firm of Messrs. Cat and Condor?" This question has a thousand times been put
by a thousand different querists: the answer has ever
been, "An Old House in the City." Such are the
words, but conveyed in no less than a thousand different tones: some replying in a note of explosive surprise, some with a pitying sneer at the interrogator,
some with a chuckle at his boorish ignorance, some
with deep solemnity, taking especial care to dwell
upon the "Old."

Having produced the gravest testimony as to the antiquity of the house, we may now venture to add our
evidence to that of serious, matter-of-fact witnesses.
We have in many a reverie read the walls of the house
— we have dived into their mysteries — we have de-

ciphered their hierographs, and, rapt by our discoveries, we have lost sight of the bricks ; as, in reading Homer or Shakespeare, we are wholly oblivious of the printer and the papermaker.   Thus our " House" has at times seemed to us built up of human bones, a mansion composed of the spoils of the churchyard. We have seen the pithless joints of the old and the young — we have beheld the skull of the widow and the orphan cemented in one compact mass — and still the walls grew higher and higher, as new materials fell into the hands of the builders — and every bone had its legend, every skull its curious history.

Anthony Cat — merry, simple-minded man — whilst seated in his leather-bottomed chair, conning his daily ten hours'. task, never dreamed of out-of-door opinions. He knew the walls of the old house were in good condition, for they had been surveyed ; but for any types or texts to be found in them, he no more thought of such superstition than the fly in a painted paper cage thinks of the daubing of its prison. Anthony Cat professed himself a Christian, and proved himself a man of business. For ourselves, we care not so much for professions as for deeds ; therefore, waving what Anthony said, we may state what he seemed — for in mind he may have been an infidel, but in practice he was (in pounds, shillings, and pence) a true believer. Anthony owed his first advance in life to his humanity. In the first American war, though he only held a situation partaking of the errand boy and the junior clerk, he was at once a philanthropist and an admirer of his master's daughter. Being on principle averse to the war, he

conceived that, by lessening the resources of his
country, he might best accelerate the advent of peace
— to which end, whenever despatched for stamped
sheets, he six times out of ten supplied the office from
his own garret, putting the purchase-money in his own
pocket. How, it will be asked, was the cheat effected?
By the unassisted genius of the simple Anthony, who,
to while away the dreariness of his lesiure, would cut
the stamps from old, extinct bonds, and with the most
praiseworthy dexterity, with a nice ingenuity worthy
a Chinese, would let them into plain parchment.
" This was the way to thrive ;" and Anthony had
the double satisfaction of assisting the cause of national
peace and individual profit. This is a truth, a truth
without one thread of fiction. In time Anthony became the second clerk — still his heart grew bigger,
still his purse dilated. However, a proposal for his
fair young mistress was met by the indignation of her
father, and Anthony was about to be discarded, when
an accidental discovery of a false stamp procured him
another interesting interview with his master. The
old gentleman was full of virtuous indignation, and
talked of hanging. Anthony fell upon his knees, and,
to the horror of the elderly lawyer, confessed a long
catalogue of forgeries ; nay, more, avowed himself
ready to publish to the world the name of every client
whose property had been placed in jeopardy by a
spurious stamp. Of course the master gave quills,
ink, and paper to the penitent for the purpose of justice? Not so ; the lawyer was a discreet man —
were the iniquity of his clerk made known, his business, his connection was gone ! Anthony rightly in-

terpreted the silence of his master, and again and
again proposed to make a " clean breast." The good
man got up a visible shudder at what he termed the
consequences of a prosecution — he could not see an
old, though worthless servant hanged ! Will it be believed by the modest reader? The instant Anthony
was assured that his master would not consign him
to the gallows, he again prayed that he might take
his daughter to the church. The master paused at
the request ; but at length, wisely thinking that the
best way to stop the mouth of his clerk would be to
give him a wife, he consented to the match. This
auspicious beginning was followed by " thick-com-
ing" successes, and in the course of a few years, behold Anthony Cat partner of " An Old House in the
City." He looked worthy of his prosperity — his face
was ever in a glow of satisfaction, his voice rung
like glass, and he would rub his hands with an air
that told you they were as pure as his own pounce.
And yet no man had a sterner eye to the " inevitable
decencies " of life. Though he was outwardly smiling, meek, and gracious, he had in his way of business a heart more than Roman. Little knew they of
the interior of Anthony Cat who judged him by his
short laugh, his venerable jest, or his one ballad at
the club — nay, they who paused at his Hoxton Villa,
garnished with potted myrtles and geraniums, and
saw the owner pacing his lawn with a pink 'twixt
his fingers brushing his nose, did him wrong if they
confounded him with the same Cat setting a suit in
his " Old House in the City," or following it out at
Westminster.

Augustus Condor, the second partner, seemed expressly sent into the world to do two things — to keep accounts and eat a dinner.   He accomplished the double purpose of his being with surpassing ability. No man had greater powers of calculation and digestion.   His moral lining was, we are convinced, composed of a Ready Reckoner and a Cookery Book. Place him before the cedars of Lebanon, and his first thought would be to calculate the height and girth of every cedar tree, and next its market price.   Fix him on the shores of the Ganges, and his first inquiry would be, if turtle swarmed there ; and Condor knew himself, and so knowing, left the difficulties of consultation to his more mercurial partner.   Cat looked to the pockets of the house, and Condor to the belly.

Having introduced the reader to the two partners, we will now take him into their office.   So, being entered, one gentle question, dispassionate reader. (We suppose it to be the first time our friend has entered the office of a lawyer.)   Do nothing new and strange strike upon your sense?   Be there no " odors " here?   Do you feel assured that there are no subtile particles flying about you, no peculiar emanations? Do you not yearn and gasp for the sweet air of even a London street?   Do not your heart sink and your lips part in sickness?   Has nothing fatal to your genial every-day flow of blood entered your system? Your finger to your pulse — now, as there is an immortal soul in truth — are you the same man you were ere you crossed the threshold?   No ; for you are not made of oak or quartz ? — You share the common attributes of our common nature, and you are a changed man. **You ask why is this?** We who have felt the influence of the *genius loci* — we whom no experience can blunt to it — cannot clearly divine the mystery — we can only speculate. Look at those piled rows of japanned boxes. We think much of the evil; a great portion of the malaria issues thence: there are the deeds of the dying, the dead, and — but we will not increase the number of the parties, though we sacrifice alliteration. Surely within all those tombs all cannot be sound — no, there is the decay of truth, the rottenness of falsehood. Though some may be wholesomely embalmed with honest ink and wax, all do not " smell sweet, and blossom in the pounce."

Thence rise the vapors, thence the noxious exhalations. And hark? Hear ye no sounds? A voice of wailing and misery, a sobbing, a groaning, as from a crucified spirit? though the notes are fine, an ear unsophisticated may catch them. From whence, you ask, this anguish? from whence this rending lamentation? We answer, from poor common sense locked up, gyved, disfigured, racked by a thousand menials, some called Whereas, some Notwithstanding, some Aforesaid, and some with names of gibberish, counting more syllables than the Spaniard. Even as the dainty spirit Ariel was imprisoned in the pine by Sycorax, that " blue-eyed hag," so is poor common sense captive to an unrelenting beldam. And, reader, did you ever see the thumb-screw or the steel boot? You have; and your cheek has wrinkled and your heart fallen as you gazed on those inventions of the devil, and thought of the blackened flesh, the spurting blood, the cracking bone, and broken marrow of the victim? Well, screw and boots may be made from the skins of inoffensive sheep; from rags cast from a beggar, and — but we must pause. We have given loose to a morbid imagination. We have (it is our failing) been dreaming a day-dream, in which have mingled all kinds of monstrous horrors, whilst, indeed, we were comfortably seated in the office of Messrs. Cat and Condor. We have taken a journey to a den of guilt and misery, while our feet reposed on the matting of an "Old House in the City." It is fortunate we are awake, or we know not how basely we might have misrepresented that young pale-faced sandy-haired clerk, with a very white shirt-collar. Who knows how we might have typified the respectable partners themselves, the worthy Cat and Condor, those solid pillars of the "Old House in the City." We have now to dismiss from the mind of our companion all that we have said : we are not justified in attempting to shake the nerves of any man ; therefore the reader may as frequently as he pleases defy the atmosphere of an attorney's office ; for our part, being naturally delicate, we love sweet air, and respect our health.

"Very sorry, very sorry, indeed ; but, sir, money is money, and people are so difficult! "

For the wisdom enshrined in these words the reader is indebted to Mr. Cat, who, with one of his blandest smiles, his eyes twinkling through his spectacles, his body gently inclined, and the tip of each thumb and finger nicely touching the tip of its brother, assured a client that money was money ; and to give Cat his due, he was capable of no better definition.

To his client, however, money was liberty, peace of mind, everything; he bit his lips, his eyes glared, and it was with some effort that with apparent composure the stranger asked, "When may I have the money?"

"To-morrow, sir, to-morrow."

The tone and manner of Cat were most convincing, and yet they evidently failed to assure his client, who, it must be conceded, ought to have been impressed with the promise of his agent, as the worthy man had almost every day, for the previous fortnight, repeated it. To-morrow bubbled from the mouth of Cat as freely as water from a source — but Lieutenant Lacy, we regret to say it, was a suspicious man, and when looking at the support of the "Old House" from the crown to the gaiters, he turned upon his heel, and said, "Then I'll come to-morrow." It was but too plain that he quitted the office an unbeliever. Indeed, to confess all, as he descended the staircase, a mutilated oath escaped his lips, an oath in which Messrs. Cat and Condor were very deeply interested. However, something must in charity be allowed to the ignorance of the man. How was it possible that he, a sailor, could judge of the difficulties of what Mr. Cat ever delighted to call " a financial operation "? What may appear very fair and simple to an unlearned mariner, abounds with perplexities in the eyes of prudent attorneys like Cat and Condor. Two and two may make four on the quarter-deck, but such false calculation is not to pass in an "Old House in the City."

Lieutenant Lacy, in addition to his majesty's commission and three body-wounds, had a wife and five children. Whilst his laurels were growing at sea, his olive branches had flourished at home; and though they were all fair and beautiful, Elizabeth, a girl of seventeen, was the fairest, the most beautiful — " an angel, if ever an angel walked," to use the words of a young gentleman transfixed one summer evening by her graces; and the exclamation must be received as a triumphant evidence of the loveliness of Elizabeth, for certain we are that the speaker was not one of those happy people who, in their dreams, awake or sleeping, see angelic faces; he had no standard of beauty, but paid an instinctive homage to its influence. Charles Bars was himself the child of an officer, and when, on the 2d of May, his eyes met the bright orbs of Elizabeth, as, accompanied by her mother and younger sister! she walked in the Temple Gardens, he felt an admiration so uncontrollable, that he three times thrust his head beneath her bonnet; nay, so powerful was his emotion, that it absolutely drove her from the spot. When she vanished from his sight, and he was prevented by a sense of delicacy (for we are almost certain that he despised the uplifted cane of a meddling gentleman) from following her, so profoundly was he touched, that he flung away an almost whole cigar, and for that evening ceased to smoke. Vesuvius itself could not give a stronger evidence of what Mrs. Siddons once called " desperate tranquillity."

Let the reader suffer a day to have elapsed, and we will then return to the office of Cat and Condor. Enter Lieutenant Lacy; he is met with a smile so gracious, so cheering, by the partner of the " Old House," that he returns it with a look of perfect satisfaction. " How have I wronged this excellent man ! Doubtless there were many difficulties in the **way of** the negotiation ; **money, on the best of security, is** scarce." **Now, though Lieutenant Lacy spoke no** syllable of this, **every word of it passed through his** brain, **as Mr. Cat,** having again carefully deposited himself in his chair, **stretched forth his right leg, and** began with an encouraging air **to pat its calf. He** then placed **both his hands in his breeches pockets,** and — credulous Lieutenant Lacy (for **he thought** he heard the crumpling of bank-notes) — observed, " I am **very sorry."** As he said this, his client leaped **to his** feet **with a noise that even** awakened the **calculating** Condor, **who, dropping** his jaw, coolly ran his tongue round his upper lip, and stared **at the disturber. Cat** widened his mouth, smiled with **great industry, and** to some **very rapid and homely queries of the Lieu-** tenant, **again exclaimed, " To-morrow."** Here — we regret **to record it** — the sailor lost all respect for the **representatives of the " Old House," and in a tone** not **to be mistaken demanded back his papers.** Cat smiled **consent, and opening the door, asked** one of the clerks **in the outer office for "** Lieutenant Lacy's *bill*."

The Lieutenant was a brave man, but at the sound **of the word** *bill,* he looked **the veriest coward. The clerks of the " Old House " were celebrated** for despatch, **and in a trice the last item, viz., the** consultation of that **day, was added to the account,** and placed between the **fingers of the debtor, who found** himself " written down " forty pounds in the books of Cat

4

and Condor. Somewhat recovered from the first
shock, the Lieutenant promised payment, but again
loudly demanded his papers. Again Condor gaped,
and again Cat smiled. "Certainly, Lieutenant Lacy
— to be sure, when our bill is paid." Now Lieutenant
Lacy had not forty shillings.

We have said the Lieutenant was a suspicious man,
and we hate suspicion, for ninety-nine times out of a
hundred, it takes away more than it secures. A man
whose road lies through a wild forest, if told that
the place be infested by a ravenous wolf, suspects
everything that moves about him to be no other than
the wolf; if a fox, a hare, or a poor rabbit start at
his feet, he trembles, fearing it the wolf; nay, if a little squirrel crack nuts on his native branch, the suspicious man stands aghast, assured he hears the wolf;
and if a few yards within his journey's end a pretty
glow-worm glisten in a bush, he runs hallooing home,
and gathering all his neighbors about him, vows he
hath escaped by a miracle, having beheld the very
eye of the very wolf! Now, had nobody filled the
poor fellow's head with terrible stories of the beast,
he had scarcely thought of it, but had gone through
the wood enjoying the singing birds, the waving trees,
and the breathing flowers!

We know not whether Lieutenant Lacy had given
ear to any malignant gossip touching the "Old
House," or whether his present valuation of Messrs.
Cat and Condor was the result of his unassisted ob-
servations; but certain we are that he viewed the still
smiling Anthony with that kind of interrogative
glance which the reader may have seen put by one

gentleman in a crowd when the inquirer has lost his pocket-book or repeater. "Are you a thief?" demands the despoiled with all the force and eloquence of eyes. When Mr. Cat made the surrender of his client's papers provisional on the payment of his client's bill, Lieutenant Lacy, though silent, put a question, and Cat, though he spoke not, smiled an answer. Cat was a philosopher, it is true; for a libel written or spoken he had a vein of unexampled tenderness, but for mere dumb opinion, for the thoughts that dwell within the chambers of men's brains, they no more affected him than they could wound the cynic through his tub. No, Cat was a liberal; he was for the free exercise of thought so long as thought went about its business, speaking no word and scrawling no pot-hook. It is clear Lieutenant Lacy was poorly matched against such a man, who was so strong in the consciousness of his own integrity, that when his intemperate client "prepared to chide," the lawyer beckoned in the senior clerk to listen to the vituperation. Whether the Lieutenant felt his want of eloquence, or whether, like a high-minded player, he refused to exhibit before so poor an audience, we cannot decide. Sure we are, that the instant the sailor caught the eye of the clerk, that instant the speaker became dumb; and more, without deigning to accept an invitation significantly put to him by the smiling Cat, he swung from the office of the "Old House" with a promptitude and decision worthy of Drake or Blake.

We spoke of an invitation on the part of Cat, and must trespass a few lines in the way of comment:

Has the reader — we beg his pardon ; of course he has —beheld a beautiful pair of lips, red and ripe as cherries, that, placed within the reach of even Origen himself, would win him to their audible cry of, " Kiss me ? " Show us the man who hath the marble entrails to withstand the invitation, and we shall honor him for a true philosopher, or despise him for a cowardly fool. Now, we place Lieutenant Lacy in the hands of the reader : it is for him to decide on the future character of the client of the " Old House," when we state an equal instance of his forbearance. For be it known, that as the Lieutenant prepared to depart, looking death at his attorney, Mr. Cat, with an improved smile, with both hands in his pockets, the tails of his coat accidentally hanging over his arms, and his head unusually advanced, approached the Lieutenant, and again grinning, " Perhaps to-morrow," turned his back upon the officer. It was a critical moment for the tempted Lacy ; for if ever, in her immortal life, Venus, without speaking, cried, " Kiss," Cat, by his smiling look, and the dexterity with which he took the most tantalizing position, cried, " Kick."

A maiden gazing at the full moon is a beautiful object ; an astronomer surveying its valleys, plains, and mountains challenges our admiration and respect ; an Indian trembling at an eclipse, beating his tambour and yelling, to scare the dragon from swallowing the planet, calls up our pity at his darkness ; a magician writing his riddles on the moon's bright face carries us into the boundless realms of imagination ; — but each and all of these, in the various emotions which they feel and excite, are, in our opinion, powerless, compared to the sensations glowing, swelling in the bosom of Lieutenant Lacy, as he surveyed the presented disc of Anthony Cat, lawyer — as he looked on the broad stone of honor of " the Old House in the City." Happy are we to say we know nothing of anatomy, and seek not to know; for were we acquainted with the minute, the delicate machinery with which we are intrusted, could we enjoy, as in our present ignorance, our dinner and plurality of bottles? No; — wearing, as we should, our eyes in our bellies, we should shudder at the despotism which we daily exercise over a thousand tender subjects, with whose names and duties we are now unacquainted; and trembling at the cruel taskmaster Appetite, we should confidently predict intestine revolution — dissolution. It is thus that their deep knowledge makes all the faculty temperate as chameleons; no true physician, no real surgeon, cares for his meals — empirics may gormandize, but science rarely dines. However, this much anatomical knowledge we have arrived at from the deportment of the Lieutenant in the hour of his temptation, — we think there can be no muscle from the heart to the toe, or fearful we are that the Lieutenant's toe had gone up. The invitation on the part of Mr. Anthony Cat was so unequivocal, that how Lacy, as a man of common courtesy, rejected it, he can best explain — we cannot. The Lieutenant descended the staircase. Mr. Cat returned to his seat with a look of disappointment, and the senior clerk vanished to his desk, balked of what at first promised to be a very pretty assault.

Lieutenant Lacy was a man of the highest courage;

a ship's crew had presented him with a sword for his
signal bravery in an awkward affair of " cutting out."
He merited to the full so flattering a testimonial of
his active gallantry ; but how much greater the recom-
pense due to him for the passive magnanimity we
have recorded ! In such a case, and with such provo-
cation, not to kick appears to us the grandest triumph
of human equanimity. Cat himself was astounded
at the moral elevation, which, however, brought its
reward. Ziska's skin, specially bequeathed by the
wearer to cover a drum, though no doubt capable of
the loudest and most terrible sounds, was, we are
certain, thin and weak as gold beater's, compared to
our Cat's skin, sounding a charge of assault at Westminster. Convinced we are that several eminent
persons might, at their deaths, forever silence the
fame of the aforesaid drum, would they but leave, for
a similar instrument, that which by good kicking
hath been so admirably prepared on the living animal.
At present we must dwell no longer on the subject ;
— yes, we must record a startling instance of good
fortune bound up with kicking.

A worthy man, happily intrusted with the guid-
ance of public taste, owed the full blazon of his prosperity to this summary, and, as it would seem, intelli-
gent operation. It chanced that a gentleman from a
great London house sojourned, in the way of business,
at the country factory of our man with the toe, and
was at once astonished and delighted to hear the application of the said toe threatened upon the lightest
blunder or disobedience of the people employed.

" Can it be ? " asked the visitor, with a look of

mingled pleasure and credulity. "Is that your way of governing? Do you really kick?"

"I do."

The querist folded the respondent in his arms, then, as Ophelia describes Hamlet, surveyed him at a distance, clasped his hand, and with an exulting voice, fairly crowing at the discovered gem, and an eye swimming with transport, exclaimed, "Come to London!" The operator quitted his country business, and in a trice was placed in the Metropolitan House. It is true, he was doomed to undergo a practical lesson from an amateur, in the very art in which he had dubbed himself *regius professor* before he himself had given a solitary lecture. But passing that slight annoyance, he had cause to rejoice at the discovery of kicking, which — enthusiastic in the remedy — he held, like Shakespeare's "barber's chair," to be equally adapted to all parties. Little knew an admiring world, when it gazed on the enchantments of the London repository, when it beheld dancing nymphs and flying Cupids, that even such delicate creatures were marshalled in their graces by the threatened foot. Processions, triumphal choruses, battles, weddings — all were kicked up! Next to the Pope, no man had such a toe! To proceed with our history. An unforeseen and critical event increased the disappointment of the Lieutenant. Arrived at his lodgings, he found a letter from Portsmouth, calling for his instant return to his vessel, the ship being under sailing orders. The papers must be obtained from Messrs. Cat and Condor at any sacrifice; he must dispose of the reversion of a trifling freehold, inherited by his wife on the death of her mother. He had debts to pay, butchers, bakers, schoolmasters to satisfy, and money must be had.

With this deep conviction, Lieutenant Lacy addressed himself to a solicitor, who promised an instaneous recovery of the documents from the " Old House." For the client, he knew not what to make of the procrastination of Mr. Cat, who, three weeks before, on almost the first glance at the papers, declared them to be immediately convertible ; money might be had upon them, ay, by noon the next day. Nothing was more easy ; the Lieutenant might depend upon the cash. From that time, however, until the final interview, there was some new, some unexpected difficulty — always, it is true, explained away by the zealous Cat, who always cried " to-morrow," and always smiled with increasing complacency.

Lieutenant Lacy was seated in the front parlor of Number ——, St. ——'s Court. His daughter Elizabeth, making the most of the light of a June evening, as it sickened through the windows, was employed on a crayon portrait of her father, a dear memorial for hearts at home, when he was " far amid the melancholy main." Elizabeth had heard of the hasty summons and worked in silence. The sailor never showed greater heroism than at that hour. His heart was heaving for his wife and children, — he was about to quit them, perhaps forever, — to leave the beautiful creature before him intrusted to a tempting world ; and yet, with these thoughts piercing his brain, he kept a smile upon his face for the gentle artist. Lieutenant Lacy had looked with unblenched gaze on the guns of an approaching enemy; but in that dreadful pause of life he showed less noble self-control, than when, with a mind racked by household wants, he looked with a smile into his daughter's eyes. Great are the battles gained on field and deck, but greater far the triumphs won by the struggling spirit at the desolate fireside.

Father and daughter were thus employed, when a knock at the door proclaimed a new arrival. The circumstance, commonplace as it was, afforded a relief to Elizabeth, who longed, but knew not how, to break the silence.

"It is not mamma," she said; "she will not be at home this hour."

The landlady briefly informed Lieutenant Lacy that a gentleman wished to speak to him. The Lieutenant quitted the apartment, but in two minutes returned followed by his visitor, who, beholding Elizabeth, seemed struck with amazement.

"I will but retire to my room, and then be with you immediately," said the Lieutenant to the stranger, in a tone partaking as much of a request as of a simple intimation.

"At your leisure, Captain — I beg pardon, Lieutenant Lacy," replied the gentleman, venturing a second look at Elizabeth, who was about to follow her father, when a glance from him told her to remain.

"Most happy, Miss Lacy, at the unexpected delight of this second meeting; most happy indeed, upon my honor."

Yes, reader, the visitor was no other than Charles Bars, the saunterer from the Temple Gardens.

"Really? — What! your father?" exclaimed the young gentleman, with the most enviable confidence; and he took the drawing from the table, and stared at it very like a patron of the fine arts. "Humph! indeed, a fine-looking man. Well, never mind, matters must blow over; and depend upon it, Miss Lacy, your papa will be a post-captain." Had Charles Bars been first lord of the admiralty, he could not have taken a higher tone of prophecy. "But really, Miss Lacy, it's hard your papa must leave his family; is there no way of keeping him?"

"I fear, sir, none; he must almost immediately set off for the fleet."

"No, no;" cried Charles Bars, "not so bad as that — not immediately. I feel I can on my own responsibility allow the Lieutenant some further time; indeed, I came with the best intentions."

It was clear to Elizebeth that the visitor was some functionary of the Admiralty; his confident tone betrayed his power and importance.

"Do you indeed, sir?" said the girl, forgetful of even the face of Charles Bars under her bonnet; "you will make my mamma so happy! we must all thank you."

"Not at all, Miss Lacy; for my part, if you desire it, your father shan't budge — anything to please you, my dear Miss Lacy;" and with every word he spoke, Mr. Charles Bars approached a step nearer to Elizabeth; and when he uttered the last syllable, his audacious arm surrounded her waist.

Lieutenant Lacy was a man of marked decision; and entering the room at this instant, without one

word or breath of warning given, Charles Bars, by
some extraordinary process, was flung with his head
under the fire-grate, his neck uncomfortably supported
by the edge of an iron fender. There he lay, and
lying, bled like Cæsar. We, however, have one excuse for the wounded. It was his firm conviction
that Lieutenant Lacy had quitted the house by some
back door, or by scaling the roof, and descending a
neighboring chimney. But why, it may be asked,
should the Lieutenant shun an interview with the visit-
or? Why treat with such contumely the son of an officer? The truth is, when we spoke of the profession of
Charles Bars's father, we forgot to state his precise
service. Be it known, then, that he was neither military officer nor naval officer, but officer to the sheriff!
And Charles himself, though young, enjoyed no less
a dignity, in support of which he had that evening
visited Lieutenant Lacy at the suit of Messrs. Cat
and Condor, for services *not* rendered, The prostrate legalist, calculating that the courage of his assailant "preyed not upon carcasses," lay motionless
as Bracton; but he proved that his lungs were of corresponding brass with his face, and he roared, " Bob
Sykes!" who, listening in the street, loudly responded
to the call with the brass of the street door knocker.
The landlady, with feminine quickness, jumped at
right conclusions, and admitted the clamorous gentleman without, who rushed into the parlor, and, blind
to the blood of his companion, in the pursuit of his
duty, cried, "Where's the Leaftenant?" Where, indeed? All we know of his escape is this: — The
landlady, ere she admitted Robert Sykes, with a

strength proceeding from the hatred of her visitors, fairly clawed the gallant seaman from the parlor, and carried him off ere he himself was aware of the abduction. Where the woman hid her victim we know not. In what household fastness, in what domestic crypt, the Lieutenant lay shut up from the searching kindness of Robert Sykes remains to this day undivulged. The Lieutenant himself would never confess it.

"A pretty business this, marm; suppose he had killed the man?" asked Bob Sykes of Mrs. Smith, when, having given up the search for the Lieutenant, he had time to sympathize with the maltreated —— "Suppose he had killed the man?" again he asked; and again Mrs. Smith rubbed her hands, and gave one of her quiet looks.

If we know ourselves, we are made up of gentleness and mercy; we would no more kill an officer of the sheriff than we would tread on a poor beetle. But as human nature at the best is weak, and as the father of evil, indefatigable in his business, ever watches about the meekest and the purest, should we ever be betrayed into the indiscretion of slaying a sheriff's officer, — should we ever be guilty of the absurd weakness, — our only hope is, that we may be tried for the peccadillo by a jury of matrons. If there be only one Mrs. Smith among the dozen, the serenity with which we shall appear in the prisoners' dock will, as Mr. Pepys would say, "be pretty to see."

The blood from the nose of Charles Bars continued to meander down the finest shirt and the gayest waistcoat of his multitudinous wardrobe. The truth is, his father " held that night a solemn supper," where all the world was invited. We speak advisedly, for among the guests there were many veteran officers and their families, half a dozen bill-brokers, and a sprinkling of hard-working attorneys, particular friends of the hospitable host. Charles Bars had risen from the hands of the hair-dresser, and, aided by his sister Constantia, was about to rehearse, at their grand piano-forte,

"Together let us range the fields;"

he proposing to challenge Miss Solomons to the performance of that duet in the course of the evening, when he was summoned by his father to execute a writ on Lieutenant Lacy. Charles was the model of filial obedience, and Messrs. Cat and Condor were excellent customers. However, we have already detailed the difficulties of Charles in the pursuit of his duty. Giving the writ to Sykes, he now quitted the house, and, entering a hackney-coach, drove homewards, speculating by the way on the amount of damages. Lieutenant Lacy emerged from his mysterious hiding-place, and immediately set off for the private house of his new solicitor. He was within sight of the door, when, somebody calling his name, he turned round and felt a paralyzing hand on his right shoulder.

"Lieutenant Lacy, you must come with me." The speaker was no other than the discerning and ubiquitous Bob Sykes, who, by a lamp, had caught a glimpse of the Lieutenant's features as he rapidly passed him. True it is, Bob had never before beheld his prisoner;

but with restless observation he had scrutinized the
drawing at the Lieutenant's lodging, and the readiness
with which he therefore recognized the original was
a high compliment to the powers of the artist.   Nothing now remained but to enter into a new negotiation
with the partners of the "Old House," who consented
to withdraw their action, avowing themselves ready
to take their bills from the proceeds of the sale of the
Lieutenant's property — a sale which they now hoped
immediately to effect.   They had never wished to
distress the Lieutenant — not they ; but he had been
so unadvised, so very impatient.   Lacy even apolo-
gized to Messrs. Cat and Condor for his hasty mis-
interpretation of their motives.   But time pressed ; he
must immediately have the money — in two days the
fleet sailed — he had that morning seen the news in
the papers, and so, in truth, had Messrs. Cat and Condor ; and knowing, as they did, that the subsistence,
nay, the very reputation of their client depended upon
joining his ship, — knowing, in fact, that he had not
an hour to spare, — they wished, at any sacrifice, to
effect a sale.

"In the evening, Lieutenant Lacy, I have no doubt,
we may sign and seal."

"Evening, sir !" exclaimed Lacy, frantically, dashing his fist upon the desk.   "In an hour, Mr. Cat, in
an hour, or I am a lost man !"

And he sank again into his chair, and a tear burned
in his eye.

Be composed, my dear sir, pray be composed," cried
Cat, looking himself the spirit of tranquillity.   "As
the gentleman, who, we believe, is desirous of pur-

chasing the cottage, is our client, we will immediately send to him. Edward, here! No; wait until I write, and take this note to Mr. Fortescue, and be sure and bring an answer."

The junior clerk vanished with the missive, and Mr. Cat proceeded to mend his goose-quill. The operation finished, he politely handed the newspaper to Lacy, who, after a vain endeavor to read it, arose, and, with vacant looks, gazed out of the window. He was, however, shortly called to a recollection of things by the sharp whistling of a man below, who sauntered backwards and forwards, evidently as if waiting for somebody. Lacy thought he recognized the gait, the costume of the loiterer. Yes, he was not mistaken; the whistler was Bob Sykes. For whom, for what could he be waiting? Edward, the junior clerk, was fleet as a greyhound; and Mr. Fortescue, being luckily at home, in a few minutes personally answered the letter from the " Old House."

" Mr. Fortescue is come, sir," said Edward.

And Mr. Cat, with a slight bow to the Lieutenant, quitted the office, we presume to settle preliminaries with the visitor. After a short absence he returned, ushering in Mr. Fortescue. He was, in reality, a man of about two-and-thirty ; but we suppose it was either the smoke of his fireplace, or a continual cast of thought, which gave to his features, in themselves not regularly handsome, the aspect of eight-and-forty. Mr. Fortescue had been a party to many of the " financial operations " of the " Old House," and thus must have possessed considerable wealth. Indeed, the fact was roundly asserted by Messrs. Cat and Condor, who would facetiously (we know not with which of the partners originated the joke) call him their golden calf. In sober truth, they had talked so much of his wealth, that the poor man passed for an incorrigible miser; and neither his dwelling nor his garments were calculated to falsify the opinion. Indeed, what can be said of a man who dwells in the top apartment of a magazine for old bottles, old rags, old iron, at the bottom of Saffron Hill, and yet bargains for and purchases twenty houses in the year — beautiful mansions, rich acres, parks, woods, fisheries? What can be urged in defence of him who, by his dealings, we should judge capable of wearing each day a new suit of gold cloth, whose whole wardrobe, were he turned out from it clean as Adam, would be no good pennyworth at fifteen shillings? The case was plain: Mr. Fortescue was a muck-worm; yet, with all the paralyzing passions of a miser, he had retained the lively sense of benefits received. He was bound by a feeling of gratitude, heart and soul, to Messrs. Cat and Condor, who, in a most difficult law case, in a cause which perilled the whole of his worldly property, had, with their proverbial sagacity, effected his triumph.

Lieutenant Lacy started when introduced to Mr. Fortescue. The appearance of the stranger was not prepossessing: harsh, dark features, completely mapped by the small-pox — a large, black, cowering eye, and a mouth wide and rigid, as though modelled by a horse-shoe, rarely appeal with success to the confidence of the superficial; and Lieutenant Lacy, though a worthy man, we do not set up for a sage.

A faded green coat, with honest copper buttons, the deceptive gilding having long since disappeared, a blue plush waistcoat, brown breeches, boots with clay-colored tops, a hat of the like hue, verdantly turned up, and a cotton neckerchief, pattern white ground, with a small dark-blue lozenge, composed all the visible obligations of Mr. Fortescue to the sophistications of dress. The business was soon commenced: and luckily Mr. Fortescue was a man of few words; we say luckily, for his voice was not one of those living harmonies the ear loves to dwell upon, at least it was not on the present occasion, but perhaps Mr. Fortescue had a cold.

"Mr. Fortescue is prepared to give one hundred and fifty pounds for the cottage."

"One hundred and fifty!" cried Lieutenant Lacy. "Three hundred, Mr. Cat — three hundred was the sum."

"You asked? Yes, Lieutenant, I remember, and in other times worth the money; nay, I think now, cheap at the amount; but Mr. Fortescue *has said* a hundred and fifty."

We must account for a peculiar emphasis on Mr. Fortescue *has said*. Briefly, then, Mr. Cat always eulogized his rich client for one stern virtue in dealing; he never rose or fell in his first offer. He was a man to die a martyr to his first *dixi*.

"But surely, Mr. Cat, Mr. Fortescue is not aware of the extent of the property, of the natural advantages — "

"Fully aware, my dear Lieutenant. I have shown him the plan, taken by our Plymouth agent; he is

5

fully possessed of everything, and he is ready to put down for the purchase "— and here Mr. Cat met the eye of Mr. Fortescue, who looked upon the ground, and turned away his head with an air of indifference, and said very gruffly, —

"One hundred and fifty."

"Never! Nothing shall force me to the sacrifice," exclaimed the Lieutenant. "Nothing! A hundred and fifty for — "

He seized his hat, and was about to rush from the room, when the shrill whistling of Bob Sykes below, like the voice of the snake-charmer, fixed him motionless. The sweat broke in beads upon his forehead, his eyes glowed, and a hectic flush came to his cheek, as he said in a tone almost tremulous with entreaty, "Say two hundred."

Mr. Cat said nothing, but threw open the palms of his hands and looked at Mr. Fortescue, who remained dumb.

"Say two hundred," repeated the Lieutenant.

"Mr. Fortescue?" cried Cat, awaiting his answer. "Mr. Fortescue?"

Mr. Fortescue again averted his face, and, as it appeared, with a slight convulsive elevation of the shoulders, again replied, "One hundred and fifty."

"It will not suffice, sir, it will not suffice," cried Lacy; and then, in a lower tone, deepening as he proceeded, "I have engagements to meet, debts of a most pressing, delicate nature to discharge, children who — Mr. Cat, you promised three hundred!"

"Very true, Lieutenant, and I still think the house

a bargain at the money; and, moreover, I have no doubt, since Mr. Fortescue will make no advance, but in a day or two another purchaser — "

"A day or two? You know, sir, I must quit London to-night. To-morrow I must be on board my ship, or I am a ruined, a dishonored man. Mr. Fortescue," cried Lacy, in a tone that seemed to pierce the spinal marrow of the purchaser, for again his shoulders leaped at the sound, but his head was turned away, and he replied no syllable. There was a dead pause in the sanctum of the "Old House;" the Lieutenant looked livid with repressed agitation; Mr. Cat gently rubbed his hands, and looked over his spectacles; Condor raised his eyes from his book, and again passed his tongue round his upper lip, and Mr. Fortescue rocked to and fro, his head sunk on his bosom. Then Lacy, gazing wildly about him, his eye fell on the newspaper, and the line, "naval intelligence," struck on his brain like fire. Falling in a chair, he cried, or rather groaned, "Give me the money." The deeds were signed, the hundred and fifty pounds paid, and then Mr. Fortescue immediately departed. The original bill of Messrs. Cat and Condor, for negotiating the purchase, was forty pounds, to which must be added the expense of the arrest, which they so deeply regretted. These demands were of course discharged by the Lieutenant, who had then but little more than a hundred pounds to provide for claims to twice that amount. Puzzled how to make one guinea perform the duty of two (in this tragic comedy of the world, a most frequent but no less difficult double), Lacy prepared to return to

his lodgings. "Tarry a little, Lieutenant; the law
hath yet another hold on thee." It is enacted in too
scrupulous England, that a man shall not, even in the
way of relaxation, break the nose of a sheriff's officer
gratis. Now, Charles Bars had admirable grounds
of action; the family surgeon could conscientiously
testify to the battered condition of the nose of his
patient by violent contact with the knuckles of the
sea Lieutenant. No time was lost to inform the assailant of his delicate predicament; still it was insinuated that Christian charity was not extinct in the
family of the Bars; a compromise of sufficient weight
might be received. Now, Lieutenant Lacy, recol-
lecting a wise axiom of warriors, that to get rid of a
troublesome enemy it is lawful to build for him a
bridge of gold, applied a principle of the field to
remove a civil difficulty, and thus relieved himself of
the broken nose of Charles Bars, by a sacrifice of ten
guineas; in proper phrase, by building for him a
bridge of gold.

Ten guineas for the single nose of a sheriff's officer!
If so small a portion of the sheriff's face divine be so
costly, what must be the value of the whole animal?
Little knew an excellent friend of ours, whose whole
heart was cream and honey, what magnificent sport
he was preparing for the world, when he gave it as
his firm conviction, that once a year every honest
man, duly equipped for shooting, should be permitted unrestricted sport in and within the vicinity
of Chancery Lane! Of what worth would be a single
head of game, when it is seen that the market price
of one nose is ten guineas! But then, on this expen-

sive scale, what an opportunity would be offered to the rich to display their wealth! Thus, no banquet, however luxuriously composed, would be deemed complete, unless, instead of being invited to partake of pheasant, teal, or woodcock, a carver could observe, " Permit me, sir, the happiness of helping you to a little sheriff's officer." Of course at first the invitation might create a start, a tremor among many guests, but the luxury would soon be understood, and as a luxury highly relished. Our gross ancestors served up the boar, the swan, nay, the porpoise. Let us prove our advancement in civilized and rational life, by dishing sheriff's officers. However, to leave the delicacies of the table for our narrative.

Lieutenant Lacy took a hurried farewell of his wife and children, and threw himself into the mail for Portsmouth. The sacrifice which he had been compelled to make, rendering the discharge of all claims upon him wholly impossible, he could not feel secure of his liberty until far upon the road. Disappointed in certain views for the provision of her family in London, Mrs. Lacy and the children prepared to return to their native place — a village two or three miles from Plymouth — at which seaport, twenty years before, an event occurred, which, gaining for the Lieutenant general esteem and admiration, we think had some influence on the affection of his future wife.

Lacy, at the time whereof we write, was about nineteen, a midshipman on board H. M. S. ——. The ship's crew had received long arrears of pay, and all on board was clamorous merriment and high festivity. The slopsellers in Plymouth thronged the vessel to ply their dreadful trade. The first thing a sailor buys is a watch. Now, Mr. Lazarus, a patriarchal slop-seller, had sold some twenty chronometers among the ship's company ; but by some unaccountable error of the maker or makers, one and all of the watches stopped, as by general consent, on the second day. The day after, Mr. Lazarus, attended by his son, a boy of about ten years old, came on board — no doubt as an assiduous and honest tradesman, to inquire into the merits of his various timepieces. Mr. Lazarus was between sixty and seventy — a man uniting to the keenest views of business a singularly mild and venerable outside. He would dilate on the excel-lences of a Guernsey frock with the winning sim-plicity of an antique shepherd. Touched by his tongue, trinkets of copper glistened in the eyes of the buyer virgin gold. There never was so meek, so picturesque a slopseller. Behold him with imper-turbable tranquillity surrounded by a crowd of sailors, every man exhibiting a watch — some roaring, some growling, some sneering, some blaspheming — and not a few grasping the frail memorial of time, as though meditating a cast at the seller's skull. In this tempest of bad words and unequivocal glances, Mr. Lazarus was motionless and patient as the figure-head — a composure highly annoying to his cus-tomers, who began to close about him — and push him, now to the right and now to the left — now backwards and now forwards, until — how the ac-cident came about not one of the crew could ever tell : the venerable Mr. Lazarus was — pushed into the sea ! " Man overboard ! " is a cry that thrills through the heart of a ship's company ; but whether in the present instance the general festivity had made men deaf to the call, or whether the cry was not sufficiently loud to be generally audible, we cannot venture to determine ; but this we know, the tide, running strong, was carrying away the old Jew, cumbrously and heavily clothed, and in a few seconds Plymouth would have mourned its oldest slopseller, had not a young midshipman leaped into the sea, and, being an admirable swimmer, come up with the sinking Israelite as his gray hairs were fast disappearing in the deep. Young Lacy supported the drowning wretch until a boat received them. The old man's son, who had shrieked in helpless agony as he saw him borne away, fell on his knees at the feet of the young officer, embracing his legs in speechless gratitude. All Plymouth rang with praises of the humanity of the midshipman for his wonderful philanthropy in saving even Mr. Lazarus. However, Lacy had his reward ; for, as we have hinted, we doubt not he owed to the circumstance the first affection of his wife.

Arrived at Portsmouth, Lacy lost not a moment, but hastened to go on board. What was his despair to see the whole fleet under sail ! It had weighed anchor an hour before ; the wind was fair and freshening — to come up with his ship was impossible — he saw her — with a sailor's eye he marked her canvas lessening as he looked. He seemed fixed, motionless with misery. Another moment, and he leaped into a waterman's boat. " Five pounds," he cried to the two men, " if I reach my ship."

" Which is she, sir?   What's her name? "

" The ——."

" Impossible, sir — she is the fastest frigate in the
navy, and the breeze, you may see, is getting up —
impossible."

" Make the trial, my good fellow — if I lose my
ship, I am lost forever. My family —" Lacy could
speak no more.

" What do you say, Peter?" asked the waterman
of his companion.

" Say?" replied the man, looking suspiciously at the
fleet, and arming himself with a mouthful of pigtail —
" it's impossible, you know ; but, poor gentleman, we
must do it."

The boat was pushed off, the sail hoisted, and the
men, with arms of iron, plied their oars. For some
time the Lieutenant sat gazing at his receding ship in
silence.   Every moment she gained upon them.

" Lay to it, boys, lay to it," said Lacy, despairingly.

The appeal was needless.   The men toiled at the
top of their strength — their faces were scarlet, and
their stout oars bent and quivered like rods of steel —
the boat, a taught, trim craft, shot like an arrow
through the water — still she seemed to close upon
the frigate.

" Damn her," said one of the men, casting a backward look at the vessel, and speaking in a tone of
mingled disappointment and admiration, " damn her,
she flies like a gull."

" The wind is getting up," said Lacy, hopelessly.

" No, sir ; if anything, going down," answered
Peter, though he looked as if he knew well enough it
was not so.

"They are setting studding-sails," said the Lieutenant, as though he gave up all for lost.

" The more credit for us if we beat 'em," answered the encouraging Peter.

Again Lacy was silent, though in the waywardness of suspense he could have talked to the boat as to a creature instinct with life and reason. Then, as he cast his eyes upon the sea, he beheld not the green fields, the vales, and groves, which a seaman struck by the calenture sickens for; but he saw mirrored in the deep, still following him and still looking on him, the face of his wife — the faces of his five children.

"My turn now," said Lacy, tearing himself from the vision, and relieving one of the men at the oar.

For another hour they pulled in almost unbroken silence. At the last, the man cried to his resting companion, "It's no use, Peter." Lacy felt that every stroke of the forward oar became less and less powerful — that his ship became less and less distinct — the whole fleet looked no more than a flight of wild swans. "It's no use, Peter," repeated the man; and he ran in his oar.

" We are gaining on them, we are gaining fast," said Lacy; "for God's sake, men, do not fail me."

" It's no use, sir," replied the man; and the sweat ran down his very fingers.

"My good fellow!" cried Lacy, imploringly to Peter.

Peter gave another look at the fleet, and then echoed his partner — "It's no use, sir."

Lacy sprang to his feet, stretched out his arms,

and, with a look of agonized madness, glared over, the boat.

The men, startled, rose with him.

At that instant, as with a charm, the wind fell.

" Where's the wind ? " said Peter, as the sail fell to the mast.

" A dead calm," cried his wondering companion.

" Come you aft," said Peter, and again he seized the oar — " now, sir," cried he, " the blessing of God, and a long stroke, and we board her."

Again Lacy and Peter bent to it — the oars rang in the rowlocks, and the water boiled as the craft shot through it. It was a long, a hard pull ; but Lacy stood on the deck of his own ship.

His brother officers crowded about him with congratulations, and even the captain, strict disciplinarian as he was, hardly repressed a smile as he said, " Better late than never, Mr. Lacy."

In the solitude of his cabin, reviewing the hurried events of the past few days, Lacy remembered and drew from his pocket an unopened letter. It had been delivered to him as he was about to get upon the mail. Fearing it contained no pleasing communication, he cared not to break the seal. He now opened the letter, and found it enclosed two hundred pounds in bank notes. Bewildered by the treasure, and still more rapt as he proceeded, he read as follows : —

" Sir : It was some comfort to me, in the bitterness of this morning, to find you did not know me. Twenty times I could have fallen at your feet, and begged you to trample upon me. O, sir, I saw it all again — I saw the old man strangling in the sea — I saw your blessed hand pluck him back to life. If ever my eyes beheld my old father, they saw him in that office — there where I was brought to cheat, to rob you. Never before did I feel what it was to be a scoundrel. At the first glance I knew you, and I felt as if I had swallowed burning coals. The money I send you will make up the fair value of the house. For your compassion of an old man in the hour of peril, may the God of Israel forever bless you.

"DAVID LAZARUS, *alias* FORTESCUE.

"P. S. Any attempt to discover where I am will be useless. I shall free myself from the bondage in which you saw me, and leave England for some place where I shall be unknown. God bless you, dear sir."

It was even so — Mr. Fortescue was no other than the tool of Messrs. Cat and Condor, the poor nominal purchaser of all their bargains. "But," says the reader, "you spoke of a lawsuit, in which all the property of Fortescue had been preserved by the partners of the 'Old House.'" Very true, for his only property was his neck. He had been brought through a very ugly business by Cat and Condor, who afterwards secured him for their own mercantile purposes. He had, however, by some means saved three hundred pounds, with which he contemplated speculations on his own account, when his meeting with the preserver of his father's life, a victim to a conspiracy in which he himself played a most odious character, struck upon his heart, and made it flow with gratitude. The miserable wretch, scurfed as he was with his daily villanies, at one touch of nature shook off his moral leprosy, and stood a healthful man. With his one hundred pounds he went abroad, and lived and died a flourishing and wealthy citizen. For once Mr. Charles Bars might claim the reputation of a prophet; for in a few months the fleet returned to Portsmouth, and in two days afterwards a communication from the Admiralty greeted Lacy Commander. But what of Messrs. Cat and Condor? what of the partners of the " Old House "? On an eventful feast, in the fourth plate of turtle, Condor went off in an apoplexy. His fortune, inherited by a profligate nephew, passed in two years into the hands of black-legs. For Cat, he became a bigoted believer in supernatural signs and tokens. He sank to mere imbecility, and may now be seen in a certain asylum, pacing the court-yard, vacantly smiling, rubbing his hands, and crying every minute, —

" To-morrow, sir! to-morrow!"

1835.

SOME ACCOUNT OF THE LAST PARA- CHUTE.

CONSIDERABLE excitement was on the —th ult. manifested throughout the populous district of Walworth. It had been industriously, though confidentially, whispered that Mr. Minnow, a fishmonger and vestryman, distinguished no less for his public spirit than his private virtues, was about to share in the perilous ascent of Mrs. Graham. A new parachute, invented by Mr. Minnow, whose scientific attainments had long been the theme of admiration among a select circle of friends, was to be tried on the occasion. And, with that liberality which had ever characterized the conduct of the above-named gentleman, a bushel of live oysters, supplied from his own warehouse, was to accompany the aerial voyagers at least five miles above the earth, and then to descend in a parachute, in order that the timid and sceptical might be assured and convinced of the perfect safety of the conveyance. In his zeal for science, Mr. Minnow now resolved that his own infant — the youngest of an interesting family of ten — should be the favored tenant of the parachute; but, as it had been only three days short-coated, Mrs. Minnow, in her natural anxiety for the health of her offspring, suggested that the dear baby might possibly take cold; and when it was considered that oysters would do quite as well, the maternal hesitation on the part of Mrs. Minnow must find some allowance in the bosoms of the most curious and the most scientific.

We should waste time, ink, and paper were we to attempt to demonstrate the vast utility of the parachute. Its extraordinary influence on the comforts of society is, happily, not now to be disputed. To be able to shoot from a balloon to the earth, when the balloon itself would afford that transit, is to enjoy the most gratifying sense of independence. Who would descend the stairs of a house when a safe and rapid flight into the street might be taken from the garret window? However, to the eventful proceedings of the day.

At an early hour the ground was thronged. The balloon was inflated, and, by its tugging motion, seemed, like a young eagle, to desire to wing its proud and lofty way into that bright and circumambient air wherein it was soon to soar in gentle grace and glittering beauty. At three o'clock Mrs. Graham appeared upon the ground, and was received with marked enthusiasm. She looked at the balloon, bowed, and smiled confidently. She was dressed in a brown gown, white straw bonnet, and blue ribbons. We had almost forgotten to state that she also wore a chinchilla tippet. By those who stood near her she was understood to inquire for her fellow-passenger, Mr. Minnow.

At this moment, as we are credibly informed by an ear-witness of unimpeachable character, Mr. Minnow came upon the ground. He was at first received with silence; but, on several persons exclaiming, " That's he — that's Minnow! " an indescribable shout seemed to rend apart the very heavens. Mr. Minnow put his hand upon his heart, and bowed. He was a remarkably respectable-looking man, having on a handsome blue coat with bright buttons, drab breeches and gaiters, a white hat turned up with green, a gold watch (he took it out to inquire the hour), and large appendages. He carried in his hand what — and we think, too, we state the general impression — we took it to be a gig umbrella. Reader, it was the NEW PARACHUTE! Who that looked upon the machine could have suspected it? Who, when the mystery was unfolded, can describe the delight of the intoxicated multitude? At length all was prepared, and —

And here, readers and fellow-countrymen, we are compelled to pause to call upon you to applaud the vigilant benevolence of the district magistracy, who had caused Inspector Lynx, of the "I" division, to prohibit the ascent of the oysters — we are bound to say there was a full bushel — unless it could be satisfactorily proved to him, upon scientific principles, that no accident could accrue to them from the experiment.

We were delighted at this interference for two reasons. The first is, it proved the humanity and activity of the magistrates; and the second afforded us the pleasure of hearing Mr. Minnow shortly, but lucidly, lecture on the principles of his new parachute, and convince Inspector Lynx that it was impossible the descent from any height could be so violent as to break in pieces *both* shells of the oyster; that, if the bottom shell were broken, the top would be unin-

jured, and *vice versâ*. On this, in the most handsome manner, — on this Inspector Lynx suffered the
bushel of adventurous aeronauts to be placed in the
parachute; and we deal in no hyperbolical figure
when we state that expectation was upon tiptoe.

Mr. Minnow handed Mrs. Graham into the basket-
car, and, with no visible emotion, followed. A third
passenger, a studious-looking man, — as it was whispered, the editor of a journal of considerable weight,
— took his seat upon the " cross-bench." The word
was given — the ropes were cut — the balloon rose
very, very slowly. Mrs. Graham flung out several
bags of sand, and Mr. Minnow lightened his pockets
of several packs of cards, eagerly sought for by the
crowd as mementos of the soul-stirring occurrence.
We were happy in securing one of these precious
tokens, the subjoined *fac-simile* of which we are
proud to lay before our readers: —

PETER MINNOW,

Shrimp and Shell-Fish Merchant,

NEW CUT, LAMBETH.

The only Warehouse for the real Parachute Oysters.

Sent in Barrels to all parts of the United Kingdom.

———

N. B. PERIWINKLES IN EVERY VARIETY.

Although many **bags of sand and** several packs of the
above cards were flung **from the car, the** balloon rose
lazily, and some of the **lower order of** spectators had

their mouths ready formed to hiss, when Mrs. Graham darted a glance of suspicion at the editor. With some confusion in his manner he put his hand to his coat pocket, and hurriedly flung an unsuspected copy of his own journal from him ; and, extraordinary as it may appear, the balloon, with the parachute attached to it, shot like a rocket into the air, Minnow just before exclaiming to his wife, " Mind, Betsy, the left box ! "

The crowd huzzaed, Mrs. Graham, Minnow, and the second gentleman each waving a flag of a different hue.

We are happy to say that here our task concludes, for we have now to report the words of that daring aeronaut, Peter Minnow, himself : —

" We rose with a gentle and steady breeze. For at least five minutes — so clearly could we discern objects — I could distinguish the mustache of Potlid, the master tinman of Lambeth Marsh ; nor was it until two minutes more had elapsed that we had wholly lost sight of his tip.

" We crossed the Thames between Waterloo and Blackfriars. By the reflection of the sun upon a black cloud, and by the aid of an excellent glass, we plainly discerned the copper edge of a bad sixpence presented to, and taken by, the unsuspecting tollman.

" The coal barges looked no larger than old shoes, and the fan-tail hats of the coal-heavers like patches on the cheeks of a lady. The pearl buttons on the velveteen jacket of a ticket-porter, as Mrs. Graham

6

assured me, presented quite an era in the history of aerostation.

"We looked from time to time with intense interest on the passengers in the parachute, all of whom appeared perfectly tranquil. We felt assured, from their unaltered demeanor, that no timidity on their part would prevent a fair trial of the powers of the new machine.

"The weather was beautiful. As we steered eastward St. Paul's became a conspicuous and animating object. We hovered above it like an eagle flapping his fan-like wings in the molten sun.* Here we descended so low, and there was about us such a death-like calm, that we heard, or thought we heard, the half-pence chink at the door of the cathedral. Mrs. Graham playfully remarked to me that the statue of Queen Anne, observed from our point of view, looked very like a Bavarian broom-girl.

"As we were wafted gently onwards Bow Church arose in all its simple dignity. By a strange coincidence Bow bells were ringing. We were borne tranquilly onwards until we found ourselves above the Stock Exchange. Here many persons looked very small indeed, and here we experienced a dead calm. In order that we might rise into another current we cast more sand out, and feared, from the confusion we saw below, that we had unconsciously flung a great deal of dust into the eyes of several contractors.

---

* We trust we do no wrong to Mr. Minnow, but we shrewdly suspect that his companion, the editor, has helped him to a figure or two.

" We rose and found another current, and, to our inexpressible satisfaction, were carried due west. Even at such an altitude we were able to make out objects. I saw what I am sure was the line of stakes belonging to the Golden Cross, but Mrs. Graham insisted that it was the National Gallery.

" I observed to the gentleman that accompanied us that the rarefied air produced in me symptoms of sudden hunger. At this he significantly asked if it were necessary that the whole bushel of oysters should descend unopened. To this I replied, with firmness, that I could not break faith with the public — the parachute must go the whole bushel.

" We were now driven on with great speed, and were about the desired five miles above the surface of the globe, when Mrs. Graham remarked that we had sailed a great distance, and that, consequently, we should have an equal distance to return.

" I had promised the spirited proprietor of the Victoria Theatre to present myself upon his stage at half past eleven at night. (I may be here permitted to express my regret that, as an old neighbor of that gentleman, I was compelled to refuse the terms of the proprietor of the Surrey Theatre. I could *not*, with justice to my family, take two pounds, and include the bushel of oysters. My tub is still at his service for the dress-boxes.) Half past eleven at the latest ; the hour was stated in the bills, and I expected a great crowd in my rooms when the play was over. On this I preferred to let the parachute descend.

" It was an anxious moment. I cut the cord, the

aeronauts — the whole bushel — shot quicker than lightning down the blue abyss. We rose, but, owing to the skilful direction of Mrs. Graham, suffered no inconvenience. The balloon was almost immediately at our command, and we prepared to descend, that we might join as soon as possible our brother aeronauts.

"We alighted in a paddock, the property of Mr. Fuss, late of Houndsditch, at the picturesque village of Pinner. To himself, his amiable lady, their lovely family, and various domestics, we owe the greatest thanks for assistance in our descent.

"Mr. Cuts, schoolmaster of Pinner, in the most handsome way despatched his fifty boys in various directions in search of the parachute, liberally offering sixpence from his own pocket to the fortunate finder.

"We were then ushered by Mr. and Mrs. Fuss into their front parlor, where we partook of a cold collation — shoulder of mutton, pickled walnuts, ale, &c.

"We made a hearty meal, but were naturally anxious for the fate of the parachute. At length our fears were dissipated by the appearance of a male and female gypsy, followed by some of the boys of Mr. Cuts, who brought to us the uninjured parachute and all the — shells!

"The gypsies were rigidly cross-examined, but were firm in their statement that the oysters came to the earth ready opened. When the peculiar lawlessness of this class of people is taken into consideration, their statement will weigh nothing with the scientific; for it is plain that the same force that opened an oyster must have had some effect upon the frail fabric of the parachute, which will, for the next six weeks, be exhibited in my rooms for the satisfaction of the curious, whether they take their oysters raw or scalloped.

" He indeed must be the most sceptical or the most envious of men, or both, who can ever venture to question the safety and utility of my parachute.

" After enjoying the hospitality of Mr. and Mrs. Fuss, the balloon and parachute were packed up, and we arrived at the stage door of the Victoria Theatre at five-and-twenty minutes past eleven, where we were cordially welcomed by the lessee ! "

Thus far goes the simple statement of Mr. Minnow. It is now our duty to declare that no sooner was his arrival made known, than a loud shout was set up for him, when he instantly appeared upon the stage, led on by the manager. A supernumerary in the background carried the parachute.

Mrs. Graham was next called for, when that lady appeared, and courtesied an acknowledgment of the honor.

A vehement cry was next raised for the proprietor. He came on after some hesitation, and was welcomed with a loud burst of applause. He was so affected by the novelty of his situation that he was led off, leaning on the arms of his friend, the stage-manager.

Mrs. Minnow and numerous family were next recognized in the left hand stage-box. They were loudly applauded, and severally returned their mute yet eloquent thanks.

The friends of science will, we feel assured, be

delighted to learn that it is next season the intention of Mr. Minnow to ascend every evening with his parachute, beginning on Easter Monday, until further notice.   1837.

———◦◦◦———

MY HUSBAND'S "WINNINGS."

A HOUSEHOLD INCIDENT.

"Most men in something cheat their wives." — THE HONEYMOON.

"THERE, Mary, my love, take my winnings," said Mr. Joseph Langshawe; at the same time laying a sovereign and a sixpence upon the breakfast table.

"Won again, Joseph!" cried Mrs. Langshawe, with one of her prettiest looks of astonishment; "won again!"

"Take my winnings," repeated Mr. Langshawe, and, suppressing a sigh, he languidly stirred his coffee.

The reader may be assured that, for a winning man, Mr. Joseph Langshawe had one of the longest faces out of Chancery; yet, at the time at which our story commences, he appeared to his wife the chosen of good fortune; there never was such a lucky man! It seemed enough for him to touch the cards to turn them to trumps. Joseph Langshawe had won again!

Certainly the continued prosperity of Langshawe was to his wife marvellous: he never sat down to cards that he did not rise money in pocket. Had Joseph made a terrible compact with that crafty general dealer who continually roams about the earth, seeking cheap pennyworths? Had he trucked his immortal jewel for pasteboard diamonds as he chose to evoke them in this world? Had he surrendered himself to the great demon for a magical influence over tens, and fives, and sequences? In a word, was Joseph Langshawe become the fated Faust of five-card cribbage? Mysterious fears of future evil mingled in the marvellings of Mrs. Langshawe!

" When I think of Joseph's continued good fortune," observed Mrs. Langshawe to a female friend, " I own to you it sometimes makes me tremble."

" Why, my dear?" asked Mrs. Bridgeman. " Why? I thought you told me, that, like a good creature as he is, he always gave you his winnings."

" And so he does," replied Mrs. Langshawe ; " invariably."

" What a good soul!" exclaimed Mrs. Bridgeman. " Dear fellow! it proves him so free from any selfish motives — shows that he merely plays for innocent excitement. And does Langshawe never lose?"

" Never," replied Mrs. Langshawe ; " and it is that which makes me so very unhappy."

" Makes you unhappy! Well, you are the strangest creature," cried Mrs. Bridgeman.

" That is," rejoined Mrs. Langshawe, " when I fear that his continued good luck may some day tempt him to play for a ruinous sum ; for it is impossible, my dear, that such fortune as Joseph's can last. I should be so happy if he'd never touch a card again!"

" Why, you bought that beautiful chain, and your
diamond drops, and all out of your husband's winnings," exclaimed Mrs. Bridgeman.

" Very true," allowed Mrs. Langshawe; and then
she repeated, with a deep sigh, " but such fortune as
Joseph's *can't* last."

Certain we are that the reader, after some further
acquaintance with Langshawe, would not wish
Joseph's fortune to continue. A brief extract from
the conversation of the night previous to the presenta-
tion of the sovereign and sixpence may explain the
mystery of Langshawe's winnings.

" Well, Langshawe," cried a friend from an opposite table, as Joseph rose to go home, " how have
you fared to-night? "

" As usual," said Joseph, and he tried to whistle;
" as usual — there's no standing Bridgeman's luck."

" What! " exclaimed Fourpoints, " lost again?
Why, you always lose."

" I should say always," replied Joseph; " never
mind — it's all right; yes, I've just enough; " and
Langshawe held in his hand a sovereign, and a half
crown, and a sixpence.

" Brought down to that, eh? " asked Flush, looking
at the three pieces of coin.

" All that's left," answered Langshawe, " out of
five and twenty pounds. Never mind, there's just
enough : half a crown will pay for my coach home,
and then — yes, that will make a very good show; "
and Joseph surveyed at a distance the little piece of
gold and lesser piece of silver in his palm; " a very
good show for my winnings."

"Winnings!" exclaimed a new member of the club — "winnings! I thought, sir, you had nothing but losses?"

"That's very true, sir," replied Langshawe; "notwithstanding, I always make it a point in my domestic economy, whatever my losses may be, to take home my profits to my wife. You perceive," — and Joseph exhibited the coin, — "when the coach is paid for, although I've lost to Bridgeman nearly four and twenty pounds, here's just a sovereign and a sixpence for my winnings."

"A sixpence! Why be so particular with the sixpence?" inquired the new member.

Mr. Joseph Langshawe looked one of his gravest looks in the face of the new member, and, after a compassionate shake of the head, observed, "I should say, sir, you were a bachelor; I should say, — pardon me if I'm wrong, — that as yet you know nothing of conjugal confidence, otherwise you would perceive that the sixpence was a — a clincher."

"A clincher!" repeated the simple new member.

"The sovereign by itself," observed Joseph, "might appear suspicious; but don't you perceive there's a reality in odd money. Mrs. Langshawe will see truth, sir, truth in the tester."

And the next morning, as we have already shown, Joseph handed over to the partner of his worldly goods a sovereign and a sixpence — his winnings!

"And who played last night?" asked Mrs. Langshawe — we must again ask the reader's attendance at the breakfast table — "who played? Bridgeman?"

"Bridgeman," answered Joseph, shortly.

"My dear Joseph," said Mrs. Langshawe, very gravely, "I wish you'd exert the influence of a friend over Bridgeman; he confesses nothing to his wife, poor, dear woman!—but I'm sure his losses must be very heavy. Everybody hasn't your good fortune, Joseph." Langshawe buried that expressive feature, his mouth, and half his nose, in his tea-cup. "It would make me truly unhappy, Joseph, if I thought you won any of his money," said Mrs. Langshawe.

"Make yourself perfectly easy on that point, my dear," said Langshawe, internally wincing at the absurd suspicion; "my hands are clean of Bridgeman, though I played with him."

"I'm delighted to hear it," cried Mrs. Langshawe. "And now, Joseph, if you'll promise me to leave off play altogether—"

"I have serious thoughts of it," said Joseph.

"You'll make me completely happy. For, depend upon it, as I have said again and again, your present fortune can't last."

"I've thought so too," said Langshawe; who might have added, "and that's why I have gone on."

"And if you give up cards, perhaps the example may have a good effect upon Bridgeman; for the Bridgemans are not like us, Joseph; they want, I fear, that mutual confidence in one another, without which marriage must be—"

"To be sure, my dear," said Langshawe, acutely anticipating his wife's period—"to be sure. No—I shall give up play."

"I hope you will—I sincerely hope," said Mrs. Langshawe, as she took up the sovereign and the six-pence, "that this will be the last of your winnings."

Noon had scarcely passed ere a passionate knocking at the door of the Langshawes announced a visitor.
" Bless me ! yes, it is — it is, dear Mrs. Bridgeman,"
said Mrs. Langshawe, with mingled surprise and
pleasure, as she heard the silvery voice of her friend
on the staircase. " Dear Mrs. Bridgeman ! "

As the visitor was introduced, Mrs. Langshawe
jumped from her chair to run and kiss her best acquaintance, when Mrs. Bridgeman smiled somewhat
severely, half dropped a courtesy, put her hand to her
brow, and sank into a seat.

" What's the matter, dear ? " asked Mrs. Langshawe.

Mrs. Bridgeman entered into no details of her
complaint, but simply observed, " I shall be better
presently."

" Anything happened at home ? " inquired Mrs.
Langshawe. " How's Bridgeman ? "

Hath the reader beheld the countenance of an
invalid when prescribed a certain drug, of all drugs
his worst abhorrence ? Hath the reader himself felt
the cold shiver running through his vitals, twisting
the very tips of his toes — the indescribable nausea
that hath puckered up his countenance divine, and
given his head a shake of most expressive loathing ?
Any one, so experienced, would have thought from
Mrs. Bridgeman's manner that Mrs. Langshawe had
spoken, it might be, of rhubarb, and not of Bridgeman — of assafœtida, perhaps, and not of a husband.

" I hope he's well ? " said Mrs. Langshawe, anx-
iously.

" I believe Mr. Bridgeman is very well," said his

wife; " but you know he never tells me anything.
Yes, last night I did gather from him that he had
played at cards only with Mr. Langshawe."

" So Joseph told me," observed the innocent Mrs.
Langshawe.

" Ha! you are blessed with a fortunate husband,"
said Mrs. Bridgeman, dryly. " Some people, it is
plain, are born with lucky fingers."

" I'm afraid it is so: however, Joseph has almost
promised me never, never to play again."

" 'Twill be a happy circumstance for some of his
friends," remarked Mrs. Bridgeman, significantly.

" If, however, he will play and win, I am resolved
— for it lies heavily upon my conscience to spend the
money upon myself — I am determined to devote the
money to some benevolent purpose: and, since the
thought has taken me, I am so delighted that you are
come to advise me! What do you think, my dear
Mrs. Bridgeman," and Mrs. Langshawe drew herself
nearer to her friend, — " what do you think of the
Society for the Conversion of the Jews?"

" Do you intend to subscribe Mr. Langshawe's winnings of last night to that estimable body ? " asked
Mrs. Bridgeman, biting her lips.

" How kind the suggestion!" exclaimed Mrs.
Langshawe. " What a good creature you are! I
did not think to do so, but now I certainly shall."

" For five-and-twenty pounds," said Mrs. Bridgeman, with a terrible smile, " no doubt you may be a
life governess."

" Five-and-twenty pounds!" cried Mrs. Lang
shawe, laughingly.

" The losses of Mr. Bridgeman last night," remarked his wife; " he played with Mr. Langshawe,
and, I presume, as usual, the fortunate man gave you
his winnings." This was said in a cold, cutting tone,
sharp enough to sever every silver tie of female
friendship.

" My dear Mrs. Bridgeman, there must be some
mistake. Joseph gave me his winnings, certainly, but
they were only a sovereign — "

" A sovereign! " exclaimed Mrs. Bridgeman, con-
temptuously.

" And a — sixpence," added Mrs. Langshawe, with
her usual meekness.

" And a sixpence! A sovereign and a sixpence!
My dear," said Mrs. Bridgeman, with awakened
sympathy, " you are a deceived, an injured woman."

" Do you really think so? " asked Mrs. Langshawe,
unconscious of the calamity.

" Mr. Langshawe won five-and-twenty pounds —
I have secret but certain means of knowing — of
poor, innocent Bridgeman : five-and-twenty pounds,
madam; and the crafty man makes his winnings a
sovereign and a — a — well, the effrontery of some
people! And had you no suspicion of your husband's falsehood? Why, that very sixpence — the
affected scrupulousness of the thing — would have
made me doubt him. My love, I have seen more of
the marriage state than you, and I know that men are
never so very particular, except when they mean to
deceive us."

" I'm sure I can't see why Joseph should misrepresent his winnings. I don't see the motive," said the artless Mrs. Langshawe.

"Perhaps not, my love; perhaps not. How should you know what he does with all his money? It's plain he has some object in deceiving you," was the charitable opinion, expressed with more than sufficient force, of Mrs. Bridgeman.

"It would really seem so," said Mrs. Langshawe, almost trembling at her doubts.

"Be sure of it," said Mrs. Bridgeman; "you haven't a twentieth part of his winnings, and where they go —"

"Many pardons," cried Langshawe, who had suddenly opened the door; "trust I break upon no secrets. How's Bridgeman?"

Mrs. Bridgeman looked at one hand, then at the other, and, with an effort, said, "I hope — that is, very well."

"Where are you going, love?" asked Langshawe, as his wife moved towards the door.

"Entertain Mrs. Bridgeman for a minute; I'll return directly," said Mrs. Langshawe; for she felt her eyes filling with tears as she looked upon Joseph, and thought of his duplicity, the sovereign, and the sixpence.

"Bridgeman very well, eh?" said Langshawe, in his easy, pleasant style.

"All things considered, remarkably well," answered Mrs. Bridgeman.

"Nothing happened?" inquired Langshawe, struck by the serious manner of the lady. "Eh? bless me! all right at home I hope? — no domestic loss — no —"

" Some people, Mr. Langshawe, would call it one.
·Mr. Bridgeman's income, though sufficient for all
reasonable enjoyments, is hardly adequate to the calls
made by cards upon it, together with the constant
good fortune of his bosom friends."

" Bridgeman plays now and then, to be sure," said
Langshawe, in mollifying voice, " but then, he always wins."

" Wins ! " exclaimed Mrs. Bridgeman ; " you know
better than anybody, you know — that last night he
lost five-and-twenty pounds."

" Is it possible ? " cried Langshawe.

" Possible ! " echoed the lady. " Losing would
seem a matter of certainty when he plays with some
people. It is as certain for Mr. Bridgeman to lose as
for Mr. Langshawe to win."

Langshawe, hurt by the words, yet more by the
piercing looks of Mrs. Bridgeman, resolved to clear
himself of the odium of constant success. With this
determination, first glancing towards the door, he
took the lady's hand. " My dear Mrs. Bridgeman,
I'm sure you can keep a secret."

The compliment at once disarmed Mrs. Bridgeman : she, too, looked towards the door, and then
said, " I can, Mr. Langshawe."

" Then, between ourselves, my dear madam," said
Langshawe, in a low, soft voice, " I never win."

" Never win, Mr. Langshawe ! — "

" Never. The truth is, Mary — bless her ! — is
such a rigid economist in everything that concerns
herself, is so averse to laying out a shilling upon
the smallest trinket, that I am compelled to use a

little harmless deceit, to induce her to commit the least expense."

"Then your winnings last night, Mr. Langshawe?"

"Quite apocryphal, I assure you — all, what I may call," said Langshawe, "a conjugal fiction."

"Mr. Langshawe," said Mrs. Bridgeman, with a subdued fierceness that made Joseph stare, — "a man may from habit consider himself justified in attempting the most unblushing fraud upon his own wife — habit goes far in all matters — but, sir, that you should hold my common sense in so contemptuous a light — "

"My dear madam, I protest!" exclaimed Langshawe, coloring to the eyelids; "I protest that I have the profoundest sense of — "

"Adds, sir — adds to the meanness of your first duplicity. You know that Mr. Bridgeman, your dear friend, as you are pleased to call him, last night lost five-and-twenty pounds."

"I vow I know nothing of the matter," cried Joseph.

"And more, and worse than all, that Mr. Langshawe was the winner."

"Now, my dear Mrs. Bridgeman," said Joseph, almost amused at the extravagance of the charge, he himself having been the sufferer, "it is very true that I spoke of winnings to Mary — I — "

"I know, sir — I know; one piece of gold and a sixpence, Mr. Langshawe," cried Mrs. Bridgeman, for a lady very sternly — "I am astounded at your double falsehood — I blush for your meanness — I — "

Langshawe could say nothing. For the first time he regretted that he had ever appeared to his wife a winning man.

"Mr. Langshawe!" exclaimed Mrs. Bridgeman, with new energy, "may I solicit of you one — a last — favor?" ·

"Twenty, my dear Mrs. Bridgeman," answered the obliging Joseph.

"One — one will suffice, Mr. Langshawe. Promise me never to play with my unfortunate husband again. Heaven knows what his losses may have been! His poor wife knows nothing. But where there are great winnings, there must consequently be — you understand me, dear Mr. Langshawe?" — and Mrs. Bridgeman tried to forget her passion, and to smile Langshawe into acquiescence. "Poor Bridgeman," she added, in a very equivocal tone, "is really no match for you. You are — you know you are — I hear it upon all hands — such an invincible player; whilst simple Bridgeman, in the vanity of his heart, thinks himself your equal. Now, do pray take pity of his weakness — don't, don't play with him;" and Mrs. Bridgeman solicited the compassion of Langshawe, as she would have entreated the mercy of a highwayman: indeed, despite the peculiarity of Joseph's winnings, he felt himself before Mrs. Bridgeman somewhat in the situation of a pickpocket. "There is a fate about you," said Mrs. Bridgeman — "as might be said of Macbeth, you bear 'charmed' cards — therefore, do spare my silly man — do spare."

"Mr. Bridgeman," said the servant, opening the door.

"Bridgeman!" cried his wife and Langshawe.

"My mistress is with him, sir," said the domestic, and disappeared.

7

It was too true. Whilst Mrs. Bridgeman and Mr. Langshawe had been left to conversation, Mrs. Langshawe and Mr. Bridgeman — the gentleman entered the house as Mary quitted Joseph — had discoursed of the gain and loss of the preceding evening.

"Mr. Bridgeman, I am so glad you're come!" said the gentle Mrs. Langshawe. "Your dear wife is up stairs."

"Indeed!" observed Bridgeman, very tranquilly. He then asked, "How's Langshawe?"

"Very well; he is with your lady. O, Mr. Bridgeman! I cannot express to you how much I am annoyed at the circumstances of last night."

Mr. Bridgeman put his hand to his chin, gently exalted his shoulders, and spoke not.

"I wish to my heart that Joseph would not play, for his fortune is so extraordinary," said Mrs. Langshawe.

Now, as Mr. Bridgeman was fully aware that, although Joseph always lost to him, he invariably, as in the case of the sovereign and the sixpence, took home winnings to some amount to Mrs. Langshawe, he did not feel quite at ease in his present situation with that lady. "Fortune," he endeavored to observe, "does act extraordinarily with Langshawe."

"And then there is something to me so uncomfortable, to say the least of it, in winning the money of our friends;" and Mrs. Langshawe looked innocently in the perturbed face of Bridgeman.

"Cards are like love, Mrs. Langshawe, as I take it; friends are not to be considered in the matter," replied the impartial Bridgeman.

"I can't think so. I think there is something almost mean and sordid in these continual attempts on the purse of those for whom we profess an esteem, a friendship," said Mrs. Langshawe.

Mr. Bridgeman, with the weight of many pounds of his friend Langshawe about the neck of his conscience, began to think the interview less pleasant than it might have been. It was plain, however, from her looks, that Mrs. Langshawe expected some reply; therefore Mr. Bridgeman nodded his head affirmatively.

"But the worst of all is, Mr. Bridgeman," said Mrs. Langshawe, with animation, "that falsehood, positive falsehood, comes of the practice. Never — never before has Joseph deceived me!" (Poor little dear!) "And now I have found him capable of the least deceit — of misrepresentation in the simplest things — it has made me truly wretched. Without mutual confidence, Mr. Bridgeman, there can be no happiness in the marriage state."

Mr. Bridgeman bowed very solemnly — perhaps it was so.

"To be sure, he may have been ashamed of the sum — really, too much to win of anybody, and, more than all, of a friend."

"Has Langshawe really confessed to having lost? Did he bring home *no* winnings?" thought Bridgeman.

"Tell me, pray tell me, Mr. Bridgeman, was not the loss between you last night five-and-twenty pounds?"

Mrs. Langshawe's manner had so surprised Bridgeman, her sudden energy had so confused him, that the color rose to his face, and he began to stammer, as he thought, " It's plain Joseph has confessed his losses — it's plain."

" Five-and-twenty pounds? " again pressed Mrs. Langshawe.

" Not — not quite," answered Bridgeman.

" It is true, then," cried Mrs. Langshawe ; " Mrs. Bridgeman's right ! "

" Mrs. Bridgeman ! " said her husband.

" It was she who told me the real amount of money lost, and not Mr. Langshawe. That Joseph should have won nearly five-and-twenty pounds of you — of you, his old, his early friend ! I shall hardly know how to look in Mrs. Bridgeman's face again — I shall — "

To the inexpressible relief of Bridgeman — who, really being the winner of his friend's money, felt with double acuteness the reproaches inveighed against the innocent — Langshawe entered the apartment, — Mrs. Langshawe as instantly quitting it.

" Bridgeman," said Langshawe, in a low voice, and with an accusing shake of the head, " this is really very wrong."

" There's something wrong somewhere," replied Bridgeman.

" My dear fellow," cried Langshawe, " if you wanted to account for five-and-twenty pounds to your wife, you needn't have laid the loss upon my shoulders."

" I account to Mrs. Bridgeman ! I lose five-and-twenty pounds ! 'Twas just my winnings. The

fact is, Langshawe — not that I am under the influence of my wife — "

"No more am I — not at all — no man less," said
Langshawe. "If I have fabled a little as to my winnings, it was out of affection, not fear — no, no, it
was to keep Mary happy, and the house quiet —
nothing more."

"I was about to say, if you must win large sums of
money, you might, out of respect of the feelings of
Mrs. Bridgeman, win them of anybody but her husband."

"But I never win large sums; never, never but
once, when I told Mary that I had won thirty guineas,
cause I wanted her to buy a pair of diamond drops,
which otherwise she wouldn't consent to purchase.
Never a large sum but then," said Langshawe.

"Nonsense! Mrs. Langshawe feels assured at this
minute that you won a large sum of me last night,"
cried Bridgeman.

"And if she does," replied Langshawe, "it is because Mrs. Bridgeman told her as much; and who
told Mrs. Bridgeman I needn't declare to you."

"Langshawe," said Bridgeman, "we have known
one another many years, and I should be sorry to
quarrel with you."

"Should equally regret it, Bridgeman," answered
Langshawe; "but when men can't keep matters like
these to themselves — when their wives must be made
parties to everything — there's an end of the very
principle of manly friendship."

"I think so too," was the gloomy reply of Bridgeman.

"At all events, then, Mr. Bridgeman," said Langshawe, endeavoring to clothe his lengthened face
with dignity, — "at all events — " Unhappily, or we
should rather say happily, the appearance of the
ladies not only cut short the wordy encounter of the
gentlemen, but the smiles and beamy looks of the
wives suddenly lighted up the faces of their husbands.
The ladies requested that nothing more might be said
of the matter, and hoping that their husbands would
leave filthy cards forever, all shook hands, and, at
the usual hour, sat down happily to dinner.

Mr. and Mrs. Bridgeman had departed for their
home, and Mr. and Mrs. Langshawe still sat at their
hearth.

"I forgive you, Joseph, this time, but never tell me
a fib again," said the pretty Mrs. Langshawe.
"Moreover, if you must play, promise me not to win
of Bridgeman. His wife found out his loss in the
oddest way: he had taken out fifty pounds to pay a
bill, and returned home — how she discovered that I
can't tell — with less than half the money: the bill,
however, was not paid, for 'twas called for before he
was up." (The truth is, that Bridgeman had not
taken the note with him, but replaced it in his desk.)
"When she heard that he had played with you, knowing that you always won, she of course concluded
that you had the money. And how naughty of you
to tell me such a tale about a sovereign, and — but I
have promised not to scold you;" and Mrs. Langshawe patted the blushing cheek of Joseph.

"She's a very violent woman, Mrs. Bridgeman,"
said Langshawe.

" Very : I was quite surprised at her passion — besides, it showed an avarice that — O, Joseph ! I wouldn't have had you keep those winnings for any consideration."

" Keep them ! Why — eh ? — Mrs. Bridgeman seemed suddenly in excellent spirits — you never returned the money — you — "

" Not exactly the money, Joseph," said Mrs. Langshawe, who smiled with some meaning.

Mr. Langshawe gaped, stared, and said, " Not exactly money — what then ? "

" O, I hit upon an excellent plan. You know my diamond drops that I bought out of your winnings?"

" Thirty guineas ! " cried Joseph Langshawe, turning a little pale.

" Mrs. Bridgeman was always admiring them. So to-day, whilst you and her husband were alone, after a little persuasion, I induced Mrs. Bridgeman — to accept them."

" You did, Mary ? "

" I did, Joseph ! " said Mrs. Langshawe, delighted at her dexterity.

" Your diamond drops ! " cried Langshawe.

" And as they cost thirty guineas, and as last night you took less than five-and-twenty of Bridgeman, why, his wife having the diamonds, you may now be said to have won less than nothing," said Mrs. Langshawe.

" Much less," groaned Joseph.

We believe, though we cannot vouch for him, that from that time Langshawe forswore cards. Of this,

however, we are certain; if he did play, Mrs. Langshawe was never again perplexed with her "husband's winnings."

1838.

———◆◆———

MIDNIGHT AT "MADAME T.'S."

HE could judge little of the deep meaning of a
very deep face, who, standing on Wednesday
last in the lobby of Madame Tussaud's Rooms, Baker Street, Portman Square, saw nought remarkable
in the visage of Mr. Gabriel Marmoset as he slowly
approached the serious money-taker. With a brooding air, he placed his left hand in his pocket, and in
a low, sepulchral voice, demanded —" How much?"

"Nothing, sir," said the money-taker; "as one of
us, you know, you are on the free list."

"Bless me!" exclaimed Mr. Gabriel Marmoset;
"and so I am. I had forgotten. My poor head!"
This simple incident to the thousands who delight in
the personal acquaintance of Mr. Gabriel Marmoset
will prove beyond anything how deep that gentleman
was sunk in meditation. He passed into the Rooms,
and, with vacant eye, surveyed the wax images about
him. It was eight o'clock in the evening, and the
Rooms, according to the promise of Madame Tussaud, were "brilliantly illuminated." Almost unconscious of the presence of a throng of visitors, Mr.
Gabriel Marmoset paced the floor; from time to time
pausing before the effigy of some desperado, where,

in the quotation tastefully adopted by Madame **Tus-**
saud, might be seen his

> " Eyes, nose, lip,
> The trick of his frown, his forehead ; nay, the valley,
> The *pretty dimples* of *chin and cheek* ; *his smiles,*
> The very mould and frame of hand, nail, and finger ! "

"Humph !" communed Mr. Marmoset with himself, looking very covetously on the image of Dennis
Collins ; " humph ! he's not copyright. Something
must be done by Christmas. A gradual falling off
of three sixpences per night — humph !" Then Mr.
Gabriel Marmoset seated himself, and thought down
" hours to minutes," and thinking, fell asleep.

It deserves to be generally known, that with a
proper regard to the health and morals of her visitors,
Madame Tussaud closes her doors at ten o'clock.
That hour was arrived, and the manager, unseen, unthought of, had been locked up still in deepest slumber, dreaming of mountains of half-price sixpences —
dreaming that all the " leaves of Vallambrosa " were
insufficient to the demands for nightly checks.

" Collins is not copyright — Hume is not copyright
— none of 'em are copyright," murmured Marmoset in
his sleep ; " I can have 'em done, and show 'em at
threepence." As the manager spoke thus in his
slumber, the clock struck — twelve !

What was the astonishment of Mr. Gabriel Marmoset to find himself in the presence of living men and
women ! Yea, surrounded by the breathing, moving
figures he had before looked upon as insensible matter ! Field-marshal Von Blucher stepped with heavy
tread to Frederick William of Prussia — Francis of

Austria kissed his fingers to the smiling Mary Queen
of Scots — Napoleon, touching his hat, offered his
box to Fieschi — the " infant son of Madame Tussaud,
which," as she informs us, she had " the honor to
model" expressly for the Duchess of York, called
hastily for his " Mammy " — Daniel O'Connell exclaimed, —

> " Hereditary bondsmen ! know ye not
> Who would be free, themselves must strike the blow?"

General Washington whistled " Yankee Doodle,"
and Joseph Hume commenced upon his fingers a sum
of compound fractions. Everybody suddenly did or
said something. The whole company appeared as
if they had been relieved from the irksome duty of
remaining silent in one position all day, and were
resolved to enjoy to its full extent their midnight
holiday. *Ca ira* was sung from the " Chamber of
Horrors," Dennis Collins inveighing against all out-
landish gibberish, and calling lustily for " the college hornpipe." We have neither space nor leisure to
particularize the conduct of every individual. All,
however, seemed bent on enjoyment — on the *dolce
far niente;* and none more so than all the cabinet
ministers, past and present.

At first, Mr. Gabriel Marmoset was abashed at the
high company amongst whom he found himself. He
had never seen so many kings, save those he had paid
on a Saturday : and though a morbid modesty was
not the disease of the manager, he nevertheless required some minutes to raise his self-assurance. He
was happily relieved by the observing condescension
of Lord John Russell.

Lord John.   What! as I think Mr. —

Marmoset.   Marmoset, your Lordship, of the Royal Sanguinary Theatre.   If your Lordship will do me the honor to recollect, I was distinguished by an interview with your Lordship on three great public questions — the Savoyards, white mice, and barrel-organs.

Lord J.   I remember : you complained that they injured the interest of the legitimate drama.

Mar.   (*Sighing.*)   Ha! your Lordship; there's no standing against foreign artists and foreign music. The legitimate drama —

Lord J.   By the way, Mr. Marmoset, will you do me a great favor?

Mar.   Is it to get up *Don Carlos ?*   I am very sorry, but my leading tragedian is at present in Horsemonger Lane, and —

Lord J.   No — no; the favor I solicit is —

Mar.   To dramatize the Reform Bill?   It will be long for a play ; but if yourself or any of your friends can manage to reduce it to a farce, I —

Lord J.   No — no; the favor I ask of the kindness and intelligence of Mr. Marmoset is this.   Will he oblige me by defining what is generally understood by his profession to be a legitimate drama?

Mar.   (*Drawing himself up.*)   My Lord, that is a point on which I have spent more consideration than any man alive!   Though I say it, my Lord, there is no manager, from a peculiarity of circumstances, so capable of affording you the required information.   I have ransacked the whole globe for attraction; I may say it, I have gone, as it were, into Noah's ark

for actors. I have executed, what meaner men
would die blushing to think of—and the result of
my experience, after much thinking, is this; that the
drama is to all intents and purposes the most legitimate—you understand me, my Lord—the most
legitimate—

Lord J. Very good.

Mar. That brings the most money! I have said
it. That brings the most money, my Lord.

Joseph Hume. (*Aside to* DENNIS COLLINS.) A
very sensible man this. Who is he?

Dennis Collins. (*Aside, in a confidential voice.*)
Hush! that's Marmyset, of the Sanguinary Theatre.

Hume. Are you sure?

Collins. Cock! 'cause he come to me in Reading
gaol, and offered to buy my wooden leg for what he
called a nistorical local drammy.

Hume. And didn't you sell it?

Collins. What do you take me for, Mr. Hume?
'Cause I was in trouble, and going over the water myself, was that any reason I should disgrace my leg by
sending it afore me?

Lord J. And pray, Mr. Marmoset—(*at this
moment several illustrious and infamous persons
came up*)—but allow me to introduce to your patronage, Mr. Marmoset of the Sanguinary Theatre.
What brings him here? I was about to ask. Can-
dor, I can tell you, is his great characteristic—a
simple good creature, as full of truth as his own play-
bills.

Mar. Oh! my Lord. The truth then is, I came
here to—for among friends business is not what it

used to be — I came to look out for attraction. I
came to see my way; and to any man or men who
can bring me one hundred and fifty pounds per night,
I have not the slightest hesitation in offering five-and-
forty shillings as a weekly salary.

Lord Byron. Ha, ha! Grey, do you want an
engagement? (*His Lordship shakes his head.*)

Napoleon. Well — man! Always had a liking
for the stage; would have made Racine a prince had
he lived in my time. (*Grimly smiling.*) What do
you offer *me?*

Mar. Really, General —

Nap. General!

Mar. I beg your pardon; but in the last piece
you were always called General, and —

Nap. Last piece? eh — what?

Collins. I seed you myself in the sixpenny gallery; and more than that — hissed you like a true-
born Englishman.

Mar. Quite true; we've had you at all ages.

Nap. Had *me?*

Mar. To prove it: if you have any fancy for the
identical hat that you wore at Marengo, you can purchase it of Mr. Moses Ragby, who lent it at two-and-
sixpence a night to Covent Garden.

Nap. Indeed!

Mar. Besides your real pocket-handkerchief from
St. Helena, before the imperial crown was picked
out of the corner.

Nap. And who — who has acted me?

Mar. Everybody; the fact is, you are a stock
part, and now go with the heavy old man.

Nap. Bah!

Prince Talleyrand. Eh, Monsieur? dis donc — est-il possible que —

Mar. Beg your pardon, sir, pray speak English, because the gentleman who translates for me isn't here.

Byron. Come, Mr. Marmoset, can you make no use of the Emperor?

Mar. Don't see, my Lord, how. By the way, my Lord, that Sardanapalus of yours is a pretty thing for the closet.

Byron. Did you ever meet with it there?

Mar. Never, my Lord: only, as it failed upon the stage — that is, my Lord — I — the truth is, my Lord, it is always a point with gentlemen of my profession, when we find a piece not quite the thing for the boards, to praise it for the library.

Byron. Because then you are sure never to meet with it — eh?

Mar. (*Pushing his forefinger in the stomach of* LORD BYRON.) You're a wag still, my Lord — 'pon my life you are.

Byron. And can you do nothing with poor Napoleon?

Mar. (*Aside.*) Between ourselves, my Lord, the fleas have done for him.

Byron. Fleas! Worms, you mean?

Mar. No, my Lord, no: since the showmen have mounted him on flea-back, he's become vulgar. He's a drug even with the image-boys. I wouldn't hurt his feelings; but at the Royal Sanguinary Theatre I wouldn't let him carry a banner — that is, unless he

changed his coat, and went on without a salary. I
wish I could hit upon something to stir the town! Do,
my Lord, help me to an idea.

Byron. What do you think of engaging the House
of Commons.

Mar. To say the truth, that struck me; but some
of the railway members ask such terms, you'd think
senators were of the same consequence as singers —
for they positively demand nearly as high salaries.
If you could suggest something at once new and musical.

Byron. What! is cat-gut at a premium?

Mar. Nothing like music, my Lord, in all its
branches; last week three traders in German bull-
finches started each a carriage: music! Penny
whistles sell for twopence. Something musical
now!

Daniel O'Connell. I have it: I'll make a speech
for you.

Mar. Should be very happy indeed, sir: but, you
know, you've tried at every theatre but mine: and
I — I can't afford it. If I could get a new effect with
a striking character!

Brougham. Why not put Talleyrand in a panto-
mine?

Byron. Don't you hear, my Lord Vaux, that the
manager wants something new?

Collins. What do you say to me, my old 'un?

Mar. Ha! Mr. Collins: if you had but taken my
terms when the bloom of your reputation was upon
you.

Collins. Tell you what, old fellow! D—n the

shiners! Dennis never cared for 'em: to prove it, I'll do you what you like for twenty pounds a night, and throw you in the ornpipe for nothing.

Mar. Under other circumstances, Mr. Collins, I should have been delighted: but at present I can't clearly see my way. (*Here the Manager sees Number Seventy-Two and Seventy-Three of the collection beckoning to him, and crosses over.*) Ha! gentlemen, if your terms are moderate — if I can see my way with you —

Seventy-Two. How much?

Seventy-Three. And find our own sack?

Mar. Ha! my dear friends, if I had only had you a few years ago; but now, murder does not bring what it used to. I've played three assassinations and two forgeries this very season to less than my expenses.

Seventy-Two. Naething sae slippery as public taste, ye ken.

Seventy-Three. (*Visibly affected.*) You'd hardly believe it, Mr. Marmoset, but naebody speers at *us* now!

Seventy-Two. (*With a sigh.*) They a' gang into the " Chamber o' Horrors."

Mar. (*Aside, glancing towards the " Chamber."*) Yes; that — that, indeed, would be a hit. He's the newest upon town; and, as I believe he is no singer, his terms may be met.

John Kemble. Mr. Marmoset, are you in want of —

Mar. Nothing at all — nothing, my dear sir, in your way. And yet, Mr. Kemble, if we could come to terms —

Kemble. For a round of characters?

Mar. Not as actor, Mr. Kemble — not as actor ; you were very well in your time — very well indeed. But, ha ! Mr. Kemble, if you could write me another " Lodoiska " !

Kemble. Am I to understand that you wish to retain me solely as an author?

Mar. Solely ; and if you will write me a quadruped piece — I have a whole menagerie at my disposal, besides a dancing-woman from the Chippewahs, and very good hopes of a real mermaid.

Kemble. Is there no public taste, Mr. Marmoset?

Mar. Plenty of it, sir, if one can but be lucky enough to catch it. As a manager, I am bound to bait with everything. I had a tank made for a hippopotamus ; the animal was caught, sir — was coming over in robust health, but — I mention no names — early one morning watch the creature was found dead. As I said, I mention no names ; but I may be allowed to state this curious fact — the third mate of the ship was proved to be own cousin to a rival manager. The hippopotamus was flung into the sea. I accuse nobody — but would have given fifty pounds if that hippopotamus had been opened.

Kemble. You haven't a play-bill about you, Mr. Marmoset?

Mar. There, Mr. Kemble — a little more red in the bills now, little bigger type, too, than we *can* recollect, eh?

8

Kemble. (*Reading the bill.*) " Overflowing house ! " What is that, Mr. Marmoset?

Mar. That is, sir, when the gallery — as I am proud to say it frequently happens at my establishment — when the gallery runs into the boxes.   In summer I fill 'em, as they filter water, by ascension.

Kemble. Curious man ! Pray explain yourself. Ascension !

Mar. You see, Mr. Kemble, I've a large ventilator in the roof. I fill my pit with paper, and then turn the paper into shillings. Marry, how? you will say. Listen : When the pit is crammed full, and a thousand people more at the door — it sometimes happens — for *there* I give no orders, — that there's not a soul in the boxes; nice, cool, airy boxes, lined with real scarlet serge, Mr. Kemble. The pit thus crammed, with the ventilator open, is only moderately hot; upon this, I resolutely close my ventilator ! The effect, Mr. Kemble, is magical ! Half the pit have, in five minutes, the extra money in their hands for the boxes — a little door, generously constructed for the occasion, is flung hospitably open, and the boxes are filled, as I say, by " ascension."   That I call an overflowing house, Mr. Kemble.

Kemble. And what may you call " a brilliant audience "?

Mar. Almost the same thing : it's when I see glittering in the fingers of every person in the pit an extra shilling for the dress boxes.

Kemble. I see you state that the house " continues to be crowned to suffocation." Do you think that an inducement to others to be suffocated?

Mar. No doubt: I'd take upon myself to make an air-pump popular by exactly the same advertisement.

Kemble. What do you consider " universal and enthusiastic shouts " ?

Mar. When the applause is almost enough to drown the hisses.

Kemble. And what the " most fashionable audience of the season " ?

Mar. When the hackney-coaches in front of the theatre outnumber the cabs.

Kemble. And do you think the town believes all this ?

Mar. To speak out, Mr. Kemble, I don't think it does.

Kemble. Then why, my dear sir — why continue to print it ?

Mar. That's very well — very well, indeed, of you : but, when a manager has lied for years together, you can't think how impossible it is for him to speak the truth. Bless you ! he wouldn't believe himself if he did. Can you suggest nothing, Mr. Kemble ?

Kemble. Here is something — lent to me last night by my neighbor here. " Seventy-Two."

Mar. Ha ! It looks like a MS., eh ? What ? " The Terrific Tapeworm," a domestic drama of peculiar interest, by Dr. M——n !

Seventy-Two. He came here yestreen, and while he was feeling the knobs on my skull, I dips my hand into his pocket !

Mar. And here are parts, and all copied out. Gen-

tlemen — friends — will you go through the piece?
" The Terrific Tapeworm ! " The name's enough.
Gentlemen, allow me to cast the drama. (*Distribut-
ing the parts.*)

Collins. I say, messmate — (*about to return the
part*) — this here's no use to me ; I can't read.

Mar. My dear sir, in the present state of things
that's not of the slightest consequence. Now, gentlemen, " The Terrific Tapeworm " !   There must
be something in such a title.   Now, gentlemen:
Scene first — Enter ———

. . . .

. . . .

. . . .

In three seconds after this Mr. Marmoset awoke;
but — and the phenomenon has been satisfactorily ac-
counted for in the philosophy of dreams — in that
space of time, the whole domestic drama was perfectly represented, the gentlemen "having kindly
undertaken their several parts at the shortest notice."

Happily Mr. Marmoset retains a vivid recollection
of every syllable of the piece ; but, too distrustful of
himself, has retained us to look to the minute points
of orthography, and to soften the severity of his punc-
tuation.

The drama itself he has not yet dictated to us ; but,
with a fine sense of gratitude, he has already sent the
following dedication of the forthcoming pages to the
printer : —

"TO MADAME TUSSAUD,
WHO,
WITH AN ENLARGED HUMANITY,
TAKES FOR HER MODELS
THE BEST AND BASEST OF MANKIND;
AND WHO
UNRESERVEDLY MINGLING THEM TOGETHER,
EXTRACTS FROM THE WHOLE
THE GOOD THAT ALL MEN SEEK,
THIS DRAMA
IS GRATEFULLY DEDICATED."

Thus much for the dedication. And though we are not able, at the present moment, to lay the drama before the reader, we are happy to state that we can afford him some matter for reasonable speculation on its deep character and diversified interest in the following address of thanks to the actors employed, seasoned with criticisms on their various talents and imperfections. The manager (who, without any compunction, puts himself in the place of author) says, —

" How difficult is it to particularize where almost all alike demand our thanks! How hard the task to vary eulogy where nearly everybody is to be praised! Never, never, since Thespis begged grease for his cart-wheel, has author been so bowed with obligation. Turn my thoughts where they will, they meet a creditor. Let me, however, — hard as may be the task, imperfect as may be my words, — strive at best to stammer my gratitude!

" To his Grace, the Duke of Wellington, I can never sufficiently express my thanks: first, for the condescension he displayed in accepting a part so mani-

festly below his genius; and next, for the importance
he gave to it. The part was a part of lines; but how
great was his Grace in the lines!

"Napoleon was, perhaps, never so much at home
as in his low comedy with Fieschi. All his by-play
showed him to be a perfect master of his art. The
playful manner in which he pulled Voltaire by the
nose must form one of the most endearing and delightful recollections of all who beheld it.* Truly
does Madame T., in her historical and eloquent
catalogue, say of him, 'Unlike his person, *which was
small*, his mind was *that* of a giant!' If this gentleman would but cultivate his singing, he would be a
very great acquisition to opera; for though his organs
are weak, they are extremely mellifluous. He has,
unfortunately, too great diffidence in making use of
them.

"To Sir Francis Burdett, for having undertaken,
at a very short notice, a part so infinitely below
him, I ought to pay volumes of acknowledgment.
The part was a very trifling one; but how much can
the baronet make of a little!

"Oliver Cromwell, as the frank, light-hearted lover,
exhibited the tender passion, even to the married, in
the most favorable view; whilst his scene at the tav-
ern displayed all that buoyancy of heart, that generosity of spirit, and delicacy of sentiment, hitherto considered by the superficial as incompatible with extreme drunkenness. The illusion was perfect: to
hear him drop his words was to listen to the wine

---

* It will be seen that Mr. Marmoset writes as if "The Tapeworm" had
already been represented to "a brilliant and overflowing audience."

running from the bottle. It is plain that nature intended him to play the very highest comedy.

"To Mr. J. P. Kemble, for the undisguised manner in which, throughout the play, he exhibited his skull, I beg to return my sincere thanks. He, I know, will think the exhibition of an entire skull but a small matter to obtain praise; but I, who, unhappily, know how very few actors can, for a whole night, be induced to show the least part of one, am happy to express to him my enlarged sense of obligation.

"Lord Byron, from his excessive timidity, prevented the display of what I will venture to predict to be a very respectable talent. If he would but borrow a little of the wild jollity of William Penn, he would give a flavor to his otherwise too quiet humor.

"Sir Walter Scott only wants encouragement to become really a tolerable favorite. He delivered a message in a manner that almost surprised me. It is charming to watch the early development of talent. With great study, great time, and some luck, Sir Walter may become a very useful person in general utility.

"Mr. Washington, as a rebel drummer, elicited scintillations of lambent humor. It is sometimes so difficult to judge of young beginners! but I think Mr. Washington will do.

"If Prince Talleyrand were not so nervous, I should have high hopes of him. I much fear, however, that *mauvaise honte* will utterly blast his prospects in life.

"Mr. Joseph Hume played his part to perfection. His address to a milk-score showed the artist.

"I regret that I cannot praise Lord Nelson. There is not one particle of salt in his sailors: they are all landsmen, with frogs in their throats. In low comedy he might stand a chance.

"Monsieur Voltaire might be tolerated as Pantaloon: in no other character can he ever be accepted. I never knew so dull a person — that is, when he speaks.

"Neither Charles Fox nor George Canning can be trusted with a single line. I never heard such speakers.

"Mr. William Pitt plays too much like a proprietor; he is always looking up as if 'counting the galleries.'

"I have now to return my most sincere — most unqualified thanks to gentlemen who, true to their engagements, have withstood the base and unmanly temptations of unprincipled rivals.

"My thanks, then, are especially due to Mr. Dennis Collins — not only for the magnanimity with which he spurned the offers of a hostile manager, but for the quiet humor with which he dealt his harmless sarcasms about him; for the agility with which he danced his hornpipe, (I was proud to hear the applause of Mr. T. P. Cooke — it was hearty, generous); and, indeed, for the sweet cheerfulness with which he performed all his arduous duties.

"There are other gentlemen (Seventy-Two and Seventy-Three) — whose names, out of respect to their extreme modesty, I suppress — to whom I am bound in everlasting gratitude. Every machination was employed to deprive me of the services of those gentlemen; but they magnanimously spurned every offer in favor of the highest bidder.

"To another gentleman, a distinguished inhabitant of the 'Chamber of Horrors,' I am especially indebted. Every manager was on tiptoe to receive him; but he had given his word — and he could give no more.

"To the 'talented' Madame Tussaud, and her no less 'talented' sons, for their extraordinary and unusual courtesy in not 'suspending the free list,' in consequence of 'the great attraction' of the last corner (number three) in the 'Chamber of Horrors,' —

"In fine, to everybody concerned or not concerned in the representation of *The Terrific* Tapeworm, I beg to express the highest, the deepest, the broadest, and the largest sense of my esteem and my respect.

"G. M.

"BOWL AND DAGGER COTTAGE."

We look with inexpressible anxiety for the MS. itself; as it is evident from the above that the drama contains an extraordinary variety of parts, we are impatient to enjoy the happy art of the writer who has so cunningly introduced them, and bound them in one common interest by the peculiar originality of his fable.

Awaiting this, we seize the opportunity of stating, on our own account, that — in consequence of a great loss of property, and therefore of rank in life (having been a large shareholder, and principal director, with two or three eminent sheriff's officers, in the late Aerostation Company) — we superintend the birth of books of any size and on any subject. We therefore beg to assure the literary nobility, gentry, and public in general, that we continue to dot *i*'s and cross *t*'s on the lowest terms, and with the greatest possible despatch.

Please to direct (post paid) " H. B., Esq.,* Red Herring Alley, Moorfields."

1837.

THE TUTOR-FIEND AND HIS THREE PUPILS.

THREE fathers had each a son — they were determined, come what might, that the boys should be wisely taught — in other words, should be instructed in the mode of *getting* on. They made all inquiries after a teacher, but, for some time, with no success : one was too poor, and therefore incapable of instruction ; another, too merry ; good-nature was a losing quality. At length they heard of a person anxious, and, they believed, well fitted to take charge of youth. The parents hastened to the scholar's abode ; it was a miserable hut in the middle of a marsh : the croak of frogs and buzz of flies were the only sounds heard about the master's dwelling, which was guarded by a little ugly cur, that, yelping at the

---

* Henry Brownrigg, Esq., Jerrold's occasional *nom de plume* in The New Monthly Magazine. — ED.

approach of the visitors, caused its master to throw open the casement, and reveal himself to the view of those who sought him.

He was a man of about sixty — his whole appearance wild and meagre. His face seemed sharp and bloodless — the dry, yellow skin, tightened over his high cheek bones, came into more ghastly relief from a dead-black eye. His brow was seamed with wrinkles. His hair, of speckled black and gray, drooped in unsocial lankness. His beard seemed half-rusted wire. His long, naked arms were fearfully muscular; and his nails hooked as the bill of a parrot. He was employed feeding a nest of owlets, with some crushed snails, before him. Looking up at his visitors, he smiled, and displayed two rows of huge teeth, of pearly whiteness. He opened the door, and the visitors entered the tutor's habitation. It consisted of one room, grotesquely furnished; Indian flies were pinned to the walls — here was the jaw of a shark — there a tiger's skin — with snakes of all sorts, wreathed in knots, hanging around. In one corner of the hovel was the miser's bed — a heap of rags, with an account-book for a pillow. A mess of adder broth was on the fire, to which old Rapax (for so was the tutor called) invited the appetites of his visitors. "There are eels," said he; "but adders *go the farthest.*"

The bargain was soon closed. Rapax was to have the children; and, next morning, Scowl, Topaz, and Blitheheart set out for their future master's dwelling. Topaz laughed as he stood on the other side of a ditch fronting the tutor's hut; then springing over, he

relapsed into a gloom as he approached the habitation. Scowl neither paused nor smiled, but dashed
sulkily over, following his companion in silence.
Blitheheart had tarried behind, gathering a water-lily
— now, he comes, skipping along, bounds across,
and arrives at his future school almost ere he sees
it. Rapax was leaning through the window, pursu-
ing his occupation of yesterday. "You are welcome," said he ; " enter. — And you, sir " (addressing
himself to Scowl), " come, feed my owlets."

"Feed owlets! Not I, by the rusty holiness of
your beard. Feed owlets!"

"You, young sir " (to Topaz), " will perhaps take
the office?"

"An' they were a nest of linnets for a pretty
daughter of yours, indeed would I; but owlets are
not young men's birds."

"Gentle youth," said Rapax, turning to Blitheheart, " will you assist me?"

"Willingly, sir," replied the boy; " but shew me
the fashion."

The old man muttered to himself, "Humph! —
scornful, jesting, and ingenious! Well, well — the
same end by different ways." Then to the youths, —
" But to our business. Enter; here we must lose
nothing, and we have squandered away ten minutes
without a purchase."

"I marvel," said Topaz, " at your exact calculation — for I see no dial here."

"Nature's clock, young man — thus," answered
Rapax, as he placed his finger to his wrist. " Can
there be a better monitor than our pulse? — spurs it
not to action? — clamors it not against idleness?"

"No," replied Scowl; "it rather tells us of the uselessness of employment, for every pulsation is but the knell of life gone by."

"Prithee, good father, what are you to teach us? Come, whistle for your dragon, and let us to the moon."

"My business is not in the clouds, young man."

"Shall we sail with you in a cockle-shell? Are you a sea-magician? I should like to string pearls with mermaids mightily," said Blitheheart.

"Nor can I fathom the ocean," observed Rapax.

"Will you then take us into the mines of earth? Shall we play at hustle-cap with diamonds? Shall we go into the earth?" asked Scowl.

"Ay, in good time."

"Truly, yes," sneered Topaz, "and without your necromancy. — Come, what will you teach us?"

"To be rich."

"Then why art not rich thyself?" said Scowl.

"How know you that I am not? I am rich."

"Are you so?" answered Scowl, with bitterness. — "Poor man!" and he looked sneeringly at the wretched abode.

"He who hoards gold," replied Rapax, "does it not for the insensible love of its glitter; but he looks abroad — he sees of what the eminence of human flesh is composed — he scrapes together wealth — and knowing that he can be splendid when he may, cares not to be so. Such am I."

"And this mystery," said Scowl, "you are to teach us? How?"

"Enter and learn."

The youths entered the hut, and they seemed as though struck with sudden plague. The old man took from a little box a piece of brilliant gold, impressed with cabalistic figures; and throwing it upon the table, desired the youths to look at it. "What think you of this metal? Each answer me. What is it?"

Scowl unceremoniously took it from the table, and throwing it up, and catching it in his hand, again cast it down scornfully, muttering, "Gold — the price of human brains!"

"But do you not value it?" demanded Rapax.

"I hate myself and all the world, that I must sometimes value this piece of ore beyond the flower or pebble trodden under foot. I value it not — but scorn it as I bow to it."

"And you, young man?" said Rapax, glancing to Topaz.

"I look on this metal," answered the youth, "and I say to myself — 'This life is a mockery; man hath made it a miserable one; and then he forms a partial antidote to its wretchedness, to be obtained by guilt, folly, or craft.' Well, I have this antidote. I ask, 'How can I use it to pleasure me?' Fancy gives the answer, and — farewell gold!"

"For me," said Blitheheart, "were I in a meadow, or by a road-side, with this gold in my hand, and some miserable wretch, with pistol at my head, should ask me for the coin, I'd freely give it him; and, pitying his poverty who made gold his only wealth, I'd raise my empty hands towards heaven, and in the lasting beauty of creation, count me beyond all princes — rich!"

" Look on this gold," cried Rapax, in a deep, commanding voice. — There was fascination in the metal. The youths looked silently and intensely ; their souls were in their eyes, and they were spell-bound. Their bosoms heaved, their mouths gaped, their fingers clutched the air, and tears rolled down their cheeks. The fiend had entered their hearts. The old man's face was wrinkled with delight, and a ghastly smile lurked at his shrivelled lips. The youths were changed, as if by magic — they were the bondsmen of sin and rapine !

It was evening when the scholars quitted the hut. The old man gave to each a piece of coin. They had not proceeded far ere they were accosted by a wretched, starving woman, with a half-naked babe. She first addressed herself to Scowl — " In the name of Heaven, young sir, and as you hope to change this miserable world for one where sorrow never enters, give me charity for the sake of my poor babe ! "

" And will you live to beg? — in the grave there is independence. Seek it ! " — and Scowl passed onward.

The woman then turned to Topaz. " You are merry, my good woman ; you will but try us ! Have beauty, yet ask for charity? Go to cities — go to cities ! "

She then appeared to Blitheheart. He was about to speak — then paused, and at length stammered an excuse — " he had no money."

The youths proceeded on their way. For a time they were silent. At length Scowl observed, " Surely our master works by magic — else I had not denied

that woman.   But a short time, and though I frowned
at man and all his wants, yet would I have taken out
my purse, and, laughing at the objections of nature,
emptied its contents to the crowd, to see them — like .
hungry fowls for barley — fight, and peck, and sidle
for the grain.   Now I would dash among the feeders,
and scaring them hence, fill my own pouch with
their corn, even though it grew mouldy whilst its
rightful owners starved.   A short time since, I
scorned the world's misery and corruption — now
I will prey upon them.   My heart is, on a sudden,
hard and moistureless.   Good thoughts have vanished from my brain — tears are dried up in mine
eyes."

"And where I would have smiled or meditated,"
said Topaz, " now I would sneer and answer groans
with jibes."

"Never before," cried Blitheheart, " could I have
resisted that woman's appeal.   I told a lie, and yet I
did not blush.   Surely we are bewitched ! "

" But awakened to reason," replied Scowl.   " The
film is taken from our eyes.   The eye of worldly
reason looks farther into earth than the vision of
romantic youth pierces the heavens."

" How long," asked Blitheheart, " do our wise
fathers propose to keep us at this academy?   When
are we to enter the world ? "

"I know not — but soon, I hope," said Topaz ;
'' for I long to have a match with its cunning
creatures."

" All in good time," remarked Scowl.   " We are
a while to look on the game before we play.   Fare-

well; the night is coming on — and now her gew-
gaws have no charms for me. Good night!" — and
each betook him to a different route, although one
road led to their several habitations.

Every morning brought the scholars to Rapax.
The fathers — though they complained of a growing
lack of obedience in their children — could find no
fault with the progress of their education. Indeed,
they were charmed with their scholarship — they had
grown so subtle and so disputative! Rapax was a
rare master!

One morning, as Scowl was about to visit the
pedagogue, a girl — a young and beautiful girl —
stood in the pupil's path. "Jane!" he exclaimed, in
a tone of mingled wonder and remorse. He glared
fiercely at the girl, and her lineaments searched by
his eyes awakened thoughts and images maddening
and confounding. He threw himself upon a bank,
and groaned heavily. "Jane!" he repeated. The
girl was at his side. His manner became more composed and solemn. He shook his head, as the eyes
of Jane seemed eagerly to penetrate his mystery — he
shook his head, and with a sickly smile exclaimed,
"You seek in vain."

"Alas! have you not happiness?" mournfully
inquired the girl.

"What is that?" answered Scowl — "that same
enigma, *happiness?* — that common jilt — that sound
of all lips — that mockery of all hearts? Fools lisp
its name, and gray-bearded men crimp their wrinkled
visages, and clasp their yellow hands, and look at the
sky when this happiness is named. What is it? I

would learn — thou art a fair teacher. Have you
known it? — what was it like? — how was it
called?"

"Once I thought it bore the lineaments of your affection; I thought its name was yours — your love!"

"My love! Pshaw! I have neither face nor form
for woman's sublimer fancies. On my brow there are
no curls to catch fair ladies' hearts; my lips are not
honeyed, but steeped in gall; I am puny — misshapen
— not at all the creature for a fair one's love."

"Thou knowest my heart — thou knowest it
wholly thine!"

"I might have loved you once — but now., — Away,
girl! Seek some pliant, thoughtless fool, who marries
from fashion, because his neighbor weds, or his own
blood burns. Show not to me Love's wreath of
flowers — my breath would taint the buds — my eye
wither them!"

"O, what a change is this!" exclaimed the heart-
broken girl. "I ask not for myself — do as you will.
But your parents — why are you thus changed
towards them?"

"Parents! I have none — they divorced me from
them — they drove me from their hearth, and placed
me with another. He has taught me to scorn them
— or at least to value them but as the common mass
around me. Yet there is one I love — thanks to my
good master! — whom I love — dearly, fiercely love;
to whom I would sacrifice father, mother, thee — all
ties that keep me to the world — all thoughts of man
and man's affection — "

"And who — what is it hath this fearful love?"

"Self! That is my god! I make all else bow down and worship it! Farewell — we part forever. When you see me turn yonder hedge, think me fallen into an unfathomable gulf. Farewell!"

"Stay!" exclaimed the girl; and then, in speechless agony, she held forth her clasped hands, looking imploringly at Scowl, who retreated a pace or two, and, with calm brutality, surveyed her posture of frenzy and despair.

"Truly," said he, "an inspired modern Sibyl! Your attitude has all the eloquence of speechless misery; and yet I think the neck is too — " (She shrunk back.) — "So — well improved! Now, would I were a sculptor! I would carve your image thus, to say my — ha! ha! — my prayers to — a stone! You would be a fitting partner for my heart. Seek you a human husband. All affections are dead within me — all feeling save one — an eternal and all-consuming pang — the pang of hunger — the longing after gold!"

"You ambitious of such dross! — you, who have — "

"Laughed, mocked at it. My master hath taught me better. Mark me, girl — then shun me. So wild, so universal, is this craving after wealth, that, did I think these yellow locks could, by chemical art, be made to yield one grain of gold — could your heart's last drop be petrified by death into a gem, although I saw beseeching angels kneel around you, I'd lock my hand within your hair — tear forth your living heart — and leave you, tombless, to the birds. Have I not said enough?"

He spoke to a senseless image. The girl fell, stricken by misery, to the earth; and the student pursued his way to the hut of the schoolmaster.

"How now, son?" said Rapax; "why thus late? What have you to show in exchange for so much time?"

"A woman's broken heart," returned Scowl.

"Ha, ha!"—and the haggard fiend crowed in the laugh—"put it by with the baubles. But come, what say you, my lads?—we have tarried long enough here? Are you for moving? Will you all follow me?"

"We will!" was the sudden and unanimous response.

"Then," said the master, "prepare to meet me at twelve to-night upon the beach. I have skiff, sail, and compass. By my art I have learned, that where the sun sets is gold; and thither we will steer. Bid adieu to your friends, and be punctual."

"Adieu!" muttered Scowl. "As surely as the wave breaks upon the beach, so surely will I be there. For adieus!—But no matter. I say I will be there."

"And I," said Topaz.

"And I," cried Blitheheart, "will but run home to see what I may pick up to help me on the voyage, and then for the ocean."

The young men departed from the hut, and the master busied himself securing his bags of gold, his jewels, with provisions, and all else needful for the enterprise.

The night came. Scowl was the first at the appointed spot. It was a narrow point, jutting into the sea, which beat over vast fragments of rocks fallen from the surrounding precipices. The night was chilly; the moon and stars were in the skies — yet there seemed a desolation in the heavens. The heavy beating of the waves was in monotonous accordance with the apathy of his soul, who, seated on the rock, raised his eyes from the deep to the cloud-veiled moon, as though they asked, " *Why* moves this water?" The moon returns him in mystery to the wave; and the sea-weed, that listlessly he plucks from the rock, adds to the whole riddle, and all is darkness. His existence seemed to pause in the question of " What *is* existence?" Night seemed again to shed some part of its former influence over him. After vainly venturing to search the hidden springs of nature — the wave's motion, the wind's chamber, the moon's glorious light — he wept at his darkness. He lay, for a time, the smarting penitent to nature, stricken down by self-accusation, whilst compunction triumphed over him, and like the scorpion near the flame, he writhed, stung with his own venom. He prayed for the rock to yawn and swallow him; he asked for annihilation, or to change his being with the weed or shell-fish clinging to the clift. His prayers were scoffed — he still must live, and bear the human stamp.

Thus for a time he lay, passively suffering the embraces of one who had watched and followed his steps where even the nest-seeking school-boy had feared to tread. By degrees, the vacant look of Scowl changed from its wandering dulness, and his eyes flashed fire. He looked with a demon's glance at the girl; and, his voice rattling in his throat, he cried, "Have I not said enough?"

The girl answered not. She sank upon her knees, and, pale and trembling, with outstretched hands and averted head, in silence waited her destiny. Scowl, raising himself from the rock, hurried to and fro on the little space allowed by the uneven surface — then stopping and looking at the girl, he exclaimed, "Jane!" She turned her face towards his, but rose not. "Jane, you have seen me weep — have heard me groan; you have beheld me snatch in hope at the fruits of heaven, and heard my teeth gnash at finding them ashes; you have twisted a shining serpent in my path; you have —" And he approached her with madness in his features.

"O God! and will you?" shrieked the girl, as, trembling, she seized the arm that grasped her.

"What! fear you death? Look at the beach beneath. But a moment, and, when your fragile form shall dash upon its bed, you will be as insensible as the pebble you displace. The rising tide will bear you to the ocean's vault; and — ha, ha! — sighing nymphs will mourn the love-murdered maid. Why have you haunted me? Was it not enough that I gave up heaven, man's social feelings — pity, love, benevolence? Did I not already stand the grim, uncouth image of man? — must the mockery be painted with blood?"

"Are your wishes blood?" replied the girl, for a moment moved beyond herself; "I thought they were gold!"

"And gold is blood!" fiercely answered Scowl. "Could gold weep for the means by which men obtain it, a new Red Sea would swallow misers in their homes."

"I have gold. Here" (and she presented to Scowl a small, well-filled leathern bag) — "here is gold — madness — infamy eternal! Ask not how I gained it!"

"Girl! what have you done?"

"Loved you — lost myself!"

"That woman so should fall! But, come, let me know your story — else, unwittingly, I may want gratitude."

"This gold — I thought my heart would stop, my arm be palsied, as I touched it — was my father's. It is — O! shall I say — it is my husband's!"

"Husband! I must trudge and sneak about the world, filching from all men. A wife is an encumbrance to a social ruffian. Were I a proclaimed bandit, then you should be my robber-queen — should kiss my sword for good fortune when I went forth, and wash my hands from blood at my return. But I cannot war so. I take your offering, but leave your hand for another."

"O Heaven! you cannot mean! — Scowl! I have lost all for you! I must — I will follow you! — O, look not so, for you cannot madden me. — Be merciful!"

"I will. Jane, this is your dying hour! Say, is not death sweet amid these rocks, with the waves and the stars to witness the fleeting soul?"

"Death! — O! to die with guilt so newly on me! Heaven have mercy! Save me — save me!"

Scowl seized the shrieking girl, who, after a short struggle, broke from his grasp, and rushed to a higher point of the rock. He follows her; she falls; and the next moment the beach bears a mangled corse!

A low, long whistle echoed among the rocks. Scowl leapt from point to point, gained the beach, and there beheld his master and his comrades. He threw himself into the skiff, and plied violently at the oar, as though he would numb the mind's action by bodily exertion.

For a time they proceeded in silence. At length Rapax exclaimed, " What! lads homesick already? What! Scowl — dull?"

" Have I proved dull since we first met?"

" In truth, no; you are an apt scholar."

" 'Tis well you had me. Had I learned from another master, I might have been as great a spend-thrift as I will now be miser. — But whither are we bound, and with whom are we to mingle?"

" Our destined land," replied the master, " is a fruitful one, and the inhabitants as nature made them. They worship the stars, and offer fruits, flowers, and shells to the spirits of air, earth, and ocean. Their land is a bloodless one, and their lives pass in the constant intercourse of what civilization calls benevolence!"

" What! " said Scowl, " have they no holiness? — holiness that burns and tortures one another? So, then, be my trade hypocrisy!"

" I," said Topaz, " will teach them to divide and subdivide their lands. I will show them how to make man-traps and spring-guns, and how (best art!) to make a mystery of common sense."

" And I," cried Blitheheart, " will create disease, and then be physician infallible."

" Truly," said Scowl, " our vessel hath a goodly freight — superstition, law-making, and physic ! "

" Welcome to your inheritance ! I give this land to your practices ! " exclaimed Rapax, as he pointed to the shore, which, with miraculous speed, they had already approached.

. Followed by his pupils, he pursued his way into the island.   At length they beheld a multitude of people seated on the grass.   The women were lovely, and the men seemed worthy of their partners ; their limbs indicated a pliant vigor, and in their features was that dauntless independence which surely adorned men in the early day.

It were long and vain to tell the means by which the strangers lured the people from their happiness and independence — by which they set parent against child, and child against father.   In fine, the land was civilized ; slaves were made, and taxes were levied ; some few fed to repletion, whilst thousands pined and died with hunger.   Rapax and his scholars controlled the work.   Trees were felled — houses built — the earth ransacked for iron for locks and bars, and swords, and bayonets.   Palaces arose — then an in-quisition, halls of justice, and a school of anatomy. There were several prisons, and some admirable powder manufactories.   There were likewise tax-gatherers and executioners.   The people were civi-lized.

At length the seeming divinity of the task-masters became a question.   Some brave hearts spoke out.

" What ! " said they, " are millions to be fools and

wretches, that some two or three may be idlers and knaves?"

At length King Rapax—for king he was—approached the crisis of mortality. He ordered his riches to be displayed about his chamber, and his blood-shot eye gleamed with horrible delight as he beheld the glittering heaps to which his soul was yet adhering; and he grasped a handful of gold even whilst its tinkling was responded to by the convulsive rattles in the miser's throat. When death gave the last charge, Rapax screamed and groaned, as though he would fight him still; and, in the agony, he crushed the metal in his hand till the blood started from the withered flesh. Tearing away his vestments, he threw himself amidst a heap of gold, as though *there* he could defy his follower; and as he writhed among the ore, he scrambled for the jewels and the vessels that were about him, supplicating the assistance of the beholders to stand before him and his foe. A terrific laugh of triumph extended his jaws, as he stretched forth his hand to seize a massive piece of gold to hide his head from the attack. Just as, with almost supernatural force, he poised the weight above him, his eyes start—his tongue works in his mouth—the ore rattles with the struggle of his limbs—and the uplifted mass, falling with a crash, thunders the knell of the miser!

The ministers paused not a moment. The ghastly corse, heaped round about by gold, appalled them not. Each was rushing on to take possession—when shouts were heard—then the trample of multitudes. The doors were burst open, and the people, thronging

onward, recoiled as they beheld the naked body of
their dead enslaver. The pupils, one and all, pounced
upon a small casket still held in the gripe of the
corse. Scowl was master of the prize, and, in an
instant, eluding the vigilance of the populace, disappeared. Topaz and Blitheheart likewise escaped.
The streets were empty — the houses deserted : the
old men, women, and children had been removed,
under a strong guard, to a secure retreat, whilst the
attack was made upon Rapax and the younger des-
pots. Scowl, with two or three of his minions, tossed
burning brands into the unguarded habitation ; the
winds rose, the flames raged, and destruction seemed
to hover over the devoted city. Again Scowl led on
his mercenaries ; again he was defeated. The dwell-
ings consecrated to the fair stranger-deities (for
such Rapax and his pupils had been deemed) were
consumed to ashes — nearly all who fought for the
bad cause, relentlessly slaughtered. A few, faithful
in adversity, by Scowl's orders launched the boat
which here first touched the island, and which had
been venerated as something little less than sacred.
There was no other refuge save the howling sea for
the gold-worshipper. All day he lay hidden ; and,
when night came, he hurried timidly to the spot
where, in an obscure creek, lay the boat. His at-
tendants were waiting his arrival. Scowl, unwilling
to venture with such a number in so fragile a bark,
despatched all, save one, to his late hiding-place, in
the excuse of having left there a treasure of great
value. No sooner had the party quitted him, than
he leaped into a boat, and, bidding the man follow,

was launching the craft into the sea, when his name was called, and, looking round, he observed his companions, Topaz and Blitheheart, rise from a pit which they had dug in the sand.

"My brother!" said Blitheheart, "we have watched for you. Let us away from this cursed spot!" and, approaching, they were about to enter the boat.

"Stay!" said Scowl; "this is all mine. Shall I not be rewarded for my work? What do you give for your passage?"

"You do but jest! What! friends barter for an act of grace!"

"I jest not. Pay me, and you shall make the voyage. Offer to palter, or to touch the gunwale of the craft, and —"

As he spoke out, he seized the oar, and stood in the act to strike.

"I will humor you, though you do but jest," groaned Blitheheart; and he gave him some twenty gems.

"More! more!" exclaimed the insatiate Scowl. Blitheheart fairly quivered with hate, as he surrendered up all his hoard to the griping hand of Scowl, who then permitted him to take his seat in the boat.

"Surely you will not leave me!" cried Topaz, in an agony of fear.

"Ay, will I," replied Scowl, "unless you pay."

"Alas! I have no means. I have lost all — all! But my future profits shall be yours."

"I am no speculator, brother," answered Scowl, with malicious coolness, at the same time pushing the boat from the strand.

" Blitheheart! will you pay my passage?" screamed
Topaz, as he waded into the sea, stretching his hand
towards the drifting skiff.

Blitheheart turned aside his head. Topaz, in
madness, seized the boat. Scowl, catching up a
sword, struck at the petitioner just above the wrist.
With a piercing howl, he let go his hold — his hand
hung but by the slightest filament! His shrieks were
lost in a sudden shout. The party of Scowl were
seen rushing down the beach, followed by the enraged
multitude. His followers begged Scowl to return —
he laughed! One of the men, seizing a musket, fired ;
but, missing his aim, wounded the innocent companion of Scowl and Blitheheart. The man was, in an
instant, tossed into the sea ; the sail was hoisted ; the
wind sprang up ; and on the boat flew from the
island. The passengers heard the tumult of the
affray — clash of swords — groans and maledictions.
The boat sailed on : they were shortly girted round
by the wild and dreary sea.

And the islanders were civilized. They knew the
value of gold and iron : they bought slaves with the
one, and made war with the other. They had prisons
for debtors ; and they could kill at two hundred
paces. They were civilized!

.   .   .   .   .   .

The old pilgrim quitted the companions of his
travel when he reached the city. He looked at every
house with suspicion. There was in his face the assumed meekness of devotion ; but his eyes had, at
times, a wolfish glare, that made the beholder gasp
as it flashed upon him. The devotee appeared aged

and travel-worn; he seemed to walk and move from the impulse of some deep, unquenchable passion, rather than from the ease of natural motion. Frequently he paused as he slunk through the streets, and then hurried from the door he was about to knock at. He arrived at a mosque, and, as if instinctively, bowed his head. He sat upon the steps, and, wearied with travel, slept. His old limbs were crouched all night upon the marble. When the morning came, numbers stood about, looking at the sleeper, who, according to the charity of the beholder, seemed something more or less than human. To some he appeared a sleeping fiend. His black, distended eyelids were in strong contrast to the bloodless pallor of his cheeks; his sharp nose, as though protruding through the skin; his fallen jaw, discovering his firm-set teeth; and his arms, hugging his breast, gave him, with different minds, the appearance of a saint or devil.

At length a youth approached the sleeper, and pulled his garment. The pilgrim, as under the influence of some dream, sprang up, and seizing the affrighted youth, shouted, "Where, where?" then, with the rapidity of thought, felt at his breast, and smiled as he seemed to grasp something. Then a sudden cramp, the effect of his cold bed and the night air, shooting through his legs, he fell; and his forehead striking against the edge of the step, the blood gushed from the wound. The people closed about him to render assistance; but, although stunned, he threw forth his legs to keep off the multitude, and never once loosened his grasp from his garment. At length the **people** resolved to **carry him to a** neighboring surgeon ; and the pilgrim, fainting **from** the loss of blood, was borne to a **low hovel in an obscure** lane.

Here dwelt the leech, a rare compound of **quaint humor,** cheerfulness, **and** avarice. The **wounded man was left alone with the surgeon, who** bound up **the hurt, and strove to unclinch the** pilgrim's hands. **Insensibility gave the patient greater** strength ; and **already the man of healing trembled for his fee.** He **administered** violent **restoratives to the patient, who at length breathed more freely — he panted, and his hands fell for an instant upon his knees. The surgeon thrust his arm into the sick man's bosom —** a **deep** snarl rattled **in the pilgrim's throat, as, recovering his consciousness, he grasped the arm at his breast, and threw back his head to confront the danger that menaced him.   There was a terrific** interchange **of look :** eye flashed on eye — **the face of each was distended —** their lips **worked, as though in disgust and hatred of** the name they **uttered — as " Scowl," " Blitheheart,"** fell, like venom, **from them.**

The **companions were again** united.   The hunters **had again met.   A hatred of** each other **in** youth had become **more deadly in age : but dissimulation could** give a seeming **sanctity to the** purpose **of a fiend.**

" **Dear brother,"** cried Scowl, "you have **a good** trade."

" **Poor, wretchedly poor,"** answered **Blitheheart.** " What then?   I am not what I was.   Now **wealth hath** no charms **for me."**   (Scowl glanced about **the hut.)** " **Believe it — I have more silver in my beard** than my bag. But come, you are wearied. Though we wear turbans we can drink wine. — Come, come, we are too old to be choked with a grape-stone. I have no money, but I have credit — we will have wine, boy; and drink to the memory of our old master!" So saying, Blitheheart left the hut on his liberal errand.

Scowl had well scanned his early companion. He had read him with eyes of distrust and hate. No sooner then had Blitheheart quitted the hovel than Scowl cast his greedy looks around — every corner, every cranny, was ransacked — the search was unsuccessful. Waiting his companion's return, Scowl took up a knife to cut a thorn from his foot — he cut, and still his face was cold and colorless: he whetted the knife upon the stone floor — it stuck at a small iron ring. Scowl seized it, and bending every nerve to the effort, lifted up a huge granite slab. He staggered half blind from the spot, and the low roof echoed the rejoicing of the demon. A blaze of gold and jewels shone upon him. At this moment the door opened, and Blitheheart entered. Scowl threw himself before the treasure, and, with the knife firmly grasped in his extended hand, dared the approach of his "dear brother," who, wildered at the discovery, moved not, spoke not, but breathed a deep groan of agony, let the pitcher fall, and, subdued to utter imbecility, threw himself upon his knees: he held out his clasped, trembling hands; the tears rolled down his withered cheeks; he tried to speak — but articulation was lost in guttural moanings.

"What! I have found a treasure!" exclaimed Scowl.

" My all, my all ! " sobbed Blitheheart, tremu-
lously.

" All ! " echoed Scowl, and drawing his finger
down the edge of the knife, and his eyes flashing with
triumph, he cried, in a mingled tone of mockery and
menace, " Halves, brother ! "

The lips of Blitheheart quivered, as though struck
with sudden ague. The veins worked like young
snakes in his brow. Still he strove to call up a
ghastly smile into his face. " Halves — ay, ay —
we'll see — but the wine is gone — we must have
more — we — "

" Regale yourself — here is my banquet. Brother
(by which dear name I claim half your substance), I
say halves ! Why so," he pursued, as he searched
among the treasure, " this is well ; a good trade, in
faith, this physic. Brother, how many men died
in this ? " and he held up a piece of coin, and then
again turned over the store. The tinkling of every
piece of metal added torture to Blitheheart — his
clinched hands struck each other in impotent frenzy,
and he rushed forward. Scowl dashed back the terrified wretch ; a struggle ensued ; and the tenant of
the hut lay dumb and insensible. Scowl searched
amongst the heap of wealth : he was speedily loaded
— indeed, he was almost held to the spot by the
weight of his pilferings. He took up a large golden
vase — twice he put it down, and then resumed it.
It could not be he must relinquish it — with hate
and selfish disappointment he dashed it from him,
and the metal tinkled against the bald skull of the
dumb and prostrate man. Blitheheart groaned heav-

ily, and Scowl, with a fiendish chuckle, crossed the threshold.

.   .   .   .   .   .

"Is there no mercy?" asked a manacled wretch; and the rattling of his chains seemed to answer — "None." The prisoner was a thin old man, whose face, though meagre, was animated with strong contemptuous feeling: his lips seemed festering with satire. He slunk to a corner of his dungeon, and lifting a stone, took from under it a small bag: it was filled with precious gems. He sat down, and taking up a loose pebble, drove the jewels between the crannies of the dungeon walls. "If they kill the birds, they shall not have the plumes," he muttered, as he studded the cell of death with gems fitting a diadem. "I fix them thus low, that they shall not glare upon men's eyes; for even in a dungeon man does not look down; his hopes will fly upward, even though they lose their pinions through the bars." As he accomplished his work the jailer entered — a friend was at the gate. "Friend!" echoed the captive, sneeringly — "say I have no legacies." The visitor would take no denial: it was Scowl who came to console the captive Topaz. Scowl held forth his hand. "What!" cried Topaz, with a malignant grin, "have you another sword behind you? — nay, leave one hand for the cord of the hangman."

Scowl approached Topaz, and touching his chains, cried, "Death, ha?"

"Yes, a little sleep after a long walk."

"And these are the men we cultivated. We taught them to dig for gold, and they hang you for

usury. 'Tis a jest, though not a blithe one. Come,
no bequest for a friend? — no wealth?"

"Wealth, I have none, though these fools hunt
me for it. They surely think I have a vein of gold
where other men have marrow. Yet I will bequeath
you something!"

"What?"

"The rope that hangs me, will serve you for a
penitential cord."

The jailer entered — the friends must separate.
They approached each other with outstretched arms.
Think, brother, do you give nothing?" cried Scowl.

"Nothing?" was the answer. Scowl, turning his
back on his companion, quitted the cell, and the
usurer was led forth to death.

Scowl, as his vessel sailed from the land, beheld the
carcass of the miser hanging to the winds.

.   .   .   .   .   .

All was bustle at the village of ———. Scowl had
returned to his native home. He had built a stately
and gorgeous palace, yet the edifice had but few inhabitants. Two or three palsied old men from the
poorhouse tottered in the halls; and the roofs that
might have sheltered monarchs echoed the shambling
tread of the pauper. Here Scowl would live in solitude, as though he communed with his riches, giving
them natures and dispositions. He would talk to
them — for his mind was sinking — as they were his
ministers and friends.

At length he ventured upon a task imposed upon
him by his late master. It was a dark, wintry night
when he hobbled to the marsh where once stood the

cottage of old Rapax. Scowl began to dig the earth, and after a long and wearisome toil, he beheld the buried riches of his master. Here night after night he toiled, removing the treasure stealthily to his mansion. One night he beheld a man moving slowly towards the pit — he saw him leap into it, and heard him rattle his wealth. Scowl sprang upon the robber, seized a bag, and swinging it with all his strength, dashed it against the head of his opponent, who fell, screaming inarticulate sounds. Scowl repeated the blows, then throwing in the earth, buried the unknown corse of Blitheheart with his idol. Scowl caught up the bag, and hastened to his mansion.

" It must be," exclaimed Scowl ; " none else could know the spot !" And then he sought to place the bag with his stores : he felt in his bosom — groaned, and let the bag fall. The noise awakened his servants : the old men ran to their master, whom they found aghast and trembling. Scowl wildly cried, " My keys ! my keys ! gone — buried !" One of the old men took up the bag — Scowl darted forth to seize it, then staggered back — as he beheld it wet with the blood of his victim. The servants cut it open, and the gold fell about the floor. Scowl stamped and shrieked as he saw the old men fighting and struggling for the coin. He rushed to the iron door of his treasures, forbidding all approach. Here, in madness, he raved for hours. The old men, terrified, and their suspicions awakened by the appearance of the bag, soon gave tongue to their fears. The civil authorities, with a crowd of villagers, were in attend-

ance.   They burst open the bolted door of the apartment which led to the retreat of the miser, beheld
him stretched at the door of his treasury.   They
raised him up — he was dead.   In his madness, he
had flung himself violently against the door, and a
deep wound on his brow showed the indention of
one of the iron rivets with which it was studded.

These are the deaths of the three pupils of Rapax.
One was gibbeted — the other murdered by his
fellow — the third fractured his own skull against
the barrier of his wealth.   They all *got on* in the
world.   1831.

THE LITTLE GREAT AND THE GREAT LITTLE.

EXTRAORDINARY is the mind of man!   He
sails in mid-air ; he compasseth the globe ; he
blunts the lightning ; he writeth *Hamlet*, *Paradise
Lost*, the *Principia*, and he chaineth a flea by the
leg.   He maketh the strong elephant to bend his
joints, and he subdueth a flea, if not to " hew wood,"
at least to draw water.   These, the later triumphs
of the human essence, are now on exhibition somewhere in that long ark for modern monsters, Regent
Street !   Yes, the " Industrious Fleas " at once delight and shame fashionable idlers, sending them to
their beds to ruminate on the sagacity of the living
world about them.

We love a monster as much as ever did *Trinculo;* hence we have been bitten; that is, we have made acquaintance with the "Industrious Fleas." Let us shortly enumerate their separate capabilities. One flea, a fine muscular fellow, worthy, did fairies die, to be mourning coach-horse at the funeral of Queen Titania (how long since the fairies had a coronation!), draws a very splendid carriage, constructed from the pith of elder. He curvets, and bounds, and shows his blood (he must have been fed in some royal stable — he hath surely fattened on kings) with the proudest royal coach-horse, on — as they say at public dinners — " the proudest day of its life." Having seen its legs, we shall think more seriously of the kick of a flea ever after. Then, to talk of a " flea bite," as a proverb for a wife — a mere nothing; let those who speak thus vainly contemplate the terrible proboscis of the aforesaid chariot flea, and then think of the formidable weapon, plunged through one's tender skin, and sucking up by quarts (we saw, we looked through a microscope) our hearts' best blood! To go to bed appears no wonder, but to be able to rise again after what we have beheld, seems to us a daily miracle! To proceed. Another of the " industrious " takes the air with a chain and a weight to his leg, the wonder consisting in its resignation to its destiny. A third flea, also manacled, draws water. A fourth flea has a more awful duty — to bear Napoleon Bonaparte, late of France, but now of St. Helena — there he is, the victor of a hundred fights, majestically seated on flea back. An enthusiastic Frenchman may, if he have good eyes, see in the

miniature emperor, the sallow, thoughtful face, the
" brassy eye" (*vide* Haydon's account). of the original
despot — could the figure take snuff, the illusion would
be perfect. Two other fleas, soldiers, fight a desperate
combat, affording in their proper persons a triumphant
refutation to the celebrated dogma of the philosopher,
that " fleas are not lobsters." We understood from
the *cicerone*, that their deadly enmity was excited
towards each other by a mutual tickling. We were
also informed, that one of the fleas (" epicurean
animal!") had the honor to sup off the hand of the
Princess Augusta. This fact was shamefully hushed
up by the magas of the *Court Circular*, else how
would it have astonished the world to have read,
that " last night her Royal Highness the Princess
Augusta gave a supper to the fleas "! Certain it is,
the document contains at times news of less interest.*
This condescension on the part of her Highness,
though it speaks much for her affability, has been the
cause of grievous heartburnings and bickerings among
the society. It is extraordinary the airs that every
flea gives himself about " his blood." However, it is
to be hoped that a herald will be appointed to settle
the claims of each disputant, and to favor the whole
with a genealogical tree. Who knows whether one
of these fleas' ancestors did not bite Sancho Panza, or
the Dulcinea del Toboso, or the *Carters*, who were
" bitten like a tench"? Speaking on our own responsibility, we are afraid that each of these little
creatures, after all its vanity about pure blood, has

---

* Her Majesty the Queen, and Prince George of Cumberland, stood the
whole of the sermon !! — *Court Circular*, April 8, 1832.

been somewhat capricious in its appetite ; a fault, by the by, which often puzzles the heralds in their labors, for certain other little animals are very angry, when they speak of blood, too.

We quitted the exhibition, and walking at a melancholy pace, with our long, lean visage bent towards the earth, we were accosted by a man — an odd-looking person, with a box at his back — who begged we would stop and see his show. We were in a sight-seeing humor, and at once consented. The box was placed on a trestle, our eye was at the glass, and our ears open, when the man commenced his description : —

" The first view presents you with a grand state coach of the Great Mogul ; it is drawn by a thousand curious animals ; they are, as you will perceive, very finely dressed in rich harness, tall feathers, and flying ribbons ; they come and tie themselves to the coach, and feel•it an honor to be bridled ; they snort, and caper, and kick mud into the eyes of the bystanders.

" The next view shows you one of these animals with a long chain and a heavy log. This chain was fixed upon his leg when he was born ; and though he has sometimes tried to file away the links, he has had his knuckles so smartly rapped, and been called so many names, — been so preached to that the chain and log were for his own good, and that it would ruin him to take them from him, — that 'tis likely he will, for the public benefit, be made to wear them to the end of his days.

" The animal in the next view, that is chained and draws water, is one of the Great Mogul's million of

slaves. Although he draws bucket after bucketful
for the Mogul's house and his household, for his
horses, and his dogs, and his kitchen, and his flower-
garden, he is often perishing himself for one half
mouthful; his lips are blistered, and his tongue black,
with the water drawn by his own hands, running
about him.

"The fourth animal is mounted on a fiery dragon,
that, belching flames, kindles forests, fires towns, dries
rivers, blasts harvests, and swallows men, women,
and sucking babes. Look to the left, and the dragon
is turned to a something no bigger than a mouse, and
with its stinted rations of butter and cheese.

"In the fifth and last view you see ten thousand
of these animals ferociously killing, biting, tearing
another ten thousand, whom they never saw till a few
minutes ago, and with whom they have no quarrel.
But they kill one another because they are tickled to
do so. That is, certain animals go about with tickling wands called 'glory,' 'deathless renown,'
'laurel,' and other titillating syllables, poking in the
ribs of the poor benighted creatures."

I took my eye from the glass. — "My good man,
what have you shown me?"

"Fleas, sir."

"Fleas! — nonsense; the fleas are shown above."

"Yes, sir; but mine are the fleas with two legs;
though, *if* I must be honest, I can't say I see any
difference between the fleas in my show-box and the
fleas above."   1832.

POPE GREGORY AND THE PEAR TREE.

HUGO BON COMPAGNO was one of the gay-est of the gay children of the south. He had archness and vivacity — a bright eye and a ready tongue. He was the favorite of the neighbors, and was predestined by the monk who taught him Latin to make a great figure in the world. Hugo had formed a close friendship with a youth about his own age — the son of a gardener; in all respects his inferior, save in that plastic quality of temper that moulded itself to the will of others, and which, by its docility, made, very frequently, a far deeper impression on those who knew him, than the more apt and vivacious qualities of his patronizing companion. However, the two lads were firm friends, and in the day-dreams of boy-hood, ere the warm impulses of our nature become chilled in the school of selfishness — ere, in our prog-ress through the world, we imperceptibly imbibe so great a portion of its clay — the youths had but one hope, saw but one fortune for both. Wealth, if they gained any, was to be equally shared by them — honors, if they came, must be participated by either. So dreamt they in the delicious time of youth; so lived they in one of the loveliest spots of Italy — at a village some few miles from Bologna. The world as yet lay before them, an undiscovered country; they saw it, as the great navigator saw, in his dreams, the distant yet unknown land; a halo of glory was about it; it was rich in fruit and flowers, and spicy forests, and mines of gold.

At length the time arrived when this romantic region was to be explored. Hugo was to go into the world. At the period of which we write, the church was the surest road to honor; and Hugo, as we have before implied, had that keen and subtle temperament, that untiring perseverance, and that aptitude for book-learning, which, in those days, were considered the indispensable requisites for one who, in ostensibly devoting himself to God, sought to grasp at temporal sway; and who, as he bowed with a seeming inward reverence to the cross, leered with a miser's eye at Mammon and his heaps. Hugo was devoted to the church; he quitted his native village, and, grown beyond childish years, and having cast away "all childish things," he became a monk, and in his function pored over that awful volume, so blotted with crime, so stained with tears, so confused, so scrawled with error — that mystery of mysteries — the human heart. Thus he labored, all his thoughts and feelings attuned to one purpose — worldly ambition. His home, his relatives, the companions of his youth, the scenes of his boyhood — all, all were forgotten — the monk had killed the man.

"Well, Hugo," said Luigi, with a saddened air, "to-morrow you quit us: to-morrow you leave the village, and the saints alone know if we shall ever meet again."

"Meet again, Luigi? and why not? You will come and see me. I shall sometimes come here. We shall see one another often — very often."

"Yes — see one another! But you will only be to me as the ghost of a dead friend!"

" The ghost of a friend! Can I ever forget Luigi!
— my earliest playmate — the brother of my heart,
though not of my blood? Trust me, I shall ever love
you."

"A monk love! — a monk has neither parents nor
friends!"

" No: he loves, with an equal affection, all mankind!"

"Ay — and only with all must Luigi take his
share. Farewell, Hugo, and the Virgin bless you:"
and Luigi turned away with ill-concealed emotion,
and endeavored to proceed with his work. Hugo
was likewise sensibly affected by the sincere passion
of his friend. And let not the reader too hastily
condemn the scene as weak and puerile — hitherto
Luigi, although he had known and conceded to the
superiority of Hugo, yet felt proud of the excellence
that had cast its favor upon himself. — He now saw in
it the cause of separation; he now felt that he was
the humble Luigi, the gardener, destined to eat from
his daily toil, and that Hugo, his earliest and choicest
friend, was to be severed from him to pursue a path,
it might be, of glory and renown. Luigi continued
at his work.

"What are you going to plant there, Luigi?"
asked Hugo.

" A pear tree, — and it is said to be of a rare kind."

" Stay; let me help you," rejoined Hugo; and approaching Luigi, he assisted him in planting the
young shrub, for it was little more. Whilst thus employed, they uttered not a word — each drew a sombre
picture of the future, and for the time Hugo felt

that he could give up all hopes of the power and
splendor promised to him in his dreams, and in those
reveries more delicious, though often as equally vain,
as the visions of the night — that he could forego all
temporal pomp, all spiritual domination, rather than
wound the honest heart beside him. — For a moment
the genius of the place seemed to ask him — " Why
not abide here in the home of thy father — why not
rest with us, and get thy food from the earth — why
pant for the commerce of the world, ' as the hart
panteth after the water-brooks?'" Ere the young
tree stood supported by the earth, this feeling had
subsided, as it had never risen, and Hugo stood again
about to say farewell to Luigi, who looked at him
with a look of mingled sorrow and distrust.

" Luigi!" exclaimed Hugo, with sudden animation,
" let this tree be as a covenant between us. As·it
stands, it is no unapt type of your friend. The rich
earth is about its roots, and the ' dew will lie upon
its branches;' with the blessings of the saints, it may
put forth swelling buds and leaves, and rich and
odorous fruit — and men may pluck refreshing sweetness from its boughs, and rejoice beneath their shade.
So it may grow up, and so may it adorn the land that
doth sustain it; and, Luigi, it may be that it may
pine and shrink, and never put forth one green leaf
— or blight may eat its buds, and canker gnaw its
heart, and so, cut down, it may be cast upon the fire,
and so may perish.

" Thus stands your friend: I shall be planted in the
church, Luigi, — in that soil, rich with the flesh and
blood of saints — heaven may rain its dews upon me,

and I may put forth glorious fruit, and, Luigi (the voice of the speaker became slightly tremulous), these hopes may be a melancholy mockery of my fate — for I may perish, unknown, unhonored, unregretted. I know not how to account for it; my mind is possessed by a sudden superstition.   I feel — and it is an odd, perhaps an unchristian fancy — that this tree will be the symbol of my destiny; if it flourish, I shall prosper; if it fade, Hugo will decay too.   But, however it may be, Luigi, the hearts of our youth shall, in their friendship, be the hearts of our old age.   And though we shall meet, yes, often meet, yet here I promise, that there is no time so distant, no state so high, that even though, parting here as youths, we never meet but as gray-headed men — that here, embracing in this humble garden, we next encountered in the halls of kings — I give my solemn word that you shall be to me the same Luigi, I the same Hugo."

Luigi grasped the hand of the speaker — "Heaven prosper you. Hugo — and forget not your friends. Remember, remember the pear-tree."

Hugo quitted his paternal home; years passed on, and whilst Luigi, a happy aad contented man, tilled his ground, and propped his vines, and saw his ruddy offspring flourishing around him — whilst he enjoyed that great gift of Paradise, "a country life," and lived in an atmosphere of serenity and sweetness, Hugo was toiling through the devious paths of church-craft, a childless man. He was a politician and a priest — then, more than ever, twin-flowers upon one stalk — he had advanced in dignity, and had almost within his grasp that bright reality, the shadow of which had shone like a star upon his tide of life, and tempted him to ford all depths, to dare all dangers, to hold all toil as nought.

And Luigi lived on, and became an old man. His children's children frolicked under the shadow of the pear tree, which shot up, and spread out, as though some spirit were specially charged to tend it.

" Ha ! " cried Luigi, " 'tis a rare crop ; " as two of his grandchildren, perched in the boughs, plucked the fruit, and threw it into the laps of their little sisters, who piled it in two large baskets — " 'tis a rare crop," repeated Luigi, " and if Hugo bear but half as much, there are few richer among the brotherhood. He said, as this tree flourished, so should he prosper : he was a true prophet ; though 'tis well he left something behind to inform me of his increasing greatness — it seems I should never have known it from himself."

Hugo had, shortly after his departure, forgotten his friend, who, however, continued to tread the same humble, happy path, in which he had at first set out. He had had nothing to disquiet him, no losses, no family afflictions ; the dove, Peace, had always nestled in his cot — and it was not until the old man was bending downwards to the grave, that misfortune threatened his hearth-stone.

A man of high birth and immense wealth had built a magnificent palazzo in the neighborhood of Luigi's cottage. This man was connected by marriage with the family of Hugo. He was purse-proud and despotic, making of his gold a sword against the poor.

One day it was his arrogant whim that the cottage of the gardener interfered with the beauty of the prospect from the palazzo. It was almost instantly conveyed to Luigi, that he must seek another abode, as the land on which the house was built, together with the gardens, belonging to his potent neighbor, was to be devoted to other purposes. The intelligence fell with a heavy blow upon the old man. To leave the cottage — the roof under which himself, his fathers, were born — to quit his gardens, his trees, things which, next to his own children, he loved with a yearning affection — the very thought of it appeared to him a kind of death. He refused to quit — he remonstrated — implored — it was of no avail — the cottage interfered with the prospect.

One evening the old man, half bewildered, had returned from a fruitless journey to the palazzo. He sat down in his garden, and looked with swimming eyes upon his mirthful grandchildren (heedless pretty ones, whose very happiness gives a deeper melancholy to a house of sorrow) ; shocked and wounded by the tyranny of his landlord, he glanced at Hugo's Pear Tree — (for so he always called it). The old man leaped from his seat ; his resolution was taken ; he would go to Rome — he would, as a last hope, strive to find some part of his boyish playmate, Hugo, in the wrinkled, politic churchman. All things were soon ordered for his journey, and he quitted the cottage, bearing with him a small basket filled with the finest pears plucked from Hugo's tree. Luigi arrived in Rome ; and now with a sinking heart, now with a confidence based on honest pride, he sought the pres-

ence of the Holy Father. Appearing before the servants of his Holiness, Luigi asked for an audience
with Messer Hugo Bon Compagno. When reminded of this unbecoming familiarity, Luigi replied,
that he knew not Pope Gregory XIII., but was a dear
friend of Hugo's, and therefore demanded to see his
companion, not caring, he said, to trouble the pope.

To this Luigi obstinately adhered, continually
urging, with great earnestness, that he should be admitted to the presence of his early comrade. There
was a simplicity in the old man's manner that for
once won upon the minions of the great; and the
strange demand of Luigi being reported to his Holiness, he was with great ceremony ushered before the
sovereign Pontiff— before the man who was courted
by emperors, flattered by kings. All retired, and the
rustic and God's vicar upon earth were confronted.

How changed, since the friends had last met! —
Then, they were, at least in fortunes, almost equal.
Now, one was bent beneath the load of empire —
worshipped as one only " a little lower than the
angels " — the triple crown upon his head — St.
Peter's keys within his hand. What has the poor
gardener to show against all these? — A basket of
pears!

" Now, my son," said Pope Gregory — " you
sought Hugo Bon Compagno — you find him in
Gregory the Thirteenth. What ask you at his
hands?"

" Justice, most holy father — justice, and no favor."

" Speak."

" I made with another, in my time of youth, a

II

mutual compact of kindness and protection — we vowed that whichever should prosper in his fortune, should serve and assist the other."

" It was a Christian promise. Well! Stand you in need of succor?"

" Most grievously — oppression has come upon me in my old age."

" And your friend forsakes you in your need? Have you witnesses to the compact of which you speak?"

" Yes — this basket of pears!"

" Pears!" cried the Pontiff, and light darted from his eyes as he fixed them earnestly on Luigi.

" We planted the tree on which they grew — ' Let this tree be a covenant between us' — were the words of my companion. He and the tree have flourished: for forty years that tree has never failed; for every year it hath brought forth a crop of luscious fruit — and I have sat beneath that tree and wondered how it could be so bountiful to me, when he who helped to plant it, he who was bending beneath his honors and his wealth, had forgotten to send me even a single pear."

" Luigi — Luigi," exclaimed the Pontiff; and with a face crimsoned with blushes, he threw his arms about the rustic! — *Their gray heads lay on each other's shoulder*. Thus they continued for some moments, and then Luigi, stooping to the basket, presented a pear to Gregory: he took it, and looking at it, burst into tears.

Luigi kept his cottage.

1831.

SOME ACCOUNT OF A STAGE DEVIL.

THE "principle of evil," as commonly embodied in the theatre, has been a sorry affair; — the stage devil, in a word, a shabby person. From the time of the Mysteries at Coventry to the melo-dramas of the phosphoric pen of the blue-fire dramatist, the father of iniquity has made his appearance in a manner more provocative of contempt than of fear; a candidate for our smiles, rather than a thing of terrors: we have chuckled where we should have shuddered.

That the stage devil should have been so common-place an individual, when there were devils innumerable wherefrom an admirable selection of demons might be "constantly on hand," made it the more inexcusable on the part of those gentlemen invested with the power of administering to, and in some measure forming, public taste. What a catalogue of devils may be found in the Fathers! Let us particularize a few from the thousands of demons with which the benevolent imaginations of our ancestors have peopled the air, the earth, and the flood. Poor humanity stands aghast at the fearful odds of spiritual influences arrayed against it; for it is the fixed opinion of Paracelsus, that "the air is not so full of flies in summer, as it is at all times of invisible devils;" whilst another philosopher declares that there is "not so much as a hair-breadth empty in earth or in waters, above or under the earth"!

Cornelius Agrippa has carefully classified devils, making them of nine orders. The first are the false gods adored at Delphos and elsewhere in various idols, having for their captain Beelzebub; the second is of "lyars and equivocators," as Apollo — poor Apollo! — "and the like;" the third are "vessels of anger, inventors of all mischief," and their prince is Belial; the fourth are malicious, revengeful devils, their chief being Asmodeus; the fifth are cozeners, such as belong to magicians and witches — their prince is Satan; the sixth are these aerial devils that corrupt the air, and cause plagues, thunder, fire, and tempests — Meresin is their prince; the seventh is a destroyer, captain of the Fairies; the eighth is an accusing or calumniating devil; and the ninth are all these in several kinds, their commander being Mammon. Of all these infernal creatures Cornelius Agrippa writes with the confidence and seeming accuracy of a man favored with their most intimate acquaintance.

In addition to these, we have, on the authority of grave philosophers, legions of household devils, from such as "commonly work by blazing stars," fire-drakes or *ignes fatui*, to those who "counterfeit suns and moons, and oftentimes sit on ship masts." Their common place of rendezvous, when unemployed, is Mount Hecla. Cardon, with an enviable gravity, declares that "his father had an aerial devil bound to him for twenty and eight years." Paracelsus relates many stories, all authenticated, of she-devils "that have lived and been married to mortal men,

and so continued for certain years with them, and
after, for some dislike, have forsaken them." Olaus
Magnus — a most delightful liar — has a narrative of
" one Hotheius, a king of Sweden, that, having lost
his company as he was hunting one day, met with
these water-nymphs and fairies, and was feasted by
them ; " and Hector Boethius of " Macbeth and Banco,
two Scottish lords, that, as they were wandering in
the woods, had their fortunes told them by three
strange women." For the " good people," the wood-
nymphs, foliots, fairies, they are, on the best authority,
to be seen in many places in Germany, " where they
do usually walk in little coats some two feet long."
Subterranean devils are divided by Olaus Magnus
into six companies ; they commonly haunt mines ;
" and the metal-men in many places account it good
luck, a sign of treasure and rich ore, when they see
them." Georgius Agricola (*De subterraneis Ani-
mantibus*) reckons two more kinds, that are " clothed
after the manner of metal-men, and will do their
work." Their office, according to the shrewd guess
of certain philosophers, " is to keep treasure in the
earth that it be not all at once revealed."

On the 20th of June, 1484, it is upon record that
the devil appeared " at Hamrud, in Saxony," in the
likeness of a field piper, and carried away a hundred
and thirty children " that were never after seen."
I might fill folios with the pranks and malicious
mummeries of the evil spirit, all, too, duly attested by
the most respectable witnesses; but shall at once
leave the demons of the philosophers for the spirits

of the play-mongers — the devils of the world for the
devils of the stage.

Why is it that, nine times out of ten, your stage
devil is a droll rather than a terrible creature? I
suspect that this arises from the bravado of our in-
nate wickedness. We endeavor to shirk all thoughts,
all recollections, of his horrible attributes, by endowing
him with grotesque propensities: we strive to laugh
ourselves out of our fears: we make a mountebank
of what is in truth our terror, and resolutely strive to
grin away our apprehensions. Surely some feeling
of this kind must be at the bottom of all our ten
thousand jokes at the devil's expense — of the glee
and enjoyment with which the devil is received at
the theatre; where, until the appearance of Mr.
Wieland, he has been but a commonplace absurdity
— a dull repetition of a most dull joke.

Wieland has evidently studied the attributes of the
evil principle; with true German profundity he has
taken their length, and their depth, and their breadth:
he has all the devil at his very finger-ends, and richly
deserves the very splendid silver-gilt horns and tail
(manufactured by Rundell and Bridges) presented to
him a few nights since by the company at the English
Opera House; presented, with a speech from the
stage-manager, which — or I have been grossly mis-
informed — drew tears from the eyes of the very scene-
shifters.

Can anybody forget Wieland's devil in " The Daughter of the Danube"? Never was there a more dainty
bit of infernal nature. It lives in my mind like one
of Hoffman's tales; a realization of the hero of the

nightmare — a thing in almost horrible affinity with human passions. How he eyed the Naiades! how he languished, and ogled, and faintingly approached, then wandered round the object of his demoniacal affections! And then how he burst into action! How he sprang, and leaped, and whirled — and, chuckling at his own invincible nature, spun like a teetotum at the sword of his baffled assailant! And then his yawn and sneeze! There was absolutely poetry in them — the very highest poetry of the ludicrous: a fine imagination to produce such sounds as part of the strange, wild, grotesque phantom — to give it a voice that, when we heard it, we felt to be the only voice such a thing could have. There is fine truth in the devils of Wieland — we feel that they live and have their being in the realms of fancy; they are not stereotype commonplaces, but most rare and delicate monsters brought from the air, the earth, or the flood; and wherever they are from, bearing in them the finest characteristics of their mysterious and fantastic whereabout.

Wieland's last devil, in an opera bearing his fearful name, is not altogether so dainty a fellow as his elder brother of the Danube; whose melancholy so endeared him to our sympathies, whose lack-a-daisical demeanor so won upon our human weakness. In "The Devil's Opera," the hero is more of the pantomimist than of the thinking creature: he is not contemplative, but all for action: he does not, like the former fiend, retire into the fastness of his infernal mind to brood on love and fate, but is incessantly grinning, leaping, tumbling: hence he is less in-

teresting to the meditative part of the audience,
though, possibly, more attractive to the majority of
play-goers, who seem to take the " evil principle"
under their peculiar patronage, laughing, shouting,
and hurrahing at every scurvy trick played by it on
poor, undefended humanity, though with a bold aim
of genius on the part of the author, the devil, in the
opera, is made the ally of love and virtue, against
blind tyranny and silly superstition. The devil is
chained, bound, the bond-slave of the good and respectable part of the dramatis personæ to the confusion of the foolish and the wicked. This is certainly putting the " evil principle" to the very first
advantage. The best triumph of the highest benevolence is, undoubtedly, to turn the dominating fiend
into the toiling vassal ; and in the new opera this
glory is most unequivocally achieved.

To Wieland we are greatly indebted for having
reformed the " infernal powers " of the theatre ; for
having rescued the imp of the stage from the vulgar
commonplace character in which he has too long disguised himself, or, I ought rather to say, exposed himself ; for there was no mystery whatever in him : he
was a sign-post devil — a miserable daub ; with not
one of those emanations of profound, unearthly
thought — not the slightest approach to that delicacy
of coloring, that softening of light into shade, and
shade into light, that distinguish the devil of Wieland.
No : in him we have the foul fiend divested of all his
vulgar Bartlemy-fair attributes ; his horns and tail,
and saucer-eyes, and fish-hook nails, are the least
part of him ; they are the mere accidents of his nature,

not his nature itself; we have the devil in the abstract,
and are compelled to receive with some consideration
the popular and charitable proverb, that declares
him to be not quite so black as limners have shad-
owed him.

By the rarest accident, I have obtained some account of the birth and childhood of Wieland.   It
appears that he is a German born, being the youngest
of six sons of Hans Wieland, a poor and most amiable doll-maker, a citizen of Hildesheim.   When only
four years old, the child was lost in the Hartz Mountains, whither his father and several neighbors had
resorted to make holiday.   The child had from his
cradle manifested the greatest propensities towards
the ludicrous; it was his delight to place his father's
dolls in the most preposterous positions, doing this
with a seriousness, a gravity, in strange contrast with
his employment.   It was plain to Professor Teufelskopf, a frequent visitor at the shop of old Wieland,
employed by the Professor on toys that are yet to
astound the world, — being no other than a man and
wife and four children, made entirely out of pear tree,
and yet so exquisitely constructed as to be enabled to
eat and drink, cry, and pay taxes, with a punctuality
and propriety not surpassed by many machines of
flesh and blood, — I say it was the opinion of Profess-
or Teufelskopf that young Wieland was destined to
play a great part among men — an opinion, we are
happy to say, nightly illustrated by the interesting
subject of this memoir.   We have, however, to speak
of his adventures, when only four years old, in the
Hartz Mountains.   For a whole month was the child

missing, to the agony of his parents, and the deep
regret of all the citizens of Hildesheim, with whom
little George was an especial favorite. The mountains
were overrun by various parties in search of the unfortunate little vagrant; but with no success. It was
plain that the boy had been caught away by some
spirit of the mines with which the marvellous district abounds, or, it might be, carried to the very
height of the Brockenberg, by the king of the mountain, to be his page and cup-bearer. The gravest
folks of Hildesheim shook their heads, and more than
two declared that they never thought George would
grow up to a man — he was so odd, so strange, so
fantastic; so unlike any other child. The despair of
Hans Wieland was fast settling into deep melancholy,
and he had almost given up all hope, when, as he sat
brooding at his fireside one autumn night, his wife —
she had quitted him not a minute to go up stairs —
uttered a piercing shriek. Hans rushed from the fireside, and in an instant joined his wife, who, speechless with delight and wonder, pointed to the nook in
the chamber where little George was wont to sleep,
and where, at the time, but how brought there was
never, never known, the boy lay in the profoundest
slumber; in all things, the same plump, good-looking
child, save that his cheek was more than usually
flushed. Hans Wieland and his wife fell upon their
knees and sobbed thanksgiving.

I cannot dwell upon the effect produced by this mysterious return of the child upon the people of Hildesheim. The shop of Hans Wieland was thronged with
folks anxious to learn from the child himself a full ac-

count of his wanderings — of how he happened to stray away — of what he had seen — and by what means he had been brought back.   To all these questions, though on other points a most docile infant, George maintained the most dogged silence.   Several of the church authorities, half a dozen professors, nay, the great Teufelskopf himself, questioned the child; but all in vain — George was resolutely dumb.   It was plain, however, that he had been the play-fellow, the pet, of supernatural things; and though there can be little doubt that his fiends and devils, as shown upon the stage, are no other than faithful copies of the grotesque originals at this moment sporting in the neighborhood of the Brockenberg, Mr. Wieland, as I am credibly informed, though a gentle and amiable person in every other respect, is apt to be ruffled, nay, violent, if impertinently pressed upon the subject of his early wanderings.   When, however, we reflect upon the great advantages obtained by Mr. Wieland from what is now to be considered the most fortunate accident of his childhood, we must admit that there is somewhat less praise due to him, than if he appeared before us as a great original.   Since I commenced this paper I have been informed by Mr. Dullandry, of "The Wet Blanket," that the goblin in "The Daughter of the Danube," a touch of acting in which Mr. Wieland gathered a wreath of red-hot laurels, is by no means what it was taken for, a piece of fine invention on the part of the actor, but an imitation, a most servile copy of the real spirit that carried George away from his father and friends, tempting the little truant with a handful of most

delicious black cherries, and a draught of kirschen-
wasser; that every gesture, every movement, nay,
that the leer of the eye, and the " villanous hanging
of the nether lip," the sneeze, the cough, the sigh —
the lightning speed, the

"*Infernal* beauty, melancholy grace,"—

all the attributes of mind and body of that most delicate fiend of the Brockenberg, were given in the hob-
goblin of the Danube. Hence, if Mr. Wieland be
not, as we thought him, a great original, he is most
assuredly the first of mimics, and has turned a peril
of his childhood to a golden purpose. Dullandry declares upon the best authority — doubtless his own —
that the devil of the Brockenberg, when little George
cried to go home to his father and mother, his brother
and sisters, would solace the child by playing on a
diabolic fiddle — the strings of wolf's gut, and the
bow strung from the snowy hair of the witch of the
Alps — dancing the while, and by the devilish magic
of the music bringing from every fissure in the rocks,
every cleft in the earth, and from every stream, their
supernatural intelligences to caper and make holiday
for the especial delight of the poor kidnapped son of
the doll-maker of Hildesheim. If this be true, — and
when Dullandry speaks, it is hard to doubt, his
words being pearls without speck or flaw, — if this
be true, we here beg leave to inform Mr. Wieland
that from this minute we withdraw from him a great
part of that admiration with which we have always
remembered the spasmodic twitch of his elbow, the
self-complacency about his eyes and jaws, the lofty

look of conscious power, the stamping of the foot, and the inexhaustible energy of *bowing* which marked his " Devil on Two Sticks," all such graces and qualifications being, as from Dullandry it now appears, the original property of the devil of the Brockenberg. However, to return to our narrative ; which, as I am prepared to show, has, in these days of daring speculation, the inestimable charm of truth to recommend it to the severest attention of my readers : —

Little George remained a marvel to the good citizens of Hildesheim, few of whom, for certain prudential reasons, would any longer permit their children to play with him ; fearing, and reasonably enough, some evil from contact with a child who was evidently a favorite with the spirits of the Hartz Mountains. However, this resolution had no effect on George, who more than ever indulged in solitary rambles, becoming day by day more serious and taciturn. His little head — as Professor Teufelskopf sagaciously observed — was filled with the shapes and shadows haunting the Brockenberg ! Many were the solicitations, made by Teufelskopf and rival professors to Hans Wieland, to be permitted to take little George and educate him for a philosopher, an alchemist, in fact for anything and everything, the boy displaying capacities, as all declared, only to be found in an infant Faust. To all these prayers Hans Wieland was deaf, resolved to bring up his son to the honest and useful employment of doll-making, keeping, if possible, his head free from the cobwebs and dust of the schools, and making him a worthy minister to the simple and innocent enjoyments of baby girls,* rather than consenting to his elevation as a puzzler and riddler among men. Thus our hero, denied to the scholastic yearnings of the great Teufelskopf, sat at home, articulating the joints of dolls, and helping to make their eyes open and shut, when — had his father had the true worldly ambition in him — the boy would have been inducted into knowledge that might have given him supernatural power over living flesh and blood, bending and blinding it to his own high, philosophic purposes. Hans Wieland, however, was a simple, honest soul, with a great, and therefore proper sense of the beauties and uses of the art of doll-making. Glad also am I to state, that little George, with all his dreaminess, remained a most dutiful, sweet-tempered boy; and might be seen, seven hours at least out of the twenty-four, seated on a three-legged stool, fitting the legs and arms of the ligneous hopes of the little girls of Hildesheim; his thoughts, it may be, far, far away with the fiddling goblins of the Brockenberg, — making holiday with the multitude of spirits in the Hartz Mountains.

This mental abstraction on the part of little George was but too often forced upon the observation of

---

* One of the most touching instances of the "maternal instinct," as it has been called, in children, came under my notice a few months ago. A wretched woman, with an infant in her arms — mother and child in very tatters — solicited the alms of a nursery-maid passing with a child, clothed in the most luxurious manner, hugging a large wax-doll. The mother followed the girl, begging for relief "to get bread for her child," whilst the child itself, gazing at the treasure in the arms of the baby of prosperity, cried, "Mammy, when will you buy me a doll?" I have met with few things more affecting than the contrast of the destitute parent begging for bread (the misery seemed real), and the beggar's child begging of its mother for "a doll"!

the worthy Hans, the young doll-maker constantly giving the looks and limbs of hobgoblins to the faces and bodies of dolls, intended by the father to supply the demand for household dolls of the same staid and prudish aspect, of the same proportion of members, as the dolls that had for two hundred years soothed and delighted the little maidens of Hildesheim. It is a fact hitherto unknown in England, that in the Museum at Hildesheim — a beautiful, though some-what heavy building of the Saxon order — there are either eleven or twelve (I think twelve) demon dolls made by young Wieland, and to this day shown to the curious — though the circumstance has, strangely enough, remained unnoticed by the writers of Guide Books — as faithful portraits of the supernatural in-habitants of the Hartz Mountains. I am told, how-ever, that within the last three years one of the figures has been removed into a separate chamber, and is only to be seen by an express order from the town council, in consequence of its lamentable effects on the nerves of a certain German princess, who was so overcome by the exhibition, that it was very much to be feared that the whole of the principality — ex-tending in territory at least a mile and a quarter, and containing no less than three hundred and twenty subjects — will pass to a younger brother, or, what is worse, be the scene of a frightful revolution, an heir direct being wanted to consolidate the dynasty. This unfortunate event, though possibly fatal to the future peace of the said principality, is, nevertheless, a striking instance of the powerful imagination, or rather of the retentive memory, of young Wieland.

The doll, like all the others, is a true copy from diabolic life: how the painful story attached to it should have escaped all the foreign correspondents of all the newspapers, is a matter of surpassing astonishment.

We now arrive at an important change in the life of our hero. His father had received a munificent order for three dolls from Prince Gotheoleog, a great patron of the fine arts in all their many branches. The dolls were intended by the prince — he was the best and most indulgent of fathers — as presents for his daughters; and therefore no pains, no cost, were to be spared upon them. After a lapse of three months the order was completed; and young Wieland, then in his seventh year, was dressed in his holiday suit, and — the dolls being carried by Peter Shnicht, an occasional assistant of Hans Wieland — he took his way to the palace of the prince. It was about half past twelve when he arrived there, and the weather being extremely sultry, George sat down on the palace steps to rest and compose himself before he ventured to knock at the gate. He had remained there but a short time, when he was addressed by a tall, majestic-looking person, clothed in a huntsman's suit, and carrying a double-barrel gun, a weapon used in the neighborhood of Hildesheim in boar-shooting, who, asking our hero his name and business, was struck with the extraordinary readiness of the boy's answer, and, more than all, with a certain look of diabolic reverence peeping from his eyes, and odd smiles playing about his mouth. The stranger knocked at the gate, gave his gun to a servant, and bade the little doll-maker follow the domestic, who showed him into a sumptu-

ous apartment. The reader is prepared to find in
the man with the gun no other person than Prince
Gotheoleog himself, who in a few minutes reappeared
to George, asked him, in the most condescending
manner, various questions respecting his proficiency
in reading and writing, and finally dismissed him
with the reward of ten groschen for his extraordinary
intelligence. Six months after this Prince Gotheoleog
was appointed ambassador to the Court of St. James's,
and young Wieland attended him in the humble, yet
most honorable capacity of page. This appointment
Hans Wieland, in his simplicity, believed would ef-
fectually win his romantic son from his errant habits,
would cure him of day-dreaming by plunging him
neck deep into the affairs of this world. Alas! it had
precisely the reverse effect upon the diplomatic doll-
maker : from the moment that he found himself associated, though in the slightest degree, with politics,
the latent desire to play the devil burst forth with in-
extinguishable ardor. A sense of duty — a filial regard for the prejudices of his father — did for a time
restrain him from throwing up his very lucrative and
most promising situation in the household of Prince
Gotheoleog, and kept him to the incessant toil, the
unmitigated drudgery, of diplomatic life ; but, having
one luckless night gained admission into the gallery
of the House of Commons on the debate of a certain
question, to which I shall not more particularly allude,
and there having seen and heard a certain member,
whose name I shall not specify, sway and convulse
the senate, George resolved from that moment to
play the devil, and nothing but the devil, to the end

12

of his days. He immediately retired to Bellamy's, and penned his resignation to Prince Gotheoleog, trusting, with the confidence of true genius, to fortune, to his own force of character, or, what is more likely, without once thinking of the means or accidents to obtain the end of his indomitable aspirations — an appearance as the devil. Unrivalled as Wieland is as the representative of the fiend in all his thousand shapes — to be sure the great advantages of our hero's education in the Hartz Mountains are not to be forgotten — it is yet to be regretted that he ever

"To the playhouse gave up what was meant for mankind."

It is, and must ever be, a matter of sorrow not only to his best wishers, but to the friends of the world at large, that those high qualifications, those surpassing powers of diabolic phlegm, vivacity, and impudence, which have made Mr. Wieland's devils the *beau ideal* of the infernal, had not been suffered to ripen in the genial clime of diplomacy. In the full glow of my admiration of his diabolic beauties — that is, since the facts above narrated have been in my possession — I have often scarcely suppressed a sigh to think how great an ambassador has been sacrificed in a playhouse fiend. Indeed, nothing can be more truly diplomatic than the supernatural shifts of Wieland. Had he acted in France in the days of Napoleon, he had been kidnapped from the stage, and, *nolens volens*, made a plenipotentiary.

It is a painful theme to dwell upon the strugglings of modest, and, consequently, unsupported genius. Therefore I shall, at least for the present, suppress

a very long and minute account of the trials that
beset our hero in his attempts to make known the
wonders that were in him.   I shall not relate how he
was flouted by one manager, snubbed by another, de-
risively smiled upon by a third ; how, at length, he
obtained a footing in the theatre, but was condemned
to act the minor iniquities, less gifted men being pro-
moted to play the devil himself.   In all these trials,
however, in all these disappointments and occasional
heartburnings, the genius of our hero continued to
ripen.   His horns still budded, and his tail gave
token of great promise ; and, at length, he burst upon
the town from top to toe, *intus et in cute*, a perfect
and most dainty devil.   Great as his success has
been, I should not have thus lengthily dwelt upon it,
were I not convinced of its future increase.   There
are great mysteries in Wieland — a part of his infant
wanderings in the Hartz — yet to be revealed.   I feel
certain from the demoniacal variety of his humor, that
there are yet a legion of spirits, fantastic and new,
yet to be shown to us ; all of them the old acquaintances of our hero's babyhood, all from the same genuine source of romance as his " Devil on Two Sticks,"
his " Devil of the Danube," and his " Devil of the
Opera."

Having discussed the professional merits of Mr.
Wieland, the reader may probably feel curious respecting the private habits of the man so distinguished
by his supernatural emotions.   I am enabled — it is
with considerable satisfaction I avow it — to satisfy the
laudable anxiety of the reader, and from the same authentic materials that have supplied the principal part
of this notice.

Mr. Wieland is a gentleman of the most retired and most simple manners. After the severest rehearsals of a new devil, he has been known to recreate himself in the enclosure of St. James's Park; and further, to illustrate his contemplative and benevolent habits, by flinging to the various water-fowl in the canal — by the way, in imitation of a great legal authority — fragments of cakes and biscuits. His dress is of the plainest kind, being commonly a snuff-colored coat buttoned up to the neck, a white cravat, drab small-clothes, and drab knee-gaiters. A gold-headed cane, said to have been in the possession of Cornelius Agrippa, is sometimes in his hand. He is occasionally induced to take a pinch of snuff, but was never seen to smoke. His face is as well known at the British Museum as are the Elgin Marbles, Mr. Wieland having for some years been employed on a new edition of the " Talmud." Although a German by birth, Mr. Wieland speaks English with remarkable purity, having had the advantage of early instruction in our language from a British dramatist, who, driven from the stage by the invasion of French pieces, sought to earn his precarious bread as a journeyman doll-maker with Mr. Wieland, senior. We could enter into further particulars, but shall commit a violence upon ourselves, and here wind up what we trust will henceforth prove a model for all stage biographies.

The inquiring reader may possibly desire to learn how we became possessed of the valuable documents from which the above narrative is gathered. To this we boldly make answer: we blush not whilst we avow that our dear friend Dullandry has a careless

habit of carrying his most **valuable** communications
for " The Wet Blanket" in his coat pocket : and that
only on Thursday last we overtook him, **with his papers** peeping from their sanctuary, **when, — when, in**
a word, the **temptation was too** much **for us, and the**
consequence **is, that the readers of " The New** Monthly" **have " Some Account of a Stage Devil."**

Why should all dramatic truths be confined to the
impartial and original pages of " The Wet Blanket"?

1838.

THE CASTLE-BUILDERS OF PADUA.

GIULIO and Ippolito were sons of a farmer living near Padua. The old man was of a quiet
and placable temper, **rarely** suffering **any mischance**
to ruffle him, **but, in the firm and placid hope of** the
future, tranquillizing **himself under the evil of** the
present. If blight came upon his corn one year, **he
would say 'twere a rare** thing to have blights in two
successive seasons ; and so he would hope that the
next harvest, in its abundance, might more than com-
**pensate for the scarcity of the last. Thus he lived
from boyhood to age, and retained in the features
of the old man a something of the lightness and vi-**
vacity of youth. **His sons, however, bore no resem-
blance to** their **father. Instead of laboring on the**
farm, they wasted their time in idly wishing that fortune had made them, in **lieu of** healthy, honest sons of

a farmer, the children of some rich magnifico, that so they might have passed their days in all the sports of the times, in jousting, hunting, and in studying the fashions of brave apparel. They were of a humor at once impetuous and sulky, and would either idly mope about the farm, or violently abuse and ill-treat whomsoever accident might throw in their way. The old man was inly grieved at the wilfulness and disobedience of his sons, but, with his usual disposition, hoped that time might remedy the evil; and so, but rarely reproving them, they were left sole masters of their hours and actions.

One night, after supper, the brothers walked into the garden to give loose to their idle fancies, always yearning after matters visionary and improbable. It was a glorious night; the moon was at the full, and myriads of stars glowed in the deep blue firmament. The air stirred among the trees and flowers, wafting abroad their sweetness; the dew glittered on the leaves, and a deep-voiced nightingale, perched in a citron tree, poured forth a torrent of song upon the air. It was an hour for good thoughts and holy aspirations. Giulio threw himself upon a bank, and, after gazing with intentness at the sky, exclaimed, —

"Would that I had fields ample as the heaven above us!"

"I would," rejoined Ippolito, "I had as many sheep as there are stars."

"And what," asked Giulio, with a sarcastic smile, "would your wisdom do with them?"

"Marry," replied Ippolito, "I would pasture them in your sageship's fields."

" What ! " exclaimed Giulio, suddenly raising himself upon his elbow, and looking with an eye of fire
upon his brother, " whether I would or not? "

" Truly, ay," said Ippolito, with a stubborn sig-
nificance of manner.

" Have a care," cried Giulio, " have a care, Ippolito ; do not thwart me.   Am I not your elder
brother? "

" Yes ; and marry, what of that?   Though you
came first into the world, I trow you left some manhood for him who followed after."

" You do not mean to insist that, despite my will,
despite the determination of your elder brother, you
will pasture your sheep in my grounds? "

" In truth, but I do."

" And that," rejoined Giulio, his cheek flushing,
and his lip tremulous, " and that without fee or rec-
ompense? "

" Assuredly."

Giulio leaped to his feet, and, dashing his clinched
hand against a tree, with a face full of passion, and
in a voice made terrible by rage, he screamed, rather than said, " By the blessed Virgin, but you do
not ! "

" And by St. Ursula and her eleven thousand virgins, I protest I will."   This was uttered by Ippolito
in a tone of banter and bravado that for a moment
made the excited frame of Giulio quiver from head
to foot.   He gazed at the features of Ippolito, all
drawn into a sneer, and for a moment gnashed his
teeth.   He was hastily approaching the scoffer, when,
by an apparently strong effort, he arrested himself,

and, turning upon his heel, struck hastily down another path, where he might be seen pacing with short, quick steps, whilst Ippolito, leaning against a tree, carelessly sang a few lines of a serenata. This indifference was too much for Giulio; he stopped short, turned, and then rapidly came up to Ippolito, and, with a manner of attempted tranquillity, said, "Ippolito, I do not wish to quarrel with you; I am your elder brother; then give up the point."

"Not I," replied Ippolito, with the same immovable smile.

"What, then, you are determined that your sheep shall, in very despite of me, pasture in my fields?"

"They shall."

"Villain!" raved Giulio; and ere the word was well uttered he had dashed his clinched hand in his brother's face. Ippolito sprang like a wild beast at Giulio, and for some moments they stood with a hand at each other's throat, and their eyes, in the words of the Psalmist, were " whetted " on one another. They stood but to gain breath, then grappled closer. Ippolito threw his brother to the earth, huddling his knees upon him; furious blows were exchanged, but scarce a sound was uttered, save at intervals a blasphemous oath or a half-strangled groan. Giulio was completely overpowered by the superior strength and cooler temper of his brother; but, lying prostrate and conquered, his hands pinioned to his breast, and Ippolito glaring at him with malicious triumph, he cursed and spat at him. Ippolito removed his hand from his brother's throat, and ere his pulse could beat, Giulio's poniard was in his brother's heart. He gave a loud

shriek, and fell a streaming corpse upon his murderer. The father, aroused by the sound, came hur-
rying to the garden; Giulio, leaping from under the
dead body, rushed by the old man, who was all too
speedily bending over his murdered child. From
that hour hope and tranquillity forsook the father; he
became a brain-sick, querulous creature, and in a few
months died almost an idiot. Giulio joined a party
of robbers, and, after a brief but dark career of crime,
was shot by the sbirri.

Ye who would build castles in the air — who
would slay your hours with foolish and unprofitable
longings — ponder on the visionary fields, the ideal
sheep of Giulio and Ippolito.

THE "LORD OF PEIRESC."

THERE are readers who may, possibly, prepare
themselves to receive the "Lord of Peiresc"
as the hero of a tale of chivalry, of old romance —
of a story full of the marvels of the world in its
simplicity of age, when the dreams of the fabulist
were a part of the realities of life, imparting to life
its characteristic tone and color. We hasten to dis-
appoint such, assuring them that "Nicholas Claudius
Fabricius, Lord of Peiresc," was really and truly a
denizen of this world — a man with a heart brimful
of love towards his fellows — a man who was at

once a pattern of the gentleman, the nobleman, and the scholar. Nothing can be more beautiful than the details of his long, amiable, and useful life, as written with affectionate regard by his friend Petrus Gassendus; and, believing that the taste of the general reader is not yet become too vitiated by the sugared nothings of many of our present phrase-mongers to relish the fine homeliness of the early biographer, we shall, in due course, proceed to select from him two or three passages, in which, by a few artless strokes of truth, the " Lord of Peiresc " is painted to the life; in which he looks, and moves, and has his being.

We have three reasons for attempting the present paper. The first is the real interest appertaining to the subject; the second arises from a hope of winning a reverent attention to an all-but-forgotten name; the third, from a belief that the biography of Peiresc is not commonly met with, and, at a first glance, may seem to promise but meagre entertainment to the general reader. There is, we allow, some husk about the book: but it possesses a kernel sweet and toothsome to those who have fed at the simple, healthy tables of the old writers, and have drank purity and strength from their maple cups. Sterne glances laughingly at Peireskius, and D'Israeli, in his " Curiosities," has a passage in honor of his scholarly sagacity; but we know of no book, no essay, which has, in popular form, exhibited the kindliness, the simplicity, and the utility of the sage and the philosopher to the admiration of the general reader. And yet was Peiresc the friend and correspondent of the worthiest Englishmen — Camden, Selden, Sir Robert Cotton, Spelman, Harvey, John Barclay, and others. Throughout France, Holland, and Italy, he was sought for and honored by all the learned; the sweetness of his disposition and the innocency of manners endearing him to men of every shade of faith. Peiresc, as limned by Gassendus, is the living picture of a scholar of the seventeenth century, of a man rising above the superstition of his time, yet with a mind slightly tinged by the romantic spirit of his age. We see in Peiresc the hearty struggle between new-born inquiry and ancient dogma: his mind boldly asserts itself in natural speculation, when not narrowed and hampered by the tyranny of early teaching. For instance, in 1608, it was reported by the husbandmen that a shower of blood had fallen, which "divines judged was a work of the devils and witches, who had killed innocent young children." This, however, Peiresc "counted a mere conjecture, *possibly*, also, injurious to the goodness and providence of God," and therefore sought for a natural solution to the seeming wonder. An incredible number of butterflies had preceded this "red rain." Peiresc shut up "a certain palmer-worm which he had found, rare for its bigness and form." In due time "the worm turned into a very beautiful butterfly, which presently flew away, leaving in the bottom of the box a *red drop* as broad as an ordinary sous." He thus satisfactorily accounts for the shower of blood; doubtless to the discomfiture of those who, benefiting by the ignorance of their hearers, might have turned it to a profitable account. There was, it appears, a shower of blood in the time of Childebert — in the time of King Robert; that is, if we may take the comment of Gassendus in the discovery of Peiresc, there were in those seasons innumerable butterflies.   However, the intelligence that enabled Peiresc to defeat superstition in its "showers of blood," did not serve him to snatch "sorcerers" from its wild and cruel hands.   It was his opinion that "though magicians have not so much commerce with the devil as is supposed, yet ought they to be punished for their *bad mind.*"   For the signs, the *stigmata* by which the sorcerer was popularly known, Peiresc doubted their genuineness; "they might be natural, and belong to some peculiar of that disease which is termed elephantiasis."   Our philosopher was doubtless wrought into this opinion by the agonies of a priest of Marseilles, "accused of magic, but freed by the court, having been first *pricked all the body over*, to find out these same insensible places stigmatized by the devil, which could nowhere be discovered."   What a melancholy, though instructive lesson is this!   Peiresc, the humane, enlightened philosopher, a cold advocate for the accused sorcerer; the champion of light bearing witness for darkness!   This was in 1608; some years, it is true, before the appearance of our own Sir Thomas Browne, at Bury St. Edmunds, the destroyer of "Vulgar Errors," errors learned too against his own exploded witches.

Nicholas Claudius Fabricius Peireskius, was of noble family, coming, says Gassendus, from the Fabricii of Pisa, who settled in Provence in the time of Saint Louis.   He was born in the castle of Beaugen-

sier, on the 1st of December, 1580, whither his
parents had retired from Aix, in consequence of the
plague then raging in that city. His father was a
senator of Aix, and his mother, selected for her come-
liness by Catherine Medicis to receive " the honor of
a kiss," on the Queen Mother's visit to that place,
was descended from nobility. Nicholas assumed the
name of Peiresc " from a town in his mother's juris-
diction." The following circumstance displays the
spirit of the times. Gassendus says, " His parents
having lived together divers years without a child,
his mother, for that cause, as soon as she perceived
she was great, took up a resolution that the child's
godfather should be no nobleman, but, such was her
piety, the first poor man they should meet with ! "
And so it happened ; the poor man giving our scholar
the name of Claudius, to which was prefixed, by the
special request of his uncle, who hastily arrived at
the fount, that of Nicholas. An accident that befell
our baby scholar shows that wicked spirits marked
him for their early victim. For —

" It is reported, that when he was hardly two
months old, an ancient woman, that was a witch, entered the chamber, and threw down before his mother
a hatchet which she had in her hand, saying that she
had brought it her again."

From what follows, it would appear to have been
very dangerous in the year 1580, in Beaugensier, to
return a borrowed hatchet ; for from the moment
the dame brought back the weapon " the mother
lost her speech, and the child his crying ; and both
their heads were so depressed upon one shoulder, and

held so stiffly in that posture, **that they** could not bend them." The story says further, ."that when his uncle knew it, he caused the old woman to be beaten, who was found in the chimney with her neck upon one of her shoulders, who, as soon as ever she lifted up her head to signify that she had *beating enough*, and to desire them to hold their hands, she said, which appeared to be true, that the mother and child were both well."

On this Gassendus sensibly remarks, " Doubtless 'tis a very strange thing that an old hag, bowing her own neck, should dart out spirits with so strong a nerve as to turn the head of one distant from her in like manner aside ! ". Perhaps Sir Kenelm Digby would account for it by the presence of " powder of sympathy," touching the powers of which he made a wise discourse " in a solemn assembly of nobles and learned men at Montpellier in France." The young Peiresc, despite of all the uncomely old women of Provence, passed through his boyhood unhurt by witchcraft, every day displaying new proofs of that restless curiosity which in all its after successes made him the oracle of his contemporaries. No trifle escaped his observation — no accident, however slight, but ministered to his thirst for a knowledge of the principles of things. He is eighteen, " washing himself in the lesser streams of the river Rhodanus," when he finds the ground, " which was wont to be even and soft," grown hard, with " little round balls or bunches, like hard-boiled eggs when their shell is peeled off." This sets him wondering, but his astonishment is increased " when, after a few days, returning to the river, he finds those little balls or lumps turned into perfect stones." On this he begins to study " the generation of stones." In Italy — for he departs for Rome in his nineteenth year — he sees in a museum " a sprig of coral which grew upon a dead man's skull," and he resolves " to go and see men fish for coral." In his progress to Rome he was entertained by the learned, who wrote verses to him as " the genius of Provence in France." On their own grounds, in their own academies, Peiresc was enabled to solve antiquarian doubts, to discover truths, and correct errors, to the delight and astonishment of native wise men and philosophers.

" But in what esteem he was in at Padua " — we quote Gassendus — " this one thing does testify ; that, whereas the print of a sapphire being sent thither from Augsburg, with an inscription, in which the word *Xiphia* did puzzle all the curious antiquarians, Pimellus writ unto him referring unto him the examination and judgment thereof. I omit how he satisfied their doubts and gave light to that word, chiefly from Strabo, who, from Polybius, makes mention of the hunting of *Xiphia*, which was a sea-monster."

The reputation of young Peiresc reaches the Pope himself; for our scholar and his brother being desirous to see his Holiness wait upon the poor men " whom he daily feeds," thought of this expedient : they " bought the turns of two poor men, and putting on their clothes, they were present among the rest ; and though the Pope knew who they were, yet he pleasantly dissembling his knowledge, and taking no notice of them, they saw all."

Peiresc was in his twenty-third year when he yielded to the oft-repeated desires of his uncle, and received the degree of a doctor; which degree "he carried with so much alacrity and vigor, that did ravish all the by-standers with admiration." Two days after, he conferred the "doctoral ornaments" upon his younger brother, making a discourse which "filled the minds of his hearers with sweet content;" the argument of which may not be familiar to every reader:—

"For from a certain statue of Metrodorus, with his hat, Arcadian cap, and labels, with his philosopher's cloak, and ring on his left hand; also from certain statues of Hippocrates with the like cloak and an hood upon it; from a certain inscription of Eubulus Marathonius, and a statue with labels not about his neck, but his head; from the like statues of Plato, Theophrastus, Phavorinus, and others; out of certain gothic pieces, upon which there were mitres, not much unlike caps; in a word, out of innumerable other monuments, he showed how the use of those ornaments came from the Greeks to the Latins, and so down to us; and how, from the *philosophers and ancient priests*, it was by degrees introduced among the professors of several sciences in our *modern universities!*"

The degree of doctor is yet upon Peiresc "in its newest gloss," when he receives the king's patent appointing him to the dignity of senator of Aix, his uncle having resigned in his favor. He, however, declines for a time the privileges of the patent, and, "having obtained a delay, he applies his mind to more free studies, to court the sweeter and more delightful Muses, to advance good arts, and to help as much as in him lay the promoters of **learning."** And to these high, ennobling ends he devoted **all his life,** waving a profitable **match in favor of his brother, and** betaking himself to the **sea-coast " to search out all** the monuments of **antiquity, and to get in travel the rarest plants, which were to be sent to the garden of** Beaugensier." Our fair readers will, we are certain, **be happy to know to whom they owe " flowering myrtles," with the accident — so prettily told by** Gassendus — that led Peiresc to its discovery.

" **About this time (1605), when Peiresc went from Marseilles to Beaugensier, he would** needs **take his way by Castellet to visit** the parish priest called Julius, **whom he** already dearly affected by reason **of** his ingenuous curiosity. Being by him led a **little** without the village, they met **a muleteer carrying a** branch of myrtle **with a broad leaf and full flower, such as Peireskius had never seen, nor knew that there was such a thing in nature. Wondering, there-**fore, at the **plant, he would be brought into** the middle of the wood where it grew, and caused the same **to be taken up, that it might be manured and** propagated. . . . This I thought good to mention, because a myrtle **tree with a full flower was a thing** unknown in Europe ; **and the thanks are due to** Peireskius that it is now **to be seen in the king's gardens, at** Rome, in the Low Countries, and other **places."**

In the same **year (1605), we find Peiresc at** Paris, courted by **Thuanus, Isaac Casaubon, and** Bagarrius, " keeper of the king's jewel-house of rarities ; " to the last of whom our antiquary explained **the** hitherto unknown inscription on an amethyst, marked with *indents*, " which had long perplexed inquirers." It immediately occurred to Peiresc " that these marks were nothing more than holes for small nails, which had formerly fastened little *laminæ*, which represented as many Greek letters." Peiresc drew lines from one hole to another, and the amethyst revealed the name of the sculptor! In the following year, Peiresc accompanies the French king's ambassador to England. For the benefit of the thousands who cross the Channel, we quote the means adopted by our voyager to prevent extreme sea-sickness : —

" Peireskius, to prevent the same in himself, left the rest of the company, and sat by the mainmast, where he was not so sick as they were. The reason being asked, he said there was least agitation in that part of the ship, and that, therefore, he withdrew himself thither, that he might not be stomach-sick, as the rest were, who, being in the head or stern, were much tossed."

Peireskius is graciously received by James, who " tenderly respected him ; " and who desired to have " from his own mouth" the story which had preceded him — of how, drinking with a toper of great reputation, one Doctor Torie, he baffled the drinker by " craftily qualifying" his own wine with water! With James a little humor went a great way, and thus on a small stock of that much-abused commodity, Peireskius might have passed with the English Solomon as an extraordinary wag. From England our philosopher goes to Amsterdam. Whilst staying at the Hague, " he would not depart until he became acquainted with Hugo Grotius," then a young man. From the Hague he stepped aside to Scheveling, where was the famous flying wagon.

" On my return from Leyden through the Hague (quoth Doctor Slop, *not* Gassendus), I walked as far as Scheveling, which is two long miles, on purpose to take a view of it."

" That's nothing," replied my Uncle Toby, " to what the learned Peireskius did, who walked a matter of five hundred miles, returning from Paris to Scheveling, and from Scheveling to Paris back again, in order to see it, and nothing else."

In 1607 Peiresc assumed the senatorial dignity, when he so executed " his office, that nothing was found wanting him," and still was left to him time enough " to study good arts, and to maintain his correspondence with learned men." At the latter end of this year, he lost his Uncle Claudius, whose " most faithful dog followed the corse all along, stood waiting upon the bier, could not for many days be gotten from the tomb, and after he was brought back to the house, stood a long time still *before his picture.*" (This last touch of affection is not unworthy of the consideration of Landseer. What a mourner would he conjure up by the exquisite magic of his art!) In 1609 Peiresc was affected with a severe fever, when he recovered, as he avers, by eating muskmelons, which in after years became his principal medicine. From this time he busies himself with the coins, weights, and measures of the ancients; and whilst engaged in these studies, has a dream in which he meets with a " goldsmith at Nismes," when the goldsmith offers to sell him a golden piece of Julius Cæsar's coin "for four cardecues," which incident actually occurred to him in his waking hours next day, but which "he reckoned only amongst those rare cases which are wont to amaze the vulgar."

From 1609 until 1630 we find Peiresc in constant communication with the learned of various countries — now deciphering inscriptions — now establishing a weekly post between Beaugensier and Paris — and ever intent upon the introduction of exotics, plants, and fruits into Provence. To him we owe the Chinese jessamine, "first brought from China, planted at Beaugensier, and from thence propagated." It was he who first cultivated in France "the gourd of Mecca, or silk plant, because it bears plenty of threads not unlike silk, fit to weave into stuffs." He planted cocoa trees, "and saw them bud; but whether through the coldness of the air, or because they were not well looked to, they came not to that perfection which he desired." We next learn that "ginger did wax green in his garden."

"I say nothing (we quote Gassendus) of the broad-leaved myrtle, with the full flower of the storax and lentisc tree, which yields mastic; and other plants mentioned before. Much less shall I speak of the great American jessamine, with the crimson-colored flower; nor of the Persian, with a violet-colored flower; nor of the Arabian, with a full flower; of the orange trees, with a red and parti-colored flower; of the medlar and sour cherry, without stones; Adam's fig tree, which Peireskius conceived to be one of those which the spies brought back that went to view the land of Canaan; the rare vines which he had from Tunis, Smyrna, Sidon, Damascus, Nova Francia, and other places."

There have been volumes enough, and too many, recording the guilt and madness of conquerors, whose lives were a curse to the bleeding world. The kind, gentle, enlightened benefactor of his race, who silently makes his foreign conquests grow and blossom in our gardens — who carries away the jessamine captive, and clothes our walks with its beauty, and scents our colder air with its sweetness; who gives to the poor the cheap and the lasting luxury of flowers — deserves a grateful memory among men, a memory growing and spreading with his gifts. The victories of the Cæsars are recorded by a few medals, shut up in the cabinets of museums, in the drawers of the virtuoso: the glories of men like Peiresc are still green among us — still glitter with the dews of the morning — still, with their constant sweetness, "scent the evening gale." Nor must we fail to record that the benevolent labors of Peiresc were continued, whilst he suffered acutest tortures from a disease which at last exhausted him. In the Easter of 1631 he was, " sitting without his door, at the entrance of his garden," struck with a sudden palsy, which deprived him of motion and speech. This he suffered for a whole week, when " somebody singing curiously an hymne of the Lives of the Lily and the Rose, he was so taken with the sweetness of the song, and the elegancy of some strain or other, that, like the son of Crœsus, desiring to utter some words, and particularly these, ' How excellent is this! ' he forthwith uttered them, and at that very moment his limbs were all freed from the palsy." In this year an extraordinary foreigner arrived at Toulon — no other than an elephant lately exhibited at Rome. Peiresc caused the stranger to be led to Beaugensier, where he took a cast of his grinders in wax, and had him painted in a lying posture, " that his joints might be seen," to the confusion, we presume, of the sceptics, who denied any such advantages to the quadruped. In 1633, Peiresc entertained " the famous poet Santamantius " at Beaugensier, who had a brother, a traveller, who had seen in Java " live-wights, of a middle nature between men and apes; " whereupon Peiresc quotes the authority of another traveller, a personal friend, and a physician, who had seen in Guinea " apes with long, gray, *combed* beards, almost venerable, who stalk an alderman's pace, and take themselves to be very wise." Our readers may have possibly beheld animals of this species.

In 1634 we find Peiresc studying hard at anatomy, which he follows with a degree of enthusiasm perhaps not altogether justifiable to the non-professional reader. Smitten by the theory of Asellius with respect to the " milkie veins in the mesentery," which " could not be discerned save in a creature living and panting, and that therefore they could not be observed in a man, whom to cut up alive was wickedness, yet did *he not therefore despair*." To be brief, a poor wretch condemned to be hanged — before sentence was performed — was by the order of Peiresc " fed lustily and securely," and an hour and a half after death was carried to the theatre of anatomy, where the wished discovery was effected.

Peiresc, having suffered intolerable agony for a month before his decease, died in the sixty-fifth year of his age. The account of his sufferings is written by Gassendus with that graphic simplicity which makes the charm of the book, but which, in deference to this over-nice age, we will not venture to copy. The portrait of the philosopher is in the happiest style of the unaffected biographer.

" He was, therefore (to begin with his stature), of a middle and decent pitch, neither too tall nor over low. The habit of his body was lean, and consequently his veins conspicuous, both in his forehead and hands. His constitution, as it was subject to diseases, so was it none of the strongest; which made him in his latter years to go with a staff. And for the same reason, his members were easily put out of joint; especially his left shoulder, which was three times dislocated. His forehead was large, and apt to be filled with wrinkles when he admired anything, or was in a deep study. His eyes were gray, and apt to be blood-shotten by the breach of some little vein. He fixed his eyes either upon the ground when he was seriously discoursing upon any subject, or upon the auditors when he perceived they were pleased with what he said. He was a little hawk-nosed; his cheeks being tempered with red, the hair of his head yellow, as also his beard, which he used to wear long. His whole countenance carried the appearance of an unwonted and rare courtesy and affability : however, no painter had the happiness to express him such as he was in deed and in truth."

To our mind this portrait is painted with all the

force of life.   We see rare old Peireskius; we see
the learning and the contemplation of the scholar —
in his large forehead, " apt to be filled with wrinkles "
— tempered and made gracious by the kindliness of
nature and the breeding of a gentleman.   He is clearly
one of Montaigne's men — a fine specimen of the simple, sterling book-men, with stored skulls and gentle
hearts.   What a capital contrast is Nicholas Fabricius to the literary coxcomb, —

> "Who, having writ a prologue with much pains,
> Feels himself spent, and fumbles for his brains " !

What a relief from the " *pardonnez-mois* " of literature — the be-scented and be-lioned petlings, who
spoil " wire-wove " with Babylonish verse and prose
— who, drawing their fingers through their raven
locks, swear, " By Gad ! " they've " writ a d—d fine
book," and vote all men vulgar fools who dare gain-
say it.   To continue from Gassendus : —
    " Though he was careful that the clothes he wore
abroad might not be unsuitable to his dignity, yet he
never wore silk.   In like manner, the rest of his
house he would have adorned according to his condition, and very well furnished ; but he did not at
all, in a manner, regard his own chamber.   Instead
of tapestry, there hung *the pictures of his chief
friends*, and of famous men.   His bed was exceeding plain, and his table continually loaded and
covered with papers, books, letters, and other things ;
as also all the seats round about, and the greatest
part of the floor."
    In his gardens at Beaugensier he was " delighted

with the pleasant verdure of plants, beauty of flowers, gentle murmur and purling noise of brooks and water-streams, together with the various songs of little birds, which, in the winter, we are told, he caused to be fed with corn, forbidding any one to catch or molest them.

"Moreover he preferred the singing of birds before the voices of men or any musical instruments — not but that he was therewith delighted, but because, after the music that men made, there remained in his mind a *continual* *agitation, drawing his attention, and disturbing his sleep;* the rising, falling, and holding of the notes, with the change of sounds and concords running to and fro in his fancy ; whereas no such thing could remain in the birds' music, which [we dispute the " because " here advanced]. because it is not so apt by us to be imitated, it cannot therefore so much affect and stir our inward faculty. He would also, for the same cause, continually breed up nightingales and such like small birds, which he kept also in his own chamber, and of which he was so careful, that he learned, by divers signs and tokens, what they wanted or desired, and presently would see them satisfied. They, therefore, as out of gratitude, would sing unto their benefactor hymns of praise ; and whereas, in his absence, they were for the most part silent, as soon as ever, by his *voice or staff*, they perceived he was coming, they would fall to singing."

The above presents us with a charming picture of the kind old scholar amidst his books and manuscripts, his medals, vases, and singing nightingales !

There were, however, other inhabitants of the chamber, though we are left unsatisfied as to their conduct towards the minstrels. "And *by reason of mice*, which did gnaw his books and papers in his chamber, he became *a lover of cats*, which he had formerly hated: and whereas, at first, he kept a few for necessity sake, he had, afterwards, a great company for his delight. For he procured out of the East ash-colored, dun, and speckled cats, beautiful to behold; of the brood whereof he sent to Paris and other places to his friends."

(In this ingenuous avowal of Gassendus there is the gem of a delicious essay. How many a man has become the lover of a cat in some shape — of a cat formerly despised — "by reason" of devouring mice! How many have been brought to endure and love the lesser evil when found to be the only remedy for the greater plague! There was — to quote one instance from a hundred — Jack Spangle, the gay prodigal Jack Spangle, a fellow shapely and agile as Mercury. He had the loudest laugh, the blackest mustache, and the whitest teeth of any spark of the day. Mrs. Sybil, the rich, withered widow of a scoundrel money-lender, looked feloniously upon him — she was determined to become the wife of Jack Spangle. Jack saw and shuddered at her purpose. O, how Jack Spangle abominated, loathed, anathematized Mrs. Sybil! In the depth and intensity of his hatred, he invented new terms of horror and disgust: it was merriment for his friends to hear him swear at the widow Sybil. Three years passed away, and a former companion met Jack and the widow man and wife. "The fact is, my dear fellow," said Jack, stepping forward to his acquaintance — " the fact is, I lost every farthing I had — was flung by creditors into jail — hadn't a penny to — humph ! eh ? — I — Allow me to introduce you to Mrs. Spangle." Jack was a second " Lord of Peiresc ; " we do not mean to assert that he became a devoted lover of his ancient wife ; but she was rich, he was penniless and in prison, and he married her " by reason of the mice." The " mice " have married many besides Jack and the widow.)

" The Lord of Peiresc " displays, in all his bearings, a finished portrait of the scholar and philosopher of the seventeenth century. There is the simplicity, the modesty, the kindliness of a truly great and well-regulated mind. It is to such men — lightly as their labors may be esteemed by a more imaginative generation — that we owe the greatest benefits. They were the collectors of facts to be employed by their successors — the gatherers of materials to be worked up into a thousand shapes of beauty and utility by those who should follow them. In the time of Peiresc, when the hard student — an anchorite amid his books — was considered by the vulgar as little less than liegeman to a magician, if not a necromancer himself, — when the large black dog of the scholar was the *malus genius* of his mysterious and devil-doomed master, — our philosopher was peculiarly fortunate in the advantage of birth and means : they afforded him, in station and power, a security and respect among men not too liberally awarded to the indigent bookman. He was " The Lord of Peiresc," and the patent of the senator gave grace and authority to the investigations of the philosopher.

The purpose of this slight paper has been to beg
of the " general reader" a short pause for the consideration of the lineaments of a great, though almost
unregarded benefactor of letters; to take him from
the candid conceits of these our most refined and delicate times, to the healthful simplicity of earlier days.
Not that, with rash, bigoted judgment, we would
sneer at the antiquarians of 1837: there are among
them wise, profound teachers; men of great discoveries ; men who have seen

> "———— the portrait of a genuine flea,
> Caught upon Martin Luther long ago " ;

and will, therefore, walk upon tiptoe to their graves,
drawn up by a prodigious sense of their own greatness.   Let them have their " peppercorn of praise ; "
and let small lecturers to the weariness of boarding-
schools talk their hour of nothings: all we ask is,
some passing attention to the early student — the
pioneer in the field of letters and of science.   Whilst
we do not envy, but wonder at the rich appointments
of well-paid sciolists, let us refresh our memory with
a view of our old philosopher in his study, and sometimes let our heart "leap up" as cheerfully as his
own nightingales at the staff of the " LORD OF
PEIRESC."

1837.

BREVITIES.

FORTUNE is painted blind, that she may not blush to behold the fools who belong to her.

Fine ladies, who use excess of perfumes, must think men like seals — most assailable at the nose.

Some men get on in the world on the same principle that a sweep passes uninterruptedly through a crowd.

People who affect a shortness of sight must think it the height of good fortune to be born blind.

He who loses, in the search of fame, that dignity which should adorn human nature, is like the victim opera-singer who has exchanged manhood for sound.

Lounging, unemployed people may be called of the tribe of Joshua, for with them the sun stands still.

Fanatics think men like bulls — they must be baited to madness ere they are in a fit condition to die.

There is an ancient saying, " Truth lies in a well." May not the modern adage run, " The most certain charity is at a pump "?

Some connoisseurs would give a hundred pounds for the painted head of a beggar, that would threaten the living mendicant with the stocks.

If you boast of a contempt for the world, avoid getting into debt. It is giving to gnats the fangs of vipers.

The heart of the great man, surrounded by poverty and trammelled by dependence, is like an egg in a nest built among briers. It must either curdle into bitterness, or, if it take life and mount, struggle through thorns for the ascent.

Fame is represented bearing a trumpet. Would not the picture be truer were she to hold a handful of dust?

Fishermen, in order to handle eels securely, first cover them with dirt. In like manner does detraction strive to grasp excellence.

The friendship of some men is quite Briarean — they have a hundred hands.

The easy and temperate man is not he who is most valued by the world; the virtue of his abstemiousness makes him an object of indifference. One of the gravest charges against the ass is — he can live on thistles.

The wounds of the dead are the furrows in which living heroes grow their laurels.

Were we determined resolutely to avoid vices, the world would foist them on us — as thieves put off their plunder on the guiltless.

When we look at the hide of a tiger in a furrier's shop, exposed to the gaze of every malapert, and then think of the ferocity of the living beast in his native jungle, we see a beadle before a magistrate — a magistrate before a minister. There is the *skin* of office — the sleekness without its claws.

With some people political vacillation heightens a man's celebrity — just as the galleries applaud when an actor enters in a new dress.

If we judge from history, of what is the book of glory composed? Are not its leaves dead men's skin

— its letters stamped in human blood — its golden clasps the pillage of nations? It is illuminated with tears and broken hearts.

1831.

<hr>

PIGS.

ADDRESSED TO THOSE " ABOUT TO LEAVE BUSINESS."

MISERABLE are those thrifty traders, who, having crammed their bags " e'en to bursting " with gold and bank paper, shut up shop, and endeavor gradually to accustom themselves to the sight of green turf, ere they are called upon to sleep under it. Mr. Pettitoes was one of those unhappy beings. He had, in his day, shed oceans of pigs' blood, and had grown immensely rich by the sanguinary employment. One day, however, his evil genius whispered, " Pettitoes, sell your business, and go live at your ease in the country." We much doubt whether the suggestion of the genius would have of itself prevailed, had it not been most opportunely backed by the whirling by of the handsome carriage of Mr. Figdust, late grocer of Oxford Street, but then Cincinnatus of Battersea Rise. Enough: Pettitoes " sold his business : " behold him in the country.

Pettitoes had a fine family — three daughters, born, it would seem, with a mortal hatred of pigs — a splendid house, gardens beautifully laid out, gra-

peries, pineries, arable land, peacocks strutting on the
lawn, and golden pheasants glittering in the wire
preserves.   To these delights may be added *The
Morning Advertiser*, every day ; and had he deigned
to consult them, the twenty new novels (subscribed
for by the young ladies) every week.   What greater
delight could fall to the fate of a retired pork-butcher,
tainted with the touch of the romantic?   And yet,
after a time, Mr. Pettitoes lost his customary suavity,
became careless of his attire of gentlemanly cut, and
once or twice struck his family with consternation,
by handling, in an absent and mysterious manner,
his father's ivory-hafted killing-knife, religiously preserved by his pious son.   Mrs. Pettitoes and her daughters — unanimous for once — declared that Mr. P. "was
not at ease.   What could be the matter with him?"

Unreflecting souls — they had their new novels,
the last new songs of the butterflies, lectures on chem-
istry, and the Egyptian hieroglyphics, to occupy their
minds — but not so Mr. Pettitoes : he, indeed, in the
eloquent language of his sympathizing family, " was
not at ease."   Could they have entered into his mind,
they would have seen how grotesquely were reflected
there all the beauties of surrounding nature.   To his
mental vision, every oak, beech, or elm seemed to
take the shape of a huge " hand " or " leg " of swine's
flesh — a hedge of hornbeam was but a Brobdignag
loin — the row of poplars so many gigantic skewers
— Sylph, the Italian greyhound, had bristles in his
back, and the peacocks did not scream, but grunt.
Gentle reader, let not this description of our hero's
mind appear forced and extravagant.   It is the com-

mon malady of the retired trader to assimilate the
objects of rustic life to the things of his former and
happier state. As the sailor beholds "green mead-
ows in the salt seas, and hears the bleating of the
sheep," so does the retired tea-dealer or pawnbroker
(we, of course, mean those with whom books are
nought) clothe the fields and hedges with hyson and
souchong, and see the three balls, glistening like Virgil's golden branch, from every tree. Could they
write their confessions, what drolleries would they
not give us — what hackney coaches running in the
milky way — what skylarks singing the two-penny
postmen's bells — what Naiads and Hamadryads
frisking it in comely whitey-brown aprons and
elbow sleeves. Thus it was with Mr. Pettitoes: all
his dreams, his waking feelings, ran on pigs; it was
in vain that he tried to divert his mind by reading.
He sent for "Hogg's Tales," but was disgusted and
disappointed. Shakespeare was only saved from his
contempt by two lines. "'Where hast been, sister?'
'Killing swine!'" O, acutely wretched is that gold-
en wretch, who, dragged by Plutus from the joyous
town, creeps over fields and adown hedges, twisting
buds and flowers into numerals and £. s. d. The
glorious sun is to him but a bright new shilling, and
when he gazes at the moon, he reads there "Georgius
IV., Dei Gratia Rex!"

Our friend Pettitoes wrestled with circumstances,
but it was in vain; he succumbed to the ruling passion, and, like a true philosopher, it was observed
that he displayed a greater serenity of mind, when it
was evident that he knew the worst. His fami-

ly wondered at his composure; they were still more astonished when they discovered its cause; for it is a curious fact — a fact well worthy of the attention of those "about to retire from business" — that from the moment Pettitoes had resolved once more to keep pigs, from that moment he became more civilized and companionable. Great, however, was the terror of the wife and daughters when they discovered that, to receive the purchased pigs in due state, it had been deemed necessary by Mr. Pettitoes to demolish a magnificent green-house. The fuchsias, the geraniums, the ranunculuses, gave way to boars and farrow sows, with long-tailed pigs, short-tailed pigs, pigs with crispy tails, and pigs minus such decorations. Mrs. Pettitoes was astonished — the young ladies vehemently remonstrated. Pettitoes, however, flew from domestic strife, and solaced himself at the pigsty. There, at all times, might he be seen, his eye gliding up and down some plethoric porker, as though, in his mind's vision, he was cutting up the breathing animal into hands, legs, loins, and chops. Had Pettitoes been transformed by Circe, he would have surely wept when set again upon his two legs. In order, as he thought, to mollify the ire of his wife and daughters, our tradesman christened his grunting family after the heroes and heroines of modern poems, novels, and songs. There might be seen, located in various sties, "Pelham," and "Eugene Aram," the "Lost Heir," and "The Man of Refinement." "Satan" was a great boar, and "Alice Gray" had a farrow of thirteen. This desecration of all that the female Pettitoes held beautiful only served to whet their disgust at pork, and to send **Mr. Pettitoes** from his carpeted **room**, hung round with genuine Morlands, to obtain tranquillity and enjoyment at **the piggery**. For some time was our tradesman satisfied with looking at the objects of his affection: it was enough for him to see the backs of his darlings widen, and the legs to become massive with the best of fat. At length, however, he felt his native thirst for blood, and it was observed that, after a time, he never visited the piggery without fumbling about at his knife. It was in vain — he gave himself up to fate — he would take his old shop. He *did* take it, paying the tenant an immense premium to go out. When Pettitoes' wife and daughters learned his resolution, they fainted; it is said that for three days horrible shrieks were heard in the neighborhood. Fortunately, however, for the gentle sex, "a woman," as Madame de Warens might have said, " who screams is not dead." Pettitoes was not called upon to go in sables. The ladies, of course, did not accompany Pettitoes to town; no, they kept the country-house, and lived with their fitting companions, the peacocks and the golden pheasants.

Pettitoes re-opened his shop: the day he again appeared in public his face had a fresher glow — his steel glittered in the morning sun — his apron and his sleeves never looked so blue. In fact, he appeared more than a vulgar butcher — there was a certain regimental air about him; indeed, it might have been said of him, as of a great general, he looked " butcher to the king." By degrees the piggery at Battersea Rise was cleared of its inhabitants. A large part of

"Childe Harold" was minced into sausages — "Eugene Aram" was once more anatomized for the benefit of the public — the family of "Alice Gray" went at from seven to ten shillings each — "Satan" was drained into black puddings, and "The Undying One" hung for two days, with a gash from ear to ear.

Of course the family never deigned to visit Pettitoes at the shop. Too proud, however, was the husband and the father, if his wife and daughters, at their country residence, would suffer him to send them down a joint of pork. They had their novels, their harps, and their auriculas — but Pettitoes was again in business; he had his apron, his knife, and his pigs. 1832.

SILAS FLESHPOTS; A "RESPECTABLE MAN."

"AY, indeed," cried the stone-cutter, "a most respectable man." This declaration of the giver of posthumous fame was intended to emphatically confirm the opinions of a previous speaker, — as we afterwards learned, the sole executor of the lauded deceased. We cannot, for a certainty, publish the true cause of his whereabout at the time of which we write — but we speak from the indubitable evidence of our senses when we avow, that last week, passing through the suburban village of Longerdash, we saw Mr. Timbrel in the stone-yard of old Cherub, then gravely and patiently at work on the virtues of the defunct Silas Fleshpots. Cherub, albeit he had polished the same alehouse bench every night for the last forty years — albeit he had married thrice, and had economically divorced himself once — although he had been a Tory with Mr. Pitt, a Whig with Mr. Fox, and a Radical with Mr. Henry Hunt — yet lived and breathed in an atmosphere of charity for all men. His calling had taught him benevolence. Like a true philanthropist, he conceived that what the superficial — in the poverty of language — call vice, was nothing more than a mistake; and thus, in the philosophy of Cherub, a most inveterate scoundrel was no other than an habitual blunderer. How could it be otherwise with one whose crude theories were ever and anon demolished by elaborate practice? Let the most egregious lie — said a great politician — be repeated for a year, and it will be universally believed. On the like principle, if, gentle reader, you have at times been disturbed by your neighbor beating his wife, or cruelly horsewhipping his children — if you have known him to refuse a single shilling to an old deserving acquaintance, and have heard him blaspheme in his last sickness — all such vague impressions of his iniquity shall fade from your mind, if compelled to labor, chisel in hand, at his epitaph. How can a man with any self-respect consider another a brute, when he may have toiled for hours to declare, in freestone or marble, that he was a loving husband, an affectionate father, and a warm friend? Every chipping of the stone knocks away a bit of uncharitableness, and

what, considered in the whole, would have been rejected as a fulsome lie, becomes, from the minute and
patient labor bestowed upon every atom of it, a radiant truth. (Historians, who very properly trust more
to style than the dulness of fact, know full well the
value of this process.) And why have we speculated
so far down the page on the causes of the charity of
stone-cutters? Why, simply out of respect for old
Cherub; for — we must own the doubt — had the
sepulchral chronicler been questioned at the Hare-
and-Hounds touching the moral qualities of the lamented Fleshpots, it is just possible (for there is a
potent mischief in some ale) the world had wanted
our opening eulogy. But we repeat, it is hard, after
sweating to establish the respectability of a person,
to be called upon to deny our own handiwork.
Thus " respectability " being chiselled at large in the
tombstone of Fleshpots, the artist could not well pro-
nounce him to be any other than " a most respectable
man."

Perhaps Mr. Jonas Timbrel — for he was allowed
to be the most precise and business-like of any of the
five trustees of Frankincense Chapel — stood at the
skirts of Cherub, to perform the pious duty of super-
intending his orthography (for the ill spelling in
epitaphs is a triumphant evidence of their distracting
pathos on the artist) ; it is not impossible, on the
other hand, that he watched the workman for this
cogent reason — he could find nothing else to do. Be
this as it may, we have proved no less than many
profound antiquarians who have written on Stone-
henge and the Round Towers ; we have demonstrated

where he was, and may surely leave the purpose for which he was there a matter of dark yet interesting doubt.   Timbrel, having made a rapid fortune in the exercise of a most laudable calling, as slop-seller at Shearness, having for many a year " relieved the hardy Tar," had retired to the village of Longerdash, to await, with the calm dignity of a Roman senator, the approach of the barbarian, Death.   In this he did but imitate the wisdom of the best philosophers, who, withdrawing from the foul contact of the world, have sought to purify and elevate their spirits in solitude and contemplation.   " Pitch defileth : "   Timbrel felt, we may say all over, this important truth.   In the pursuit of his vocation, he had been thrice tarred and feathered.   It has been thought due to the memory of Fleshpots — due to his wise appreciation of character — to say thus much of his chosen friend, to whom we are indebted for the following history.

(It is a curious and not an idle employment to mark the rise and progress of a particular word, when that word has become the distinguishing motto of no mean portion of the world ; to observe its different shades and manifold diversions from its original line and bent ; to note how it has passed of current value in one reign, and then been cried down with the clipped coin and pocket-pieces in the next.   To us, who have trifled away some time in this inquiry, " respectability," in its various modifications, has been of no light interest.   We have followed the word through centuries, and having been made to stare by some modern interpretations, we stopped dead short at the emphasis of the stone-cutter.   Particular words may be indeed, like the men who **abuse** them, of a noble origin — synonymous with honor, greatness, glory : they come at last to dignify meanness **and disguise deceit.** " Tact," " talented," **though now** in tolerable odor, consider-**ing the hard** duty they are put to, may in half a century change their present application ; and what **is** now liberally bestowed upon patriots and players **may be** the exclusive **property** of highwaymen and **pickpockets. We mark** this **paragraph in paren-theses, in the hope that the " light reader" will avail himself of** the privilege it bestows.)

We shall narrate the biography of Fleshpots in our own words, the style and phraseology of Timbrel — who had evidently, though without acknowledging it, built himself on the author of *The Urn-Burial* — be-ing, we **fear, at once too gorgeous and too** dusty for our purpose. **We shall serve his words as** Cato — really a respectable man — was accused of dealing with the remains of his brother Cæpio ; we shall pass **then through our own sieve, to separate the gold** from the cinders ; and **this gold we shall** melt, and twist, and hammer after **our "** own sweet will."

To the honor of Silas Fleshpots, be it said, he came **of no** questionable origin ; **for the bar** sinister in his **shield** had been duly proved — that is, sworn to — before **a** leash of magistrates ; thus there remained no doubt to puzzle future heralds ; the parish had its book — its *libra d' oro* — and the overseers of St. Sepulchre have ever been famous for a **fine bold hand.** Hannah Shields lived at ——— : **as the house yet** remains, and its present landlord **intends to apply for leave** to play a fiddle and piano, we will not name the sign :

the peccadillo of sixty years since might, indeed ought, to weigh with a scrupulous magistracy. It is enough to say, that the mother of Silas, before she was his mother, lived in the primitive capacity of maid. After his birth, she, of course, quitted her vocation; from a mere maid she became — indeed it often happens — a most respectable housekeeper. But let us not anticipate.

Hannah's young mistress, the eldest daughter of the landlord, was, in the graphic words of her expressive father, " a perverse [we will take it upon ourselves, though we lose a letter, to substitute] puss." Even her sisters owned she was not ill-looking; but then her temper was most extraordinary. Though bred where she had the peculiar advantage of viewing every shade of character, from the lightest to the blackest, her manners were alike to all; though for twenty years she had listened to the English language, in its most various and energetic developments. her own vocabulary was poor as a nun's. When a " gentleman at the bar " — as her paternal guardian was wont to say — swore to her beauty, he might, for the effect it produced upon her, as well have declared himself to the sign over the door. This insipidity could not but irritate the best of fathers. Her sisters had married wealthily; and Ellen was twenty, and still single. Her father could not but tremble for the effect of her coldness; and once overhearing a ticket-porter swear that " she wasn't flesh and blood, but a pictur," the miserable parent gave her up as lost. His fears, however, made him precipitate. She was not to be lost; for a rich distiller declared his love, and in proof of his passion drank his nightly ten glasses of brandy-and-water, mixed by the compelled hand of Ellen, although the bibulous suitor more than once vowed that her fingers froze it. We regret to say it, nobody spoke well of Ellen — if we except the beggars that hung about the door — and a certain pale-faced young man, one Thomas Roper, the aforesaid distiller's clerk, whose praise, it will be owned, was worse than blame — since, though receiving fifteen pounds per year, to be divided with his widow mother, Thomas Roper wasted his master's time in reading poetry, and, what was worse, trying to write the same. It was a profound secret; but at the time of which we speak, he had appeared in print.

The distiller grew more ardent — the father more imperative. Ellen's eyes became redder, her cheeks whiter; Ellen was to be married! At this interesting juncture, Hannah forfeited the esteem of the best of masters — she who had been so trusted, so caressed, she who would have been left with untold gold, had her master ever left gold in that predicament! Let us be brief. The landlord commenced with his son-in-law elect, the distiller called in a friend, a pious, excellent man, and — what else could be done? — Hannah was charged to confer the honor of paternity. Hannah showed her conscience, and kissed the book! We would wish here to drop our pen; in charity to the weak persons who honor literature, we would be dumb; but what was to be expected of a youth who wrote verses — love verses? Of course the father was the distiller's clerk! We are grieved to add, that the young man, not being persuaded even by the solemn oath of the betrayed victim, rejected the proffered honor; and when blandly asked by the proper authorities to marry her, he swore too — swore, and refused. He had no money — had no friends: he was therefore, in default of marriage, sentenced, in the patriotic words of the magistrate, to serve on board a man-of-war, in defence of his king and country. In one little week, poor Thomas — that is, Thomas — was scraping a ship's timbers at the great Nore — his mother was weeping, day and night, in the poorhouse; Ellen had been supported, like a corpse, to the altar with the distiller, and Hannah had been carefully lodged in two very comfortable attics. Ellen did not survive the birth of her first child. Sorry are we to say that she spoke of death as a happy release; when dead, there was found among her little trinkets a leaf of the *Gentleman's Magazine,* in which was "Lines to Ellen," with a lock of hair enclosed in what was meant for a letter, but which bore only the words "Tower Tender, Decem —"; the writer having been surprised in his attempt at illegal communication "with the shore." In two years the distiller died of apoplexy; and, until of late, it was feared that many important chemical secrets, of great value in his business, had died with him. Happy are we to say, there is every reason to believe that such is not the case.

We now come, and our readers must pardon our long preface to the event, to the birth of our hero. By an extraordinary coincidence, he was baptized Silas — a remarkable accident, for such happened to

be the sponsorial appellation of the pious yet humble
friend of the late distiller.   And yet a little thought
clears away the mystery, and places the gratitude of
Hannah Shields in the most ineffable light.   Impressed,
no doubt, with the paternal care — the elder Silas was
sixty — of that excellent man, as exhibited in his indignation at the false young clerk, she bestowed upon
her child the honored name of her disinterested champion.   There was a thankful delicacy in the act not
to be mistaken.   Nor were her obligations confined
to the loan of the name ; she likewise owed to the
senior Silas the furniture of the before-named two
attics.   This was true benevolence, for the good man
never vaunted of the act ; his dearest friends knew
not of his charity, nay, he had kept it a secret from
the wife of his bosom.   Pity that a carnal defect in
his education should have caused the slightest inconvenience to so worthy a creature.   But we are
pained to state that ere his godson — yes, we may
as well own it, the little Silas found in him a godfather — was two years old, the sponsor had been
elected treasurer of an uncertain Benefit Society.
The members could not have made a worse choice ;
the ingenuous, simple soul knew no more of figures
than of Chinese ; he was a signal victim to his ignorance of arithmetic.   Of this defect was he so trem-
blingly conscious, that nothing could induce him to
pass his accounts.   Though earnestly sought after by
all the members — nay, though invited by newspapers
and handbills — he was so morbidly alive to his want
of skill in numbers, that he replied to no single inquiry.   Such sensibility it may be hard to believe,

but he would not even show himself. Retiring from
public life, he many years after died, and in his bed.

Saint Sepulchre's — indeed from his earliest days it
was expected — did its final duty by the youthful
Silas; he was placed apprentice to a conscientious
tallow-chandler at Limehouse. His mother at this
time had dwelt for three years housekeeper to a tide-
waiter in the same neighborhood. Now, the good
soul, though she became, Sunday after Sunday, and
love-feast after love-feast, more practically serious, —
though she had thrown into the flames her well-
thumbed copy of George Barnwell, and was become
a yearly shilling subscriber towards the conversion of
the Jews, — still, as the sequel will exemplify, she
persisted in the indulgence of a most extraordinary
piece of fiction; and this it was: Her son had grown
for twelve years under the honored name of Shields;
She now insisted that he should commence his apprenticeship as Fleshpots. What the woman meant
by such caprice we know not, especially as she became more vehement in this her resolution, after hearing an eloquent discourse on the sinfulness of false
witnessing. Briefly, to the wonderment of several
authorities, Silas was bound in the name of * * * *,
the ex-treasurer. We can only say with Mr. Otway,
" women have strong constitutions."

Silas, it must be owned, was a sharp, shrewd lad;
his master never doubted his cleverness; but when,
in the first week of his service, he had sent into circu-
lation two bad dollars and a shilling, many a time
unsuccessfully proffered from the till by his employer,
he from that moment rose in the estimation of Mr.

Sol; but only rose to rise still higher, when — on two of the counterfeits being brought back by the customers, the one the wife of a sailor, and the other a little girl — he, in the most civil, but withal determined tone, declared they must be mistaken; neither dollar nor shilling could have issued from " their " till; they were not in the habit of taking bad coin; besides, people should look at their money before they left a shop. On his next club night Mr. Sol could not refrain from speaking of the extraordinary sharpness of his apprentice, though he did not particularize the special cause of his eulogy. After this time, Silas waxed great in the house; what medals of victory are to the soldier, the three pocket-pieces were, in the eyes of his master, to our apprentice, who wisely argued, that if bad money were unfortunately taken, bad money should be "got off." Are not many respectable people of the like just opinion?

Mr. Sol was growing rich. Despite the heavy excise, he continued to flourish; and we may say not too much when we avow that Silas flourished with him. He would have been completely happy but for the persecution of Betsy, the housemaid, who, whether he would or not, was determined on loving him. He had hinted this to his mother, who failed not to bestow the most virtuous abuse on the " forward hussy ; " at the same time declaring that women were horribly altered since she was young. Besides, Betsy was absolutely a parish apprentice. She was, it is true, buxom and good-tempered; and yet, with all this, she would love Silas; who, it must be confessed, was too respectable in his views to encourage two young

ladies at the same time.   Amelia Sol, a gentle
maiden not quite thirty, had fixed the apprentice;
though whether by the prospect of her father's shop
and good-will, or whether by her own beauty, — for
she had, with other equal charms, a furtive expres-
sion of eye, sometimes called a squint, — we know not.
Certain it is, they burned with a mutual flame; and
Silas, when the term of his apprenticeship had but a
few hours to run, with an undaunted face opened the
business to his excellent master.

"Why, see ye, Silas," — and Mr. Sol looked and
spoke like any one of the five hundred cosy old gentlemen in the old comedies, — "Amelia is certainly beyond your match.   It is true you have been a very industrious lad; but then Amelia expects great offers.
You have — I don't deny it — behaved very respect-
fully — up early and down late — saved me many bad
debts.   But then Amelia cost me a great deal of
money; the card-cases and the tea-rug are her own
work.   I own you understand your business; but
then Amelia — "

At this interesting moment Mr. Sol was called into
his shop, and from thence went into his room, accompanied by three, evidently unexpected, visitors.   This
interruption was particularly unfortunate; for Mr. Sol
had made his mind up to give Amelia to Silas, but
very prudently withheld a sudden consent, in order to
make the gift more precious.   Though Silas knew
not that the line had been written, he then felt that
" the course of true love never did run smooth " — for
the first time in his life this respectable apprentice
could have sworn.   Intense love made him needlessly

impatient; for, on the same evening, his worthy
master re-opened the business with a clear determination to " make two lovers happy." With this laudable view, he commenced, and had got as far as,
" Well, Silas, as a virtuous woman is a crown of
glory," when the apprentice interrupted him.

Silas rose from the chair to which he had been politely invited by his patron, and with praiseworthy
deference, his hands hanging at his sides, and his
head inclined somewhat forward, thus addressed
him : —

" Your pardon, worthy sir, for my presumption this
morning. I have considered the error of my ways,
and now repent of my audacity."

" Well, well, it was a bold deed : but you're a lad
of spirit, Silas; and a faint heart never won — eh ?"
And here the master chuckled a laugh, and gave a
searching wink, though, for its effect, he might as
well have winked at a dead man, or a dead wall; for
Silas, unmoved, proceeded : —

" Feeling, sir, that your excellent daughter is far
above me —"

" Ay, ay; but I'm the last man to brag of family.
If we come to the truth, all the same flesh, Silas; and
so —"

Silas was not persuaded by the philosophy of his
master; for he continued to apologize, until, op-
presssed by his repentant diffidence, Mr. Sol jumped
from his seat, ran to the stairs, and called Amelia; at
the word the modesty of Silas strengthened into resolution. With an assured air he was retiring towards
the door when the maiden entered; it was a critical

moment.   Taking Amelia by the hand, her parent advanced to Silas, who, shrinking, still retreated, — his master still talking, and following him up, and the gentle virgin blushing a deeper red at every syllable.   In this manner the three had just completed the circuit of a tolerably large room, and Mr. Sol, with a gush of affection, accompanied with admirable pantomime, just "like one of those harlotry players," had exclaimed, "Take her, and bless ye both," when Silas vanished.   Had the floor opened and swallowed him, father and daughter could not have been more astounded; they stood, each with an open mouth, petrified by his retreating steps, which in the awful silence told with horrible distinctness!   How long their astonishment might have lasted passes our speculation to say, had they not been violently brought back to this world by the street door, which, turning on its infernal hinges, "grated harsh thunder"!   On this a flood of tears relieved the forsaken Amelia, whilst a torrent of oaths comforted her father.   The benevolent soul was struck to the core by the ingratitude of his late apprentice — for, from twelve o'clock that day, the indentures of Silas had been waste parchment.   Was it possible that he could know of the mishap of the morning?   O, no!   Had Silas been aware that the best of masters was exchequered to double the amount of his worldly goods for only defrauding the excise, he would have been the last to leave him; for left him he most assuredly had; as on the instant and anxious search of father and daughter, it was but too apparent he had sent away each and every of his three deal boxes.

15

" The scoundrel came to my house with a bundle no bigger than my fist, and he quits my service with three boxes ! "

Something must be allowed to human infirmity; poor Mr. Sol was not so much disgusted at what Silas had taken, as what Silas had left. Amelia, who really loved the runaway, wept and said nothing. Beautiful is woman's gratitude ! and Amelia was grateful for past favors: for Silas was the first and only " monster wearing the human form " who had ever said a civil word to her !

But we must not give up Silas undefended.   It was not his fault if his master suffered his parlor keyhole to hunger for paper.   He had no wish to pry or listen ; but if people would talk in alt, whilst he moved like a mole about his business, family matters would cleave the ear, which, however it tried, could not be deaf.   If Silas felt annoyed at the delinquency of his master, he was absolutely shocked that it should be found out ; but the profligacy of Mr. Sol being made so public as the light of his namesake, was it prudent for a young man, just entering life, to ally himself to such a connection ?   His heart bled for Amelia ; but the illiberal world would not discriminate : in quitting her, he felt he left his dearest hopes ; but would it be proper to marry " into such a family " — would it be respectable ?

As we are touching on the various accidents of this one eventful day, we must not forget to chronicle an accident which befell Betsy — the despised, the discarded Betsy.   About an hour after the visit of the three mysterious persons, of whom we have before spoken, it was notified to the housemaid — though we almost feel convinced that Silas heard no syllable of the discourse — that she was suddenly become the mistress of little less than five hundred pounds.   A lottery-ticket and a blue-coat boy account for the windfall.

Silas was scarcely emancipated from the thraldom of apprenticeship, when he was doomed to endure — in addition to the loss of Amelia — another, and if possible, a more bitter privation.   The tide-waiter had been some time dead, and Mrs. Hannah Shields, retired on her means, lived as she could.   Her son was the perfection of filial compliance; for his mother, having in a hasty moment commanded him never again to appear before her (Silas had been somewhat energetic in filthy money matters), he obeyed her to the very letter; nay, though he heard she was in her mortal sickness, he did not dare to violate her orders.   Once, indeed, he approached the door, but was scared from the threshold by the appearance of the doctor's boy, about to deliver for the patient at least half a dozen phials.   Silas wondered how the man of physic was to be paid.   He had no money to spare; and in his outset of life — for he would wisely harp on that string — to saddle himself with responsibilities which he had, as he conceived, no present means of paying, was not honest, was not respectable.

Death, however, despite of the doctor, marched sternly to his purpose, and, deaf to the shrieks and ravings of the poor soul, carried off his victim.   Silas now conceived himself released from the injunctions of his mother, and with filial haste rushed to the lodging, which, to his horror, he found stripped of nearly everything. He entered the room at the moment the nurse was curiously trying a small packet, in order to come at its contents without risking the felony of breaking the seal. Silas snatched at the missive, which he found directed in his mother's hand — that was never to be mistaken — to himself. Casting a disappointed glance about the walls, he descended the stairs to hide his emotion, and to break the parcel. He found it to contain minute directions for his mother's funeral, and — but why mention money at such a moment — it likewise contained a hundred and fifty guineas. In a terrible letter, addressed to her son, the miserable woman denounced herself as the worst of sinners, and with this deep sense of her own unworthiness, charged Silas not to lay out a penny more than was absolutely necessary on her burial. The young man, impressed with this solemn adjuration, as he conceived, most aptly fulfilled his duty by not spending one farthing on the ceremony. He was so affected, that it was full ten days ere he could trust himself near his mother's late dwelling; and then what was his mortification on learning that she had been interred at the parish charge! The authorities, urged by the nurse, applied to Silas for reimbursement; at she same time hinting at the probable contents of the parcel, which, as he refused to pay, they required to see. On this point Silas was decided; the packet contained family secrets, of no importance to any but himself; and would the overseers wish to rake up the errors of the dead? No;

they were too considerate to desire it; and, for himself, he trusted he was too respectable to permit it.
The overseers were vanquished; and Silas felt that
the spirit of his mother was, on one point at least,
appeased; for she had been put into the earth at the
very least possible expense. With this comforting
assurance, and wiping away some natural tears, Silas,
with quite dry eyes, looked out for a shop.

But a very few weeks elapsed ere our hero was a
householder. Would we were equal to the task — it
would cast a perpetual halo round our humble pen,
could we faithfully describe the feelings of Mr. Silas
Fleshpots running riot over Chinese bridges, vaulting
over elephants' backs, and now expanding at the
forms and plumage of parrots and paroquets, and now
brooding, with halcyon wings, on oriental lakes. Let
not our reader marvel at these exotic images, though
transported to London. We speak of Silas on the
first Sunday of his housekeeping; when, lying in bed,
the sun shining (for this happened to be the summer, when the sun was visible in every street in
Limehoûse), steeping in eastern light the bed curtains which encompassed the young beginner, and
cast on him a trance of inexpressible delight. It was
then the bed furniture, enriched with its multitudinous
patterns of beast, bird, fish, and tree, exercised a
mystic power on the rapt beholder. The elephants
grew bigger, and twisted their little trunks in token
of glad greeting — the palm trees grew and grew —
the birds fluttered — the water rippled — yea, and a
stream of melody floated underneath the tester! To
the ecstatic eye of Fleshpots everything was real, was

true; and his ears drank in a living music. Whence, inquires the reader, all those wonders? Again we say, from the bed curtains. We think we can satisfactorily explain the miracle. Thus it was. When Silas, at twelve years old, was first brought to the unfortunate Mr. Sol, that beneficent man was confined to bed — suffering from a late supper of questionable mussels. — Sneer not, reader; lampreys have dethroned kings! — The parish boy was naturally awe-struck; every article in the presence-chamber was instaneously burnt, as with a branding-iron, into his tender memory. His moral being had, in that one minute, if we may use the word, stereotyped every object presented to his senses. Let the wonder of the boy explain the ecstasy of the man; for the very curtains which impressed the child from St. Sepulcre's, actually hung, on the morning of which we speak, about the housekeeper of St. ——. Every elephant was become his own, every tree, and every feather. We feel that a whole volume of metaphysics might hereon be written; the matter for the task being no more recondite than faded bed furniture, and Silas Fleshpots, boy, contrasted with the same Silas, man. If the reader be a philosopher, we think he will understand us; if he be not, we own, with him, the whole paragraph to be unutterable nonsense.

So carried away were the feelings of Silas, so possessed was he, by the changes of the past years, and the hoped glories of the future, that he had wholly forgotten a late most important ceremony. Yes; his young wife, the good-tempered, red-faced Betsy lay unthought of by his side. As the marriage, in consequence, no doubt, of the recent death of Mrs. Shields, had been so quietly celebrated, we may be excused for omitting to speak of it until the present moment. Silas, we conceive, vindicated his claim to the softer emotions by his union with Betsy : the poor girl — although, as we have before remarked, she was amiable and good-looking — loved him, and though his bosom was yet bleeding with the thoughts of Amelia, a victim to the misconduct of her father, he manfully determined on a self-sacrifice to pity, and, caring but little for Betsy, magnanimously married her. It was odd, but the sum won by his bride from Cooper's Hall was a few pounds over the amount required for the good-will of his late master's establishment. Silas might, indeed, have had time granted to pay the money ; but scorning all obligation, he thought it most independent to marry. With his previous savings, and — Plutus and his executive officer alone know how money grows with some people — other trifles, he contrived to purchase the greater part of the furniture of his quondam employer ; among which were the elephantine bed curtains. On the very day which rose on Silas Fleshpots, stationed for the first time at his own shop door (as he stood with his sharp frost-colored face, and his intensely-mangled sleeves and apron, he looked the embryo possessor of at least half a plum), Mr. Sol exhibited himself to the philanthropists of Fleet Market, cooped in the iron cage for wicked debtors. And did Silas never think of Amelia? Sorry are we for human weakness to answer — Yes. It was she who ruffled the honeymoon with the first quarrel ; for Mrs. Fleshpots, having occasion to enlarge the wardrobe of her husband by half a dozen new shirts, called in a foreign needle to assist her own. Now, Amelia was reduced to ply as a daily sempstress, and it was with considerable emphasis that Mr. Fleshpots accused his spouse of want of common feeling for her late mistress ; for, in his own words, he had no doubt that the " poor thing would have come just as cheap."

Every day added to the wealth and respectability of Fleshpots ; indeed, there seemed with him a subtle sympathy between cash and character. They were the " twin cherries " on his household stalk : in very truth they were so alike, that even Silas himself would at times have been puzzled to decide which was which ; fortunately his philosophy raised him above nice distinctions. It was not long ere Fleshpots rose to an overseer ; from overseer he dilated into contractor — a love of purely financial operations then fell upon him, and he became, in quite an unostentatious way, bill-broker. Here was a wide field for his philanthropy ; we might, but we will not, cite a thousand instances of its operation. Did a young couple set up, especially in the tallow line, in his neighborhood — it was not long ere the kindest offers were made to them ; not indeed by Fleshpots ; no, he shunned the applause of such public goodness — but by his almoner, a friend who — on merely the written signature of the party — would sometimes pay down hard guineas. Palpable, glittering gold, for a few scratches of the pen ! It cannot be disguised that certain results, never contemplated by the original

benefactor, would distress all parties ; but these accidents would only more strongly illustrate the worth
of Fleshpots.   He was not the man to oppress young
beginners by clamoring for instant restitution ; no, no
— he would give them months or years ; — and when
grasping neighbors, he could have named, were making fifty per cent. he in scarcely one instance required more than forty-five.   And what bettered these
transactions was the secrecy with which they were
effected ; he knew that it might hurt the credit of a
young tradesman, if a certain lease-security, or bond,
or mortgage were known, and so, with delicate consideration, never breathed a word about it.   On the
contrary, where he had most served, there would he
most praise : thus it was not unusual to hear the
name of Fleshpots quoted as an example of consum-
mate liberality — as of a man who " would live
and let live."   Of course, a few malign and envious
spirits would spit their bitterness.   It is painful to be
compelled to believe, that in one very hard winter,
when Mr. Fleshpots, in the benignity of his nature,
dispensed one pound of candles to each of fifty pauper
families of six, there were people who sneeringly
remarked that the donor had not long had the con-
tract to supply the parish.   Such aspersions were
weak as they were wicked ; they could no more dim
the bright respectability of Fleshpots, than they could
tarnish the splendid silver wine-cooler presented to
him on his retirement from office by a grateful vestry.

   " Wisdom is found," says an obscure poet, " with
childhood about its knees ! "   Let this be granted,
and there never was a wiser being than our kind

hero.   No man took a more lively interest in the Sab-
bath and parochial schools of **Limehouse**. The acu-
men with which he examined the awe-struck scholars,
his impressiveness when he came to the Decalogue —
and here we are reminded of a touching circumstance,
powerfully illustrative of Fleshpots' high sense of
moral justice — of his exceeding fitness as an amateur
instructor of youth. Being of the vestry, our hero
received a small premium with a lad from the work-
house, a boy whom — for he had no children of his
own — it was his wish to make a great deal of. The
boy was dull and delicate; but his delicacy, as his
master said, might have been looked over, had he
been honest. Fleshpots, who taught two schools
" not to steal," failed to impress the commandment on
Peter.

Our friend, **as overseer, was, of** course, appealed
to by many worthless people — by persons who not
only had very equivocal claims to any relief, but who
certainly had no claim at all on the benevolence of
Limehouse. Sailors are, proverbially, the most in-
considerate and ignorant of men: thus Fleshpots
was often pestered by the importunity of starving seamen, who swore they were of his parish, when he
swore — for he would swear before seamen — they
were not. One day — time runs on; Silas had been
five-and-twenty years in trade — a wretched seafaring
man, of more than middle age, came as claimant on
the overseer, who, in terms not to be misunderstood,
bade him troop for an impostor. The man — there
was starvation in his looks — quitted the shop with a
wicked oath, and Silas returned to his nap in his

back parlor. No sooner had he closed the door, than Peter ran into the street, and beckoning to the sailor, put into his hands a part and parcel of his master's lawful property. Fortunately for public morals, the boy was detected; and, at the instance of Mr. Fleshpots, confined in the proper asylum for all disobeying apprentices.

The cook of Mr. Keelhaul, ship-owner, in the freedom with which she parted with the refuse of the kitchen, bore a flattering testimony to the wealth of her employer. She had that day sold her merchandise to the tallow-chandler, and that comprised not only the usual perquisites, but five collops of fat meat, accidently, no doubt, thrown into the vessel. The transfer of this property had not been made ten minutes before the sailor, lawfully rebuffed by the overseer, quitted the door. Peter had seen the man — had heard his master — and yet Peter, as he thought, unobserved, purloined the identical pieces of meat, and ran and placed them in the hands of the tar.

Let us not dwell on youthful depravity: suffice it, the boy was confined; in his confinement enlarged his acquaintance, who, in the end, tempted him to run from an excellent master. From small pickings, he went on to serious thefts; and — but what was to be expected? — Peter was hanged for highway robbery. This painful incident displays the wisdom of Fleshpots — had he not, in the first instance, prosecuted Peter, the boy might have robbed, with impunity, till he became gray-headed; whereas he was providentially cut off at seven-and-twenty!

Some three or four weeks after the theft of Peter,

as Fleshpots and Timbrel were settling some affairs
of partnership, — this was soon after the removal of
the latter gentleman from Sheerness, — the overseer
was summoned on a coroner's jury. Attending at
the due place and hour, he learned that the deceased
was a sailor. On view of the body, he moreover discovered it to be that of the importunate beggar, for relieving whom Peter was then suffering durance. The
man had been found dead; how he died was not
known; some of the jury thought of too much liquor
—some of too little food; Fleshpots inclined to the
former opinion. However, the verdict ran that
" Thomas Roper was found dead!" Our readers
must recollect the name of the deceased; yes, the
dead man — as proved by certain papers about him —
was no other than the verse-writing distiller's clerk —
the profligate youth, who had rather chosen to
scrape the hard ribs of a man-of-war than to endure
the loving arms of Hannah Shields. We are happy
to think, that in the body of Thomas Roper, Silas
did not recognize that of his parent. No, we believe
the delicacy of Hannah had always kept from her
son the name and state of the author of his being.
What would have been the anguish of Fleshpots, had
he known he had been sitting on his own father!

The event, however, passed not without some slight
pain — though all in the way of business — to Fleshpots. Mr. Timbrel partook with himself the delight of
affording assistance to destitute seamen. Money was
lent them on their wages and prize-money; and it so
happened, that among other documents, faithfully delivered by Mr. Timbrel to his partner, was an instru-

ment which, ultimately, brought them in six hundred·
per cent.   It was no other than the right to receive
prize-money due to one Thomas Roper, and sold by
him for something less than an old song to Mr. Timbrel.
How one recollection awakens another !· It was
then, and for the first time for many, many years, that
Fleshpots recollected a certain paper, bequeathed to
him by his mother, with the addition of seventy-five
guineas, to be given to one Thomas Roper, sailor,
whom in her own words she had " cruelly treated."
Now, among the many thousand sailors, how was
Silas to find out Thomas? And as for any cruelty
on the part of his mother, it could not be ; the poor
woman was beside herself with the terrors of near
death.   If he had known it had been the same
Thomas !   And this he said to himself — kind creature ! — at least fifty times.

And Silas continued to flourish.   His wife, at the
time of his retirement from business, — for we approach that golden epoch, — had been dead some
fifteen years.   Silas felt her loss, was lone and solitary ; for, about the same time, he had been wounded
by base ingratitude.   A young tradesman, to whom
he had lent a considerable sum, failed in his pay-
ments, and escaped to America.   It will illustrate the
peculiar benevolence of our hero, when we inform
our readers, so far from visiting the innocent partner
of the villain with reproach and contempt, he, on the
contrary, received her — though comparatively young
and inexperienced — under his roof, in the trustwor-
thy situation of housekeeper.   Poor thing ! she received his dying words, and an annuity.

Fleshpots died fairly laden with respectability. He was the patron of twenty charities, and, towards the close of his life, never ate of a hot joint on Sundays. He died, and died in peace; for the reports that in his last moments he raved about twenty women in white squirting fire at him — of half a dozen devils, with pigtails, and in sailors' jackets, roaring about him — of vats of boiling gold, and such distempered nonsense — were, we believe, fully traced to the malice of a disappointed undertaker.

Silas Fleshpots was a respectable man : this cannot be doubted. It is chiselled in his epitaph, — chiselled in large letters, — for it was especially ordered in his will that his respectability should go forth, and stand forever — large.

1835.

——•◦•——

THE TRUE HISTORY OF A GREAT PACIFICATOR.

THOSE of our readers who have had the good fortune to visit the Hague will probably recollect the White Hart, a humble, but remarkably neat hostelry, situated in an agreeable part of the most delightful of all European villages, a village particularly interesting to an Englishman and scholar from the great names associated with its air of learned retirement. The whole place seems a large college, with museum and gardens. We walk there, and

think of Sir William Temple, and Bolingbroke, and
Boyle, and of twenty others, whose memories turn a
Dutch village into an elysium of letters, who take us
back a hundred years and more, and make us people
of the past, real flesh and blood of the eighteenth
century. We doubt not that such have been the feelings of thousands of our readers who have visited
the Hague; but we know not whether we ought to
express a regret that the enjoyment of such learned
abstractions is in future denied them on their return
to the circle of the Dutch court, for certain we are
that they will no sooner learn the history of the illustrious individual whose birth has given a glory to the
White Hart than they will forget English ambassa-
dors and English philosophers in the lively curiosity
that will incontinently take them to the aforesaid public house. To begin our " true history."

It was at the White Hart, on the 2d of December,
in the year one thousand eight hundred and seven, in
the left front chamber on the second story, that Diedrich Van Amburgh saw the light. He was pro-
nounced by the vrow Kinderkid — a woman whose
word, from her long experience in such matters,
passed as an authority throughout the whole of the
Netherlands — the finest man-child that in all her
many days she had ever seen. Great was the rejoicing at the White Hart on the birth of little
Diedrich. A Holland's tub was tapped, and everybody, from the solid burgher to the drudging boor,
was pressed to drink long life and happiness to the
new comer.

We can, without any perturbation of conscience,

declare that during a journey undertaken for no meaner purpose, we have met with no story, no legend, illustrative of the peculiar genius of our hero during the first six months of his eventful existence; in fact, with nothing that, philosophically considered, can be viewed as a dawning or promise of Van Amburgh's after glory; for we are inclined to receive as apocryphal an anecdote offered to us for two guilders by a Rotterdam Jew, who professed himself ready to give an authentic pedigree of the story, an anecdote involving the character of the White Hart cat, said to have been *looked* into a palsy, in her attempt to steal the pap of Diedrich, the child lying at the time before a fire of glowing turf, within eye-shot of the delinquent.   If the story be true, — though we must not forget that men are but too prone to invent wonders for wonderful individuals, — it is an extraordinary instance of the early development of that faculty which has subsequently achieved such triumphs in the brute world.   The cat (we speak on the authority of the Jew) was so completely fascinated, subdued, terrified by the glance of the babe that, in four-and-twenty hours the animal became, from a most beautiful jet black, a dirty gray-white.   Now, he who at six months old could look a black cat white may be reasonably expected at thirty years to change lions into puppy-dogs, and tigers into doves.   Having given our faith to the first story, belief in all subsequent wonders is easy to the meanest capacity.

We are, however, happy to state that we approach a period of our hero's life at which we meet with well-authenticated facts, with accounts of his ex-

traordinary influence over the lower animals, subscribed to by three burgomasters of Rotterdam, and,
therefore, documents pure and speckless as Runject
Singh's large diamond.

It was the good fortune of little Diedrich to have a
godfather who was fully impressed with a sense of
the child's abilities; for, at the Amsterdam fair, he
purchased a very splendid coral, hung round with
twelve bells in little fancy oranges, — a delicate compliment on the part of the goldsmith to the house of
Nassau, — silver gilt, all toned according to harmonic
principles, the benevolent object of the sponsor being
that his godchild should cut his teeth to the accompaniment of the very sweetest music.   The coral was
hung about the babe's waist, and a pretty rattling and
ringing he kept up, laughing, and crying, and cooing,
and teething all the while as if nothing was the matter.   Diedrich was ten months old when his father,
who, in sooth, was never happy when the child was
from his arms, took his babe with him into the cel-
lars; for, even in Holland, where British brandy is
not, there are certain mysteries to be performed in
vaults, which probably it is wisdom in those who love
cellar comforts not too curiously to inquire into.
There was the child crawling upon the ground, ringing his coral, squalling, crying, laughing; our host,
Van Amburgh, now chirping to his last-born, now
singing a snatch of a Dutch melody, and now swearing affectionately through his teeth at some playful
transgression of the pretty babe.   At this moment
Kidneyvat, the burgomaster of Rotterdam, alighted
— if we may use such a word for so huge a man —

at the door of the White Hart, and instantly there
was a loud calling through the house for Mynheer
Van Amburgh. Our host rushed from the cellar,
strange to say, forgetful of the child in his precipi-
tancy to do all honor to a Rotterdam burgomaster,
who, on some official business, the object of which
we have failed to discover, took the landlord from his
house, keeping him until the late hour of ten at night
from the hearthstone of the White Hart. He had
left the house about three hours, when suddenly there
arose a yell throughout the hostelry for the child.
Every place was searched but the right one; night
drew on, and O, the horror, the consternation, that
reigned throughout the White Hart! Happily, however, the host returned to his house at seven minutes
to ten, and — the sternness of history refuses to con-
ceal the fact — very drunk indeed was he, even for a
Dutchman. His wife — but we refuse to describe, as
we might, the affecting picture of maternal love; it is
enough to say that the words, " The child, Diedrich,
darling, angel, innocent lost one ! " poured from the
lips of the landlady, tears dropping from her eyes as
she accosted her spirituous husband, somewhat staggered by her uneasiness, and a little moved by the
burgomaster's cheer. " Where — where's the child ? "
exclaimed vrow Van Amburgh ; when Diedrich, after
the confusion of a moment, looked very wise, and,
whilst a smile broke over his broad face, making it
shine like a tub of butter in the sun, he softly grunted
forth, " The cellar ! "

At the words a shriek burst from the assembled
household. " The cellar ! " And instantly armies of

rats, every rat as big as any hare, galloped through the affrighted imaginations of the servants, for the vrow Van Amburgh fainted dead as stone. "The cellar!" No man, woman, or child stirred a foot: every soul seemed petrified with horror; stood as though motion was useless, the child having, of course, been shared in little pieces among the ravenous vermin — swallowed in small bits, flesh and bones, cap, and bib, and tucker. Rats had been seen in that most rat-frequented cellar big as moderate-sized dogs: they had, one hard winter, shown considerable disposition to attack Van Amburgh himself, taking, by the way, a shameful advantage of his having, contrary to his usual custom, entered their domain without a stick. Was it, then, to be thought of, came it within the wildest dreams of hope to imagine, the dear little innocent Diedrich safe? No; the lovely little one was dead, and though buried, was carried about the cellar in mince-meat, entombed in the bowels of the pitiless rats.

No man stirring towards the cellar, the host himself proposed to descend, when he was followed by all the guests and the servants — for the vrow Van Amburgh remained insensible — to the death-place of " dear little Diedrich." The cellar was exactly thirty feet six inches (we mean, of course, English measure) below the street, and was approached by a narrow, winding staircase, which admitted, and that with some difficulty on the part of the experimentalist, only one Dutchman to ascend and descend at a time; seven servant girls, of irreproachable character, had left the White Hart simply because they were found of too luxuriant a figure (Venuses run large in the Netherlands) for the narrow capacity of that cellar staircase.

Mynheer Van Amburgh descended first; his opposite neighbor, the cooper, a man of unblemished veracity, followed, and, as we have already stated, a long train of the affrighted and the curious descended one by one, and not a word was spoken, not, save now and then a sigh, a sound was heard. Hence the party, when within some ten feet of the cellar, heard, to their astonishment and deep delight, the musical ringing of little Diedrich's coral bells; and more, they heard his dear, sweet little voice cooing away, and laughing, and, in the innocency of its little heart, trying to hum a tune to the dulcet accompaniment of mellow silver. Every man and woman paused. and exclaimed a short thanksgiving as the bells still rang.

" Let's see what the younker's about," said the father, and, as cautiously as his condition permitted him, entered his spacious cellar, which was speedily thronged by his followers. They looked around, and though they saw a faint glimmering of a light, — for the host had left his lamp in the cellar (fortunately the babe was dressed in woollen), — though they heard the bells and the voice of the baby, they could not immediately discover where the infant was. At length the father led the party through a long lane of Holland's tubs, and there in a corner, to the wonder and admiration of the spectators, they beheld — what? Little Diedrich Van Amburgh seated — how the child got there was not the least wonder — on the head of a gin-tub, shaking his silver-gilt coral, and nodding his head, and conceitedly trying to snap his little, thick, turnip-radish fingers, and, in a word, by intuition, of course, delightfully imitating the graceful airs of great composers, who flourish their glittering *batons de mesure* to the gratification of an audience, and the perfect unconcern of an orchestra! There he was, shaking his coral bells ; but, reader, we have not yet told you to whom : in a word, then, to no less than a hundred and fifty rats, — for the cooper counted them, — the least of them as big as terriers, dancing and caracoling, and, at the voice of the babe, running up the gin-tub, and licking his face, and subjectedly, as if in token of homage, rubbing their noses against his toes.

It would be a waste of time and paper to attempt to describe the astonishment of the beholders ; let the reader imagine himself in the cellar of the White Hart, at the interesting juncture whereof we write, and consider what would have been his measure of surprise. The feat of Diedrich made even Dutchmen marvel. They were silent in their astonishment ; yea, their tongues were like bits of ice in their mouths, from sheer wonder. A greater wonder, however, almost immediately thawed them.

They had gazed in dumb abstraction at the gambols of the rats, at the subjection of the vermin to the voice, looks, and gestures of the infant pacificator ; but when, at certain inarticulate words uttered by Diedrich, six of the largest rats ran up the tub, and two, standing on their hind legs, rested their fore paws upon each of his shoulders, when a third rat sat, as in the act of begging, on the crown of his head, two other rats crouched upon his knees, and a sixth rat, taking his tail in his mouth, hung, like a necklace, round the throat of their baby dominator, — when the Dutchmen beheld this, — no more, in fact, than an adumbration of the future group of lions and tigers, — when the Hollanders beheld this, they *did* shout!

It was extraordinary, however, and certainly the strongest evidence of the mysterious influence of young Van Amburgh over the hearts and minds of the vermin, that, though several gin-tubs jumped from their bottoms, — the motion caused by the vibration of the Dutchmen's shout, — the rats never moved a muscle! They looked steadfastly in the faces of the Dutchmen, and, catching the eye of their nursling master, kept their places.

Fortunately this circumstance is so well attested, the triumph of young Van Amburgh over the ferocity of the rats is so finally established by events subsequent to the scene in the cellar, that all the malignity of envy — and Mr. Van Amburgh, who has " robbed the lion of his heart," cannot despoil the serpent of its poison — cannot shake it! We have talked to people, most respectable persons now dwelling at the Hague, who well remember to have seen young Van Amburgh, when only four years old, drawn about the village by twelve of his father's rats, in light pig-skin harness, attached to a small, shell-like vehicle, unfortunately, only seven years since, burnt in a house at Leyden, whither it had been sent for the inspection of the curious.

At four years old, drawn by rats, would young Van

Amburgh pass through every corner of the Hague, nay, proceed as far as Scheveling and back; and though many and many a cat sat in the doorways, and licked his lips as he leered at the plump and whiskered team of the infant pacificator, yet no cat dared to pounce, for this reason — the eye of Diedrich Van Amburgh was upon him.

To this wonderful organ, be it understood, our hero ascribes all his triumphs in the brute creation. Great conquests have certainly been made by the same instrument in the higher walks of animal life; but in the inferior parts of the *règne animal*, Diedrich Van Amburgh is a conqueror unrivalled — the Hannibal of hyenas, the Cæsar of leopards, the Napoleon of Bengal tigers.

We had almost been guilty of an important omission in this our veracious history; we had well nigh forgotten to state that the coral of the baby Diedrich is now to be seen in the museum at the Hague, if we mistake not, in the case to the left of the wooden chair in which General Chasse sat at the bombardment in the fortress of Antwerp — a relic which the Hollanders are very justly proud of. The coral, by the way, has been despoiled of one of its bells, it is supposed by a curious Englishman on a visit three years since to the museum.

To resume our biographical narrative.

Our hero is now four years old, and every day brings with it further evidence of his surpassing genius; he continues to grow the marvel and delight of the good people of the Hague. When at eight years of age, an event occurs which doubles even the enthusiasm of that most enthusiastic race of people, the Dutch; for the pet of the village, Diedrich, was wont to be absent whole days, from morn till night, from the paternal roof, usually returning very hungry and very wet. Every means were tried to learn the cause of his absence, to discover where he passed so many of his valuable hours; but Diedrich maintained a dogged silence to all queries, or essayed to laugh them aside by some playful quip or quirk. At length, having pondered on the matter some time, Mynheer Van Amburgh set spies upon the movements of his son; and hence we are enabled to gladden our readers with one of the strangest recitals, perhaps, ever yet recited.

" The small village called Scheveling," says an " English Gentleman," who, in 1691, wrote upon the Hague and its adjacent places, " is inhabited chiefly by fishermen, where is a curious, hard, sandy shore, admirably *contrived by* nature for the divertisement of *persons of quality*." This village is approached from the Hague by " a late-made way, cut through vast, deep mountains of sand, paved through with curious stones — a work fit for the ancient Romans;" and to this village, and its " admirably contrived sandy shore," would Diedrich Van Amburgh, when eight years old, daily resort; and thither was he watched by the spies set upon his steps.

Fables have been invented that may be considered as somewhat bearing upon our narrative; but the circumstance only proved that the fiction was but the shadow to the " coming" truth. For instance, the elder Pliny — a gentleman of considerable fancy —

informs us that a little boy scraped an acquaintance
with a dolphin, and by bribing the fish with a portion
of his morning's bread and butter, would induce it to
carry him on its back to school, from Baiæ to Puteoli,
and from Puteoli to Baiæ. The boy, catching the
measles, died; "when," says Pliny, "the dolphin
pined and died, and was buried in the same grave
with his little playmate!" "These be truths!" The
younger Pliny, trumping the card of the elder, tells a
story of a dolphin, " at Hippo in Africa," who, meeting a boy swimming wide from his companions, dived
under him, took him on its back, and bundled off with
its affrighted burden into the " open sea," when, having swum a league or two, the dolphin tacked, made
for land, and carefully deposited the child upon the
shore. The story ran through the town, and the next
day the strand was thronged with people, curious to
see if the dolphin would come again; when, about
half past eleven, lo! it came, and, playing all sorts
of inviting tricks, the people walked up to their knees
into the river, and stroked and patted it, the women
kissing and calling it pretty names. The boy, who
had on the former day backed the fish, then put himself again astride it, and, doubtless, amidst enthusiastic exclamations, was carried out into " blue water " by the dolphin, and again faithfully brought back.
The historian adds that " the deputy governor " of the
province believed that the affable fish could be nothing but a god in disguise ; and, therefore, on an early
visit of the creature to the shore, ordered some precious ointment to be poured upon it. From that moment the fish lost its spirits, became sick and feeble,

and in a short time was never seen again.   The truth is — a truth that has escaped the sagacity of the younger Pliny — that the dolphin suspected the precious ointment to be fish-sauce, and, though grieved for the sake of its personal safety to discontinue its visits, prudentially concluded that people who had such an abundance of fish-sauce might some day be in need of fish to eat with it.   Such were the dolphin's speculations, and wisely, as we think, it turned its head to sea.   "Here be truths."   To return to Diedrich Van Amburgh.

He is now, gentle reader, in the ninth year of his age ; and one bleak, tempestuous morning he is seen, as we think somewhat presumptuously, treading the " hard, sandy shore," made for " persons of quality," at the wild, dreary, yet picturesque, village of Scheveling.   The youngster walks the sands with a sturdy foot, and as he walks, looks out, and whistles towards the ocean.   He has walked and whistled but five minutes, when lo! six porpoises tumble towards the shore.   Diedrich walks fearlessly towards them, jumps upon the back of the biggest, and away goes he, hurrahing, laughing, shouting, riding like a cork upon the crest of the billows ; twenty Dutchmen, among whom are the spies appointed by his father, with the fishermen of the village, their wives and families, fixed upon the strand, transmuted into stone by the daring of that " marvellous boy."   The story flew through the Hague, and when, after a somewhat exhausting ride of four hours, young Diedrich turned his porpoise for the shore, he saw it covered with the inhabitants of the Hague, with an odd thousand or two from Delf and other places, congregated there to receive him with due honors on his coming in. He came with the porpoises bounding and tumbling about him, each porpoise having a bell round its neck, unlawfully taken by Diedrich from his father's hostelry for his own ocean pets. We pass the scene of his welcome by the Dutch public, the delight of Diedrich's father, the tears of his mother. Young Diedrich was presented at the Dutch court, and there were several cabinet councils held to consider the propriety of employing him as courier of the mail-bags by sea between Holland and France, when, with a waywardness, alas! too frequently a baneful ingredient in the composition of genius, young Diedrich destroyed the hopes of his family in his advancement by clandestinely eloping with a Dutch skipper, a frequent visitor at the White Hart, bound for Batavia, where, as the captain assured our hero, he might assuage his raging thirst for leopards, tigers, and lions in any number. These brilliant prospects were too much for the filial duty of young Diedrich; and in the tenth year of his age he quitted the White Hart, and hid himself in the obscure port of Amsterdam until the skipper should be ready for sea, Diedrich seeing, if he remained at home, that he would inevitably be appointed to some lucrative place under his own government. However, one of those accidents to be found in the lives of all truly great men prevented his shipment for Batavia, having been shamefully lured aboard a South Sea whaler only the night before her departure for her three years' voyage, the captain of the ship, with a base regard for personal interest only to be found in the very meanest natures, having concluded that the wonderful genius of Diedrich Van Amburgh might be of considerable advantage to himself and owners in the South Seas.

The captain was not mistaken. He returned to Holland with the spoils of five-and-twenty first-rate fish; but for the honor of our common nature we almost blush to state that, at the dinner given to him by his owners at Rotterdam to commemorate his triumphant success, — *his* success ! — the skipper by no one word had acknowledged the wonderful services of Diedrich, to whom, indeed, the prosperity of the voyage was wholly and solely to be attributed. Our readers may probably be aware that the whale fishery is a toilsome and most hazardous employment. Diedrich Van Amburgh, however, by the force of those great gifts awarded him from his birth, made what would have been a long, miserable three years' voyage nothing more than a long excursion of pleasure. What Diedrich had been in his infancy to the rats, that was he in his boyhood to the spermaceti whales.

Was a whale in request, the captain immediately ordered Diedrich, with a telescope of the highest power, to the mast-head, where, having spied the monster, Diedrich could fascinate him with his eye through the glass, and in an instant leviathan would " swim a league," tamely present himself alongside the ship, and, patient as a lamb, meekly suffer himself to be harpooned, young Van Amburgh, be it understood, whistling " Yankee Doodle " or " Old Kentuck " — melodies taught him by an American,

one of the crew — to quiet him during the operation.

The captain in a very long speech, fully reported
in the *Abendblatt*, spoke of his own trials, the sufferings of the sailors, but not one word of that miracle
of a boy, Van Amburgh, who, by the way, stung by
a sense of injustice, had deserted from the ship on
the back of a white shark, a young grampus following him on shore with his bundle, when homeward
bound for Amsterdam.

Diedrich, still fixed upon the lions, entered himself
on board a ship bound for Ceylon. Many disappointments, however, combined to thwart his determination to escape into the woods, where, by the
mere force of character and power of eye, — such
being the only means employed by Van Amburgh to
subdue all beasts, — he resolved to beard the lion in
his den, and, in fact, carry civilization and all its hu-
manities amongst the feline tribes of the wilderness.
Enough for us that Diedrich Van Amburgh had carried into practical perfection the benevolence of his
early theory ; that he has shown how

> " ———— education forms the brutal mind,
> And as the *stick* is used, the beasts incline ; "

and that if there are lions who eat rajahs, tigers that
have a propensity for child-stealing, and leopards
nurturing in their savage breasts a preference for living flesh, no matter whether of man or beast; the
evil arises solely from the misfortune of their ignorance ; that they know no better, and are to be pitied
for their darkness.

We have placed Diedrich Van Amburgh at Ceylon. We regret, deeply regret, to state that here there is *hiatus in manuscriptis;* we lose sight of him for some years, until we again meet with him in England, a purchaser of one of our new lions, then a cub, — a nursling, —

"With the most innocent milk in its most innocent mouth."

On the breaking up of our national establishment in the Tower, in defence to a senseless cry of — But no; we started on the broad ground of benevolence, and we will not betake ourselves into the smoking corner of politics. The lions were sold from the Tower, and happy was the cub that fell into the hands of Van Amburgh; he, the beast himself, may possibly be ignorant of his great happiness; but we — poor mortals as we are, knowing full well the powers of temptation, with the difficulty of overcoming them — we cannot but admire the acquired temperance and meekness of that lion, who, with a young lamb rubbed against his lips, with its white wool tickling his whiskers, turns from it, like a lady from a second glass of wine! We should like to see the stock-broker, with lambs of the 'Change offered to him, who would gently put them aside! It would delight us to know the exact style of countenance of the small, yet noisy patriot, tempted by a baronetcy, or the fleecy hosiery of place, stanch to his " principles," and rock to the blandishments of a minister. We know what it must have cost the lion to be able to turn away from a remarkably healthy child — vaccinated and all — with bloodless lips: and admiration is the fruit of that knowledge!

We have now little more to speak of than the discipline employed by Mr. Van Amburgh for the subjugation and instruction of his brutes; and it will, we are sure, delight our readers to learn that Mr. Van Amburgh, quite in opposition to the general belief, rules them with the downiest feather. To speak literally, the heaviest weapon employed upon them in their hours of schooling is a stick of cinnamon; and this, be it understood, he uses upon the hides of his pupils, not as a means of physical punishment, but as conveying to them a sense of degradation — as he has assured us, a far more bitter chastisement upon a lion or tiger of any natural goodness than stripes or chastisement. It is really delicious to witness the interview of Van Amburgh with the beasts in their time of relaxation, when not stirred up to please a vulgar audience by an affectation of ferocity; it is most gratifying to witness the interchange of caresses between the master and his servants — the mild intelligence on the one side, the confidence and gratitude on the other.

It will be seen that Mr. Van Amburgh's treatment of the brutes is almost wholly intellectual. He reasons with them, and has at length succeeded in conveying to their minds surprisingly clear ideas of right and wrong. He now and then finds it expedient to read something dramatic to them, when desirous of tranquillizing their rising passions. The manager has generally placed at his disposal the MSS. of tragedies, comedies, farces, &c., for the purpose. But we have it on the assurance of the great teacher himself, that, if he wishes to wholly subdue the whole menagerie, he finds nothing so efficacious as the *libretto* of a new opera.

We are, however, happy to state that this civilization of the brutes of the forest by the great benevolent professor is only the first of a series of improvements contemplated by him in the body social. What he has done for lions, tigers, and leopards, he professes himself ready to do for men of all conflicting opinions, passions, and interests. We have not the address of the brute-trainer, neither are we in possession of the terms required by him per lesson; but if any of our readers, male or female, will apply personally to him, having made up their minds to conform to the self-same harmonizing system worked out with such success upon the lower animals, they need not for an instant doubt of the same gratifying results.

It is with this feeling — it is from a consciousness of the higher uses of Mr. Van Amburgh's system — that we have been induced to give this lengthened notice of it, to go thus comprehensively into what we trust will prove a most valuable exposition.

1839.

MICHAEL LYNX; "THE MAN WHO KNEW HIMSELF."

"SIR, will you buy any rhubarb — most excellent Turkey rhubarb?" asks the turbaned dealer, in his best English, of the thousandth passenger, who, with a wily glance at the drug, and a shiver from the crown to the sole, hurries past, deigning no syllable in reply. It is not that he despises the medicinal qualities of rhubarb; by no means — he knows them to be admirable; but then, ninety-nine times out of the hundred, he believes, or tries to make himself believe, that he has no need of them. To his brothers and sisters, to his wife, his sons and his daughters — indeed, to all his relatives, friends, and acquaintance, he may be all but convincingly eloquent on the " sovereign remedy " of rhubarb ; but, for himself, he knows his constitution — he never requires it. A man who presents a history, containing professedly rigid lessons, is a vender of drugs ; a book with an avowed moral is — rhubarb.

Shall we then, at once, avow the tendency of the narrative of Michael Lynx — " the man who knew himself"? No; we eschew such peril, begging to assure our friends that if, in the following pages, they find, not a string of moralities, but anything like a single moral, it must be to their own searching sagacity, and not to our premeditation, that they will owe so questionable a discovery. Thus, assuring a large portion of the reading world that we

17

mean nothing, we think we are justified in the most reasonable hopes of fixing its attention.

Michael Lynx was born — as it is allowed that the joyful event took place precisely nine months and three days after the marriage of his mother, the friends of the lady — and we take our readers to be immediately such — are not authorized to call upon us for the precise date of the parish register. It is sufficient, for every reasonable purpose, that Michael was most unequivocally, most undeniably, born. We care not to dwell upon the event, it not being with Michael, as with crowds of heroes, one of the two most remarkable accidents of his existence. How many thousands are no more than human candles! They are lighted, and they — burn out. Not so our Michael. His " brief candle " first saw the light in a garret, fearfully elevated above the classic ground, east of that spot where, in the time of Richard the Second, grapes, it is said, were persuaded to ripen, but where, in the present degenerate times, oxen are at certain days congregated, though not to tread, the fruitage of the legendary vine. We speak of Smithfield. If Michael's taper of life burnt irregularly, something is to be allowed for the influence of early accident : the window-frames of the room in which he was born were most impartially fitted with brown paper. It is true great, steady, shining lights have come down to us from garrets ; but Michael was not one of these. He was deprived, by the local obscurity of his birth, of even the playful boast of Pope Sextus the Ffth, who, born in a hovel, which admitted the sun through a thousand crannies, vaunted that he was *nato di casa*

illustre — "born of an illustrious house." Now, as
to his house, Michael — and it is saying much —
might have counted flaw for flaw against any pope
in Christendom ; but though he had all the defects,
he could not boast — in the peculiar place, and under
the circumstances in which he was born — of that
light which made them illustrious ; for it is sometimes
better to be the bastard of Apollo, than the lawfully
begotten of Plutus.

We have to excuse another defect — a defect implanted in Michael from his earliest years. It cannot
be disguised that Michael's taper, ere it was one
third consumed, was often placed in a bottle. Now,
seeing that all men are but so many candles, it should
be allowed that the steadiness with which they beam,
the clearness and the duration of their light, the absence of volatile insects which make them waste and
flicker, the lack of winding-sheets, and other weaken-
ing superstitions that beset the tallowy torch of flesh,
depend almost entirely upon the quality and the
currents of air in which it is doomed to be lighted
and to burn. If this be a vulgar error, like the
broken-down gentleman who cried mackerel, we
earnestly hope that nobody has heard it.

A candle in a bottle ! We have made it our business through life to narrowly mark a candle when
so placed ; and we fearlessly assert, defying contra-
diction, that no candle, thus situated, ever burnt
fairly and truly, with credit to itself, and full honest
duty to its master. Mark, ye philosophers ! behold,
ye chemists ! how the gross stream winds itself
around the vitreous neck of the destroyer, meandering

down in twenty ducts into one dull, noisome pond
of fat! Is there a breathing man who hath not seen
this? If there be, let him seek to know the great
moral lesson; and when he sees — as surely he will
see — the substance of the taper running into darkness, the bright wick grown dull and black, with
sooty lumps, thick as blotches on a drunkard's nose,
— loading and deforming it, — then let him take heed,
and never hope to burn his candle in a bottle.

Michael passed the first seven years of his life in
healthful dirtiness, flourishing in filth. He was a
well-planted root, and shot up firmly from the soil.
As for the prejudice against what is vulgarly called
dirt, like every other prejudice, its nursing mother
is ignorance. It is only necessary to observe any of
the tens of thousands of little imps waddling, creep-
ing, running, screaming, hilloing, bellowing, beyond
the confines of clean respectability, to feel assured of
the sovereign excellence of dirt. There they are, a
part and parcel of the mud-pies they knead and
chaffer with. Our heart leaps up when we behold
" a brood of unclean children," — little new-made
Adams, — so dirty, there seems but part of their clay
dried into flesh. Pride may read a fine lesson of humility in such faces; yea, there is a deep primitive
truth in their very earthliness. Let pampered vir-
tuosos feed their sickly sensibilities with paintings
and carvings; let them be rapt with Raphael's form,
with Titian's color; let their mouth's water at the
small prettiness of a Cellini; let them treasure their
blooming canvas, their images in marble and ivory,
in bronze and gold; let them treble-lock their muse-

ums and their cabinets; but leave to us the true,
the inimitable *terra cotta*, of rare human flesh. Thus
every alley is our gallery — every *cul-de-sac* our ample studio! We could, we feel it, write upon the
subject until dirt changed under our pen as at the
touch of Midas's finger. We could read a great moral
truth in a begrimed cheek; we could — and how
many pious fathers might we evoke from their dusty
cells to bear testimony — prove the deep sagacity of
many by-gone saints in their contempt of water.
How many of those excellent men — of those noble
.pillars of their faith — have come down to posterity
with anything but clean hands? in how many thousand instances (see the lives of anchorites, popes,
ancient sulphur-breathers, and modern rantipoles) has
the odor of sanctity been any other than the absence of
linen? We have read a list of thousands of relics, all
duly authenticated, and have not met with one shirt
in the whole catalogue. Thus far to combat a morbid
sensibility of what are absurdly called the decencies
of life; henceforth let our readers — which are only
three other words for all the world — look with an
instructed eye upon external uncleanness; let them
not turn away from the unseemliness of the mere covering, but hug it closer to their hearts for its foulness.
Gods! had we time and space to write an encyclo-
pedic chapter on dirt, what saints, what heroes, what
politicians, what poets, could we pick out of the mud!
To our story.

And Michael grew in a congenial soil. We regret
that, up to his seventh year, no particular event announced the dawning of that light which in after days

brightened and dazzled his circle.   Passing over two
brief captivities in the Compter, with one private
whipping, as matters unworthy of the historian and
of Michael, let us set out with him in the wide world.
Stay: to disarm scandal, we may as well explain
that Michael's first imperfect knowledge of criminal
law arose from his love of apples — a love, as it appears, so deeply implanted in our common nature;
so involved in its profane accidents!   An apple —
but the story is trite as pippins — taught Sir Isaac
Newton true gravity; an apple taught Gregory the
Seventh a lesson for popes; an apple saved Clym of
the Clough from the gallows; an apple might have
educated Michael Lynx for that final destination.   We
have now no time to discuss it, but trust the reader is
fully impressed with the importance of the subject.
Much may yet be said of the apple!

Beholding Michael at ten years old, we cannot but
believe that Nature and Destiny, like inexorable old
women as they are, wrangled at his cradle.   Nature
endowed the child with her rarest gifts, but the beldam Fate long denied their profitable exercise.   It is
thus the opposing powers sit, brooding over the world,
pleased at nothing so much as at thwarting each
other.   It is thus Nature makes her beautiful, her best
creatures, and then Destiny snatches away the glorious
handiwork, and locks it forever in a corner cupboard.
Again, Nature produces some poor misshapen thing,
— some half made image, loathsome without, and
dark within, — when her sister hag, with a grim
laugh, pounces on the abortion, hugs it, dandles it,
and ringing its nose with gold, hanging priceless

jewels at its ears, high uplifts the gilded ugliness.
Think of it, ye who, from the nursery to the family
vault, walk upon lamb's-wool — think how many
noble slaves hath the witch Destiny " acting her ab-
horred behests," daily sweating " in the eye of the
sun," pining in the darkness of the night. How
many are bowed by her invisible chain ; how many
prisoners in the city ; how many serfs in the field !
She has her captives ; and yea, with a false and foul
religion, she has her idols for her slaves to worship —
her consecrated crocodiles — her solemn monkeys.

Nature had given to Michael the easy means of a
carriage and liveries, but Destiny would not readily
encourage the coachmaker and tailor. The bountiful
goddess had made our hero musical and imitative ;
but Destiny, who for a time made the god of music
himself a shepherd, marked Michael for someting less,
and Smithfield for his Arcady. Now, had Michael
been born within the purlieus of Drury Lane, had
he been even pot-boy to a theatrical public house,
how different had been his fate — how primrose-
decked his path to fortune ! Of what availed his
powers of song, his gifts of mimicry? It is true he
was the idol of the critics at the Three Jugs ; but,
like their numerous brotherhood, though they could
let fall showers of praise, they could not give the
smallest piece of pudding. (By the way, why does
not some lecturer on pneumatics define the precise
time that a man may live upon mere. praise? We
should like to see a popular poet in a moral air-pump.)
Michael would imitate every domestic beast of the
field, and was judged — a rare and happy accident

to the performer — by persons who really knew something of the subject. Had he to mimic a goat, a hog, a calf, an ass — there were among the auditors the most competent judges of the performance. Happy Michael! how many a playwright has yearned for such critics, and only sometimes found them! Here were gifts, had the professor been the favorite of Destiny. To hear Michael, was to fancy Noah's ark sounding in his larynx: indeed, " he was no vulgar boy!" and had Fate only thrust him into a play-house, with such convertible talents, in a very few years he might have had a bank account, and green and gold liveries. Had he only lived in these days, when, like a Turkish pacha, the dramatic muses have horse-tails for banners, Michael had surely emerged even from the obscurity of the Three Jugs; but in the dark times when Michael roared, and growled, and brayed, and neighed, jackasses were of no stage value: Mr. Garrick had no taste; besides, unlike all his brethren, he had a touch of envy.

From ten to seventeen did Michael tend sheep as a profession, and imitate them as an enjoyment. A marked change then ensued: he had hitherto been a sloven, he now became a fop; he cast aside a thatch of worsted, which, for at least twenty years, under various owners, had usurped the name of cap, and assumed a straw hat of more than brimstone brightness; there was, moreover, a cunning knowledge of life in the tie of the black ribbon that girdled it — a true knowledge of the magic worth of appearance — of, as in later life he would say, the use of the exterior. He had a deep-blue frock, one pair of leathern breeches, and shoe-buckles, if not all silver, at least copper, very preciously and thickly cased. Thus habited, a switch in his hand, and a sprig of lavender in his mouth, — so fitting, looked as though it grew there,— Michael would drive his flock. Virgil's shepherds (they *had* their faults), in all their glory, were but cow-boys to Michael. If he did not play upon a pipe, he smoked one with an air very far beyond the pastoral; if he did not milk sheep, no hand could more adroitly kill them ; if he were not called upon to guard his ewes from wolves, no youth, especially twice a day, had a more craving regard for mutton. Another change, besides the vulgar mutation of dress, came upon Michael ; or, it may be, it came with the dress — the shirt of Nessus had its poison, and shirts and new coats, on skins unused to such delicacies, have sometimes a subtle and mysterious influence — " there is magic in the web." How the refinement came, we pause not to inquire ; but certain it is, from the day that Michael first appeared in his reformed costume, he gave up his brutal imitations, at least of the lowest of what the humility of man calls lower animals. He would still mimic a few of the nobler creatures ; but it was only when he was in very excellent cue indeed, and at the pressing request of friends, — a request very often put, and consented to, — that he would condescend to make an ass of himself. The goose he solemnly forswore at seventeen : how many of our wisest sages have come far short of Michael !

This determination of our hero was, however, for a time fatal to Michael's worldly prospects. When he ceased to be a vulgar beast, he ceased — and the like

may have happened to the most convivial souls — to
be attractive to his circle of former admirers. But
the truth must out — ambition was at the bottom of
this false delicacy. He had, in an evil hour for his
reputation, visited a menagerie at the festival of St.
Bartholomew. From that moment he was haunted
by the roaring of the forest kings; from that moment
he despised his former accomplishments, holding
them as worse than nought, and henceforth determined to do nothing but the lion. It was in vain that
friends dissuaded, critics sneered, and foes rejoiced;
it was in vain that he was called upon for a growl or
a bark, in both of which he was pre-eminent; he
would do nothing but roar, and his roaring was contemptible. Foolish Michael! thou mightest have
continued to the end an applauded, prosperous puppy
— but to try the lion, was to fall indeed! And yet, in
the homely history of Michael, read we not the fate
of thousands? There are greater houses than the
Three Jugs in which the same mistake is daily,
nightly made. There are persons of greater likelihood
than Michael who will attempt a roar, when the very
extent of their ability is a tolerable yelp. We might
multiply parallel examples, but leave them to the
reader, — who, or he must lack acquaintance, can
number them by the gross.

Fortune, however, did not wholly desert Michael;
for at the time of his waning popularity at the Three
Jugs he had fallen captive to the sloe eyes and
damask cheeks of a maiden, a dweller on the Barnet
Road. Divine, enduring, charitable woman! Though
Michael was a mongrel to all mankind, to Susan he

was a veritable lion! It is thus, though the poor dolt be jeered and scorned abroad, the love of woman crowns him monarch at her side; it is thus, though the silly goose be plucked bare in the world, that new " wings at his shoulders seem to play" when looked on by her eyes! Michael wooed with the regularity of a stop-watch; for, ever at appointed time he breathed the gentle signal, which, with corresponding punctuality, brought the maiden to his arms.

At the period of the fulness of his passion many sheep had been stolen. One theft was marked by peculiar daring, and the evil growing daily worse, called for vigorous punishment. A hundred guineas was the promised reward for the apprehension of the robbers. All Smithfield was in consternation: since the expedition for the Golden Fleece there was never such a stir — " a hundred guineas reward!"

We spoke of the concerted signal between Michael and Susan. It was a dark, wintry night, and the *pastor* Michael approached the habitation of his adored, a cottage constructed with a fine taste for the picturesque, and an equally fine contempt for the elements. Michael trode with stealthy footsteps of a hero of romance, or a smuggler; indeed, a custom-house officer would have paused, doubting whether the intruder came with a contraband passion or with illicit brandy. Michael, " holding his breath for a time" (at certain seasons the house of the beloved strikes solemnly upon the heart), crept as closely to the hut as prudence counselled (for Susan shared the common calamity of heroines, she had a father), and then, with his soul at his lips, uttered the well-known sound. But how to describe it! Michael, in the single honesty of his nature, spoke, as he thought, with the mouth of a mere sheep; but what bleating! how modulated — how softened — with what passion trembling in its tones — with what a tale of hopes and fears in its few vibrations! A man of ordinary sensibility hearing it would have forsworn mutton for the rest of his days. There was such pathos in the sound — such eloquence of the heart! This, sympathizing reader, is, you feel, no raphsody; you, who have heard love refine the roughest notes — you, who have known him tune harshness itself to music, will do the same reverence to the bleating of Michael. Ample justice you cannot award, for you did not hear it.

Susan tripped from the cottage; she joined her lover — she spoke — yes, in soft, low accents, twitching Michael by the arm, she exclaimed, "Hush! you fool — I'm here!" Michael answered not; he stood, as on the sudden, struck to stone: perhaps he felt the abrupt truth of Susan — perhaps he felt the cold; we cannot answer; but, certain we are, that the signal of love had found an echo in the throats of a near flock, for bleatings came through the darkness, not unaccompanied by human oaths. Michael, without a word, followed the sound; and the roused father of Susan, hearing the lover's footsteps, followed him. Michael approached the prison of the flock, an old dilapidated barn; a light glimmering through the crannies, he beheld — for he knew the ruddle, knew the faces of the innocent victims — the stolen sheep! Had he doubted the identity of the beasts, the peculiar cast of features of two men, — one employed skinning

a fat wedder, and another about to prepare a second
for the like operation — would not have convinced
him of his error.   As he stood, in that brief moment,
he felt, in imagination, the weight of a hundred guineas suddenly fall into his pocket: another second,
and, without any trick of fancy, he felt a huge hedge-
stake fall upon his back.   His first cry was " Thieves ! "
his second, " Murder ! "

We cannot here suppress a few words on what we
may call the nationality of the principal of these exclamations.   We hold it to be a signal evidence of
the immense wealth of our country, a flattering proof
of our commercial greatness, and of the universality
of property, that when man, woman, or child is as-
saulted, — though neither shall be the loser of so
much as a hair, — the cry of the assailed is " Thieves ! "
A man receives a cowardly insult ; the poltroon runs
away ; what suddenly trips up his heels — what, but
" Stop thief ? "   The cry, knocking at every man's
breeches pocket, makes him champion the distressed.
There is a freemasonry in the words, and when hal-
looed, all men proffer helping hands.   Of the two
exclamations, " thieves " is strikingly national ; —
" murder " is enjoyed by other countries.   Certainly
there is no comparison in their relative effect.   Some
fifty years ago, at a crowded drawing-room, two
countesses — beautiful as angels — were beset on
their way to their carriages.   One lost a necklace,
the other a bracelet ; one cried " thieves ! " the other
" murder ! "   The thief, with the stolen property upon
him, was instantly taken ; the murderer, pocketing the
bracelet, was suffered to walk away.   When we heard

this we vowed, were we a countess, never in any situation to trust to " murder." No; let every woman in the hour of danger — that is, if she wish for intruding succor — scorn " murder," and place her reliance upon " thieves ! "

The fine tenor shouting of Michael, accompanied by the sharp, treble screaming of Susan, whilst her father, at every blow he dealt, groaned a deep bass through his teeth, scared the varlets in the barn, one of whom, making a rush for the door, received from the paternal cudgel a misdirected thwack, which levelled him. However, he was again upon his legs, when Michael fastened upon him, and the lover and the thief, grappling each other, they both fell to the earth. There they lay, writhing and rolling, he of the hedge-stake raining an impartial shower of blows, now upon his future son, and now upon the sheepstealer, as each came uppermost. The combatants blasphemed; Susan got new strength with screaming: the father growled as he labored; the rescued sheep set up bleatings of thanksgiving; when, in the midst of the hurly, half a dozen tapers, like so many wills-'o-the-wisp, broke through the darkness, and the voice of the parish constable, with the voices of two men unknown, were heard in the distance. From that moment the thief, with oriental resignation, lay motionless; Michael sat gasping upon him; the father, with one hand, leaned upon his staff, and with the other wiped the sweat from his forehead; Susan smoothed her hair, and dried the corners of her eyes. In this condition they waited the approach of the parish functionary, who, acknowledging the greeting of

Susan's father, stopped, with his light to the ground, when Susan uttered a scream, sharp enough to pierce to the horn lantern which disclosed the horror; for the blood ran in streams down Michael's face, dripping upon the face of the thief below him, and for the time almost blotting out his identity. But Tips, the constable, was a stern thinker, paying little respect to blood; so, somewhat wiping from the features of the thief the property of Michael, there came to light the well-known visage of Jack Robinson, better known by the genial alias of Flowers-in-May. "He's my prisoner, and there's the stolen sheep!" cried Michael. "And a good night's work thou'st made of it," rejoined one of the men; "a hundred guineas, and only for a cracked crown." Questionless a hundred guineas are "worth a poor man's keeping:" but whether, in the present instance, the exchange was in the youth's favor, whether Michael's *pia mater* had been mortally injured by Susan's *pius pater*, remained a case for the surgeons and the assizes. Happily Michael's skull was no egg-shell, and though, almost immediately on the arrival of Tips, he swooned, and, at least to Susan's father, looked dangerously interesting, time and a plaster made all whole again. Perhaps, too, there was some potent anodyne in the sympathy of the paternal clubman, for no sooner did he hear of the reward than all his prejudices melted away, and nought remained in his breast but admiration for his valorous son-in-law. Besides, as both father and Michael, with an exemplary delicacy, breathed no syllable of family quarrels, the broken skull and bruised, party-colored car-

cass of our hero were put down to the black account
of the sheep stealers, on whom we shall expend but
a few words. The luckless Flowers-in-May — his
companion never came near him in his last trial —
was judged and sentenced. Michael received the
hundred guineas, and Tips a most handsome compliment from the bench, together with an extra parochial
reward for his cat-like vigilance on the night of the
scuffle. Tips had been to call a midwife; but, with
praiseworthy fortitude, he forbore to intrude upon
either judge or vestry a single word about his domestic misfortunes.

Michael and Susan were married! The hundred
guineas, which had produced a halter for Flowers-in-
May, had bought bridal garlands for the youthful
couple: hemp-seed and nuptial flowers sprang from
the same bed! That a hymeneal wreath should be
only a continuation of the yarn of the ropemaker!
Shudder not, ye gentle youths; shrink not, ye timid
virgins. When Susan pressed with her loving arm
the neck of Michael, there arose no compunctious
workings to his throat; when Michael put on his
night-cap, it brought no thought of Flowers-in-May
to Susan. No; the hangman wove no dreams for
them; they slept peacefully, as though the only gallows were in Utopia. Was not this insensibility?
Certainly not: for, much to the disappointment of an
overflowing Old Bailey, Flowers-in-May was not
hanged. The night before his intended appearance
he had broken prison, and one of his legs; certainly
no very cheap escape; still, as most men have two
legs, and none have more than one neck, when dis-

location is inevitable, it is well that the greatest evil
be shared by the greatest number. Michael at the
same time reaped the reward of — (a rare union) —
mimicry and modesty. Jove lowed his love as a bull;
Michael bleated, an innocent sheep; mark the fruits
of his humility: had he visited Susan as a lion,
would there have been any response from the stolen
flock? Would they have acknowledged by a single
note, by the slightest tremor, their fears of the destroyer? As a lion, Michael might have roared and
starved; love tamed him down to a sheep, and fortune flung about him a fine, thick fleece. That many
men would think of Michael!

Having married our hero, we shall, for some twenty years, leave him to himself and his wife. Twenty
years! If the reader startle at the change we are
about to show him, if he smile incredulously at the
shifting of the scene, and vow we pen a fairy tale,
and not a true and sober history, we —

Here, librarian, hand this sceptic a few volumes of
the *Moniteur*. There, sir, turn over, not the leaves
of twenty years, but of ten, of five, or two. A fairy
tale! Why, all the dreams of Eastern visionaries
are weak, colorless fantasies to the stern doings of
this tangible world. Should palaces, built in a night,
call up our wonder, when, in a few years, we have
seen the temples of living kings so oppositely tenanted? The stage harlequin is now a poor imbecile
— outtripped, outdone by the real antic: all others
are base impostors, things whose wickerwork peeps
through the covering; Fortune alone is the true
mountebank! See — now she borrows a regal

18

crown, as a Jackpudding, with a smirk, begs of his
audience a wedding ring: mark how she whirls it,
and twists it, and now hiding it in some base corner,
now lending it for a holiday ornament, and now
plucking it away again — and now, with a harlot's
smile, and a profound courtesy, returning it to its de-
spairing owner. And now she sits upon a palace
step, with balls and sceptres in her lap, casting them
now high and now low, like an Indian juggler. And
now she takes some forlorn nestling, and — *presto!*
— he is *pullus Jovis!* And now, after the thing has
strutted, and screamed, and called on nations to reverence its plumes, — with no more ceremony than a
farmer's wife seizes one gosling from its brethren, —
does Fortune catch the radiant bird — dishonorable
catch! She gripes him by his glorious tail — and
plucks the peacock of his every plume.

Mr. and Mrs. Lynx, at the close of twenty years,
were resolved on retreating with their honorable spoil.
The hundred guineas had rolled and gathered, giving
the lie to vulgar superstition, which, with the malice
of envy, had predicted ill luck to the sudden gain.
How many sleek, oily souls — when they count their
hoards, no matter how acquired — must chuckle at
the bugbear! Michael had, however, flourished upon
average honesty; he never vulgarly picked a pocket,
and certain we are, he never so much as dreamed of
forgery. He had grown rich, and as his purse
swelled, his tastes enlarged. Retired from the
drudgery of making money, his only thought was
how to extract dignified happiness from the four per
cents. Michael was fixed in a suburban villa, com-

manding a most extensive view of metropolitan va-
por; his house was as fine, as light, and almost as di-
aphanous as a Chinese lantern; for Michael was none
of your churls who build about their domesticities
with walls and hedges: not he. The curious traveller might have counted every mouthful swallowed by
Michael at breakfast and dinner; for, if he were not
quite as unconscious, he was as careless of publicity
as a honey-bee in a glass hive. And this, after all, is
true retirement. Solitude is not a thing of trees and
bricks, but a part of the immortal man. Michael's
retreat was all that he could wish; his garden was
very promising; his orchard, in a little more than a
quarter of a century, would " in summer yield him
shade, in winter fire;" whilst his lawn looked not
common grass, but closely, and almost as regularly
shaven, as its master, seemed like an unwrinkled sheet
of green baize. He wanted nothing; for a red and
blue macaw broke a stillness that might have been
oppressive; and for employment, Michael for the first
three months superintended the education of a perverse kitten, whose ravenous love for a dozen gold-
fish, in at least a two-quart globe, as they glanced in
the sun — Michael would sometimes think of his
guineas — he, after commendable perseverance, subdued into the coldness of mere respect. And is this
the Michael of Smithfield? Remember, reader,
twenty years! It is not half the time that yonder
elephant, cribbed in a den of cunning joiner's work,
was the rough denizen of the forest; and now mark
the tame grace with which he takes a sweetmeat
from that fair, white hand! Moralists exclaim that

all men are forgetful of nothing so much as of their end. This is a mistake: when they rise, they are more oblivious of their beginning. When Michael stood at his garden porch, holding 'twixt his lips a sprig of jasmine, plucked from his own tree, growing upon his own freehold, he would have been a cunning metaphysician who could have persuaded him that he was the very Michael of twenty years ago; at most, he might have had some vague impression, some interrupted glimmering of the fact, but nothing that he could have conscientiously sworn by. It would be a profitable sorcery that could evoke the spectres of our buried years, making them pass, one by one, before our eyes, each shadow following the meanness, the folly of its day! What a picture-gallery to " sear our eyeballs!" And yet what heart-burning, what contention with the exhibitor! For how few would own the shadow of ten, or five years back, to be their true likeness — their *vera effigies?*

Michael was completely happy. He had an enduring wife, a fine house, fine grounds, a well-stocked cellar, and, he thanked Heaven, — people generally do when prayers and the physicians have failed, — no children! If his mansion were not very durable, it could boast the brightest paint. If it were not built upon rock, the surrounding gravel walks shone like red gold. His house might have been more commodious, but not so handsome. And thus Michael lived, or, rather, stagnated, into old age, imbedded, like a jewel in cotton, in all the comforts of this our eating, drinking, and sleeping existence.

And to what did Michael owe this full prosperity? To the hundred guineas? Yes, for they brought with them more than gold; they brought self-knowledge. From the day that Michael touched the shining reward he became an altered man. It was then he " knew himself; " it was then, reviewing the folly of his past ambition, and contrasting its effects with late results, he started in the world with a proper consciousness of his powers, and a resolve never to attempt beyond them. This was the secret of his success; it was this that clothed the tatterdemalion; that housed him; that gave him " land and beeves." He might, had he persisted in his vanity, have mummed away a whole life a mountebank and vagabond; but the forcible illustration of his true powers fixed his eyes upon himself; he looked inwardly, and seeing there no lion, at the last hour " knew himself."

We might close this, our rambling story, with a budget of moral reflections: we shall levy no such tax upon our readers. In every walk of life, from St. Stephen's to St. Giles's, how many Michaels become ridiculous, misanthropic, miserable, unprincipled as lions, who might have been useful, kindly, happy, honest, as mere sheep!

1835.

RECOLLECTIONS OF GUY FAWKES.

*" When a man has once been very famous for jests and merry adventures, he is
made to adopt all the jests that want a father, and many times such as are unworthy of him."—* MOTTEUX's *Life of Rabelais.*

AT midnight, on the fifth of November, in the
year of grace one thousand six hundred and
five, Guido Fawkes, "gentleman," was discovered,
" booted and spurred," in the vicinity of St. Stephen's
Chapel, having on his person " three matches, a
tinder-box, and a dark lantern ; " and purposing,
by means of gunpowder, to blow up, says King
James, " the whole nobility, the most part of the
knights and gentry," besides " the whole judges of
the land, with *most of the lawyers*, and the whole
clerks." For this one indiscretion Guido Fawkes
has forfeited his gentility, and become a proverb of
wickedness. In boyhood, we looked upon Guido
Fawkes, gentleman, as one a little lower than the
devil: he had four horns and a dozen tails. " Years
that bring the philosophic mind " have divested him
of these excrescences and appendages, and Guido
Fawkes now appears to matured charities merely a
person of a singularly eccentric disposition.

Some five-and-twenty years ago it was the patriotic custom of the authorities of an Isle of Sheppy
dockyard to bestow upon their apprentices a few
wagon loads of resinous timber, that a bonfire worthy
of the cause it celebrated might be kindled from the
public purse — that the effigy of the arch-fiend Guy

might be consumed in a fire three times hotter than
the fire of a furnace.   Such fierce liberality was not
lost upon the town's people : their ardor in the burning
business smouldered not ; every man subscribed his
plank or log ; and, from the commission in his uniform to Bobby in his pinafore, the fifth of November
glowed in the calendar of their minds a pillar of
fire.   For a month before the day, the coming anni-
versary busied the thoughts of boyish executioners,
resolved to show their patriotism in the appointments
of their Guy — in the grotesque iniquity of his face,
in the cumbrous state of his huge arm-chair.   To
beg clothes from door to door was then the business
of every lover of church and state.   To ask for a
coat, a pair of breeches, a shirt (the frill could be
made of paper), hose and hat, was not mendicity,
but the fulfilment of a high social duty.

Guy Fawkes would at length be dressed.   A philosopher might have found good matter in his elee-
mosynary suit.   In   the   coat   of   the   bloodthirsty
wretch, he might have recognized the habit of Scum,
the slopseller, a quiet trader, afloat of twenty thousand pounds ;   in the vest of the villanous ruffian,
the discarded waistcoat of Smallgrog, the honest
landlord of a little house for sailors ;   in the stock-
ings of the atrocious miscreant, the hose of the
equitable Weevil, biscuit-contractor to his Majesty's
fleet ;   whilst for the leather of the fiend-like effigy,
Guy Fawkes was to be exhibited, and afterwards
burned, in the broad-toed shoes of that best of men,
Trap, the town attorney.

The chair, too, in which Guy Fawkes sat, might

it not have some day enshrined a justice of the peace?
and the lantern, fixed in the hand of the diaboli-
cal, lynx-eyed monster, might it not have been the
property of the most amiable and most somnolent of
all the Blue Town watchman? And then the mask
fixed upon the effigy — or the lump of clay kneaded
into human features, and horribly or delicately expressed, according to the benevolent art of the makers, — might not the same visor have been worn by
a perfect gentleman, with considerable advantage, at
a masquerade? — might not the clay nose and mouth
of the loathsome traitor have borne an accidental
likeness to the very pink of patriots? Let philosophy ponder well on Guy Fawkes.

We will now attempt our childish recollections of
the great Guy. We have waked at midnight, perhaps, dreaming of the bonfire about to blaze, and
thinking we heard the distant chorus sounding the
advent of the Mighty Terror. No, it was the sea
booming across the marsh — the wind rising and
falling. There was nothing for it but to go to sleep,
and dream of unextinguishable squibs and crackers.
At length four o'clock arrives; the cocks crow; the
boys can't be long now. There — hark! How the
chant comes up the street, like one voice — the voice
of a solitary, droning witch! We lie breathless,
and shape to ourselves Guy Fawkes in the dark!
Our hearts beat quicker and quicker as the chant
becomes louder; and we sit up in the bed, as the
boys approach the door, and, O, how we wish to be
with them! There — there they are, in full chorus!
Hark! —

> "The fifth of November. as I can remember,
>   Is gunpowder treason and plot —
> I know no reason, why gunpowder treason,
>   Should ever be forgot!"

We feel an unutterable pang, for loudest among the loud we hear the shrill voice of Jack Tarleton. "Ha!" we sigh, "*his* mother lets *him* out." The bitterness passes away with the

> "Hallo, boys! hallo, boys! make a round ring —
> Hallo, boys! hallo, boys! God save the King!"

And now the procession moves on, and the voices die in the distance, and we feel we are left alone; and, in a few minutes, we hear new revellers, rejoicing in the captivity of a suit of clothes stuffed with hay, and called Guy Fawkes! They pass on, and are followed by others, and our little brains are set at work, and seem seething in the song. Guy Fawkes! Guy Fawkes! Who — what *is* Guy Fawkes? We had been told that he had been caught with lantern, tinder-box, and matches, ready to blow up thousands of barrels of gunpowder, and so to destroy the king, bishops, and members of Parliament. It must be shocking — very shocking: still, we could not perfectly envisage the atrocity — we could not make out the full horror. We had an undefined sense of the greatness of a king, though we hardly dared to hope we should ever see one. We had a less remote notion of the nature of a bishop, having been helped somewhat in our speculation by the person of the curate at the garrison church. "Curates may come to be bishops, only bishops are very much greater; and curates have nothing upon their heads, where-

as certain bishops might wear mitres." On learning
this, we thought that bishops were merely full-grown
curates; in the same way that we had seen Poland
hens with their top-knots of feathers, only the spring
before bare-headed little chicks. It was thus, in the
irreverence of childhood, we disposed of the whole
bench of bishops. But now came we to the difficulty — what, what could be a member of Parliament?
Was it a living thing? If so, had it a voice? Could
it speak? Could it sit? Could it say yes and no?
Could it walk? Could it turn? Or was it merely
an image? Was it pulled by wires, like sister Jenny's
doll? We had been told that members of Parliament made laws. What *were* laws? Were they the
lions and unicorns on the king's arms? Were they
a better sort of cakes, too dear for everybody to buy?
Little boys ate Parliament cakes — were laws cakes
for men? If so, were they gilt or plain? — with
comfits or without?

It is no matter, we thought, being unable to satisfy ourselves: it is no matter. Guy Fawkes — that
shadowy, terrible mystery — had once lived, and had
tried to kill the king, the full-grown curates, and
those undivined riddles — members of Parliament.
We again went to our first question. Who *was* Guy
Fawkes? Did he have a father and mother? Was
Guy Fawkes ever a little boy, and did he fly a kite
and play at marbles? If so, how could he have ever
thought it worth his while to trouble himself with
other matters? There was something terrifying in
the idea of having played with Guy Fawkes. We
fancied him at taw — we saw him *knuckle-down*.

No — it could not be; the imagination of the child could not dwell upon such an impossibilty. Guy Fawkes a boy! — a baby! — now shaking a rattle — now murmuring as he fed, his mother smiling down upon him! No, no — it was impossible. Guy Fawkes was never born — he was from the first a man — he never could have been a baby. He seemed to us a part of the things that had always been, and always would be — a piece of grim eternity; a principle of everlasting wickedness.

(Is it in childhood alone — is it only in the dim imaginings of infancy — in the wandering guesses of babyhood, that we manifest this ignorance? When the full-grown thief is hanged, do we not sometimes forget that he was the child of misery and vice — born for the gallows, nursed for the halter? Did we legislate a little more for the cradle, might we not be spared some pains for the hulks?)

And then we had been told Guy Fawkes came from Spain. Where was Spain? Was it a million miles away? and what distance was a million miles? Were there little boys in Spain, or were they all like Guy Fawkes? How strange, and yet how delightful to us did it seem to feel that we were a part of the wonderful things about us! To be at all upon this world — to be one at the great *show* of men and women — to feel that when we grew bigger we should know everything of kings, bishops, members of Parliament, and Guy Fawkes! What a golden glory hung about the undiscovered!

And Guy Fawkes, we had heard, had his head cut off, and his body cut into quarters! Could this be true?

Could men do to men what we had seen Fulk the butcher do to sheep? How much, we thought, had little boys to grow out of before they could agree to this! And then, when done, what was the good of it? — what *could* be the good of it? Was Guy Fawkes eaten? If not, *why* cut him up?

Had Guy Fawkes a wife, and little boys and girls? Did he love his children, and buy them toys and apples? — or, like Sawney Bean, did he devour them? Did Guy Fawkes say his prayers?

Had Guy Fawkes a friend? Did he ever laugh — did he ever tell a droll story? Did Guy Fawkes ever sing a song? Like Frampton, the Blue Town barber, did Guy Fawkes ever get drunk? At length we put to ourselves the question of questions : —

Was there ever such a man as Guy Fawkes?
Did Guy Fawkes ever live ?

This query annoyed us with the doubt that we had been tricked into a hate, a fear, a loathing, a wonder, and a mixture of these passions and emotions, for a fib. We felt disappointed when we felt the reality of Guy Fawkes to be doubtful. We had heard of griffins, and unicorns, of dragons, that had eaten men like apples; and had then been told that there never had been any such thing. If we were not to believe in a dragon, why should we believe in Guy Fawkes? After all, was the whole story but make-game?

The child passively accepts a story of the future — he can bring his mind up to a thing promised, but wants faith in the past. The cause is obvious: he recollects few things gone, but is full of things to come. Hence, Guy Fawkes was with us the ogre of a nursery ; we could have readily believed, especially after the story of Beauty and the Beast, that he married Goody Two Shoes, and was the father of little Red Riding Hood.

But Guy Fawkes grows with us from boyhood to youth. He gets flesh and blood with every November ; he is no longer the stuffed plaything of a schoolboy or the grotesque excuse for begging vagabonds, but the veritable Guy Fawkes, "gentleman." We see him, " Thomas Percy's alleged man," at the door of the vault, "booted and spurred ; " — we behold that " very tall and desperate fellow," lurking in the deep of night, with looks of deadly resolution, pounced upon by that vigilant gentleman of the privy chamber, Sir Thomas Knevet! We go with Guido, " the new Mutius Scævola, born in England," before the council, where " he often smiles in scornful manner, not only avowing the fact, but repenting only, with the said Scævola, his failing in the execution thereof." We think of him " answering quickly to every man's objection, scoffing at any idle questions which were propounded to him, and jesting with such as he thought had no authority to examine him." And then we think of the thanksgiving of the great James, who gave praise that, had the intent of the wicked prevailed, he should not have " died ingloriously in an alehouse, or stew, or such vile place," but with " the best and most honorable company." *

Guy Fawkes is, in our baby thought, a mysterious

---

* See " His Majesty's speech concerning the Gunpowder Plot," &c., in the Harleian Miscellany.

vision — one of the shadows of evil advancing on the path of childhood. We grow older, and the substances of evil come close upon us — we see their dark lanterns and snuff the brimstone.

1837.

———◦◦◦———

THE HEDGEHOG LETTERS.

CONTAINING THE OPINIONS AND ADVENTURES OF JUNI-PER HEDGEHOG, CABMAN, LONDON; AND WRITTEN TO HIS RELATIVES AND ACQUAINTANCE, IN VARIOUS PARTS OF THE WORLD.

LETTER I.

TO PETER HEDGEHOG, AT SYDNEY.

DEAR PETER: At last I'm settled to my heart's content. For fifteen years and more I've been fighting, and punching, and screwing, and doing — the Lord forgive me! — all sorts of mean tricks to be respectable; and now I'm happy, for I've given the thing up. I've got rid of every bit of the gentleman, and drive a cab. Ha! you don't know — you can't think — what a blessing it is to get rid of all cares about what's genteel. It's like taking off fine tight boots, and stretching yourself in comforta-ble old slippers. How respectability did pinch, and gall, and rub the skin off me, to be sure! but I've done with it. I've given up the trumpery for the good, stout, weather-proof character of cabman. Respectability is all very well for folks who can have it for ready money; but to be obliged to run in debt for it — oh, it's enough to break the heart of an angel.

Well, I've gone a good round, and it's nothing but right that I should be comfortable at last. Wasn't all the sweetness of my little boyhood lost in an attorney's office? At a time of life when I ought to have been bird's-nesting, shoeing cats with walnut-shells, spinning cockchafers on pins, and enjoying myself like any other child of my age, — there I was half the day wearing out a wooden desk with my young breast-bone, and the other half running about, like a young cannibal, to serve writs; sneaking, and shuffling, and lying worse than any play-bill, and feeling as happy as a devil's imp on a holiday whenever I " served " my man. Yes, Peter, that I've any more heart than an oyster left me, is a special favor of Providence; for what a varmint I was! If it hadn't been for the play-house, I should have been ruined. Yes, Peter, but for the Coburg Theatre, I have no doubt that at this time I should have been a sharp attorney, not able to smell as much as a lucifer match without the horrors.

'Tis a great place for morals, the play-house, Peter. As I say, it quite drew me back into the paths of virtue. Old Simcox, my master, to keep me active, used to give me a shilling for every writ I served. He used to say, there was nothing like rubbing a young dog's nose in the blood, to make him sharp after the game. Well, with these shillings I used to go to the Coburg gallery. That gallery was my salvation. When I used to see the villain, who'd been so lucky all through the piece, chopped down like chopped wood at the last, — my conscience used to stir worse than the stomach-ache. And so by degrees I liked the play-house more, and the writs less. And one day when Simcox told me to go and serve a writ upon the very actor who used to do me so much good — for he was always the cock of the walk as far as virtue went — I gave him such a speech about " tremble, villain, for there is an eye," that the old fellow gasped again. When he had recovered himself enough to fling a ruler at my head, I put my cap on, and turned my back upon the law.

After this, I sold play-bills at the Coburg doors, and that's how I picked up the deal I know about the stage.

And so I went scrambling on till twenty, and how I lived I don't know. Indeed, when I look back, I often think money's of no use at all; folks do quite as well or better without it. Money's a habit — nothing more.

At twenty — how it happened I can't tell — I found myself a tradesman. Yes; I sold baked 'tatoes, and — on nipping winter days — used to feel myself a sort of benefactor to what is called our species. I had read a little at book-stalls and so on. And many a time have I, with a sort of pride, asked myself if many of the Roman emperors ever sold two 'tatoes, salt, and a bit of butter for a penny. I should think not.

Well, at three-and-twenty down came that bit of money on me ! Whether it was really a relation who left it, or not, or whether it was all a mistake, I never asked, — I took the money. And that bit of money made me swell not a little. Yes; I swelled like a toad — full of poison with it. Then I went to make no end of a fortune. I thought luck had fallen deep in love with me, and I couldn't go too far.

There was a gentleman who always came with an order to the Coburg. A few years ago I should have said he was a Jew; but now I know manners, and so call him a gentleman of the Hebrew persuasion. Well, if he couldn't talk melted butter! We were both to make our fortunes, but I was to find the money for the couple. We went upon 'Change; and, as he said, both of us were ruined. Ruin, however, could have been nothing strange to him, for he never seemed the worse for it.

From that time, Peter, I was flung upon the hard stones of London. I had too much pride to go to the 'tatoes again, and so took to billiards. Ha! Peter, it's dirty bread; it's bread with the head-ache, and the heart-ache, in it. That wouldn't do long; though how I did shuffle and hedge, and make the most of the innocent, and all to try to keep myself respectable!

I tell you, for fifteen years I fought it out like a man. I didn't care what came of it, what folks said of me — I would be respectable. A superfine coat and a prime dinner I would have; but ha, Peter! it's all been taken out of me. I've given it up, I tell you, and I'm a happy cabman.

Bless your soul! you can't think what a happy life it is. Always seeing something new, and always riding with somebody. For you must know, my cab isn't one of the new concerns that divide the driver and his fare. That wouldn't suit me, no how. No; I like to ride upon what I call an equality, and talk and learn life as I go. You can't believe the sort of people that I sometimes drive about, — and the things I get out of 'em.

But I intend to write it all down, and to save the bother of posting, and all that, to print my letters at once. Then, if my dear relations and acquaintance that are scattered in all the corners of the world don't know anything about me, 'twill be their fault, not mine.

I couldn't have thought that a cabman's life could have so improved the mind. But when we meet at the Spotted Lion — that's our watering-house — there's something to be heard, I can tell you. I never troubled my head with politics before I drove a cab: no, I was little better than an animal — but I should think that now I know something of the Bill of Rights, and all that; and all from the newspapers. When the nose-bag's on the old mare, don't I read the debates in Parliament!

I was going to write you a bit upon the Sugar Question, but old Lumpy — he's our waterman — has called me for a job.

So at present no more from your cousin and well-wisher,

JUNIPER HEDGEHOG.

1845.

Letter II.

To Mrs. Hedgehog, of New York.

My Dear Old Grandmother: Thank all your stars and two garters that you're out of England! We're all going to be made Catholics. It's a settled fact. You ought henceforth never to cook a supper of sprats without looking at the gridiron, thinking of Smithfield, and being special grateful for your deliverance.

Nobody can tell what's come to half the Bishops, and three parts of the clergy. Such a noise about surplices and gowns! The old story again. The old fight — as far as I can tell — about white and black; one party vowing that the real thing's white, whilst the other will have it that the true white's black. Yes, grandmother, it's the old battle of black and white that, as far as my learning goes, has for hundreds of years filled this nice sort of world of ours with all kinds of trouble. Nobody can tell what's set these ministers of peace — as they call themselves — all of a sudden in such a pucker — but I think I've hit upon the cause; and here it is.

All this noise in the church has begun in the playhouse. I'm sure of it. Foolish people say and write that we English folks don't care about plays. There never was such a mistake. In our hearts all of us, and especially many of the Bishops and clergy, dote upon the play-house; but then, you see, it isn't thought quite the thing for the clergy to go there.

The Bishop of Exeter — I'm cock-sure of it — has a consuming love for a pantomime; but then he wouldn't like to be seen in the boxes of Drury Lane, giving his countenance to the clown, that takes his tithe of all sorts of things that comes under his nose. The Bishop of London, too, — he, I've heard it said, got made a Bishop of by some intimate acquaintance of his that wrote plays in Greek. Well, he can't go and enjoy his laugh at the Haymarket, — or have his feelings warmed till they boil over at his eyes at the Victoria (that was once the Coburg). So you see, as the Bishops can't decently stir from the church to the play-house, they've set their heads together to bring the play-house to the church. And this accounts for all their fuss in the church, about what the play-house people call the "dresses and decorations." They seem to think that religion isn't enough of itself, unless it's "splendidly got up." Whereupon they want to go back to the old properties of crosses, and candlesticks, and so forth, to fill the pews. Well, when the Bishops — the gray, sober men, the fathers of the church — have this hankering after a bit of show, it isn't to be expected that the young fellows will refuse the finery. Certainly not. Whereupon they're bringing in all sorts of fashions, it seems. They don't think it enough to belong to the Army of Martyrs, unless they've very handsome regimentals.

In some of the churches they've revived what they call the offertory. It's this. At a certain part of the service, they send round a bag, or a pocket at the end of a stick, to all the people, to put money in. I have

seen the same sort of thing used in the streets to reach
to the first-floors, when the tumblers go about. Well,
this money is gathered for a many things. But John
Bull doesn't like it. They say the crocodile has his
tender part somewhere about his belly — John's vital
part is his breeches-pocket. Nevertheless, there's no
doubt that the Bishop of Exeter — for he's very strong
upon the offertory — has introduced it to make religion, what is so very much liked in England, select
and respectable. You see, the people who can't
afford to drop their Sunday shillings and sixpences,
won't have the face to go to worship at all, — or they
may turn Dissenters, — and so the Established Church,
like the Opera House, will be made, a place for what
the *Standard* (I can tell you *that is* a religious newspaper, though you may never hear of it) calls the
" better classes." Poor people may turn Anabaptists,
or anything of that sort that's very cheap. Purple
and fine linen ain't for everybody; no, isn't there
good stout sound cloth, and striped cotton?

The Bishop of London has been in very hot water
with the folks at Tottenham about the Sunday silver,
which they won't pay at all. Well, he says they
needn't pay it for a twelvemonth. So it seems that a
truth isn't a truth all at once; it takes a year to grow.
According to the Bishop it would seem that truth
was born like a tadpole, that wanted time afore it
came to be a perfect frog.

Well, then, there's another notion about. It's said
that the wants of the people are so many, that it's
quite out of the power of the laboring clergy to attend to 'em. It would be worse than drayman's

work. And so it has been recommended that there should be a sort of church militia raised in addition to the regulars. It was only last night that I drove down to Fulham a very chatty sort of man, — I think the under-butler of the Bishop of London. Well, he talked a good deal about this militia, — they're to be called deacons I think, and are to be considered a sort of a parson; like young ravens not yet come to their full black.

Well, it was quite plain that he hoped to be one of 'em, for he said the places would be open to anybody really pious, of the humblest parts. He was very talkative; and said these deacons would have all the comforts of the monks without any of their vows; going to people's houses; worming themselves into their families, and learning all their business, carnal — yes, I think carnal was his word — and spiritual. When I asked him if, like the monks, they were to wear gowns and hoods (as I'd seen 'em at the Coburg), he winked very knowingly, and said, with the blessing of Providence, that might come. At all events, they might begin with letters and numbers worked in gold or silver in their collars, and, something after the new police, have a pink or purple strap about their cuffs, when upon spiritual duty.

Folks are in a mighty stir about the matter; but I think Exeter and London might bring all the people of their own minds; if they only knew how to go about the business. I've just been reading Miss Martineau about mesmerism; and she says this — "It is almost an established opinion among some of the wisest students of mesmerism, that the mind of the somnambule [you must ask somebody about these words] mirrors that of the mesmerist ; " and then she goes on to say, " It certainly is true to a considerable extent, as is pretty clearly proved when an ignorant child — ignorant, especially of the Bible — *discourses of the Scriptures and divinity when mesmerized by a clergyman*."

Now, the bishops have nothing to do but to mesmerize the people, — I'm sure I've known parsons who've done wonders with sleepy congregations, — have only to get 'em " to mirror *their* minds," and they may do as they please with crosses, and surplices, and saints, and offertory, and all that. In a word, the Bishops of Exeter and London have only to send all their flocks well to sleep, to shear 'em after what fashion they like.

As yet, my dear grandmother. I haven't given nothing to the offertory, and I won't agree to the move about the surplice. But flesh is weak. I can't tell how long I may hold out. Fashion's a strong thing, and always strongest when it sets towards the church. The day may come when I may take my gray mare — as I'm told they take all the animals in Italy — *to* be blessed and sprinkled on the feast of St. Anthony,. and the Bishop of London may do the job for her. But I'll hold out as long as I can. In the mean time let me have your prayers, and believe me your affectionate grandson,

JUNIPER HEDGEHOG.

P. S. I did intend to write to cousin Bridget, but Lumpy's called me away for a long job.

LETTER III.

TO MRS. HEDGEHOG, OF NEW YORK.

MY DEAR GRANDMOTHER: We're all safe for a time; the Pope hasn't quite got hold of us yet. You recollect, when I was a boy, how I would fling stones, and call names, and go among other boys pelting 'em right and left, and swearing I didn't mean to hurt 'em, but played off my pranks only for their good. And then, when I used to get into a terrible fight, you remember how you used to come in at the last minute, and carry me off home just as I was nearly giving in. And then, how afterwards I used to brag that if grandmother hadn't taken me away, I'd have licked twenty boys; one down, another come on! Well, well; the more I see of life, the more I'm sure men only play over their boys' tricks; only they do it with graver faces and worse words.

What you did for me the Archbishop of Canterbury has done for the Bishop of Exeter. Almost at the last minute, he has wrapped his apron about the Bishop and carried him out of the squabble. And now the Bishop writes a letter, as long as a church bell-rope, in which he says he only gives up fighting to show that he's obedient — more than hinting, that if he'd been allowed to go on, he'd have beaten all comers, with one hand tied behind him. At all events, he's very glad there's been a rumpus, as it proves there's pluck on both sides. Yes, he says, —

"Whatever may have been the temporary results, *I do not and cannot regret* that I deemed it necessary publicly to assert those principles of church authority which it is alike the duty of all of us to recognize and inculcate. The very vehemence with which the assertion of them has been resisted, *proves.* if proof were necessary, *the necessity of their being asserted,* and of our never suffering them to fall into oblivion."

If this isn't talking in the dark, I don't know what a rushlight is. You might as well say, that the "vehemence" with which a man resists a kicking, "proves the necessity" of kicking him. Because folks wouldn't at any price have surplices forced down their throats, and offertory bags poked into their pews, why, that's the very reason you should try to push both surplice and bag upon 'em. As I say, it shows there's blood on both sides — and it's a comfort to know that both parties are ready for a tussle. Well, I've heard this sort of preaching from a Tipperary cabman, and never wondered; but it *does* sound droll from a bishop.

I've read something somewhere about the thunder of the church, and have now no doubt that it must be very serviceable; it must so clear the air after a certain time. Here, for months, has Exeter been thundering in the newspaper — crack, crack, crack! it's gone almost every morning, till people wondered if the steeple of their own parish church was safe; and now, at last, he sits himself down, and smiling as if his face was smeared with honey, folds his hands and softly says, " Thank Heaven! we've had a lovely storm."

Talking about thunder, I once read a poem — one of those strange, odd things that give your brain a twist — called *Festus*. There was a passage in it that certainly did bother me; but now I can perfectly understand it. Somebody says to another, —

"Why, how now !
You look as tho' you fed on *buttered thunder.*"

Now, the Bishop of Exeter — I say it with all respect, grandmother; for you know you always taught me to love the bishops — is this very man. You've only to read his letters, really so noisy, and yet, as he declares, meaning to be so soft — to be sure that what he lives and thrives upon is *buttered thunder.*

The Bishop, of course, isn't alone in his happiness at the row. One of his best friends, the *Morning Post*, believes it will do a deal of good. True piety, like physic, wants shaking to have its proper effect. The *Post* talked a little while ago about "the means which have made the church arise from its slumbers *like a giant refreshed;*" that is, getting up in a white surplice, to be refreshed with ready money from the pews. I don't know how it is, but I don't think the church ought to be compared to a giant. All the giants I know are people of very queer character. The best of 'em gluttonous, swaggering, overbearing chaps, with nothing too hot or too heavy for 'em to carry off; now, these are not at all the sort of creatures that we are likely to think of, when we're reading the Bishop of Exeter's letters. No: they rather remind us of a shepherd playing on his pipe — I've only read of these things — to his sheep and lambkins.

The *Morning* Post further says, —

" We are not among those who feel alarm at the present state of the church. *The fermentation will throw off the scum*, and what is good will remain."

Now, grandmother, you know enough of boiling to know that " the scum " always floats on the top. Now, is anything on the top to be thrown off? Don't flurry yourself: the *Post* doesn't mean that. What it means is, that a whole lot of the vulgar members of the Established Church will be so fermented by the surplice, the offertory, and other Popish ingredients — grains of Paradise as they tell us — that they'll be thrown clean out of it. You know how Bill Wiggins once poisoned the pond, so that the fish was floated dead ashore. In the same way the church may get rid of its small fry, and " what is good will remain." Then the church will be something like. Now, it's old and weather-stained, with time blotches and cracks about it. But how fine it will look with crucifixes and pictures of the Virgin inside — a clean white surplice always in the upper pulpit — and the whole building beautifully and thickly faced with *Roman* cement !

But at this present writing, it isn't all over in the city of Exeter. The Bishop having had his fling, — one of the journeymen, the Rev. Mr. Courtenay, minister of St. Sidwell's, comes in for a little more than his share of the performance. Don't think I'm profane, dear grandmother — no. quite the reverse. But you *have* in your time been to Astley's, and seen the riding in the ring. Well, the principal rider

comes, and does all manner of wonders whilst canter-
ing and galloping, and going all kind of paces.
When he's done, he makes his bow, and goes off.
And then, after him, comes the clown. Well, he's
determined to outdo all that's been done before him,
—and for this purpose goes on with all sorts of ma-
nœuvres. Now, the Bishop of Exeter has made his
bow, and the Rev. Mr. Courtenay is, at the time I
write, before the public. He *will* preach in a surplice. And that he may do so with safety—for all
the folks in Exeter are in a pretty pucker about it—
he goes to and from church, as I may say, in the
bosom of the police. O, dear! isn't it sad work,
grandmother? this noise about black and white
gowns, when churchmen ought to think of nothing
but black and white souls? Black and white! as if
there was a pattern-book of colors for heaven! However, how it will end nobody knows; but if the matter goes on as it promises, it is thought the Rev. Mr.
Courtenay will call to his aid the yeomanry, and be
escorted to St. Sidwell's by a body-guard armed with
ball cartridge. It is said he has bespoken two
howitzers to keep off the mob from the church doors.

I've hardly time to save the packet; so remain

Your affectionate grandson,

JUNIPER HEDGEHOG.

P. S. They do say that Mr. Courtenay wants to
be made a martyr of. But the days for burning are
all gone by. Besides, other folks declare that the
parson of St. Sidwell's would have been too green to
burn at any time.

LETTER IV.

TO MICHAEL HEDGEHOG, AT HONG KONG.

DEAR MICHAEL: When you quitted England, in the Hong Kong division of police, I promised to write you all the news I could; at least, such news as I knew you'd like. The crimes and evils of population were, I know, always a favorite matter with you. I'm sorry to say the evil's getting worse every day. And no wonder. You'll hardly believe it, Michael, seeing what a surplus of pauper flesh and blood respectable people have upon their hands, that there's a set of ignoramuses who absolutely offer a premium for babies; for all the world, as they give away gold and silver medals for prize pigs. I take the bit of news I send you from *The Times*. You must know, that a few weeks ago, a " Mrs. Clements, of 21 Hunt Street, Mile-end New-town," had at once " three children, two girls and a boy." All, too, impudent enough to live. Well, *The Times* published an account of the misdemeanor, and — would you believe it? — some " generous individuals," as they are stupidly called, sent, among 'em, thirty-eight pounds for the mother and little ones.

Now, what is this, as you'd say, but fostering a superabundance of population? It's no other than offering bribes to bring people into the country, — already as full as a cade of herrings; and when every trade is eating part of its members up, for all the world as melancholy monkeys eat their own tails!

Isn't it shocking to encourage the lower classes to add to themselves? There's nothing that money won't do; and I've no doubt, whatever, that, for some years to come, all children at Mile-end will be born by threes and fours. A shrewd fellow like you must have remarked how people imitate one another. You never yet heard of an odd act of suicide, or any kind of horror with originality in it, that it didn't for a little time become the fashion, as if it was a new bonnet, or a new boot. And so, among the lower orders, it will be in the matter of babies. Now, if Mrs. Clements had been sent to prison for the offence, then the evil might have been nipped in the bud; but to reward her for her three babies, who could show no honest means of providing for themselves, why, it's flying in the face of all political economy. Three babies at once at Mile-end is monstrous. Even twins should be confined to the higher ranks.

You'll be glad to hear that we've been giving a round of dinners to your Chinese hero, Sir Henry Pottinger. At Manchester he was hailed as the very hero of cotton prints. They dined him very handsomely, — and you may be sure there was a good deal of after-dinner speaking. A Rev. Canon Wray answered the toast for the clergy. I once read of a melancholy man, who thought all his body was turned into a glass bottle, and so wouldn't move for fear of going to pieces. Now, I'm certain of it, that there's a sort of clergyman, who, after some such humor, thinks himself a forty-two pounder; for he is never heard at a public meeting that he doesn't fire away shot and gunpowder. The Rev. Canon said (or rather fired) his thanks, that Sir H. Pottinger "had opened a way for the march of the gospel." Now, Michael, I never heard of any artillery in the New Testament. And he further said, —

"British arms seem scarcely ever to know a defeat. In the east, west, north, and south, our soldiers and sailors are, in the end, victorious. I cannot but think that, as Great Britain holds the tenets of the gospel in greater purity than any other nation, so she is intended by the divine will to carry inestimable blessings to all distant benighted climes."

Well, Michael, I've heard of a settler in mistake sowing gunpowder for onions; but the Rev. Canon Wray, with his best knowledge about him, thinks there's nothing like sowing gunpowder for the "scriptural mustard-seed." I suppose he's right, because he's a canon; and therefore not to be disputed with by your ignorant, but affectionate brother,

JUNIPER HEDGEHOG.

LETTER V.

To Mrs. Barbara Wilcox, at Philadelphia.

DEAR SISTER : It gave me great pleasure to learn from your letter that yourself, husband, and baby got safe and sound to your present home. You ask me to send you my portrait. It isn't in my power to do so at present; but if I should be unfortunate enough to kill anybody, or set a dock-yard afire, or bamboozle

the bank, — or, in short, do anything splashy to get a
front place in the dock at the Old Bailey, — you may
then have my portrait at next to nothing. Then, I
can tell you, it will be drawn in capital style — at full
length, three quarters, half length, and I know not
what. I've read somewhere that in what people call
the good old times — as times always get worse, what
a pretty state the world will be in a thousand years
hence! — when there were dead men's heads on the
top of Temple Bar, grinning down what people call
an example on the folks below, — that there used to
be fellows with spy-glasses; and, at a penny a peep,
they showed to the curious all the horror of the aforesaid heads, not to be discovered by the naked eye.
Well, the heads are gone; — and the spy-glass traders
too; but for all that, there's the same sort of show
going on, and a good scramble to turn the penny by
it, only after a different fashion. Murderers are now
shown in newspapers. They are no longer gibbeted in irons; no, that was found to be shocking,
and of no use: — they are now nicely cut in wood,
and so insinuated into the bosoms of families. The
more dreadful the murder, the greater value the portrait; which, for a time, is made a sort of personal
acquaintance to thousands of respectable folks who
pay the newspaper owner — the spy-glass man of our
time — so much to stare at it as long as they like.

I am certain that the shortest cut to popularity of
some sort, is to cut somebody's throat. A dull, stupid
fellow, that pays his way and does harm to nobody,
— why, he may die off like a fly in November, and be
no more thought of. But only let him do some

devil's deed — do a bit of murder, as coolly as he'd pare a turnip: and what he does, and what he says; whether he takes coffee, or brandy-and-water " cold without;" when he sleeps, and when he wakes; when he smiles, and when he grinds his teeth, — all of this is put down as if all the world went upon his movements, and couldn't go on without knowing 'em. To a man who wants to make a noise, he doesn't care how, all this is very tempting. I hope I mayn't come to be cut in wood, — but still one would like to make a rumpus some way before one died.

There's commonly an Old Bailey fashion, the same as a St. James's fashion. Just now — as you want to know all the domestic news — poison's carrying everything before it. 'Twould seem as if people suddenly thought their relations rats, and treated 'em accordingly. I never yet tried my hand upon a book, but I do think that I could throw off a nice little story with lots of arsenic in it — a sort of genteel Guide to Newgate. I've been reading about a lady, one Tofana, who made a great stir some years ago. She could give arsenic in such a manner, that she set people for death, as you'd set an alarum. She got a good many pupils, young married ladies, about her, who all of 'em put their husbands aside like an old-fashioned gown. Now, I do think that a novel called *The Ladies' Poisoning Club, or Widowhood at Will,* would just now make a bit of a stir. I don't mean to say that I could write a book; that is, what folks call *write:* but I've a knack; I know I could imitate writing, just as an ape imitates a man. The subject grows upon me. I certainly think I shall

20

make a beginning. However, of this you shall hear more by the next packet. I do think I could make a hit in what I call arsenicated literature. There's arsenicated candles — why shouldn't there be arsenicated books? — In haste.

Your affectionate brother,

JUNIPER HEDGEHOG.

P. S. If I do the book, I shall follow it up with a sort of moral continuation, to be called *The Stomach Pump*.

LETTER VI.

TO MR. JONAS WILCOX, PHILADELPHIA.

DEAR BROTHER-IN-LAW: As my last letter was to sister, it is but fair that you should have the next dose of ink. Well, Parliament's opened; and Sir Robert's made a clean breast of it — that is, if a Prime Minister can do such a thing. There never was such harmony in the House of Commons! After Sir Robert had spoken out, you might have thought all the House was holding nothing but a love-feast. I was in the gallery — I won't tell you how I got in — and never saw such a sight in all my life. All the papers, I can't tell why, have oddly suppressed an account of the matter ; therefore what you get from me will be exclusive — from your " own " correspondent. Treasure it accordingly.

When Sir Robert said he should keep on the Income-Tax for three years longer, almost the whole

House fell into fits of delight at his goodness. You might have seen Whig embracing Tory — Radical throwing his arms about the neck of Conservative — and Young England with tears of gratitude rolling like buttermilk down upon his white waistcoat. When Sir Robert had quite finished his speech, there was a shower of nosegays flung upon him from the Treasury benches, just in the same way as now and then they pelt the actors at the play-houses! Sir Robert picked 'em all up, and pressed 'em to his heart, and from the corners of his mouth smiled ten thousand thanks. Then, sitting down, he very handsomely gave a flower apiece to what he calls his colleagues. He insisted — amidst the cheers of the House — on putting a forget-me-not in the button-hole of Mr. Gladstone (who sobbed audibly at the touch of friendship) ; and then he handed a lily — as an emblem of the Home Secretary's reputation — to Sir James Graham. At this, I needn't tell you, there were "roars of laughter." To be sure, at this season of the year these flowers were artificial ; but for which reason, it was said by somebody, they were more in keeping with Sir Robert's measure. Two or three members — for form's sake — abused the Income-Tax, but nevertheless said they would vote for it. Lord John Russell called it a shameful, infamous, ignominious, tyrannical, prying impost : he would, however, support it. This is as if a man should denounce another as a coward, a ruffian, and a thief, and then — fold him to his bosom! But they do odd things in Parliament!

Sir Robert says we are to have the Income-Tax for

only three years longer. Nonsense. He intends
that we should grow with it upon us. He'll no more
take it off than a Chinese mother will take off the little shoe — that, for the beauty of the full-grown
woman, she puts upon the foot of her baby girl. The
child may twist, and wriggle, and squall; and the
mother may now and then say pretty things — make
pretty promises to it to keep it quiet — but the shoe's
there for the sufferer's life. Now, John Bull — thinks
Sir Robert Peel — will move all the better with his
foot in the Income-Tax; all the better, too, because it
most galls and crushes a lower member.

However, we are to have the duty off glass; which,
says Sir Robert, is much better than if the duty were
taken off light. It is not for such as me to dispute
with a minister, but I can't see how, if I'm to get my
house glazed duty free, it's quite as good as if there
was no Window-Tax. To be sure, if a man, as a
householder, were to new glaze himself from top to
bottom once a quarter, it might be another thing; he
might save upon the glass what he now pays for the
sun that, in London, tries to come through it. He
may certainly afford to have more windows, — but
will, I say, the saving on the glass pay for the light?
Besides, not light alone — but air is paid for. There
is at the present time a secret agitation going on
among the cats of England. The grievance is this : —
A man can't make a hole in his house for the cat to
pass in and out to mouse or visit, without the said
hole being surcharged as a window. This is a wrong
done upon the cats of the country; but whether done
out of sympathy with the rats or not, let Sir James
Graham answer.

However, one comfort will come of cheap glass. Folks who choose to visit museums, and such public places, may break what they like of the material at a decreased cost for the pleasure. Before it was bad enough. Nothing, according to law, being worth more than five pounds; so any malicious or morbid scoundrel (or both) might smash any rare piece of antiquity, and handing to the magistrate any sum over five pounds, bid him take the change out of that. I think a club might be formed for certain young chaps about town, to be called The Independent Smashers. They might subscribe to a common fund to pay fines; and each in turn draw for the pleasure of a bit of destruction. With the duty taken off the article it would be remarkably cheap sport. However, there is no doubt of it that Peel has got great glory by taking off this tax. A good deal of his reputation as a minister will be looked upon as glass; such side of his reputation in the eyes of an admiring country to be always " kept upwards."

We are to have sugar, too, at about three halfpence a pound cheaper; which Mrs. Hedgehog tells me will allow us to save at least sixpence a week: however, what we shall have to pay to protect the West Indians, she, poor soul, never dreams of, and I should be a brute to tell her. Therefore — poor thing! — she may now and then toast Sir Robert in her Twankay, without thinking of the 140,000*l.* we lose in the other way. Then, again, what we shall save in cotton is wonderful!

The auctioneers, too, are all right. They are to knock down at so much for life, instead of taking out a yearly license. It is thought that this enlarged piece of statesmanship came about out of compliment to George Robins, who in one of his familiar letters to the Premier, said he'd rather have it so.

However, everybody says Sir Robert Peel's in for life. He's married to Downing Street, — and nothing but death can them part. One thing's certain: he's got a thumping surplus.. And when any man in England gets that, folks are not very particular how he's come by it.

So no more at present from your affectionate brother-in-law, JUNIPER HEDGEHOG.

LETTER VII.

TO MRS. HEDGEHOG, OF NEW YORK.

DEAR GRANDMOTHER: It was very kind of you — though away from Old England — to have prayers put up for the Bishops of Exeter and London, and Mr. Courtenay and Mr. Ward, with all the unfortunate young clergymen who've been frightening their good mother Church, for all the world like young ducklings that, hatched by a hen, would take water. The Bishops, you will be glad to learn, are much better; and now, Sunday after Sunday, the young parsons are taking off their white surplices, and putting on their old gowns, just like idle, flashy, young dogs, who've been making a noise at a masquerade, but are once more prepared to go back to their serious counters. Mr. Courtenay and two or three of his kidney did think of putting on chain-armor under their surplices, like the Templars that you once saw in the play of *Ivanhoe;* but whether the Bishop of Exeter has interfered or not, I can't say; the thing's given up.

Mr. Ward, who has been turned out of Oxford for his *Ideal of a Christian Church,* — which means a church with censers and candlesticks, and pictures of the Virgin, and martyrs' bones, and other properties, — is going to be married; if the business isn't done already. I shouldn't have written upon the matter, only Mr. W. has printed a letter in all the papers, giving *his* notions of the holy state. They, certainly, are very sweet and complimentary to the lady chosen by Mr. Ward; for he says, —

"First, I hold it most firmly as a truth even *of natural religion,* that celibacy *is a higher condition of life* than marriage."

Now, if celibacy is the highest condition of life, how is it that Adam and Eve came together while they were yet in Paradise? Their union — according to Mr. Ward — ought to have taken place after they both fell. Matrimony should have followed as a punishment for the apple. And then, when it was commanded to " increase and multiply," was it supposed that those who obeyed the command would not be in so " high a condition " as those who neglected it? But men read their Bibles through strange spectacles!

However, grandmother, as you like to hear all the chat about the church, you must know that last week I took up a fare near an oyster shop in Covent Garden

— a very respectable sort of person ; in fact, I'm sure one of the Established Church. When he had left the cab, I found that *The Ecclesiastical Gazette* (No. 81) had dropped from his pocket. I've gone through it, and found parts of it — I mean the church advertisements — very odd indeed. You can't think how strange they read after the New Testament — if you wouldn't think the pulpit cushion was a counter, after reading 'em ! Look here, now :

A CURATE WANTED in a large market-town forty miles from London, near a railroad, population *five thousand*, where the Incumbent resides and takes his full share of the duty. He must be in Priest's Orders, have a voice sufficiently *loud* for a very large church, and, whilst holding *moderately high church views*, be chiefly anxious to *seek and save the lost* by preaching Christ and Him crucified. Stipend. *one hundred pounds* a-year. The Advertiser does not pledge himself to answer every letter.

All of 'em bargain for a loud " voice : " you'd think, grandmother, the advertisements were for chorus-singers, and not clergymen. And, grandmother, can you tell me what " a *moderate* high church view " is? Is it moderate virtue — moderate honesty — moderate *truth?* Pray tell me.

Another advertiser wants "a pious and active curate," who will double his duty with " the tuition of the incumbent's sons." That incumbent has a good eye for a good pennyworth, depend upon it.

At Bishop's Lydeard a curate is tempted with " a neat little cottage," and " *almost* certainly the chaplaincy of an adjoining union," with " other considerations " (what can *they* be, grandmother?), which

will make the salary " equivalent to 100*l.* per annum."
And for this he must be orthodox and married.

Another curate is wanted in a "small parish in
Berks," where "*the duty is very light.*" What
would the apostles have said to such an offer?

A beneficed clergyman, advertising from Camber-
well, wishes for duty " in some agricultural *and picturesque part* of the north of England." A picturesque part! You see, it isn't every one who would
like to preach in the wilderness.

Another curate is required in Nottinghamshire:
salary, 100*l.* per annum. He must have the highest
references for "gentlemanly manners," *as* " the vicar
is resident." I suppose, if the vicar was away, a
second or third rate style would do well enough for
the parishioners.

However, you'll be glad to learn that several of the
advertisers profess to be " void of tractarianism and
other novelties." Just in the same way as they write
up somewhere in Piccadilly — " The original brown
bear."

Another clergyman " is desirous of meeting with
an early appointment in town:" and, grandmother,
you may judge of the lengths this gentleman will go
to preach Christianity and save human souls, when
he adds, " No objection to the Surrey side!" Isn't
this good of him? Because, you know, grandmother,
the opera, and the club-houses, and the divans, and
so forth, are none of 'em on the Surrey side. To be
sure, there's the Victoria, and Astley's — but they're
low.

Now, grandmother, don't all these advertisements

smell a little too much of trade — don't they, for your notions of the right thing — jingle a little too much with gold and silver? As I'm an honest cabman, though I knew I was reading all about the Church and her pious sons, yet, somehow, the advertisements did put me in mind of "Rowland's Macassar," — "Mechi's Magic Strops," and "Good stout Cobs to be disposed of."

I am, dear grandmother, your affectionate grandson,

JUNIPER HEDGEHOG.

P. S. I open my letter to tell you that the Bishop of Exeter has broken out again. A Mr. Blunt, of Helston, *will* wear the surplice; and the Bishop, like a bottle-holder at a fight, backs him in his doings. Do have more prayers put up for the Bishop.

LETTER VIII.

TO SAMUEL HEDGEHOG, GALLANTEE SHOWMAN, RATCLIFFE HIGHWAY.

DEAR SAM: I'm just come home from Hampstead; and so, while the matter's fresh in my mind, I sit down to write you a few lines. You have heard of the awful murder — of course. Well, I don't know: murder's a shocking thing, to be sure; nobody can say it isn't; and yet, after what I've seen to-day — Sunday, mind — it does almost seem to me as if people took a sort of pleasure in it. Bless you! if you'd only seen the hundreds and hundreds of folks figged out in their very best to enjoy a sight of the place where a man had been butchered — you'd have thought Haverstock field, stained and cursed as it is with blood — a second Vauxhall at the least. I'm sure I've seen people going to Greenwich Fair with not half the pleasure in their faces. However, I'll tell you all about it.

I was called off the stand about eight this morning by a gentleman and lady, dressed as I thought for church. They're a little early, thought I, but that's their business. "Take us to Hampstead," said the gentleman; "and mind, as near to the murder as possible." "Do, my good man," said the lady, — bless you! to have looked at her you'd have thought she'd have fainted at the sound of murder, —" do, my good man," said she, " and make haste; for I wouldn't be too late for anything. Take care of these," said she to the gentleman, giving him a basket, " and mind they don't break." Well, it's my business to drive a cab; so I said nothing, but started for Hampstead. Bless you! Before I'd got half up Tottenham Court road, it was no easy driving, I can tell you. The road swarmed! Up and down the New Road, through Camden Town, and right to Haverstock Hill — I never saw anything like it, except perhaps on the day they run for the Derby. Everybody seemed turned out to enjoy themselves — determined to have a holiday, and no mistake.

Well, I drove as near as I could to the place; and then I got a boy to hold the horse, and got down and went along with my fare. If it didn't make me quite

savage and sick, Sam, to see hundreds of fellows —
well dressed gentry, mind you! — gaping and lounging about, and now poking the grass with their sticks,
as if it was something precious because blood had
been shed upon it — and now breaking bits of the
trees about the place, I suppose to make toothpicks
and cribbage-pegs of. And then there were fathers
— precious fools! — bringing their children with
them, boys and girls, as though they'd brought 'em to
a stall of gingerbread nuts, where they might fill their
bellies and be happy! But the worst of all, Sam,
was to see the women. Lots of 'em, nice, young, fair
creatures, tender as if they were made of best wax, —
there they were running along, and looking at the
bushes, and the grass, and talking of the blood, and
the death-struggle — just as if they were looking at
and talking of the monkeys at the 'Logical Garden.
Well, the handsomest of 'em after a time looked to
me no better than young witches, — and that's the
truth. Every minute I expected some of 'em to do a
polka, they did after a time seem so to enjoy themselves.

Well, all of a sudden, I missed my fare. Looking
about, I saw my gentleman go up to the brick wall.
Then he took a heavy hammer out of his pocket, and
knocking away, split a brick, and then knocked it out
of the wall. " This is something like," said he to me,
twinkling his eye; " something to remember the murder by." And then he carefully wrapped the pieces
of brick in a silk handkerchief, and put 'em in his
breast pocket, as if they'd been lumps of diamonds.
I said nothing — but I could have kicked him. How-

ever, he hadn't done yet — for going to a part of the
field, he said to his wife, — for so she proved to be, —
" This is the place, Arabella ; the very place ; where's
the pots?" Then the lady took three garden-pots
from a basket, and then her husband, dropping upon
his knees, turned up the earth with a large clasp-
knife, and when he'd filled the pots, he dug up two
or three daisy roots, and set 'em ; his wife smiling
and looking as happy all the while as if she'd got a
new gown, or a new bonnet, or both.   " Come,"
said the gentleman, squinting at the daisy roots, and
twisting one of the pots in his hands — " this is what
I call worth coming for.   As I say, this is something
to recollect a murder by.   Humph!" and then he
paused a bit, and looked very wishfully at the stile —
" humph! I should like a walking-stick out of that ;
but the police are so particular, I suppose they
wouldn't suffer it.   Come along, Arabella ; " and securing the broken brick and the daisy roots in the
pots, my gentleman went back to the cab.   " Now
drive as fast as you can to the church," he said ; " I
wouldn't but be there for any money."   Well, I never
did drive through such a crowd, but at last I managed
it : and at last, — but no ; I haven't patience enough
to write any more upon this part of it.   There was
nothing wanted in and about the churchyard to make
it a fair, except a few stalls and such like.   It made
me sick, Sam, to look upon this murder's holiday.

I wish you'd have seen the Yorkshire Grey, public
house!   No sooner did they open the doors, than
there was as much scrambling as at any play-house
on boxing night.   Well, the landlord didn't make a

little by his gin that day! Murder proved a good customer to him! And then to see the hundreds and hundreds struggling and pushing to get to the bar — to hear 'em laughing and shouting — and seeing 'em tossing off their liquor — upon my life, Sam, there was a mob of well-dressed, well-to-do Englishmen, that considering what had brought them there, wasn't half so decent as a crowd of Zealand savages.

Cricketing's an English sport — so is single-stick — so are bowls — so are ninepins — and after what I've seen to-day — so, I'm sure of it, is murder. For my part, it does seem a little hard to hang the murderer himself, when it appears that he gives by his wickedness so much enjoyment to his fellow-subjects.

Well, Sam, I'm now come to the marrow of my letter, and it's this. I do think if you will only take pains, and have all the murders of the year nicely got up, you may make a capital penn'orth of the lot with your show at Christmas. When lords and ladies make a scrimmage for it at police courts, and respectable, pious people take in newspapers for the very best likenesses of prisoners and cutthroats, — I'm sure you'd get custom — if the thing was well done — ay, " of the nobility, gentry, and public in general."

Now, do, Sam, take my advice. Depend upon it, the pop'lar taste sets in for blood: and so, instead on winter's nights a going about with your old-fashioned cry of " Gallantee Show" — sing out, " Mur—der," and your fortune's made. And so no more from

Your cousin and well-wisher,

JUNIPER HEDGEHOG.

LETTER IX.

TO MRS. HEDGEHOG, OF NEW YORK.

DEAR GRANDMOTHER: You ought to be in England just now, we're in such a pleasant pucker. The Church is in danger again! I have myself known her twenty times in peril, — but now, she really is at the very edge of destruction. You know there's a place called Maynooth College, where they bring up Roman Catholic priests for the use of Ireland. Well, there's a lot of folks, who will have it that this College is no bit better than certain tanks I've read of in India, where they breed young crocodiles to be worshipped by people who know no better. Sir Robert Peel intends to give 26,000*l.* a year to this place — it used to have an annual grant of 9,000*l.* — that the scholars may be increased in number, and that they may be better taught and more comfortably boarded and lodged. Well, the members of the Church of England — although here and there they have grumbled at the matter, and have called the Pope names that pass in small change at Billingsgate — have been mute as fish compared to the Dissenters. It is they who have fought the fight; it is they who have raised the price of parchment by darkening the House of Commons with clouds of petitions. It is they who have risen to a man, and have patted the British Lion, and twisted his tail, and goaded him — as you'd set a bull-dog on a cat — to tear Popery to pieces.

But, dear grandmother, don't be afraid. Before

you get my next lettter, with all this noise and boun-
cing, we shall have settled down as quiet as stale
soda-water. And then for the Church being in danger, — bless you! the very folks who are now holding up their hands, thinking it will drop to pieces —
(from its very richness, I suppose, like some of your
plum-puddings) — why, they'll sleep quietly in their
beds, and take their glass of wine and chicken with
their usual appetite, until the Church shall be once
more in trouble, once more to give 'em a pleasant,
healthful shaking, — and then once more to let 'em
easily down again. I've known some girls who've
thought they best showed how tender they were by
always going into fits: well, I do think that, just like
'em, some people believe they best show their religion when they scream and foam at the mouth
about it.

It's a settled belief with a good many pious people,
who are as careful of their religion as of their best
service of china, only using it on holiday occasions
for fear it should get chipped or flawed in working-
day wear — it's the belief with them that a Papist is a
sort of human toad — an abomination in the form of
man. Doctor Croly has surely a notion of this sort.
A few days ago he appeared on Covent Garden stage
(I think his first appearance there since his comedy
of *Pride shall have a Fall*) and called upon the
Lord, with thunder and lightning and the sword, to
kill his enemies — meaning Roman Catholics! And
then the Doctor showed how Providence had punished
all naughty kings who had cast an eye of favor on the
Pope. Capping this, the Doctor more than hinted that

George the Fourth — the first gentleman in Europe, for he had a greater number of coats than all the rest of the kings put together — was somewhat suddenly called from his loving people, because he had passed the Bill that 'mancipated the Catholics. Well, when we think how many Catholics there are in the world — when we remember the millions of 'em scattered about the earth — it does appear to me a little bold in a worm of a man (whether the said worm wears clergyman's black or not) praying to the Lord to destroy, crush, burn, whole nations of men and women, because he wasn't born to think as they do. But so it is with some folks, very proud indeed of their Christianity. Hear them talk and pray, and you would think that Satan himself — the father of wickedness — had been the creator of ninety-nine men out of a hundred, and that it was the pure, elect, and lucky hundredth that religiously begged for the destruction of the ninety-nine. But all the noise is about the largeness of the sum — the 26,000*l.* The 9,000*l.* was every year quietly voted — for I call the gaggling of two or three Parliament geese as nothing — and still the Church stands unshaken on her foundations. By this it would seem, that with some folks it is the money that a wrong costs, and not the wrong itself, that is objectionable. Thinking after this fashion, drunkenness is not to be thought a vice if it be drunkenness gratis; it, however, increases in enormity with the increase of its price; thus gin-drunkenness is merely wrong, but burgundy-drunkenness is infamous to the last degree. Haven't I read somewhere of an old Greek philosopher — if some of those chaps had lived in these times, they'd now and then have found themselves at the police office — who felt mightily disposed to do what was immoral, and only held back at the purchase-money! I think he said, he wouldn't "buy repentance at so dear a price." Now, if he could have had the sin at a cheap pennyworth, the sin itself had been light indeed. It's the weight of money that makes the weight of crime.

But, I suppose, Doctor Croly, Mr. M'Neile, and such folks — who seem to read their Bibles by the blue light of brimstone — believe that the extra money given to the Roman Catholic priests of Ireland will only be so much powder and shot with which they may bring down Protestants. Well, if money is to make converts, what has the Irish Protestant Church been about, that has always had a full money-bag at her girdle, and more than that, plenty of leisure to reclaim the fallen? She has always had a golden crook whereby to bring stray lambs into the fold, — and yet has added nothing to her flock.

Now, according to my opinion, the folks who abuse Maynooth ought rather to feel glad that more money is to be given to her priests, seeing what an abundance of money, and good things purchased by money, have done for the Irish Protestant Church. It has become slow as it has become fat. Stuff even a pulpit cushion with bank-notes, and it is strange to see how religion will sleep upon it. And therefore people ought to rejoice that the Catholic priest is to be made a little comfortable in worldly matters! Excellent, worthy churchmen, who can command the sports of the field, and all the pleasures of the table,

are not the busy, troublesome folks to go about con-
verting their benighted neighbors! And though the
Maynooth pupils may not — like their beneficed
rivals — keep fox-hounds, and enjoy the dearest turtle,
pine-apples, and all that — they will not, I think, be
in after-life more dangerous to the Protestant Church,
because — when at College — they slept not more
than two in a bed.

But there's a sort of people in the world that can't
bear making any progress. I wonder they ever walk,
unless they walk backwards! I wonder they don't
refuse to go out when there's a new moon, — and all
out of love and respect for that " ancient institution,"
the old one. But there always were such people,
grandmother — always will be. When lucifers first
came in, how many old women, stanch old souls —
many of 'em worthy to be members of Parliament —
stood by their matches and tinder-boxes, and cried out,
" No surrender!" And how many of these old women — disguised in male attire — every day go about
at public meetings, professing to be ready to die for
any tinder-box question that may come up! Yes,
ready — quite ready, to die for it; all the readier,
perhaps, because dying for anything of the sort's now
gone out of fashion.

Even Sir James Graham says the time is gone by
for ill-using Ireland. " The time is gone by!" And
yet how many men before Sir James have stood up,
and declared *their* time — the time " gone by" — was
the best time possible for Ireland; that what was
doing for her could not be improved; and, having
thundered this, have sat down secure in a majority

that has voted for the evil to continue! What a long while it is before men in power will learn to call things by their proper names! What a time it takes to teach ministers to call evil, evil — and lies, lies!

Sir Robert Peel has behaved in the handsomest manner in the matter. He says it is by no means his wish to rob the Whigs of the gratitude of Ireland for the Maynooth measure. Certainly not: they no doubt could have carried it had he joined them; this, however, he would not do; he has, however, no objection that they should join *him*. And so, they may have the gratitude, and he the patronage and power. They have helped him to open the oyster; he swallows the fish, — and they are quite welcome to the shells.

It is quite a delight to read Sir Robert's Parliament speeches. Did you ever talk to a man who seemed never to hear what you said, but only thought what he should say to pass for an answer? who seemed as though none of your words entered his ears, but all slid down his cheek? I've met with such people, and Sir Robert Peel — when I read his Maynooth speeches — does remind me of 'em. What a way he has of talking *down the side* of a speech, and never answering it direct! I hardly wonder that the playhouses don't flourish, when there's such capital actors of all sorts in the Houses of Parliament.

I had just been reading an account of two or three more Maynooth meetings, where some of the speakers talked about the true and the false religion, as though themselves had a sole and certain knowledge of what was true — what false: I had just been reading all this, when my eye fell upon a paragraph headed "Lord Rosse's Telescope." Lord Rosse, you must know, is one of those noblemen who do not pull off knockers — knock down cabmen — and always take a front seat at the Old Bailey, on a trial for murder. No: he has been making an enormous telescope; and the paragraph I write of says — "Marvellous rumors are afloat respecting the astronomical discoveries made by Lord Rosse's monster telescope. It is said that Regulus, instead of being a sphere, is ascertained to be a disk; and, stranger still, that the nebula in the belt of Orion is a universal system — a sun, with planets moving round it, as the earth and her fellow-orbs move round our glorious luminary."

Now, at one time, a man might have been burnt alive for taking it upon himself to say that Regulus was not a sphere, but a disk; and that Orion (I know nothing about him, save and except that a marvellously fine poem, price one farthing, was lately published with his name) did not wear in his belt any nebula, but a universal system! La, grandmother! when I read of these things, I feel a mixture of pain and pity for men that, instead of having their hearts and spirits tuned by the harmony that God is always playing to them—(and they won't hear it, the leathern-eared sinners!) — think of nothing but swearing that one thing's a disk, and the other a nebula, — when they only look through small glasses, wanting the great telescope to show 'em the real truth!

And so no more from your affectionate grandson,

JUNIPER HEDGEHOG.

P. S.   I blush for myself, that I had almost forgotten to tell you that Doctor Wolff has come back, safe and sound, from the innermost part of India, where he went to try to save the lives of two Englishmen, Stoddart and Conolly.   It was like going into a tiger's den to take flesh from the wild beast.   And yet the stout-hearted man went!   Such an act makes us forget the meanness and folly of a whole generation!   Captain Grover — a heart of gold, that! — has published a book on the matter called *The Bokhara Victims.*   As no doubt the New York publishers — in their anxiety to diffuse knowledge — have already published it for some five cents, do not fail to read it. As for Doctor Wolff, I wonder what Englishmen will do for him.   If he'd come back from India after cutting twenty thousand throats, why, he might have had a round of dinners, diamond-hilted swords, wine-coolers as big as buckets, and so on; — as it is, I fear nothing *can* be done for him.   However, we shall see.

Letter X.

To Mrs. Hedgehog, of New York.

Dear Grandmother : England's still above water : the sea doesn't yet roll over Dover cliffs ; nevertheless the Maynooth Grant, that I wrote to you about, is gone through the House of Commons ; and in a very few weeks the Papists, as you love to call 'em, will have the money.   Sir Culling Eardley Smith, Mr. Plumptre, and others of their kidney, may possi-

bly for a month or two appear in the streets in sack-
cloth and ashes, and with beards like Jew rabbis —
just to show their respect for the departed constitution;
but after a decent time of mourning, they will, no
doubt, be open to consolation, and take their dinners
with their usual appetite. I shouldn't wonder, if in
six months the Rev. Mr. M'Neile (of sulphurous
principles) consents to eat and drink like anybody
else; and shall be by no means surprised if Doctor
Croly is found to have regained at least all the flesh
that anxiety and grief for the Church in danger have
so deplorably deprived him of. It's wonderful to think
how certain saints and patriots get lean and fat as
sudden as rabbits! Wonderful to think, when the
whole world, according to their declaration, has gone
to bits, how well and contentedly they still continue
to live upon the pieces! But, dear grandmother, what
a blessing is Exeter Hall! What a safety-valve it is
for the patriotism, and indignation, and scorn, and
hatred — and all other sorts of public virtues — that,
but for it, or some such place, would fairly burst so
many excellent folks, if they couldn't go and relieve
their swelling souls with a bit of talk! As it is, they
speechify and are saved! Only suppose there had
been no place whereat worthy people could have
abused the Maynooth Grant — no place wherein to
air their own particular Christianity to the condem-
nation of the religion of everybody else — what would
have been the consequence? Why, they must have
exploded — burst like the frog in the fable. Day after
day, Mr. Wakley and his brother coroners would
have been sitting on the body of some respec-

ble saint and patriot — day after day we should have read the verdict — "Died by retention of abuse!" Happily, while we have Exeter Hall, we are spared these national calamities.

As I know, grandmother, your natural tenderness for all that concerns the bishops, I must — at the risk of bringing on your colic — inform you that they are again in danger. Even the *Morning Post* is beginning to neglect 'em! Some newspaper — I don't know which — has proposed, as the only true remedy for the distresses of the country, that there should be a greater number of bishops. Now, this, at the first blush, seems a capital notion. But only mark what follows. The writer would multiply episcopal blessings, by "distributing the revenues of the present sees, as they fall vacant, among a greater number of bishops!" And the *Morning Post* doesn't at once put down his infamous proposal. Only imagine one Bishop of London slit into half-a-dozen bishops — one Henry of Exeter made twenty Henrys — just as you make bundles of small wood from one large piece! After giving utterance to this wickedness, the writer goes on to think "it impossible that the spiritual lords should continue to be members of the legislature, after ceasing to be rich men." And this the *Post* calls "no singular opinion. For such is the habitual association of power and station in this country with wealth, that perhaps nine out of every ten persons that one might meet walking along the Strand, would say with this writer, that unless a prelate had his thousands a year, and his carriage, and his servants, and his grandeur of *accessaries*, he could not properly take a part in counselling the government, or assisting to make laws in the Upper House of Parliament!" And if the people think so, I've heard it said that the bishops have themselves to thank for such belief; seeing that the world often hears more of their carriages and servants than of the humility and tenderness that were shown by the Apostles! The *Post*, however, to my amazement, is for stripping Lambeth and Fulham of much of their finery. Yes; the *Post* absolutely says, "We protest against the opinion that, without the wealth, the worth of the bishops in the House of Lords would be nought. Nay, we can conceive the possibility of the influence of learning and eloquence, and venerable earnestness, being *even greater when disassociated* from wealth and worldly interests!" Only imagine, grandmother, the Bishop of London, walking down to the House of Lords, leaning on a horn-tipped staff, and not rolled along in his cushioned carriage, with a servant in purple livery to let down the steps for him! Isn't the picture terrible? — isn't it what they call revolutionary? And yet the *Morning Post* — as coldly as this present month of May — can see the possibility of a Bishop of Exeter being cut into ten or twenty bishoplings, and never swoon, or even so much as call out for hartshorn? Who is the revolutionist *now?*

The month has been a dull month: politics and all that, have been as stupid as the weather. The trees and bushes have come out, to be sure; but only, as it would seem, from a matter of habit, — because it's May by the almanac. However, the Duke of Newcastle has very kindly tried to give us a fillip. As

I've heard somebody say in some play or the other,
" Orson is endowed with reason ! "   We've had two
letters from Clumber !   You must know that in the
British Museum there are two or three mummies of
Egyptian kings, they say, who lived, I don't know
how many thousand years ago.   Now, just suppose,
grandmother, that one of these mummies — with his
brains out, be it remembered — should have suddenly
got up, and written a letter or two to Mehemet Ali
and his Egyptians, thinking 'em the self-same Egyptians that used to worship crocodiles and ibises, and
make gods of the leeks and onions that grew in their
gardens, — suppose the British Museum mummy had
done this, — well, the thing would have done no more
than the political mummy of Clumber; would have
made just the same mistake as his well-meaning
Grace, the Duke of Newcastle.

" Forget all you've been learning for these last
thirty years at least — give up the wickedness of
steam — forego the iniquity of railroads — be content
with sailing-smacks and stage-coaches — repeal the
Reform Bill — repeal Catholic Emancipation — in a
word, wipe everything from your minds gathered
there since the good old times ' when George the
Third was king ' — come out again in the pig-tails
and shoe-buckles of that blissful reign, — and I, Duke
of Newcastle, am ready to march with you !   I am
prepared, at every risk, to be the hero of the back-
step ! "   As yet, I've heard of nobody who has joined
the Duke's standard ; but if recruits should come in,
I'll let you know.

It is not unlikely, grandmother, that you may have

a few Highland families sent over to America; as they are now being carefully " weeded out " from their native places by certain landlords who think it better and more Christian-like to turn their lands into sheep-walks than to suffer them to be tenanted by mere men, women, and children. " Weeding " is a nice word — isn't it? It so capitally describes the worth of the thing rooted out. The poor man is of course the " weed ; " the rich is the " lily, that neither toils nor spins." And just now, it seems, certain places in the Highlands are overgrown with this rank, foul weed; this encumbrance to the soil; this one human thing, worse than thistle or nettle. What a beautiful world this would be — wouldn't it? — if this weed of poverty was cut up, burnt, destroyed, — got rid of any way? It's a dreadful nuisance; and yet it *will* spring up, like groundsel or any other worthless thing! And strange to say, the sun will shine upon it, and the dews of heaven descend upon it, all the same as if it was one of the aforesaid lilies, full of light and breathing sweetness. Odd, isn't it, that the sky should shine so impartially on both?

Your affectionate grandson,

JUNIPER HEDGEHOG.

LETTER XI.

TO MISS KITTY HEDGEHOG, MILLINER, PHILA-
DELPHIA.

DEAR KITTY: If I haven't written to you before this, it is because I've had nothing worth ink and paper to send you. I know that you've a mind above politics, and — may you be pardoned for the lightness! — can sleep like a cat in the sun, no matter how much the Church may be in danger. When, however, there's anything stirring among silks and satins, why, then your woman's spirit is up, and all the milliner is roused within you. Knowing this, Kitty, I shall treat you with a few lines about a Powdered Ball we've lately had at Court, when everybody, out of compliment, I suppose, to what is called the wisdom of their ancestors, went dressed like their great grandfathers and grandmothers. A huge comfort this to great people in the shades! Dear Queen Charlotte was once again at Court, very flatteringly represented by a fine piece of point-lace worn by the blessed Victoria herself. And dukes, and lords, and generals — all of 'em sleeping in family lead — were once more walking minuets and dancing Sir Roger de Coverley. Everybody for a time lived more than a hundred years ago; and, as I'm told, felt very happy at going backward even for one night. To go back is with many high folks the greatest proof of wisdom; and therefore among such people the Powdered Ball was considered a glorious stride in the right direction. Only imagine the rapture of a Duke of Newcastle, living even in fancy for a few hours, at any time from 1715 to 1745; a time when there was no Reform Bill; no steam-engines; no railways; no cheap books! Think of the delight of many old gentlemen believing themselves their own grandfathers; quite away from these revolutionary days, and living again in "the good old times"! I've heard — though I don't answer for it — that two or three of 'em were so carried away by the thought that, to keep up the happiness as long as they could, they went to bed in their clothes, high-heeled shoes and all. At this very moment, they *do* say, Lord —— is still in his embroidered coat and smalls, with a wig like a white cloud upon him. He declares 1715 is such a "good old time" that nothing shall make him go on again to 1845. He has ordered flambeaux for his servants, and now and then talks about going to Ranelagh. Moreover, by people quite worthy of belief, it is feared that this delusion, as they call it, is spreading amongst certain high folks — many of 'em thinking themselves a hundred years back, and wanting to make Acts of Parliament in the spirit of that good old time. See, Kitty, how a Powdered Ball may turn the highest heads — even the nobs of a country!

The ladies were, of course, all jewelled, and very fine. O, what a fortune some of 'em would have been to a poor man — with their stomachers! But, Kitty, there is one odd thing at these masks and balls. How is it that young ladies — with names as white as snow — sometimes take the characters, fly-spotted and damaged as they are, of sinful love-birds? You, Kitty, being a woman, can explain this : but to me, one of the ignorant, rough sex, it does seem odd that a pure young lady should dress herself as Nelly Gwynne or any other person of the sort, when the aforesaid pure lady would squeak — and, no doubt, very proper — at the living creature as if it was a toad. Can you explain this, Kitty? Do they take such characters, just as they put black patches on their cheeks, to bring out their own white all the stronger? Or is it that there's a sort of idle daring in it, just as children play with fire, though they never mean to burn themselves? I can't make it out : but how should I expect it — I, a poor, weak, ignorant man, — how should I unriddle a creature that's puzzled Solomon?

Of course, there was an account of all the dresses. Well, when I opened the *Morning Post*, and saw whole columns built o' nothing but velvets and satins and all that, if I didn't grin — like a clown through a collar for a new hat — at the vanity of life. "Look here," says I to Bill Fisher, that was sitting in the Spotted Lion, — " look at the conceit of these folks," says I, " who think that all the world's to stand still a reading about their 'gimp Brandenburghs, and buttons' — 'their buttons and frogs' — their 'blue facings and turnback' — and such mountebankery." "It's quite beneath us as men," says Bill; " not at all like lords of the creation. Now I can forgive the women — poor little souls ! — for having all their flounces and puffings put in the paper. It's nat'ral

for them." " Why nat'ral?" says I. " Why," says
Bill, " because they know it makes one another
savage. Bless you! that's what they do it for — and
nothin' else." And then you should have heard how
he laughed, as he spelt out the paper. " Look here
now," says he, " here was a lady with ' a dress looped
with bouquets of pink roses ; skirt of rich green satin,
trimmed with flounces of point lace and bouquets of
roses ; white satin shoes with high heels, green
rosettes with diamonds in the centre. Hair powdered,
and ornamented with roses and diamonds.' Now,
isn't it dreadful, Juniper, that people are to be stopped
over their honest pint of porter with stuff like this?
What's ' satin shoes with high heels' to all the 'versal
world? But then, as I say, the women do it to make
one another savage. I've often thought, since they
like so to print in the papers what clothes they wear
— that, at the same time, they might let the world
know what books they read, what pictures they
looked at, — in fact, what sort of dresses they put
upon their minds. But, to be sure, this would make
nobody savage." This is what Bill Fisher says ; but
mark, Kitty, I'm not quite of his way of thinking ;
though, after all, it does seem odd that a young lady
should think it worth while to put all her clothes in
print for all the world to spell over.

But the Ball will have done a great deal of good,
in making us look a hundred years back. How I
should like to see the thing tried upon a grand scale !
Suppose that everybody in London, just for four-and-
twenty hours, out of compliment to the great example

set by the court, should live as if it was 1745! Wouldn't it be droll? Droll to have the gas out, and set up oil-twinklers; droll to make the new police put on drab coats, and call the hours, like that " venerable institution," the watch! Droll to have all the rail-trains stopped, and only book passengers for York by the wagon! Droll to stop the steamboats on the river — the omnibuses in the street; making folks move about in nothing but wherries, hackney-coaches, and sedan-chairs! Droll, too, would it be to start for Gravesend in the tilt-boat on a two days' voyage! Well, I do hope that all this will be brought about. For if all folks in London were made to live only four-and-twenty hours of a hundred years ago — I do think that for the rest of their lives they'd shut their mouths about those precious good old times, that some people do now so like to cackle about.

There's no doubt that the Powdered Ball has been a very fine affair, but the Ball of next season will be the grand thing. A nobleman's footman, as I last night drove, told me that at the Ball of next year, all true folks will wear supposed dresses from the time of 1915 to 1945 — that is, about a hundred years ahead. There's a good many opinions as to what they'll be. Some folks declare they'll be plain as drab — and some that we shall have all gone back again to the fashion of the painted Britons, as you see 'em in the History of England. By that time, it's thought, soldiers' uniforms will have gone quite out — the electric gun and such nickknacks having killed war, body and bones. Howsomever, 'twill be odd to see how people's fancy will dress themselves for a hundred years on ; there'll be more cleverness in that, if well done, than in wearing the precise coat and petticoat of your grandfather and grandmother.

Your loving brother,

JUNIPER HEDGEHOG.

LETTER XII.

TO MRS. HEDGEHOG, NEW YORK.

DEAR GRANDMOTHER : The Maynooth Grant is granted, and the British Lion has once more gone to sleep. When either Sir Culling Smith, Mr. M'Neill, or Doctor Croly shall pinch his tail, and make him roar again, you shall have due notice of the danger. I think, however, that the Lion is safe to sleep until next May, when, of course, he'll again be stirred up for the folks at Exeter Hall. In the mean time he must be tired — very drowsy, after the speeches that have been made at him ; so let him sleep on.

Yes : Maynooth College has got the new grant ; nevertheless — to the astonishment of the Duke of Newcastle and Company — the sun rises every morning as if nothing had happened ; and, so hard does the love of shillings make man's heart, London tradesmen still smile behind their counters, never thinking that their tills are threatened with an earthquake. Newcastle and other Peers — just out of consolation to their shades — have written what's called a " Protest " against the grant : and a hundred years hence, when England is blown to atoms by the measure, very comfortable it will be to their ghosts, as they walk among the ruins, to see men reading the aforesaid " Protest," and hear them crying, " A prophet! a prophet ! "

And now, grandmother, comes the Roman Catholic Bishops. They won't have Peel's plan of education, unless all the masters are to be of their own faith. For, they say, " the Roman Catholic pupils could not attend the lectures on history, logic, metaphysics, moral philosophy, geology, or anatomy, without exposing their faith or morals to imminent danger, *unless a Roman Catholic professor* shall be appointed for each of those chairs." You see, the lecturer on history, if a Protestant, might be for making Queen Mary — Bloody Mary, as I was taught to call her at day-school — a very cruel wretch, indeed ; whereas the Queen Mary of the Catholic might be a very nice woman, who never could abide fagots, and never knew where Smithfield was. And then for logic (you must, as I've said before, look in the dictionary for hard words), — logic, it seems, is a matter of religion. What's logic to a Protestant isn't logic to a Catholic, or a Mahometan, or a Chinese ! In the same way, I suppose that a straight line in London would be what they call a curve in Dublin, and perhaps a whole circle at Canton. And then for " geology " and " anatomy." The Protestant geologist might make the earth younger or older than it really is, and all to suit his own wicked purposes. Again, look at the danger of having a Protestant lecturer on anatomy ! Why, we all know that's there's nothing certain in anatomy; that it's all a matter of faith.

Thus, if a Catholic anatomist lectured, we'll say, upon the body of a Protestant pluralist, he might out of blindness declare that the said body never had a a single atom of heart; that such pluralists always lived without the article. While, on the other side, the real Protestant lecturer, discussing on the self-same *corpus*, might declare that it was all heart, like a summer cabbage! " Professors' chairs!" When I read these things, I somehow do think of the baby chair that I used to be set up in to take my meals, with a stick run through the arms to keep me from tumbling out. The talk is so childish!

You ask me about your pet, the Bishop of Exeter. Well, the clergy of his diocese have just suffered what's called his " charge." A charge, grandmother, in which the Bishop generally contrives to put in a lot of small shot to pepper about him right and left. As usual, he talked a good deal about himself; making Exeter out such a soft, gentle person — such a lump of Christian butter — that in this hot weather, it's wonderful he hasn't melted long ago. Ha, grandmother! what a lawyer was spoiled in that Bishop! What a brain he has for cobwebs! How he drags you along through sentence after sentence — every one a dark passage — until your head swims, and you can't see your finger close to your nose! He talked about this Puseyite stuff — this play-acting of the Church — for I don't know how long; but whether he very much likes it, or very much hates it, it's more than any cabman's brains can make out. I never read one of Exeter's charges, that I don't think of a sharp lawyer quite spoiled — but this last is a

greater tangle than all.   He talked a good deal about
" the Apostolical succession," the truth of which, he
said, he would defend.   How I should like to hear
him trace himself — Henry of Exeter — *upwards!*
He then came to the new Bill that was to take the
right of divorce out of the hands of the Church.   He
said, " Let the *Liberalism* of the age be content with
what it had already achieved.   It was enough for one
generation, that men and women might be coupled together in a Registrar's office, with as total an absence
of all religious sanction, as if one huckster were
coupled up in partnership with another."   Here the
Bishop's right enough, no doubt.   For if the Bishops'
court loses cases of divorce, what lots of fees go from
them to the mere lawyers!   A wedding-ring and a
license are things almost dog-cheap; but, O grandmother! what a lot of money it takes to break that
ring — what a heap of cash to tear up the license:
and that's the reason that divorce, like green peas at
Christmas, can only be afforded by the rich.   Next,
the Bishop had a fling at what he called " the unhappy beings who went to Mechanics' Institutes and
lecture-rooms."   He said they wanted " the discipline
of the heart and the chastening influence of true religion."   I'm an ignorant cabman, grandmother; but
if so many " millions," as the Bishop said, want this,
— I must ask, what do we pay the Church for?   If so
many of us are no better, as Exeter said, than " any
of the wildest savages who devoured one another in
New Zealand," for what, in the name of pounds,
shillings, and pence, do we pay Church rates?   Why
don't the Bishops and the high preachers of the

Church come more among us? Why, thinking of the " Apostolical succession," don't they copy more than they do the fishermen and tent-makers who are their forefathers? I can't help asking this; though, as I said, I know I'm an ignorant cabman.

The Bishop, however, after scolding a good deal, tried to end mildly and like a Christian. I've read at some book-stall of an Indian leaf. One side of it acts as a blister: then take it off, turn it, and the other side serves for the salve. The Bishop of Exeter, to my mind, always tries to make his charge a leaf of this sort; though I must say it, one side is generally stronger than the other — better for blistering than healing. So no more from your affectionate grand-son,

JUNIPER HEDGEHOG.

LETTER XIII.

TO RICHARD MONCKTON MILNES, ESQ., M. P.*

SIR: As I once had the honor to drive you down to Parliament — and as I found you such an affable gentleman, with no pride at all in you (I say noth-ing about the sixpence you gave me over my fare) — I make no bones at all in writing these few lines to you, about your motion for private hanging. I see by the newspapers that you want to make a law

---

* Now Lord Houghton. The *Saturday Review*, in noticing one of his Lord-ship's books, says that " none of our readers will require to be told that Lord Houghton is a continuation of Richard Monckton Milnes." — ED.

to hang inside of the jail, in a snug and quiet way; and not to have the show in the open street. Pardon a cabman's boldness; but really, Mr. Milnes, you can't have thought of the shocking consequence of your measure, if so be it had been carried out. What! Make a law for private hanging! With one bit of parchment destroy what I'll be bold enough to call one of the chief amusements of the people? Sir James Graham knows better than this; for he generally contrives to have an execution on Easter and Whit Monday, just by the way of an early whet to the appetites of the holiday-makers. First the Old Bailey and then Greenwich; Mr. Calcraft, the hangman—and then the fire-eater and the clown. Your bill, sir,—do forgive my boldness,—was very rash, and not at all just. They've taken away bear-baiting, and duck-hunting, and dog-fighting, from what they call the lower orders; and now you'd deprive 'em of their last and dearest privilege—you'd, with one dash of the pen, rob 'em of their own public gallows? And you call yourself a friend of the people, Mr. Milnes—a stickler for their ancient sports and pastimes? I don't wonder that for once something like shame came over Parliament—that not forty conscientious members stopped to listen to you—and that, in a word, you were " counted out."

I have said your bill was unjust, shamefully unjust, unless you can prove to me that there was a clause in it to what they call indemnify the housekeepers in the Old Bailey for their loss of vested interests, seeing that they make no end of money by letting their windows at a popular hanging. Why, a Hocker's worth any money to 'em; for it's odd how hanging brings down the pride of some of the upper classes, many of the nobs enjoying it quite as much as the lower orders, only that they give one or two guineas — according to the beauty of the murder — for comfortable sitting room. If the men they call the Six Clerks were indemnified, surely you wouldn't rob the tradesmen of the Old Bailey.

But it really is shocking to see how a mere member of Parliament will set himself up against a clergyman of Newgate! Didn't the Rev. Mr. Davis preach that the whole use and beauty of hanging was to be found in making it public? According to him, if it was possible to hang a man where all England might see him strangled, why, all England would certainly be the better for it. I've no doubt that the cause of so much crime is in the smallness of the Old Bailey, that will only accommodate such a few! Why shouldn't the gallows be erected on Salisbury Plain, with cheap railway excursions from all parts on hanging days?

Pardon me, sir; but there never was such a mistake as to think to do away with the wickedness of hanging by making it private. In the first place, if to see a hanging is no warning to the beholder, do you think that to hear or read of a hanging would do all the good of an example? Does what men see, or what they hear, stir 'em the most? But let us suppose that a man is to be hanged inside of Newgate. Why, the penny-a-liners, that get their sops-in-the-pan out of the condemned cell, — why, they would write all sorts of pretty things, all kinds of interesting stories about

the last minutes of the criminal, and so the curiosity
of the town would be more agog than ever. The
picture newspapers that publish the murderers' portraits — those family papers for the instruction and
amusement of the younger branches — would give
half-a-dozen pictures where they now give one. The
secrecy of the thing would give a flavor to the whole
matter.

And now, suppose that a rich man was to be
privately hanged; a banker, we'll say, or, saving your
presence, even a member of Parliament. Well, we
know how unbelieving is man. There's thousands
of people who would never sleep quietly in their
beds, for the thought that the said banker or member
was never hanged at all; — but was smuggled out
alive in a coffin, and shipped abroad. Every year or
so, there'd be a letter in the newspapers from somebody who had seen the banker somewhere in the
Back-woods, where he had married one of the Chac-
taws, and got a family of ten children. No, Mr.
Milnes, private hanging won't do; the people arn't to
be cheated out of their pleasure after that fashion.

Besides, Mr. Milnes, all hanging's a bungle. The
gallows is condemned, marked to come down; timber by timber it's loosening, and it's no use trying to
keep it together with small corking-pins. No, Mr.
Milnes, it will better become you, be more like your
kind, good-natured self, to give a pull at the planks,
to bring the whole machine to the ground, to make
it a thing of the past, like the bonfires that burnt
witches, — and for the hangman thrown out of work,

why, small retiring allowances have been given to worse public servants.

Hoping, sir, that you'll excuse my boldness,

I remain your obedient servant,

JUNIPER HEDGEHOG.

P. S. You know my number, sir, and I'm always in Palace Yard.

LETTER XIV.

TO MRS. HEDGEHOG, OF NEW YORK.

DEAR GRANDMOTHER: September's so near we can almost put our hand upon it, and yet I'm in London. It's a dreadful confession of poverty, but I can't help it. If I'm not ashamed to be seen on my stand, I'm not a licensed cabman. The only comfort is, everybody that stays in town must be as poor as myself; and that, according to some folks' notions, is a blessing to think of. A purse that was dropped on the pavement of Regent Street lay there a week, and was at last picked up by a policeman. London never looked so poor and dull; for all the world like a fine lady in an undress gown, with all her paint wiped off. The opera is shut up, and the manager has had a silver bed-candlestick given him by lords and dukes, because he has been so full of public spirit as to make his own fortune. By the way, grandmother, I don't know how it is with the player folks in New York; but here with us, if a man or woman want a

bit of plate, they've only to take a theatre. A play-
house is a short cut to a silversmith's. There isn't a
London manager who isn't plated after this fashion,
which shows there is no place for true gratitude like
the green-room. But I ask your pardon for talking
of such matters: knowing what a low place you
think the theatres.

Parliament, like a goose that has been set upon too
many eggs, has risen with half of 'em come to nothing. But this, grandmother, is the old trick. When
the Parliament first opens, and ministers come down
with new law after law, — why, what busy, bustling
folks they seem! What a look of business it gives to
the whole thing! But half of 'em is only for show;
just so many dummies to take in what shopkeepers
call " an enlightened public." You know the bottles
of red and blue that they have in apothecaries' shops.
Well, half the folks think 'em physic, when they're
nothing in the world but colored water. Sir James
Graham's Medical Bill was just one of these things;
nothing real in it; but something made up for show;
just to give a coloring to business. Talking of Parliament, a dreadful accident happened at the proro-
gation.

You know it's the privilege of the Duke of Argyll
to bear the royal crown before the Queen. Certain
noble folks come into the world with certain privileges of the kind. One has a right to stir the royal
tea-cup on the day of the coronation — another to put
on the Queen's pattens whenever she shall walk in
the city — another to present the monarch with a pint
of periwinkles when he shall visit Billingsgate; and

so forth : all customs of the good old times, when people thought kings and queens were angels in disguise who had kindly left heaven just to give poor mortals here a lift — in fact, to make the world endurable. Well, the Duke of Argyll, walking backwards with the crown — going straightforwards not being at all the thing in the court — fell, poor old gentleman, down some steps — and, falling, dropped the crown ! Phewgh ! There was a shower of pearls and diamonds ; for all the precious stones came rattling on the floor, just as if the queen, like the little girl in the fairy story, had been talking jewels. There were thoughts, I'm told, of calling in the police to keep off the mob of peers ; but altogether they behaved themselves very well, and not a precious stone was found missing. The accident, however, caused a great fuss ; and I'm told that in order to prevent its happening again, Madame Tussaud has offered to make a Duke of Argyll in wax, that, fitted up with proper wheels and springs, may be made to go backwards, with no fear of a tumble. Should the thing succeed — and I don't see why it shouldn't — it would be a great saving in the way of salaries to the country, if a good many other court officers were manufactured after the like fashion. They would work quite as regularly, and look just as well.

I'd almost forgotten to say that the king of the Dutch has been on a visit to us — and, as I've heard, a very decent sort of king he is. Of course he played whilst here at a little bit of soldiering — guards and grenadiers were turned out in the Hyde Park, that he might review their helmets and bear-skin caps. Isn't it odd, grandmother, that the first show kings and princes, when they come to us, want to stare at, is a show of soldiers? Just to see how nicely men are armed and mounted to kill men? They don't mean any harm by it, of course; but still — I can't help thinking it — it does appear to me, if Beelzebub was to go into a strange country — if, indeed, there is any country he's not yet visited — the sight he'd first like to see would be the sight of men taught the best way of cutting men's throats. And then (if he came here to London) he'd go down to Woolwich Marshes to see what they call rocket-practice. And, wouldn't he rub his hands, and switch about his tail, to see how rocket and shells split, break, tear away everything before 'em, showing what pretty work they'd make of a solid square of living flesh, standing for so many pence a day to be made a target of? You'd think it would be some wicked spirit that would enjoy this fun; but no, grandmother, it isn't so; quite the contrary; it's kings and princes. And yet I should like to have some king come over here who wouldn't care to go a soldiering in Hyde Park; who wouldn't think of rocket-practice; but who, on the contrary, would go about to our schools, and our hospitals, and our asylums, and all places where man does what he can to help man — to assist and comfort him like a fellow-creature, and not to tear him limb from limb like a devil!

Our Queen has gone to Germany to see where Prince Albert was born. Well, there's something pretty and wife-like in the thought of this, and I like it. There was a dreadful fear among some of the nobs in

Parliament, that while the Queen was away, the kingdom would drop to pieces. But it isn't so: the tax-gatherer calls just the same as ever. The Queen took ship, and landed at Antwerp, — at the Quai Vandyke. Now, Vandyke, you must know, was a famous painter; and abroad, they've a fashion of naming streets and places after folks that's called geniuses. We haven't come to that yet. Only think of our having a Hogarth Square, or a Shakespeare instead of a Waterloo Bridge! And then for statues in the streets, we don't give them to authors and painters, but only to kings and dukes that don't pay their debts.

Still, I do feel for her gracious majesty. Dear soul! Isn't it dreadful that a gentlewoman can't step abroad — can't take boat, but what there's a hundred guns blazing, firing away at her, — as if the noise of cannons and the smell of gunpowder was like the songs of nightingales and the scent of roses! How royalty keeps its hearing, I can't tell. When the dear lady got upon the Rhine, there were the guns blazing away as though heaven and earth were come together!

It's odd enough that people will think a great noise is a great respect; and that the heartiest welcome can only be given by gunpowder. It seems that the folks were putting up a statue to a musician, named Beethoven, and the Queen of England and the Prince were just in time to pay their respects to the bronze. Mr. Beethoven while alive was nobody; but it's odd how a man's worth is raked up from his coffin! And so, it's a great comfort to great men who, when in this world, are thought very small indeed, to think how big they'll be upon earth, after they've gone to heaven — a comfort for 'em, when they may happen to want a coat, to think of the suit of bronze or marble that kings and queens will afterwards give 'em. If, now, there's any English composer — any man with a mind in him, forced for want of better employment to give young ladies lessons on the piano, — when he should be doing sonatas and sinfonias and that sort of thing, — why, I say, it must be a comfort for him to know that folks can honor genius when it's put up by the way of statue in the market-place.

One of the prettiest stories I've heard of the jaunt is this, — that the Queen and Albert went in a quiet way to visit the Prince's old schoolmaster. If this isn't enough to make all schoolmasters in England hold their heads up half-a-yard higher! Besides, it mayn't show a bad example to high folks who keep tutors and governesses.

All together the Queen must be pleased with her trip, and I should think not the less pleased where the folks made the least noise ; although, from what I read in one of the papers, everybody doesn't think so ; for the writer complains that there was " no shouting or noise, but only that *eternal bowing* which so strikes a traveller, and which would make one believe that beings across the Channel were formed with some natural affinity between their right hands and their hats." Really, to my mind there's something more pleasing, more rational like, in one human creature quietly bowing to another, than in shouting and hallooing at him like a wild Indian. But, then, people do so like noise !

You'll be sorry to hear, grandmother, that your pets, the bishops, are again in trouble. I'm sure of it, bishops were never intended to have anything to do with money: they always tumble into such mistakes, whenever they touch it! How is it to be expected that they should know the mystery of pounds, shillings, and pence, — they who can't abide earthly vanities — they who are always above this world, though they never go up, as I hear, with Mr. Green in his balloon? Well, it seems that the bishops have had a mint of money put into their hands, that they may build new churches for their fellow-sinners, whom they call spiritually destitute. Well, would you think it? — in a moment of strange forgetfulness, they've laid out so much money upon palaces for themselves, that they can't build the proper number of churches for the poor? The bishops have taken care of the bishops, — and for the spiritually destitute, why, they may worship in highways and byways, in fields and in commons. Of course the bishops never meant this. No: it has all come about from their knowing nothing of the value of money. Still, what's called the lower orders won't believe this. And isn't it a shocking thing to consider that the poor man may look at Bishop So-and-so with a grudge in his eye, saying to himself, "Yes, you've built yourself a fine house — you've got your fine cedars and all that King Solomon talks about in your own palace — but where's my sittings in church — where, bishop, is my bench in the middle aisle?"

This is so dreadful to think of, that I can't write any further upon it; and so no more from your affectionate grandson, JUNIPER HEDGEHOG.

LETTER XV.

TO MRS. HEDGEHOG, OF NEW YORK.

DEAR GRANDMOTHER: As I don't think you have any liking for railways, — being like Colonel Sibthorp, one of those folks loving the good old times, when travelling was as sober a thing as a wagon and four horses could make it, — I really don't see how I'm to write you anything of a letter. There's nobody in town, and nothing in the papers but plans of railways, that in a little time will cover all England like a large spider's net; and, as in the net, there will be a good many flies caught and gobbled up by those who spin it. Nevertheless, — though I know you don't agree with me any more than Colonel Sibthorp does, — it is a fine sight to open the newspapers, and see the railway schemes. What mountains of money they bring to the mind! And then for the wonders they're big with, why, properly considered, arn't they a thousand times more wonderful than anything in the " Arabian Nights' Entertainments?" Then we have flying carriages to be brought to every man's door! All England made to shake hands with itself in a few hours! And when London can, in an hour or so, go to the Land's End for a gulp of sea-air, and the Land's End in the same time come to see the shows of London, — shan't all of us the better understand one another? shan't we all be brought together, and made, as we ought to be, one family of? It's coming fast, grandmother. Now pigs can travel, I don't know how far, at a halfpenny a head, we don't hear the talk that used to be of "the swinish multitude." And isn't it a fine thing — I know you don't think so, but isn't it? — to know that all that's been done, and all that's to do will be done, because Englishmen have left off cutting other men's throats? That peace has done it all? If they oughtn't to set up a dove with an olive branch at every railway terminus, I'm an impostor, and no true cabman.

Yes, grandmother, peace has done it all! Only think of the iron that had been melted into cannon, and round shot, and chain shot, and all the other sorts of shot — that the devils on a holiday play at bowls with! — if the war had gone on, — all the very same iron that's now peaceably laid upon sleepers! Think of the iron that had been fired into the sea, and banged through quiet people's houses, and sent mashing squares and squares of men — God's likenesses in red, blue, and green coats, hired to be killed at so many pence a day — only think what would have been this wicked, I will say it, this blasphemous waste of metal, — that, as it is, has been made into steam-engines. Very fine, indeed, they say, is the roar of artillery; but what is it to the roar of steam? I never see an engine, with its red-hot coals and its clouds of steam and smoke, that it doesn't seem to me like a tremendous dragon that has been tamed by man to carry all the blessings of civilization to his fellow-creatures. I've read about knights going through the skies on fiery monsters — but what are they to the engineers, at two pound five a week? What is any squire among 'em all to the humblest stoker? And then

23

I've read about martial trumpets — why, they haven't, to my ears, half the silver in their sound as the railway whistle!

Well, I should like the ghost of Bonaparte to get up some morning, and take the *Times* in his thin hands. If he wouldn't turn yellower than ever he was at St. Helena! There he'd see plans for railways in France — *belly France*, as I believe they call it — to be carried out by Frenchmen and Englishmen. Yes; he wouldn't see 'em mixing bayonets, trying to poke 'em in one another's bowels, that a few tons of blood might, as they call it, water his laurels — (how any man can wear laurels at all, I can't tell, they must smell so of the slaughter-house!) — he wouldn't see 'em charging one another on the battle-field, but quietly ranged, cheek by jowl, in the list of directors! Not exchanging bullets, but clubbing together their hard cash.

Consider it, grandmother, isn't it droll? Here, in these very lists, you see English Captains and Colonels in company with French Viscounts and Barons, and I don't know what, planning to lay iron down in France — to civilize and add to the prosperity of Frenchmen! The very Captains and Colonels who, but for the peace, would be blowing French ships out of the water, — knocking down French houses, — and all the while swearing it, and believing it too, that Frenchmen were only sent into this world to be killed by Englishmen, just as boys think frogs were spawned only to be pelted at! O, only give her time, and Peace — timid dove as she is — will coo down the trumpet.

Now, grandmother, only do think of Lord Nelson as a railway director, on the Boulogne line to Paris! Well, I know you'll say it — the world's going to be turned upside down. Perhaps it is: and after all, it mightn't be the worse now and then for a little wholesome shaking. They do say there's to be a rail from Waterloo to Brussels, and the Duke of Wellington — the iron duke, with, I've no doubt, iron enough in him for the whole line — is to be chairman of the Directors.

The Prince Joinville is now and then looking about our coasts to find out, it is said, which is the softest part of us, in the case of a war, to put his foot upon us. Poor fellow! he's got the disease of glory; only — as it sometimes happens with the small-pox — it has struck inwards; it can't come out upon him. When we've railways laid down, as I say, like a spider's web all over the country, won't it be a little hard to catch us asleep? For you see, just like the spider's web, the electric telegraph (inquire what sort of a thing it is, for I haven't time to tell you), the electric telegraph will touch a line of the web, when down will come a tremendous spider in a red coat with all sorts of murder after him! Mind, grandmother, let us hope this never may happen; but when folks who'd molest us, know it *can* come about, won't they let us alone? Depend upon it, we're binding war over to keep the peace, and the bonds are made of railway iron!

You'd hardly think it — you who used to talk to me about the beauty of glory (I know you meant nothing but the red coats and the fine epaulets; for that so often is women's notion of glory, though, bless 'em, they're among the first to make lint, and cry over the sons of glory, with gashes spoiling all their fine feathers) — you'd hardly think it, but they're going to put up a statue to the man who first made boiling water to run upon a rail. It's quite true; I read it only a day or two ago. They're going to fix up a statue to George Stephenson, in Newcastle. How you will cast up your dear old eyes when you hear of this! You, who've only thought that statues should be put up to Queen Anne, and George the Third, and his nice son, George the Fourth, and such people! I should only like a good many of the statues here in London, to be made to take a cheap train down to Newcastle, to see it. If, dirty as they are — and dirty as they were — they wouldn't blush as red as a new copper halfpenny, why, those statues — especially when they've queens and kings in 'em — are the most unfeelingest of metal! What a lot of mangled bodies, and misery, and housebreaking, and wickedness of all sorts, carried on and made quite lawful by a uniform, — may we see — if we choose to see at all — about the statue of what is called a Conqueror! What firing of houses, what shame, — that because you're a woman, I won't more particularly write about, — we might look upon under the statue, that is only so high because it has so much wickedness to stand upon! If the statue could feel at all, wouldn't it put up its hands and hide its face, although it was made of the best bronze! But Mr. Stephenson will look kindly and sweetly about him — he will know that he has carried comfort, and

knowledge, and happiness to the doors of millions!
— that he has brought men together that they might
know and love one another. This is something like
having a statue! I'm sure of it — when George the
Fourth is made to hear the news — (for kings are so
very long before the truth comes to 'em) — he'd like
to gallop off to the first melter's, and go at once into
the nothing that men think him.

And besides all this, the railways have got a king!
When you hear of a king in England, I know your
old thoughts go down to Westminster Abbey, — and
you think of nothing but bishops and peers, and all
that sort of thing, kissing the king's cheeks, — and
the holy oil put upon the royal head, that the crown,
I suppose, may sit the more comfortably upon it, —
but this is another sort of king. Mr. King Hudson
the First! I have read it somewhere at a bookstall,
that Napoleon was crowned with the Iron Crown of
Italy. Well, King Hudson has been crowned with
the Iron Crown of England! A crown melted out
of pig-iron, and made in a railway furnace.

I've somewhere seen the picture of the River Nile;
that with the lifting of his finger made the river flow
over barren land, and leave there all sorts of blessings.
Well, King Hudson is of this sort; — he has made
the molten iron flow over all sorts of places, and so
bring forth good fruits wherever it went.

So no more from your affectionate grandson,

JUNIPER HEDGEHOG.

www.ingramcontent.com/pod-product-compliance
Lightning Source LLC
Chambersburg PA
CBHW051123120726
47905CB00005B/1398